GETAWAY DAY

GETAWAY DAY

Don't stop believing.

Ken White
March 2020

KEN WHITE

TATE PUBLISHING
AND ENTERPRISES, LLC

Published by Tate Publishing & Enterprises, LLC
127 E. Trade Center Terrace | Mustang, Oklahoma 73064 USA
1.888.361.9473 | www.tatepublishing.com

Tate Publishing is committed to excellence in the publishing industry. The company reflects the philosophy established by the founders, based on Psalm 68:11,
"The Lord gave the word and great was the company of those who published it."

Cover design by Jeffrey Doblados
Interior design by Jomel Pepito

Published in the United States of America

ISBN: 978-1-62994-915-4
1. Fiction / Coming Of Age
2. Fiction / Coming Of Age
13.12.10

Dedication

To my family.

A crowd of more than 5,000 filled Modesto's Del Webb Field on October 14, 1962, as the San Francisco Giants and the New York Yankees spent ninety minutes each practicing between the rain-delayed sixth and seventh games of the World Series. The once-in-a-lifetime event featured eight future Hall of Famers: Yogi Berra, Whitey Ford, and Mickey Mantle from the Yankees; Orlando Cepeda, Willie Mays, Willie McCovey, Juan Marichal, and Gaylord Perry from the Giants.

Photograph by Forrest G. Jackson Jr.

Acknowledgments

A special thanks to Heidi Sciutto for her sharp and meticulous editorial eye. And Scott Mitchell for his graphic design wizardry.

Baseball Folks: Brian Richards (Museum Curator, New York Yankees), Tim Wiles (Director of Research, National Baseball Hall of Fame), Kim McCray (National Baseball Hall of Fame, Giamatti Research Center Intern), Bruce Grimes, Rich Keller, Jim Moorehead, Arturo Santo Domingo, Mike Murphy, Chris Kutz (PR and Operations Assistant, Pacific Coast League), Earl Bloom (Orange County Register), Steve Barr (Little League Baseball and Softball), Bob Vanderberg (*Chicago Tribune*), David Haugh (*Chicago Tribune*), Scott Reifert, (Vice President of Communications, Chicago White Sox), and Leni Depoister (Coordinator of Media Services, Chicago White Sox).

Resource Folks: Michael Phillips, NBC News, Marcy Freer (California Department of Transportation, Division of Public Affairs), Jennifer Lynch (Historian and Corporate Information Services Manager, United States Post Office), Adam Yenkin (The Museum of Broadcast Communications), Travis Westly (Head of Reference, Newspaper & Current Periodical Room, Library of Congress), Janet Coles (Supervising Librarian, Transportation Library and History Center California Department of

Transportation), Tom Jabine (Library of Congress), Lance Armstrong (Valley Community Newspapers), Dylan McDonald (Center for Sacramento History), Julia Schaw (California State Library Foundation), Carson Hendricks, and Richard Stayton.

Valley Folks: Kim Normoyle, Tom Myers, Janet Lancaster (McHenry Museum), Dan Kiser, Bill Moorad (RIP), Harriet (Nard) Rivers, Jim Nard, Dennis Snelling, Skip Chiesa, Colleen Bare, Wes Page, Russ Newman, Robert Ulrich, Jack Ulrich, Joy Ulrich, Rich Keller, Mike Pratt, Lee Pratt, Robert Pratt, Don Bronsich, Frank Blanas, Marion Zoodsma, Judy Sly (Editor, *The Modesto Bee*), Joan Lee (Director of Multimedia Images, *The Modesto Bee*), Melissa Van Diepen, Forrest Jackson, Phyllis Jackson, Ismael Ontiveros, Mike Lynch, Philip Feebeck, Ann Arnold, Bill McRivette, Larry Robinson, Marsha Bond, Jennifer Mullen (Executive Director, The Modesto Convention & Visitors Bureau), Chris Murphy, Michael Harrell, Arnold Schmidt, Kevin Fox, Dr. Delmar Tonge, Dick Doll, Susan Belt, Danny Johnson, Don Bean, Ken Haub, Judy (Nicholson) Eubie, Chuck Duchscher, Wendy Lucas, Ann Veneman, Christie Camarillo (Oakdale Cowboy Museum), Jacki Conner (Oakdale Saddle Club), Mike Gorassi (Vice President, Modesto Nuts), Jim Pfaff, Phil Baird, Lance James, the Perry Family, and Henrietta Sparkman.

Teammates: Jack Leach, Lee Delano, Roger Ringsted, Mike Normoyle, Larry Simmons, Paul Cornwell, John Bellizzi, and Kim Normoyle.

High School Classmates: Mark Peterson, Sheila Harrell, Sandy Gant, Vernon Gant, Randy Clark, Ron Champion, Ed DiFrancia, Susan Allen, Paul Seideman, Peter Koetting, Larry Dempsey, Marsha Bledsoe, Ron Darpinian, Carol Harmon, Barney Eredia, Steve Couture, Brad Bassi, Jan Sturtevant, Janis Redpath-Kennedy, David Bradford, Nancy Wolff, and Catherine New.

Family: Tom White, Leona (Cannizzaro) White, Wendell White, Debbie (White) Farrell, Sammy (White) Leverone,

Sandra (Muse) Crowell, Gary Nielsen, David Nielsen, Charlene (Rogers) Orona, Don MacRitchie, Susan Crosby, and Stephan Marlow.

Inspirations: Ray Bradbury and George Lucas.

Consultants: Jim Cirile, John Reed, Alan Rinzler, Claudia Newcorn, Jan Fishler, and Ed Gray.

My love, inspiration, and rock. Robin Johnson.

Prologue

When a father gives to his son, both laugh; when a son gives to his father, both cry.

—*Jewish Proverb*

It's complicated. Fathers and sons are. It's been said that it's up to the son to live up to his father's reputation, or atone for his mistakes. Unfortunately, that's something we never can win. As sons, we are shaped by the tug of our father's expectations and the weight of his disappointments. We will always dwell in his shadow.

Fathers and sons have been rivals since forever. They have long competed for the respect of their community, the praise of their peers, and the love of their wife/mother. And, they've always had issues. Their conflict is as old as time, stretching back to BC and *The Bible*, before and beyond. Like Abraham and Isaac, or the Prodigal Son, the Good Book is full of stories about battles between men and their boys. As are myths, fables, and fiction, which tell more vivid tales of their clashes and struggles: Telemachus and Odysseus, Oedipus and Laius, the Hamlets, Geppetto and Pinocchio, George Bailey and Zuzu, Atticus Finch and Jem, Ozzie and Ricky, Mr. Cleaver and the Beaver. It's really nothing new. It's always been a kind of Greek tragedy. There were some times I hated my father, and other times I loved him. Some times I took his advice, other times I ignored it. Some times I wished he wasn't around, other times I feared my wish might come true.

For Baby Boomers who grew up when I did, it was up to the father to teach his son to be a man, to be tough in a cold, hard, unforgiving world. It was up to the mother to dress the wounds when that world kicked your butt. It was up to the father to provide qualified approval. It was up to the mother to provide unconditional love. It was up to the father to run alongside as you tried to ride your bike for the first time and shout encouragement as you did. It was up to the mother to stand on the sideline frightened you'd fall, and wipe away the tears when you did. Fathers took charge. Mothers took care. Between them, with a little help from family and friends, community and society, a baby boy would grow up to be a man – a normal, productive, well-balanced, and committed member of society. In the case of Baby Boomer boys like me, that meant being self-assured, self-absorbed, and self-conscious about changing the world and making things right, and filled with a sense of entitlement and great expectations for our own success.

Many believe a boy's struggles with his father make him a man. I never struggled with my father. That's because he, like many of the men of his generation and unlike the men of his father's generation, didn't feel the need to teach his children how to make it in a tough world because he believed his kids weren't going to live in the same world he had. It was bound to be better. My father and I didn't always agree. We didn't always see the world the same way. And we didn't always make the same choices. But, on the important issues – like family and the right thing to do, community and how you treated people, friends and taking care of each other, values and conformity for the common good, and duty – we were as one.

Sports offered one of the best ways (sometimes the only way) a father could get close to his son. By listening to, reading about, or watching the game together, by teaching the game and perhaps coaching it, by keeping score and debating the strengths and weaknesses of your idols, the two of you could spend time alone together and learn to at least respect, certainly enjoy and appreciate, even like or love, one another.

Baseball, in particular, was a game that bound together fathers and sons. Like so many things, baseball was easy and it was hard. It was graceful and clumsy, quirky and predictable, fair and foul, old and new, wild and controlled, relaxed and intense, fun and torture. Often thanks to the expectations. That you enjoyed it. That you were good enough. That you'd want to play it again. With him. That he'd have time for you now and you'd have time for him later. Baseball, in all its elegant and simple complexity, echoed the saga of fathers and sons, as well as the unbroken circle of life.

Baseball was the only sport for me; probably because summer was my favorite season. Maybe, because it was familiar. I understood it. I got it. And I could play it. There was something about the history and tradition, innocence and nostalgia, the symmetry and sense of fair play, the rite and ritual. Throwing, catching, hitting, running, and sliding all seemed so natural and effortless. It always made me think of a time when things seemed easier and better. I liked the fact that it was the player that scored, not the ball. That it included errors, since we all made them. That it valued a keen eye, quick reflexes, and good judgment. That it was a team game. That it wasn't played against the clock. That, as writer Roger Angell once wrote, "Since baseball time is measured only in outs, all you have to do…is keep hitting, keep the rally alive, and you have defeated time. You remain young forever." For me, baseball was the never-ending game. And, it felt like home.

CHAPTER 1

The torture was finally over. Replaced by rapture. The San Francisco Giants had won the 2010 World Championship of Baseball; their first since 1954 and their only since grapes-of-wrathing it west from New York.

My son and I stood where my father and I had stood on that day in 1958 when San Francisco welcomed their new team with a celebratory parade down Montgomery Street to Market Street to City Hall, led by Willie Mays and Hank Sauer sitting in a convertible Chevy Impala. My dad had taken me not because he was a Giants fan. He loved the Yankees. He took me because he loved baseball. And he loved me.

On this beautiful November day, my boy and I waited in the shadow of the TransAmerica Pyramid. Back in the Barbary Coast days, that part of the street had been known as the Montgomery Block, or "Monkey Block." At the time, it was the tallest building in the West and was home to a colorful spectrum of lawyers, financiers, writers, actors, and artists, as well as visiting celebrities like Jack London, Lola Montez, Maynard Dixon, Lotta Crabtree, Frank Norris, Ambrose Bierce, Bret Harte, the acting Booths, and Mark Twain.

We had gotten up before first light on that cool November 3 morning and headed over the Altamont from Modesto to join the rest of the die-hard fans who had staked out spots along the parade route. I had taken the day off work and my son out of school, just like my buddies and their dads used to do on opening day. We had caught BART in Dublin, jumped off at Montgomery Station in downtown San Francisco, and walked the few blocks north to the Pyramid.

The words of Kruk and Kuip describing the last pitch of the fifth game of the Series against the Texas Rangers still echoed in my ears, as we moved through the vapor-lit, early-morning streets. "And the right-hander for the Giants throws. Swing and a miss. And that's it," Duane Kuiper screamed. "And the Giants, for the first time in fifty-six years, the Giants are World Champions," Duane Kuiper yelled. "As they come pouring out of the dugout."

"I love torture," Mike Krukow added.

"We did it," Kuiper said, sounding like he still couldn't believe it.

"You never forget your first," Krukow finished.

It was magical. It was mystical. It was terrific.

Brian "Fear the Beard" Wilson had just struck out Nelson Cruz to end the game at Rangers Ballpark in Arlington, Texas, cinching an impressive 3-1 victory and clinching an improbable World Series Championship. Wilson ended the game the same way he always did. He turned away from the plate, crossed his forearms in front of his chest, and quickly looked toward the sky. A signal he adopted and adapted from Mixed Martial Arts to honor his late father, who had died of cancer when Brian was seventeen. Then he was mobbed by his teammates, as he stood his ground on the mound. When asked later by a reporter if this signal meant more than the others, he replied, "This one was the most special, sure. It showed that hard work really does pay off. That's what my dad always taught me."

As the sun came up over the East Bay foothills and the Bay Bridge, it turned into a beautiful, Northern California fall day. I balanced a Rawlings baseball on the tip of my fingertips and raised it to the burnished-red sun. Surrounded, we watched as the spectacle of people, autos, floats, and cable cars streamed by. It was literally a sea of orange and black as far as the eye could see; the biggest crowd in the city's history. There were people standing on Muni buses, hanging from streetlight standards, leaning out skyscraper windows, and cheering from apartment fire escapes. Panda-bear-hat-wearing, rally-thong-waving, rally-towel-flapping fans were everywhere. Lou Seal, the Giants' mascot, flopped on his back and made a confetti angel in the blizzarding drifts of orange and black shredded paper.

Just like fifty-two years ago, Willie Mays led the parade. He sat alone this time on the back seat of a vintage, 1958 Cadillac convertible. Ever the gracious gentleman.

It was fantastic to see the misfits, or manager Bruce Bochy's "Dirty Dozen," in person. We'd been to a few games that season, but the players mostly existed for us on TV and the radio. Seeing them as flesh-and-blood characters, as excited as Little Leaguers, made us appreciate them even more.

My son grasped an ink pen shaped like a Louisville Slugger, which had been a get-well gift to me from my father. When the cable car carrying Aubrey Huff and Pat Burrell swung in front of us, my son dashed through the crowd and ran up to the car. His half-orange, half-black painted face and orange-dyed and spiked hair must have gotten their attention, as well as the SFPD mounted patrolman who smiled, sitting astride a horse with the Giants' "SF" shaved into its rump, and let him get close enough to offer up the pen and his brand-new World Champion Giants hat. Huff set down his Bud light, grabbed both hat and pen, balanced the cap on his head, looked at the pen, mock-swung for the fences with it, signed the hat, and gave them back to my boy.

"That's quite the special piece of lumber, young man," the Huff Daddy said.

My boy just grinned back, rooted where he stood.

"What's your name, son?" Burrell asked.

"Mikey," he answered, breathless.

"Mickey?"

"No, Mikey. Like my dad. We're Giants fans."

"Your face says it all," Pat the Bat replied.

My boy smiled and touched his painted face.

"Catchy name," Burrell added.

It was. My father wanted to name me Mickey, after his hero, but my mom dug in. They compromised on Michael. So, dad always called me Mikey. I did the same with my boy. Mikey and Mikey Jr. The M&M Boys. Just like Mantle and Maris, or Mantle and Mays. MM, MM good.

We decided to skip the celebration in front of City Hall, where the parade route ended. There were way too many people and much too much traffic. We watched the replay of the entire event back home on cable TV, courtesy of Comcast Bay Area Sports. Krukow added the exclamation point to the post-parade ceremony when he said, "You are not standing alone. You are standing with the person that taught you the great story of the San Francisco Giants. Whether it be your dad or your mom or sister or your friend or your grandpa. And you have but one responsibility. And you owe it to the person that taught you 'The Good Book San Francisco Giants.' You need to pass this story on. Keep this love alive. And when you tell the story, simply tell 'em, 'We're the Giants. We're San Francisco. And we're the World Champions.'"

CHAPTER 2

That miniature Louisville Slugger bat pen was indeed special. My dad had given it to me at a get-well party in late February 1962.

The weather in California's Central Valley in February could be all over the place. Fog, rain, wind, and cold often alternated with balmy, seventy-degree weather. This day was one of the warm ones, which was why my parents held the party at J.M. Pike Park behind our house. No surprise, considering that was a second home for all us neighborhood kids. All my buddies from Garrison Elementary School and Roosevelt Junior High, the neighborhood, and Little League were there, as well as Mr. Leach, my fifth grade teacher and A-Team coach. We didn't have time for girls then; although they had our attention, none were invited. My dad barbequed dogs and burgers, while my mom made potato salad. All my favorites. The guys played a little whiffle ball. I wanted to, but couldn't yet, so I just watched.

One of the older neighborhood kids rode up on his bicycle to watch. That's how he got around, even though he was old enough to drive. My dad made us let him play although he was kind of strange. He had a hair-lip so, being the smart-mouthed kids that we were, we always made fun of him. But, he was a great athlete. He was fast and he could hit the ball a mile. One time, when he was giving us a hard time out in the park, my little brother told my mom, and she and my best friend's older sister came running out to the park carrying baseball bats and chased him off. That was the last time he ever bothered us. Mom probably felt sorry for what she had done, which was why she always talked Dad into letting him play and, as a result, so did we.

There was an empty field across from the park next to the brand new Coca-Cola plant. We had dug all kinds of tunnels in that field, like busy little ants. We'd hide things there and build fires that would smoke us out. Our parents were scared to death the earth would collapse, so they made us stop. Of course, we didn't.

I stared at the train tracks just across that field and beyond Highway 99, which had oleanders down the middle to separate the four lanes of traffic. I loved hearing the whistle blow, especially at night. That old lonesome whistle. I used to think of the Hank Williams song every time I heard the train, but I was thinking of the midnight train whining low, not the lonesome whip-poor-will, too blue to fly. It always reminded me of people going somewhere. Like George Bailey in *It's a Wonderful Life*, when he said, "You know what the three most exciting sounds in the world are? Anchor chains, plane motors, and train whistles." There were places out there I had to see.

My dad hated the train because it always made him late coming home from his full-time job and sometimes late going to his part-time job. He worked during the day as an installer for the Pacific Telephone and Telegraph Company, aka Pacific Bell, or Ma Bell, as he liked to call the parent company American Telephone and Telegraph. His office was south of the highway, adjacent to the Department of Motor Vehicles. He drove an Army-green Ford Econoline van filled with tools, equipment, and materials, as well as two ladders on top. He also worked at night and on weekends at the Barbour's Gas Station on Ninth Street, which was also Highway 99, near the Griswold and Wight car dealership. The train tracks ran right down the middle of Ninth Street. If you got caught on the wrong side, you were going to be there a while. Traffic always came to a dead stop any time the train rumbled through town. People got mad, but not mad enough to do anything about it. The state was getting ready to build a new Highway 99, an honest-to-goodness freeway, which would by-pass the commercial districts of all the towns along its spine. I guess people were getting tired of having to stop at signal lights all the way to Los Angeles.

We kids were sweaty and stinky when it came time to have black-iced chocolate cake and orange sherbet ice cream. And open presents. My teammates had pooled their allowances, which gave them enough to give me a subscription to *Sports Illustrated.* Mom gave me underwear. Embarrassing. My younger brothers and sisters gave me hand-made birthday cards they had crafted at school.

I remember removing the baseball-themed wrapping covering the small slender gift to reveal a forest-green, white-striped box. I opened the lid to reveal the baseball-bat-shaped pen and pencil set, complete with an authentication certificate from the Louisville Slugger factory. It was so cool.

"Thanks Dad," I said. He smiled.

My best buddy Gary Rawlings (yep, just like the baseball gear) grabbed the pen from my hands, pointed to the far edge of the park, and swung from the heels. Another neighborhood buddy, Chris, wadded up some of the gift wrapping paper and began pitching it to Gary.

"Give it back," I said, as I tried to get the bat away from Gary. I never liked other people playing with my things.

"In a minute, okay," he said.

"No, it's mine and I want it back." I reached for it again and he jumped back, holding it high above his head.

"Come on," I said. I squeezed my left arm close to my belly to make sure I didn't stress out my new stitches.

"Just a couple more swings."

"Forget it," I said. I turned and walked away, slumping down on the brightly colored wood-and-concrete bleachers behind the metal, chain-link screen of the baseball diamond. I wasn't there for long before my mother appeared. I couldn't look her in the eye. I knew I was being a spoiled brat. And she was going to remind me.

"Why do you always do that?" she asked.

"What?" I answered, crossing my arms.

"Why can't you share?"

"It's my stuff."

"And they're your friends."

"So."

"Some day, you'll learn that it's not always about you. That this big old world doesn't revolve around you."

"They're bugging me. I wish they'd just go home."

"They're friends and family. That's what we do."

"Who cares?"

"Growing up means letting go, Michael. So, let it go. Please just let it go."

Of course, I didn't. And couldn't. And never did. I sat there a while longer after she left before someone hit me with a water balloon. Then the battle was on.

CHAPTER 3

On TV a month earlier, my family had watched the ball drop in Times Square to usher in 1962, like we always did. We knew the New Year had officially begun when Guy Lombardo and his Royal Canadians played "Auld Lang Syne" live from the Waldorf Astoria on CBS-TV. For the rest of the year, each weekday night, we caught up on what was happening outside our living room by watching the local news at six o'clock and the Huntley-Brinkley Report at a quarter after on KCRA-TV, the Sacramento NBC affiliate station. Sometimes we'd switch over to CBS and watch Douglas Edwards. For some reason, NBC was my favorite.

That January, construction had begun on the Houston Astrodome, the new home of the expansion Houston Colt 45s, who would work out an agreement with our local minor league club – the Modesto Reds – to be a part of their farm system. In the American Football League Pro Bowl, the West beat the East 47-27. Jack Nicklaus, a twenty-one-year-old amateur golfer, made his first pro appearance and finished fiftieth at the Los Angeles Open at Rancho Park Golf Club, winning a whopping $33.33. In the National Football League Pro Bowl, the West beat the East 31-30. President John F. Kennedy visited Uruguay. Bob Feller and Jackie Robinson were elected to the Baseball Hall of

Fame. Brian Epstein signed a management contract with a rock 'n roll group named the Beatles. Two members of the "Flying Wallendas" high-wire act were killed when their seven-person pyramid collapsed during a performance in Detroit. And it snowed in Modesto, which almost never happened. It was the day before a special election that sent Republican John Veneman to the California state assembly.

That was only the first month of 1962. It was shaping up to be an interesting year, as the world kept spinning by outside the window of my home in Modesto, California, the town where summer lasted longer. Modesto belonged to me and the Central Valley Heartland was mine. There was no other place on earth like it. The lush garden first seen by mountain men like Jedediah Smith, explorers like John Fremont, and naturalists like John Muir. It was flat, dry, and desolate. Once, though, it was a sea, filled by rivers of the Sierra Nevada, with names like Tuolumne and Stanislaus. Now it was the world's most fertile, most productive farmland, thanks to irrigation. Crops could be grown here around the clock, around the year. It was put here for farming. Some had even suggested that it be used exclusively for cultivation, that all the residents should be uprooted and moved to the foothills that rimmed the valley. What was once a sea of water was now a sea of grass. Lying below the soil was the bottom of this ancient sea. It was a layer of clay, impermeable. Nothing got through. In some places, it was far below the surface; in others, it was very close to the top. Skimming the valley, as a marsh hawk would, hunting, it was dead level. There wasn't much tall enough to break the dusty monotony. But, I loved it, because it's what I knew. It was home. I took the good with the bad. I liked the flatness, unending. I liked the people, uncomplicated. I liked the weather, unbearable. I supposed it's what you got used to. I didn't care if my hometown was hot, flat, small, and foggy. It was mine.

Neither my dad nor my mom were from the valley. My dad, Timothy Owen Wright, had been born in Los Angeles.

He joined the Marines when he was seventeen and a half. My grandfather picked up his diploma for him on graduation day at Manteca High School. My mother, Cora Ann Baker, had been born in Jamestown, one of fourteen children. My parents were introduced by a friend of my mom's, who happened to be my dad's cousin. Mom was working as a telephone operator and was living in a boarding house in Stockton. Dad was back in Manteca after coming home from World War II. They met again in Strawberry, in the Sierra foothills above Sonora, where my mother was working at the snack bar and my dad was working a timber crew. It was a short courtship. They married at Stockton's City Hall. I was born a year later.

I was the oldest of five. They say firstborns learn to be resourceful, self-reliant, and tough. They demand a lot of themselves, and of others. They were organized and anxious. And were always expected to set a good example. That was me, to a "T."

I had two younger brothers and two younger sisters. Timothy "Timmy" Owen Jr. was only fifteen months younger than me, so we were pretty close. William "Willy" Christopher, who was named after one of my dad's Marine buddies, was five years younger. Since he was the youngest boy, he got picked on a lot. He handled it pretty well. Diane "Dee-Dee" Jane was next in line. She looked a lot like Dad and was pretty easy-going, just like him. Cheryl "Cheri" Gayle was ten years younger than me and probably the most like me in personality. We were a family.

What are little boys made of, made of?
What are little boys made of?
'Snaps and snails, and puppy-dogs' tails;
And that's what little boys are made of.'

What are little girls made of, made of?
What are little girls made of?
Sugar and spice, and all that's nice;
And that's what little girls are made of.'

Mother Goose must not have liked boys. Each time I heard that nursery rhyme growing up, I realized it was true in so many ways, but it made me mad at girls. We were nice, too. We just enjoyed playing in the dirt more.

On any given day, little boys were also made of greed, envy, sloth, gluttony, wrath, pride, and lust. Pretty much some variation of all the seven deadly sins. We wanted what we wanted and we wanted it now. We wanted what our friends had. We were lazy and would do as little as we possibly could, for as long as we could. We ate and drank anything and everything, any time we could. We got mad and held grudges forever. We believed the whole world revolved around us and were angry when it didn't. And we craved what we couldn't have.

My brothers and I were close because we rolled out of the womb one-two-three. I came out butt-first, but that's another story for a different time. Then Timmy. We did everything together, until Willy arrived. When he was old enough, he became the Third Musketeer. Any time you saw one of us, the other two were lurking nearby. We played sports, explored the neighborhood, victimized small creatures, threw rocks, played *Monopoly* and *Chutes and Ladders*, ran through mud puddles, dressed up for Halloween, wore hand-me-downs from older cousins, chased bees and butterflies, teased little girls and sisters, watched TV, played with matches, climbed trees, skinned knees, ran with scissors, caught polliwogs, nearly broke our necks on the Slip 'n Slide, played Cowboys and Indians and War, got brain freeze from ice cream cones, swam at Playland and in the canals, watched Saturday afternoon Westerns, rode horses at Grampa Owl's, gigged frogs with Dad, protected each other from older cousins and neighborhood bullies, sang songs, danced dances, and ate everything but peas, brussels sprouts, and scalloped potatoes.

We were boys, and boys being boys, we naturally enjoyed the same things. We were inseparable, until someone got sick or hurt. Then you'd think we had lost an arm or leg. We shared everything. Disneyland, Christmas, family vacations, Easter, friends, bedrooms and bathrooms, school, summer, wagons and bicycles, sports, clothes, enemies, pets, chores, colds, heroes, and our hometown. It was a common experience and shared memory that only the three of us would have. Ever. Nobody could take it away. Ever. We were the only ones who could finish each other's stories and dream each other's dreams.

When our sisters came along, the household priorities shifted from testosterone to estrogen; from blue jeans to pinafores; from snails to sugar. Mom finally had allies and things balanced out a bit.

"Sisters, sisters. There were never such devoted sisters." Every time I heard that song from the movie, *White Christmas*, I thought of my little sisters. They were fun to be around and it was amazing to watch them grow. I liked my brothers, too, but it was different. Brothers always seemed to be so competitive and were encouraged to one-up each other; all part of that ritual of being a man. Sisters, whether they were older or younger than their brothers, generally seemed to be much more encouraging, supportive, forgiving, and easy. Although I sometimes resisted taking my brothers along with me on various errands or adventures, I never hesitated to invite my sisters, never refused when they wanted to tag along. If they wanted me to play dolls or house with them, I did. If they asked me to be a part of their tea party, I was. If they pleaded with me to show them a new dance, we danced. I don't know how many Christmas Eves I stayed up late with Dad to assemble a bike, a vanity, or a cardboard kitchen.

Diane and Cheryl were curious about things and had a wonderful fantasy life. Whether it was dressing up the kitties in doll clothes, creating an imaginary friend, or building a world for Ken and Barbie, they never stopped exploring and imagining and dreaming, especially about growing up. They both completely enjoyed going through my seventh and eighth grade yearbooks, studying the individual portraits and the group photos of clubs and activities. They totally had fun looking at the messages in the yearbook, as well as the inscriptions on the individual, wallet-sized photos we got each year and distributed to guy friends and girlfriends, hoping to get a cool note from the guys and a sloppy note from the girls, especially from the girl of the moment. Both Dee-Dee and Cheri would mark the photos of their favorites with a little pencil tick and then they'd make up romances and lives for each of them. How they would marry, how many children they would have, and what kind of work the boy would do and what kind of hobbies or special interests the girl would have. It was all so innocent.

I had to thank my parents for being such good role models and demonstrating, with the way they lived their lives each day, that men and women were equal. That although Dad went to work each day and Mom worked at home, she worked just as hard and sometimes juggled more things and put out more fires in an hour than Dad did in a day. They respected and loved each other and recognized that the other had an important role to play in our family and in raising us kids. My parents didn't fight very often and they were never mean to the other. They didn't curse or yell or hit. And we didn't miss it.

I've heard it said that the happiest people don't necessarily have the best of everything. They just make the most of everything they have. That's what my family did. We were kind of poor. It seemed like I was always staring, with my nose pinned against the window pane, at something somebody else had. We mostly drove used cars that my dad had to work on every weekend to keep running. It seemed like he was always out in the front driveway, on a cold winter's Sunday, busting a knuckle trying to repair a fuel pump or radiator or fan belt. Just one of a whole bunch of "had to." We had health insurance through the phone company, but no dental or vision coverage. My dad had bad teeth. He never got them worked on because he wanted to save the money so he could pay for our dental work. We all had bad teeth, like he did, so a lot of money went to the dentist in those days. He let his teeth rot, so we could get ours fixed. He stayed sick, so we could stay healthy. I didn't know any better. I never thought we were poor because we always seemed to get what we wanted, thanks to our mom buying us stuff out of the Sears catalogue which, of course, kept my dad in debt and forced him to work his second job, and sometimes, a third job. I was happy and it all seemed pretty normal to me. It wouldn't be until I was much older that I could see the gap between what we had and what others had.

CHAPTER 4

In February, baseball's National League released its first 162-game schedule. Both leagues had traditionally played 154 games before that. President Kennedy banned all trade with Cuba, except for food and drugs. The Russian newspaper *Izvestia* reported that baseball was actually an old Russian game. A bus boycott started in Macon, Georgia. First Lady Jacqueline Kennedy conducted a television tour of the White House. The Soviet Union exchanged captured American U2 pilot, Francis Gary Powers, for Soviet spy, Rudolph Ivanovich Abel. The Beach Boys introduced a new musical style with their hit, "Surfin'." John Glenn was the first American to orbit Earth in Friendship 7. South Vietnam President Ngo Dinh Diem's palace was bombed, killing an American contractor – the first American to die in Vietnam. And a guy at MIT named Steve Russell created a game called *Spacewar* that ran on a computer called the DEC PDP-1.

In 1962, my family lived at 1500 Del Vista, right next to Pike Park, which was our home away from home all year long. Our very own oasis with a swing set, sand box, baseball diamond, and wide open fields. During the summer, we'd be there from sunrise to sunset. We played baseball no matter what season it was.

Except now, as February counted down. I was still recovering from losing my spleen. And it was killing me. No baseball, no running, no nothing. No matter. The weather got worse after my get-well party. When it wasn't foggy, it was too cold. When it wasn't too cold, it was raining. The streets were flooded. As usual. I burrowed inside and couldn't wait until I was better. Spring Training was just around the corner. So were the tryouts for the Babe Ruth League, which was the next step in local organized baseball after Little League. It had been three weeks since the accident and I was getting bored and antsy. I was ready to start playing ball again, now that I'd conveniently forgotten and buried what had put me on the disabled list in the first place.

It was while playing a game of lob ball on a fog holiday that I had ruptured my spleen and nearly died. There had been no school on that February day. The tule fog was so thick, it was too dangerous to drive. The city schools cancelled all classes. And us guys immediately grabbed our baseball mitts, bats, and balls and headed out to the park for a little lob ball. It was cold and wet and miserable, but we didn't care. We loved baseball. We only had enough guys to play the left side of the infield, so we closed off the right side, since only one guy hit left-handed, and made pitcher as good as first. The ball had to be hit to the left of an imaginary line that ran through the pitcher's mound, across second base, out into centerfield, and through the Coca-Cola plant across the street. Anything hit to the right of that line was foul, except when the lefty was up and we'd shift to the right side and make everything hit to the left a foul. The Coca-Cola plant had a vending machine in the lobby that had the coldest Cokes for just ten cents. We always made time for a Coke break on a hot day, if we had gotten our allowances.

I was playing short and wearing my steel baseball spikes. I'm not sure why. Maybe because I didn't want to slip and hurt myself. Maybe because they made me feel like a big leaguer. Ernie was on first. He was a year older than us and one of the neighborhood punks. He lived next to Gary and only got to play when we were short guys. Bobby, another neighborhood kid, was up. He slapped an easy one-hopper to me. A tailor-made double-play ball. I snagged it and raced to tag second before Ernie got there. We arrived at the bag at the same time. Ernie was barefoot, so he jumped to avoid getting spiked. And planted his knee in my gut.

The next thing I knew, I was on my back. I was white as a ghost, clammy, and kind of sick to my stomach. My buddies helped me up. Roy, another neighbor kid and my best friend until Gary had come along, said I didn't look so good. He grabbed my stuff and walked me home.

When we stepped inside the house, my mom froze when she saw me. Roy left and I went into the bathroom. I felt like I had to pee, but couldn't. I felt like I had to poop, but couldn't. I had a pain in my left shoulder. That was all Doctor Robinson needed to hear when my mother called. He told her to bring me in right away. When we got to his office, he checked me over, asked a few questions, and said I needed to go to the hospital. He picked me up and carried me out to the car. I was shocked because he wasn't all that big and seemed kind of old at the time. Plus, if he was doing that, I figured it must be bad. It was.

I had, indeed, ruptured my spleen. The spleen the doctors said I didn't need because it was a vestigial organ, whatever that meant. It sounded like "vestal virgins," which I had read about in Roman mythology, but I knew it wasn't the same. This was the same body part that killed jet pilots who parachuted out of their planes over the ocean, hit the water, ruptured their spleens on impact, and bled to death. The organ that had just pumped two pints of blood into my stomach cavity. Enough blood that, if my mom hadn't taken me to the doctor right away and the doctor hadn't recognized the symptoms right away and hadn't carried me out to the car in his arms right away, I could have died. I would find out from the surgeon later how really close to death I had been.

While I was recovering in my room following the surgery, Dr. Nachtmann visited me with a present. My spleen in a glass jar of formaldehyde. It was gross. When my parents arrived, he said a few words and left.

"I'm not fuzzy anymore," I proudly told my mother.

"The anesthesia must be wearing off," Dad replied.

"No," I corrected him. "I'm not fuzzy down there," I said, pointing below my stomach. The summer before I had started sprouting pubic hair and Mom had teased me about it. During prep for the surgery, they had shaved me clean.

For a week after I came home from the hospital, I would crawl into my parents' bed in the middle of the night. It had scared me pretty good and I couldn't sleep. One night, my father said, "You've got to stop doing this, son."

"But, I'm afraid," I said, as I cuddled closer to my mom.

"Then tell us a story," she said. "You know," she added, "there are cultures all over the world that have men who have looked death in the face and returned to tell stories that helped the tribe survive. Tell us a story, Michael."

And I did.

During my recovery, I spent a lot of time in bed, or on the couch in the living room. I watched TV and the world unfolded in front of me. It was a habit I couldn't break, even after I got healthy. Each day, I'd be glued to the TV, and every night, I'd get the latest news from Channel 3 then Chet Huntley and David Brinkley.

I loved old movies, even more than the new ones, and I got to watch a lot of them as I watched the minutes tick by that February. *Cape Fear* and *The Manchurian Candidate* couldn't hold a candle to *Casablanca* or *Citizen Kane*, although *The Man Who Shot Liberty Valance* was pretty good. There was something about those old black-

and-white films from the thirties and forties. I think I loved them partly because my mom did. Whenever I had a cold or the flu, even sometimes after school, I'd watch an old movie with her while she ironed clothes. Cagney, Bogey, Errol Flynn, Veronica Lake, Alan Ladd, and all the other stars seemed so much larger than life, even though some of them weren't much taller than me in real life. Mom would almost always tell me about the time she met Edward G. Robinson while he was filming a movie around Sonora. She always told that story every time we saw Edward G.

I wasn't a big fan of golf. I had never played and I thought it was as dull to watch as raisins drying, but I always watched the Crosby "Clambake" because of all the celebrities. They looked like they were having a great time. Bing, Bob Hope, Phil Harris. It was quite a cast. The golf tournament took place each February at Pebble Beach and was usually broadcast on ABC, with Jim McKay doing the commentary. The weather was always a little unpredictable, but this year it actually snowed, which didn't stop them from playing or Doug Ford from winning.

Doctor Robinson finally cleared me to go back to school and I returned to Roosevelt Junior High School to finish the eighth grade. I had missed fourteen days. I hadn't been sick at all during seventh grade and only a couple times in elementary school. I enjoyed school too much to skip any of it. I felt pretty special that morning when everyone saw me for the first time in two weeks. All the guys kidded me, all the girls just smiled. I loved being the center of attention. I really raked in the sympathy during gym class when I lifted up my shirt and showed the guys my ugly red welt of a scar. I still couldn't dress for gym or shower, so I just gave them a little peek. Dr. Nachtmann had carved a big, old lazy "T" on my stomach, with the top bar of the "T" pointing north-south, and the leg pointing east-west. The stitches hadn't dissolved, or been completely removed yet. The welt was red and looked like a fat earthworm. The skin around it was peeling from being dry. It was pretty impressive. Of course, when summer rolled around, I was embarrassed to take my shirt off any time I went swimming, so I pretty much only hung out with my family and close friends until the scar started to disappear. It took a while.

CHAPTER 5

In March, our little black-and-white television continued to beam in world events. I followed the Giants in the newspaper and got back into my school and home routines. A young folk singer named Bob Dylan released his first album on Columbia Records, simply calling it, *Bob Dylan*. The first Kmart store opened in Garden City, Michigan. Wilt Chamberlain of pro basketball's Philadelphia Warriors scored one hundred points against the New York Knicks. The citizens of St. Louis voted to build a new baseball stadium for the Cardinals. U.S. military advisors began training South Vietnamese helicopter pilots. Because the Jack Tar Harrison Hotel had a "no black policy," the Philadelphia Phillies moved to Rocky Point Motel, twenty miles outside Clearwater, Florida, for Spring Training. In the 24th NCAA Men's Basketball Championship, Cincinnati beat Ohio State 71-59. Boxer Benny Paret died from injuries suffered during his bout with Emile Griffith at Madison Square Garden. Jack Paar hosted his last *The Tonight Show* on NBC. And Cesar Chavez founded the United Farm Workers Union.

It was a very long winter. Wet, cold, and foggy. I couldn't wait for spring. And baseball. Finally, the first Spring Training games rolled around. I stepped out the backyard gate and into Pike Park.

I wrapped my fingers around the brand new Rawlings baseball and held it up to the misty sun. I was filled with wishful thinking.

In 1962, the Yankees moved their Grapefruit League facilities from St. Petersburg's Al Lang Field to Ft. Lauderdale Stadium in Ft. Lauderdale, Florida. Their new stadium cost $600,000. It could seat 8,000 and even had air-conditioning, which nobody had back then. By moving to the east coast of Florida, the Yankees were closer to four other teams, which they could now play without having to travel so far. The Baltimore Orioles were in Miami, the Los Angeles Dodgers were in Vero Beach, the Washington Senators were in Pompano Beach, and the Kansas City Athletics were in West Palm Beach. The first workout for Yankee pitchers and catchers was February 19. The first full-squad workout was February 28. The first game was March 10 against the Baltimore Orioles.

The Giants also had a spanking new facility. It was located in the middle of nowhere, outside a place called Casa Grande in Arizona. Owner Horace Stoneham had built a $2 million resort designed to be a self-contained complex. It had its own airstrip, eighteen-hole championship golf course, pool, and multi-field complex with an adjoining ballpark that could seat 3,000. Stoneham built the facility to be used as a training complex in February and March, and a luxury resort hotel the rest of the year. The Giants opened 1962 in Tucson against the Cleveland Indians.

My mother never met a holiday she didn't like; partly because each one was a day to celebrate, a day off from the day-to-day. Plus, they were all fun in their own way. One of her favorites was March 17 – St. Patrick's Day. It had nothing to do with being Irish, because she was Bavarian German. Or drinking, although she enjoyed a cocktail or two. Or shamrocks, although she was terminally superstitious. Or leprechauns, though I think she believed they really existed and would have dearly loved to find the pot o' gold at the end of the rainbow. For *Madre*, it was all about the "wearin' o' the green."

If you didn't wear green on St. Patty's Day, she would pinch you. Not an easy pinch, but a turn-the-skin-red and leave-a-white-mark twister. She loved catching us kids without our green on. Because she always trapped us first thing in the morning, when we were all still half-asleep, it was easy; easier than fooling us on April Fool's Day, but that's another story. Of course, we'd be sure to add some green somewhere before we headed off to school, since every kid there had learned the same painful lesson at home and each was eager to apply it to their classmates. When we finally donned the green, it was usually someplace invisible so we could trick our attackers, since turnabout was fair play if they were wrong. The pincher would thus become the pinchee.

I'm pretty sure Mom didn't know that the tradition originated with an Irish street ballad written in 1798. And that green, which was one of the colors of the Irish flag and the shamrock, represented the Irish rebellion from Britain, which was associated with the color red, thanks to the Union Jack and their military uniforms. Because it became a sign of Irish patriotism, any Irishman caught wearing green was hanged on the spot by the Brits. I think if my mom had known the true history, she probably wouldn't have insisted that we wear green.

As far as the pinching part of the tradition, that was purely an American invention, which reportedly started in the early 1700s. Those early colonials believed that wearing green made you invisible to leprechauns, who would pinch anyone they could see, which meant anyone not wearing green. Kind of a vicious circle. People began pinching those who didn't wear green as a reminder that the wee folk could see them, making them fair game, thus freeing the warner to sneak up and pinch the warnee before the little people did. It was silly, but fun. Because St. Patty's fell on a

Saturday this year, we didn't have to worry about getting pinched at school. But, that didn't stop Mom.

After finishing our chores, Tim and I went to Vince's house to hang out. Vince, or Vito as we nicknamed him, lived just down the street from us. He was a year younger than me and a year older than Tim. My brother and I kind of both thought he was our friend. He had a younger sister named Laura, who was Tim's age, who Tim kind of liked. She was a typical little sister. Always tattling and trying to get us in trouble. Other than that, she was okay. Vito's parents, Marco and Elaine Carrasco, both worked. Marco, also known as Mark, was a milkman, so he was up early and home early so he could nap. Elaine sold real estate part-time, which meant she was never home. They always had goodies around the house, so Tim and I loved visiting Vito. It was there that I first smelled a gardenia, so I've always associated that smell with that place. Mark and Elaine were good friends of my parents. Just about every Friday night, you'd find them drinking coffee, playing cards, and gossiping. Eventually, they moved from caffeine to cocktails.

My family loved playing games, especially card games. We started with Fish, moved up to Crazy Eights and Hearts, and on to Pinochle. Although it was relatively easy to learn, Pinochle took skill and concentration to win. My parents taught most of our friends how to play, so we'd always have enough for a table. My dad and I were pretty competitive. We were both decent players. We were never on the same team because we usually partnered up with a weaker player to balance the sides. On the rare occasion that we did team up, we were almost invincible. Dad could always figure out a way to make the bid by making his hand work, even if we both had nothing but junk.

One bone of contention between us came to be known as "Kevin's Rule." I would never bid without an ace of trump in my hand. My philosophy was that since the ace was needed for a run in trump and aces around, which was one ace in each suit, you doubled the odds of having a good hand if you had the ace. Any time I won the bid, I never called trump in a suit if I didn't have the ace. My dad, on the other hand, felt the ace was just one more card and the odds of getting it, or having your partner pass it to you, were the same as any other card. In Pinochle, when your partner won the bid, you were able to pass them four cards to help their hand and to help your team make the bid. The problem was, if you had five good cards to pass, and one of them was the ace of trump, you had to make a choice about what to send. Since I always assumed that everyone, especially when they were my partner, played Kevin's rule, I never passed the ace of trump. My father and I had a few discussions about that strategy over the years. We never worked it out.

CHAPTER 6

Every day that April, I followed the Giants. Every day, I got a little stronger. And every day, the world changed a little more. Arnold Palmer won the 26th Masters at Augusta, Georgia. *West Side Story* won Best Picture at the thirty-fourth Academy Awards, while Sophia Loren won Best Actress for her role in *Two Women* and Maximilian Schell won Best Actor for *Judgment at Nuremberg*. Stan "The Man" Musial scored run number 1,869 to set the National League record. Walter Cronkite succeeded Douglas Edwards as anchorman of *The CBS Evening News*. In the 16th NBA Championship, the Boston Celtics beat the Los Angeles Lakers four games to three. The Mets tied a National League record by losing nine straight to start the season. On the flip side, the Pittsburgh Pirates set an NL record by winning their first ten games. The Toronto Maple Leafs won the 45th Stanley Cup Championship by defeating the Chicago Blackhawks, four games to two. Ranger 6, the first U.S. satellite to reach the moon, was launched from Cape Canaveral, Florida, and later crashed on the moon. Sandy Koufax of the Los Angeles Dodgers struck out eighteen Chicago Cub batters. In the 16th Tony Awards, *A Man for All Seasons* won Outstanding Play and *How to Succeed in Business without Really Trying* won Outstanding Musical.

And Marvel Comics released the fifteenth *Amazing Fantasy* comic book, which introduced Spider Man. Orlando Cepeda and Willie McCovey were guests at the Sportsmen of Stanislaus Club in Modesto.

That month, Chet Huntley did a special on NBC about Spring Break in Daytona, Florida. It was called *Spring Break: Where the Boys Went*. Ever since the movie *Where the Boys Are* with Connie Francis came out in 1960, I guess college kids had been heading to the sun to hang out, drink beer, and get together. Out here in California, they came to Palm Springs. It was the first time I remember a TV news program showing kids drinking beer and dancing together. It was cool to see all these cars driving up and down on the beach. Some pretty wild stuff.

April was also rodeo time in California. I knew that because my grandfather was a real live cowboy.

Grampa Owl wanted us boys to be buckaroos, just like him, especially since Dad didn't want anything to do with ropin' and ridin'. My grandfather had been a ranch foreman and worked the stockyards of California his entire life, so my father grew up riding horses, mucking out stalls, and working livestock. My grandfather was a bit of a dandy, so he loved getting dressed up and riding his best pony in parades and rodeos. My dad hated it, primarily because it usually meant getting up before first light on a holiday weekend, feeding the horses, loading them into a trailer, getting all duded up, driving two or three hours, riding in sweltering heat down the asphalt main street of some small town, loading the horses back onto the trailer, returning home, and taking care of the animals before collapsing into bed. When he was older and confident enough, he told his father he wouldn't be riding in any more parades, or doing any more rodeos. That's when Grampa Owl started working on us. We called him Grampa Owl because we couldn't pronounce his first name, which was Alowishus.

Of course, we loved it. The hats, the boots, the shirts, the belts with big buckles, riding horses, going on cattle drives, visiting the stockyards in Stockton, helping brand and castrate calves. Who wouldn't enjoy being a miniature Tom Mix or Hopalong Cassidy or Roy Rogers? For us, a visit to Grampa's meant a day being around big, dusty, brown-eyed animals. We couldn't wait.

What this all meant was I would be going to the Oakdale Rodeo with a friend and not my dad.

I had met Rusty as a first grader at Washington Elementary School. My family had just moved to Modesto from Lathrop and Washington was the first of many schools I would attend, as we moved around Modesto and new schools opened. We were living on Faustina in South Modesto, near Belle Nita Park. Rusty was a 4-Her and his parents owned a cattle ranch on Paradise Road. He had ridden ponies from the moment he could walk. We had become friends at school because we both had the same Roy Rogers lunch boxes, which, of course, meant that Roy was our hero. We'd spend our recesses re-enacting the stories we'd see on his TV show, which was broadcast on NBC, and in his movies. After my family moved closer into town and I changed from Washington to Enslen, Rusty and I would still see each other at the county fair or when our Little League teams played each other, and sometimes at Modesto Reds games. He'd invite me out to the ranch to ride horses, since he knew I had ridden before. We'd canter along the Tuolumne River and pretend there were outlaws lurking in the cottonwoods and willows. Rusty was an old rodeo hand, having started mutton busting around the time we first met and moving up to saddle bronc and bareback riding as a junior rodeoer. He always did well at the Oakdale Junior Rodeo, which took place in August, and that was one of many reasons he liked the Oakdale event.

The Oakdale Rodeo was a Real Cowboy Association-sanctioned event and was one of the most popular and competitive small rodeos in the country. It was the first outdoor rodeo in the western United States. Oakdale, which was known as the "Cowboy Capital of the World," drew some of the best bronco busters, steer wrestlers, and bulldoggers in the country. Oakdale was also well known for the number of professional cowboys who called it home, including Leo and Jerold Camarillo; accomplished horsemen and hard-working ranchers whose day job had turned into a popular sport. Rodeo was the only sport that started out as a way of life. What these men, and later women, did day-in and day-out eventually became a competition with some pretty big purses. Rodeo was a Spanish word derived from *rodear*, to surround, or *rueda*, which meant wheel. The word came to mean "the gathering of cattle," or "round up." Back in those days, at the end of the day, ranch owners would place wagers to see whose hands were the best at breaking horses, bringing in the herd, or roping a steer. A simple game turned into serious money and a new athletic competition was born.

This April day was unseasonably warm for the valley. Temperatures had been hovering in the high eighties, with predictions of more hot weather to come.

The annual rodeo parade took place at ten o'clock on F Street, which doubled as the main street through town and State Highway 108. Rusty's mom and dad parked their pickup on the street and we set up our lawn chairs. I kept an eye out for my dad's cousin, who still rode with the Tuolumne County Sheriff's Posse. I had to smile as they and the rest of the parade entrants passed by because just about every one was some kind of mounted unit. I thought of my dad.

When the parade ended, we piled into the truck and drove to the rodeo grounds, which were farther down F Street, on the road to Sonora and the Gold Country. We handed off our tickets and walked through a collection of booths selling hot dogs, Rocky Mountain oysters, cotton candy, beer, clothes, and information on Oakdale, the Oakdale Saddle Club, the 4-H, and other community organizations. As we moved toward the grandstands, we saw the Camarillo brothers, dressed and ready for their team roping contest, talking with some other cowboys. It looked like a group of working cowboys standing around chewing the fat.

We had seats just above the cyclone fence line in the south grandstands. The rodeo kicked off with a presentation of the colors, followed by a procession of all the competitors, capped by the introduction of Bonnie Hawkins, Miss Oakdale Rodeo. The Christensen Brothers Rodeo Company was the stock contractor. Mel Lambert was the announcer. There were a total of 230 entries. The nice thing about a small rodeo, as opposed to rodeos like Salinas and the Grand National, was that there was only one event at a time, so you could concentrate on just that. The order of events was pretty much the same every year, bareback, saddle bronc, bulldogging, team roping, bull riding, women's barrel racing, and businessmen's roping. In between events, there was usually some kind of entertainment. Then there was the rodeo clown and barrel man, "Wild Bill" Lane and Wilbur Plaugher, who were often the only thing between a cowboy, an angry brahma bull, and a mouth-full of Oakdale dirt.

The Camarillos won their event that afternoon. The best all-around cowboy was Dale Smith of Chandler, Arizona. At the end of the day, as the sun dropped into the west and we headed home, I was kind of sorry my dad didn't like being a cowboy, because I sure did.

CHAPTER 7

Opening Day always meant the end of winter and the beginning of summer (although it was really spring). The last of the season I hated and the first of the season I loved. Every true baseball fan couldn't wait for that special day. We'd all been marking off our calendars since the last pitch of last year's World Series. On Opening Day, we could live and breathe and hope again. On Opening Day, every team was in the race. Everyone was a contender.

As the first official franchise in Major League Baseball history, the Cincinnati Reds always got to be the first team to play on Opening Day. They held the "opening of the Openers." It was said that the citizens of the "Queen City" looked upon Opening Day as "one small notch below Christmas."

Since baseball was, after all, the national pastime, Opening Day always seemed to attract politicians anxious to show the American people they were one of them, had the right stuff, and could wing a fast ball up there with the best of them. President William Howard Taft, who was a big fan – in size and enthusiasm – was the first president to throw out the first pitch way back on April 14, 1910. In 1950, Harry S. Truman, who happened to be ambidextrous, threw out balls both right-handed and left-handed. On April 9, 1962, President John F. Kennedy continued the tradition by throwing out the first pitch at Washington's new District of Columbia Stadium.

Early Wynn, a Hall of Fame pitcher who played his entire career in the American League for the Senators, Indians, and White Sox, once said about Opening Day, "An opener is not like any other game. There's that little extra excitement, a faster beating of the heart. You have that anxiety to get off to a good start, for yourself and for the team. You know that when you win the first one, you can't lose 'em all." I liked his name and his optimism.

Opening Day for the Yankees that year was at two o'clock EST on April 10 against the Baltimore Orioles at Yankee Stadium. Mrs. Claire Ruth, Babe Ruth's widow, threw out the first pitch. My dad and I were listening in. Since he worked for the phone company, Dad could pull a few strings for important things. He made a few calls to some of his service buddies who worked for the New York Telephone Company. They set up a temporary phone line so my dad could listen to the game long-distance. It was a direct line from Yankee Stadium to our little house in Modesto. He'd connected the phone line to a tiny amplifier and speaker, so we could both listen. That's how much my dad loved his Yankees. He felt bad about doing it, but only until the first pitch. He always took the day off work and let me stay home from school. We couldn't afford to go to the real thing, so we did the next best thing.

I was bouncing a tennis ball off a piece of plywood, with a strike zone marked by masking tape, that was leaned up against the garage wall, practicing fielding ground balls and trying to keep the ball away from my dog, Ring, and my little brother, Willy.

"As the great Lou Boudreau used to say," my dad quoted, "'On Opening Day, the world is all future. There is no past.'" He went on, "Some day you and your son will be listening to an opening day game just like we are today." My old man was a bit of a long-view philosopher.

My team, the Giants, was opening against the Milwaukee Braves at Candlestick Park on Candlestick Point in San Francisco. They wouldn't be playing until one o'clock Pacific Time. The Yankees would be almost done by then.

Candlestick Park had opened on April 12, 1960, with Vice President Richard Nixon throwing out the first pitch. It was kind of a miserable place to play. In the summer, it was windy and cold because, when it was hot in the Livermore and San Joaquin Valley, it sucked the fog in from the ocean. Mark Twain supposedly once said, "The coldest winter I ever saw was the summer I spent in San Francisco." *San Francisco Chronicle* columnist Herb Caen once wrote, "[At Candlestick] look at the way the wind plays with the hot dog wrappers. And remember that it's the only ballyard in the world in which a sportscaster was once heard to say: 'it's a hard drive to dead center – no – it's drifting a little – FOUL!'" It may have been no fun, but it was the only major league park in Northern California. It was ours and ours alone.

In the eighth inning of the Yankees' home opener, Mickey Mantle hit his 375th career homer off reliever Hal Brown, to tie it up.

"Picking up where he left off last year," my father commented.

"I bet Willie hits one, too," I countered.

"I don't know. Spahn is pitching today. He's pretty tough on Willie."

"I put a nickel on the 'Say Hey Kid.'"

"Never bet more than you can afford to lose."

"I just got my allowance."

"You're on."

We listened to the game in silence for a while. While I bounced the ball, Dad cleaned the BBQ grill. He was wearing his sweat-stained Yankees hat with a deep crease in the front of the crown, like he always did. I don't know where he learned to crease it that way. Maybe he did it when he was in the Marines. He played some ball for the base team at Camp Pendleton in San Diego, before being shipped out to the Pacific.

"Who was better?" I asked. "DiMaggio or Mantle?"

"That's a tough one. If Mantle hadn't caught his spikes in that drain, no telling how good he could have been."

"What drain?"

"Well, it was the 1951 World Series. In fact, it was on your third birthday. October 5. Your team, the Giants, against my team, the Bronx Bombers. It was Mickey's first Series. Willie's, too. And DiMaggio's last. As the sports writers wrote, 'The Commerce Comet arrived on the final voyage of the Yankee Clipper.' But, old Joe D. didn't go quietly," my dad added. "He told manager Casey Stengel, The Ol' Perfessor, 'There's nobody taking center from me until I give it up.' He could be a real cobb sometimes."

Funny how Mantle's and Mays' careers were always intertwined. They were the original M&Ms. Both came up as rookies in 1951. Willie won Rookie of the Year. Both played in the Series that year. And they were on a collision course again in 1962. It's kind of amazing how many times the paths of legendary players crossed in their lifetimes.

My dad went on to tell me the story of that fateful game in the '51 Series. The Giants, who were still in New York playing at the Polo Grounds, had won the National League pennant in a thrilling three-game playoff with the Brooklyn Dodgers, thanks to Thomson's legendary home run at Coogan's Bluff. The Shot Heard 'Round the World. The Mick started the Series playing right and DiMaggio was in center. It was the fifth inning of game two. Mays flied to deep right center. Both DiMaggio and Mantle converged on the ball. At the last second, DiMaggio called for it. Since DiMaggio was "Mr. Yankee," Mickey peeled off to let him take it. He sort of stutter-stepped. When he did, his cleats caught a drainage cover in the outfield grass. His knee twisted awkwardly and he instantly dropped to the ground in a heap. Witnesses said "it looked like he had been shot." He was carried off the field on a stretcher and watched the rest of the World Series on TV from a hospital bed. The Yankees would win in six.

"'Sides, it's always the center fielder's ball if he can get to it," my dad explained. "Mick was done for this Series, but he'd come back. Not as strong as before, but plenty strong. Can you just imagine what he would've been like on two good legs?"

"Not as good as Willie."

My father stopped scrubbing the grill. He put the Brillo pad down, wiped his hands, and turned around to face me.

"There's nobody better than the kid from Commerce, Oklahoma. Not then, not now, not ever."

"Willie's faster."

"Mickey was."

"Willie stole more bases."

"Better check your stats."

"Willie could hit for power and knock in runs."

"Mickey's career stats were better."

"Willie was a better fielder. He had more gold gloves. And that basket catch was so cool."

"I may have to give that one to you."

"Gotcha," I said, clapping my hands.

"But, best all-around? I'm going to have to go with my guy. A Triple Crown and three MVPs to Willie's two."

"Don't know about that. Have to check the Baseball Encyclopedia."

"You do that. You might be surprised."

"You might be wrong," I replied.

"I've been wrong before."

"Well, Willie played in twenty-four All-Star games. Mickey only made thirteen."

"Like I said, Mickey was hurt a lot. Besides, it became a popularity contest once the fans got the vote."

"Sour grapes."

"Got to protect my guy."

Joltin' Joe had retired in 1951 and returned to his family home in the Marina district of San Francisco. The "City by the Bay" was a couple hours drive away from Modesto. I had always wondered why my dad never tried to visit him. My mom always told me it was because money was usually tight, our car wasn't all that reliable, and it was just too expensive to take the bus or train. Plus, the Yankee Clipper, like my father, was a very private man and didn't like to be bothered. So he never did.

The Yankees won that first game of the 1962 season 7-6 in front of 22,978 fans. It was an omen.

My dad reached to turn off the radio. He winced and touched the left side of his stomach. He frowned.

"You okay, Dad?"

"Yeah, sure. A little indigestion. Must have been your mom's stroganoff. She always puts too much salt in it."

"It is pretty salty. But, pretty good."

"Yep, pretty darn good."

"Can I go to Gary's?" I asked. "We're going to listen to the Giants."

Dad gave me a mild stink-eye.

"His dad's a baseball fan, too. They both stay home on opening day. Just like us."

"Okay, but be home for dinner."

"Thanks, I will," I shouted over my shoulder as the side gate slammed shut.

I hopped on my bike and rode the few blocks to Gary's, the baseball cards clothes-pinned to my spokes, chattering like a roulette wheel. I kept meaning to take them off. Time to grow up.

I was, after all, thirteen going on fourteen. Just a regular, normal kid. Average size, average intelligence, average ambitions. With average problems. I weighed ninety-seven pounds and stood five feet two inches. 20/20 sight in both eyes. Freckles, dimples, butch haircut, big ears, squinty eyes, chipped front tooth. Just an ordinary guy. But when it came to baseball, I was an extraordinary fan.

As I rode up Del Vale, head down, I didn't notice the big-finned Cadillac cruise up behind me. The next thing I knew, I had been slimed with a cherry-flavored sno-cone. It hit me in the left shoulder, just like a Drysdale brush-back. I wobbled, but kept it steady. I looked up and saw the leering face of Teddy Jensen gazing out the back window of the Caddie. Teddy was the son of another local surgeon, a colleague of the one who carved me up. His old man was rich and Teddy was spoiled rotten. We were the same age and we hated each other. He looked down on me as white trash. I felt sorry for him because his mom and dad were divorced, he had no brothers or sisters, his grandmother, who was behind the wheel, was sort of raising him, and he was just plain miserable, which he used to fuel his mean streak. It was as long as he was rich. And that was very long.

In junior high, Teddy was leader of a group of kids called the "Elite Eight." They were a loose collection of wealthy, white kids who thought they were tough guys. I guess they were tough for the middle-class. They all lived in nice, big houses along the golf course at Del Rio Country Club, or in the College Neighborhood, so-named because it was near Modesto Junior College. They had the coolest clothes and hottest girlfriends, which they changed as often as they changed their Brylcreem. They were mostly punks who picked on the weak kids at school. They always moved in a pack. You never caught them alone, even in the hallways at Roosevelt. A lot of them were pretty spoiled. Both parents usually worked, so they had a lot of time on their own without anyone watching them. A couple of the Eights I knew from baseball. I could never understand why you would want to be a jerk when you could be an athlete. They all wore the same white Levi's, purple sweatshirts with the sleeves cut off, pointy black shoes they bought at Thom McAn's, long black trench coats with the collars up, and spit curls. Back then, wearing a sweatshirt with cutoff sleeves was a sign you were in some kind of gang. I thought the Eights were kind of a joke, but I stayed out of their way. I usually got even on the playing field.

I flipped Teddy the bird, which shocked him for a moment, then I peeled left onto Gary's street.

Although Gary's dad was home today, we usually had the house all to ourselves. Mr. Rawlings worked as a ditch tender for MID, the Modesto Irrigation District, and Mrs. Rawlings worked as a secretary for Kriese, Haack, and Kriese, a local insurance company. His oldest sister, Carol, was in college and about to get married, and his youngest sister, Lucy, had a steady boyfriend, so she was with him all the time.

Gary and I listened as Juan Marichal – "The Dominican Dandy" – and the Giants whipped Warren Spahn and the Braves six zip, with Willie hitting a solo home run in the first. It, too, would prove to be a good sign. Following the game, we played hot box on Gary's front lawn with Roy. Hot box, or "pickle," was a game where two guys got a third guy in a run-down and tried to put him out before he could slide safely into one of two bases, which were usually sheets of cardboard or someone's T-shirt or a hand towel, set up a specific distance apart. The trick was to get the ball back to the other player and make the tag without dropping the ball, or throwing it away, before the runner slid into the bag. We learned it from Coach Leach, who used it to teach us good base running. It was great practice for real game situations. That day, they never got me out.

CHAPTER 8

As I was growing up, all my spring and summer days were consumed with baseball, whether listening on the radio, watching on TV, playing lob ball in the park, or playing organized ball. In elementary school, it was Little League. In junior high, it was Babe Ruth. After that, I hoped I'd be good enough, or have time enough, to play high school ball, American Legion, or Pony League.

Just about all my buddies and I played Babe Ruth. Each year in April, the coaches held tryouts at the three junior high school fields for all the eligible thirteen-year-olds who wanted to play. They then met to draft teams. Once you were drafted, you usually played on the same team until you were fifteen. If you had an older brother already playing, you were put on his team. Any time a father coached a team, his sons were immediately placed on that team without having to be drafted. Some dads with really talented sons would sometimes become an assistant coach, just so their boy could be on a really good team, or play with the buddies he'd played with in elementary school. It was kind of rigged.

Coaches really were a lot like dads. They were gods, mentors, and role models. If you were lucky, your father would also be your coach. Which I was. I had only had two coaches in my life before junior high. My father and Mr. Leach. Mr. Leach had been my PeeWee coach, then my dad had been my "B" team coach and, when I moved up to the "A" team, Coach Leach took over again. At Roosevelt Junior High, I had Mr. Deaver for seventh grade baseball and Mr. Nard for eighth grade.

In my experience, there were two kinds of coaches. Those who were quiet and led by example, and those who yelled and tried to browbeat you into being better. Deaver was the former, Nard the latter. I preferred Deaver. I never responded to the coach who screamed red-faced at his players. I remember reading that Mickey Mantle hated Casey Stengel because Stengel was always riding him, which was what Mantle's father had done to him all his life. He said they were never satisfied. That didn't stop him from trying to please them.

Coach Leach taught us how to properly wear our uniforms, crease our hats, oil our gloves, and polish our shoes. He always felt that part of playing good was looking good. You had to look and act like a ballplayer before you could be a ballplayer. He kept stats all season long, so we could see how we were doing. If anyone went swimming on the day of a game, they didn't play. He wanted everyone rested. He always could tell who had broken the rule by their chlorine-bloodshot eyes. If we weren't hustling, or made a mental mistake in practice, like not backing up a base or not hitting the cut-off, he would stop practice, look at us, ask us what we did wrong, and then hit the ball a mile and make us chase it. By the time we got back, someone else was in our spot. I chased a few. It made an impression. But, he never yelled. All he had to do was give us that look. I never missed the cut-off again.

From our coaches, we learned about baseball and we learned about life. We learned about preparation, attitude, and teamwork. We learned that talent was as much a result of practice and dedication as natural ability or instincts. We learned about being confident versus being cocky. About being humble in victory and gracious in defeat. About knowing before each play what you were going to do. And about backing up the play and your teammates. We learned about taking something away from each win and loss, and then putting it all behind you. We also learned about mastering the mechanics of the game. About physical and mental conditioning. We learned about the history and tradition of the game. And about never giving up. On a game, on your teammate, on yourself.

In baseball and in life, I tried to please my dad, but not because he expected or demanded it. But, because he won it. Quietly.

I really liked my little brothers. But, sometimes, they made me mad. Like when I'd be doing something and they'd want to do it, so my parents would make me let them do it. Or, they'd be doing something I wanted to do and they wouldn't let me do it in reasonable time, so I did what any big brother would do. I'd make them. Like the time my brother Tim was swinging on our backyard swing set. I had been swinging first and got bored and started tossing the stick for Ring. When I got tired of that, I decided I wanted to swing again, but Tim wasn't ready to give it up. I thought I'd help him change his mind. I walked around behind him and started pushing him, gently. He went a little higher each time I pushed him. I pushed him a little harder and he went a little higher. Finally, I gave him a big push and he flew out of the swing, into the air, and landed with a sickening thud. And immediately started howling. My mom came running out first, followed by my dad. Mom picked Tim up and tried to console him, but he kept crying. Dad grabbed me by the arm and asked what had happened. I told him Tim had fallen out of the swing. When my dad asked if I had anything to do with it, I said no.

Tim screamed and pointed at me, saying I pushed him. I yelled back, saying I hadn't. At that point, Dad spanked me hard on the butt, pushed me toward the house, and told me to go to my room. He grabbed Tim and did the same thing. Of course, we were going to the same place because we shared a room. I could see the veins bulging in my dad's forehead. All my mom could do was stand by and watch.

Tim couldn't sleep that night. He cried and cried. My parents gave him some baby aspirin, but that didn't help. Finally, my parents figured something really bad might have happened. They took him to the emergency room at City Hospital. Turns out, I had broken his collar bone. My dad always thought twice about spanking us after that.

Thanks to baseball, I liked throwing stuff. Actually, even if I hadn't ever seen a baseball, I'd probably still like to fling things. Anything. All the time. Baseballs, sticks, footballs, clods of dirt, glass bottles, and rocks. I had already broken my share of windows and dented a wide variety of available flat surfaces. One day, Gary, Roy, and I were playing in the alley behind Roy's house. In the middle of the block lived this kid named Floyd, who was our age and went to school with us. He was kind of odd, at least to us, which made him an easy target.

Floyd always looked like he was crying when he was angry and he was very angry now, as he straddled the wooden fence of his backyard, trying to protect his domain from the pack of neighborhood kids with nothing better to do on this Saturday morning than pick on the weird kid. We were like jackals, bobbing, weaving, howling, and looking for a weakness – taunting a wounded animal we could bring down and devour. We could smell his fear. We liked it.

The rest of my buddies jumped up and down, made faces, and howled. We were social predators. It was our job to weed out the weak, ostracize those that didn't fit, didn't belong, and couldn't cope.

"I'll shoot," Floyd cried, as he pointed the bow and arrow at Gary's heart. That's when I hit Floyd with a rock. Right between the eyes. He dropped the bow and fell off the fence. When his mother came out the back door, we scattered to the wind, high-tailing it down the alley and back to the park where we would isolate our next victim.

"Why do you kids do these things?" my mother asked. "Why? That poor boy didn't do anything to you."

"He was going to kill Gary," I said, as my mother and father glared at me.

"Not likely," my father replied. "Sounds like you were picking on him and that's all he could do."

"He could have stayed inside the house."

"Not when you were throwing pebbles at his bedroom window," Mom replied.

"Who…we didn't…" I swung around and glared at Tim and mouthed, "Big mouth."

"We're going over there right now so you can apologize," my dad stated.

"For what?"

"For being a bully," my mom cut in.

That's just what we did. My dad took me by the arm and pretty much dragged me over to Floyd's house. Floyd's mom invited us in. Floyd's dad had died, so his mom was raising him. Floyd was sitting on the couch in the dim light of their living room. He had a huge, bruised, goose-egg lump just above his eyebrows. It was almost too painful to look at.

"Don't you have something to say to Floyd?" my dad prodded.

I looked up at my dad and saw there was no backing down, took a deep gulp, and said, "Floyd, I'm sorry. I didn't mean it."

Floyd glared up at me. If looks could kill, I would have been dead meat. "It's okay," he mumbled.

"Okay, good, thanks," the words tumbled out of my mouth as I pulled my dad toward the doorway. And we were gone, out the door, and back to the safety of home.

I was far from being out of the woods. A few days later, our next-door neighbor, who was kind of a wild man and liked shooting pistols, came to the front door and started yelling at my dad.

"Calm down, Bill," my dad said, as he stepped out on the front porch. "What's the problem?"

"That boy of yours," Bill sputtered.

"Which one is it this time?"

"The oldest."

"What'd he do?"

"Threw dog s— in my daughter's wading pool."

"Now, why would he do that?"

"Ask him."

"I will. Thanks, Bill."

"What about my pool?"

"We'll clean it up."

"Clean it! It's disgusting. I want a new one."

"Okay, Bob, we'll see what we can do. It's the end of the month, so money's a little tight."

"Not my problem, Wright. Make it right."

My dad found me out back throwing a ball up on the roof and catching it as it rolled off.

"Michael," he yelled and I knew there was trouble.

I walked around the corner of the house and onto the patio where he was waiting.

"Mr. Irving said you threw dog crap into his wading pool."

I didn't know what to say, or do. I had done it, but I didn't want to admit to it and, if I confessed to it, I didn't want it to sound all that bad.

"It was Ring's dog food, not his poop."

My dad just glared at me, thunderstruck.

"He said it was crap and he wants the pool replaced. You're going to pay for it."

"How?"

"With the money you make at Bi-Rite."

"I've already spent that money on some glove oil and baseball cards."

"Well, then I want you to go over to his house tomorrow and see if there are chores you can do."

"Dad…"

"Don't 'Dad' me. Tomorrow. His house." He turned and walked back into the garage and into the house.

Turns out, when my brother had been scooping up the dried dog crap, it somehow got mixed up with the dry dog food. And got into my hands. I was just trying to see if I could hit the pool next door while perched on our roof. I did all right.

CHAPTER 9

My dad was pissed. Again. I had yelled at Mom and now she was crying. She had said something, probably something really innocent like "clean your room" or "feed your dog," and it had pushed a button. We got into a yelling match and I told her, "I hate you!" Which, of course, I didn't mean. It had just come out. Now she was in tears. She left the room and I knew it would be trouble when Dad got home, so I made sure I was outside where there was room to move. He found me petting Ring on the strip of dirt next to the patio.

"Apologize to your mother."

"It was all her fault."

"Because she asked you to do your chores?"

"I was going to."

"When?"

"Eventually."

I noticed that he had picked up a thin piece of wood that had fallen off the fence. When I was younger, he occasionally used a belt on us when we'd really screwed up. He'd tell us to go to our rooms and take our pants down, while he slid the leather belt out of the loops of his blue jeans. I hated that sound. A leathery slithering. He'd follow us into our room and tell us to bend over.

All the while, we were crying and whimpering like we'd already been beaten. As he stood there, he'd almost always say, "This is going to hurt me more than you." I didn't believe it then, but I believed it later because he really hated spanking us. Sometimes, we gave him no choice. Sometimes, we backed him into a corner and there was no option. Of course, as soon as he raised the belt, we'd all put both our bare hands behind us to protect our naked butts and our hands would take the beating. Today, he was carrying a wooden stick instead of a leather belt.

"Come here," he commanded.

"No," I replied.

"Don't make me come over there."

I'd heard that line a thousand times, too, but I wasn't budging. Then I made a dumb move. I ran. I figured I'd dash out the back gate and into the park. He was still young enough and could run pretty fast, but he was a smoker. Thanks to his cigarette lungs, I figured there was no way he could catch me. Evil thoughts, I know, but I was trapped. It was amazing how quickly those thoughts flashed through my head and helped decide for me. I took off. I bolted to my right toward freedom. Out of the corner of my eye, I saw him raise his arm and fire the stick at me like some ancient hunter. Like those hunters, he hit his mark. On the fly. He led me like a pro and the stick caught me in the left temple. I dropped like a rock and rolled a couple feet. When I stopped, I got to a knee and touched the side of my face. When I saw the trickle of blood, I started crying.

"I'm sorry, Mikey. I didn't mean to," he said, as he rushed to my side and tried to help me up. By then, I was mad, too. I brushed his hand away, stood up, and walked a few feet away. He was shook up. I could tell, but I was enjoying it. *Serves him right*, I thought. I covered the bleeding with my hand, glared at him, and let him and his guilt twist in the wind.

"I hate you. And I hate her. I hate all of you. I wish I didn't have a mother," I hissed. "Or a father. I don't need any of you." That was the wrong thing to say. His eyes narrowed.

"You're all the same," he replied. "Selfish. Your brothers and sisters are just like you. You take and take and expect more. It's probably our fault for spoiling you. You get what you want, what you came for, and then you leave. And I have to pick up the pieces. I have to hold her hand and wipe away her tears when she cries herself to sleep wondering what she said wrong. Worrying that you still love her. That's what mothers do, you know. They die a little each night because of their children. We fathers have to tell her it's all right. It doesn't mean anything. They still love you. The fact is, my boy, you – none of you – will ever love her as much as I do." He pointed a finger at me. "I don't ever want you to treat her that way again. You understand?"

I did, but I wasn't going to give him the satisfaction. I turned and ran. I kicked open the back gate and dashed into the park.

When I didn't return for dinner, my mom started crying again. "He does this from time to time, Cora. You know that," my dad said. "He's probably over at Gary's. I'll go get him."

I was at Gary's. The Rawlings didn't know where I was because I was crouched beside the pigeon coop in their back yard. Licking my wounds and my pride. I came home late, snuck in the house, washed my face, and went to bed. We never talked about it again.

The Century 21 Exposition opened a week later on April 21. It would be better known as the Seattle World's Fair. The expo was all about the future, technology, and space. The organizers wanted to prove to the world that we weren't losing the "space race" to the Russians. Of course, the Russians chose not to participate and we decided not to invite some of the other Communist countries, which meant it was kind of our party. The symbol of the fair was the Space Needle. At 605 feet, it was the tallest building west of the Mississippi. It was very space age. I really wanted to go, especially since the World's Fair didn't get to our side of the continent very often. It would have to wait. There were other things on my agenda.

Easter Sunday this year was April 22. Although I was too old for Santa Claus, the Tooth Fairy, and the Easter Bunny, I wasn't too old to get in on the goodies. For Easter, that meant a basket filled with candy and an egg hunt with a few cash incentives.

Early that morning, Dad had snuck into the backyard and hidden each of our baskets and the five dozen Easter eggs we had colored the previous Friday night with our PAAS egg-coloring kit. As soon as the sun came up, we were let loose. I didn't bother with the eggs. I went for the money and then the basket, usually finding everybody else's before I found mine and taunting them with clues until they discovered theirs. Each was loaded with jelly beans, chocolate bunnies, marshmallow chicks, and cream-centered eggs. My teeth ached just thinking about all that sweet stuff. Every year, there was always an egg or two we couldn't find because Dad was too sneaky, or found an especially unique place to hide an egg. We'd find it a month or two later and it wasn't pretty.

After the hunt, it was time to shower and dress up in our new, Sears catalogue clothes and do our obligatory twice-a-year visit to the Congregational Church. The other visit being Christmas Day.

As I sat in the pew nodding out after the insulin shock of too much sugar wore off, I half-listened to Reverend Charles Spencer's sermon on Christ's death, rebirth, and resurrection. As I dozed, I silently wondered if that could actually happen to a real man.

CHAPTER 10

The following Friday, my dad came home early from work. I knew something was up because he never came home before five. And here it was just after three. My mother knocked on our bedroom door. "Michael, Tim, and Willy, I'd like you to join us in the living room." I heard her do the same on my sisters' door.

All five of us kids sat on the floor in a semi-circle in the small living room. My mother sat on the red-upholstered couch bookended by maple coffee tables. My dad walked in from the kitchen and sat down facing us in one of the overstuffed living room chairs. He didn't look good. He was pale and sweating. He grimaced and touched his stomach, which he had been doing a lot of lately.

"I just came from Doctor Battle," he started. "He's been running some tests."

"What kind of tests?" I asked.

"Shush," my mother said. "Be patient."

"Doesn't matter, son," my father replied. "Apparently, I've got something growing inside my stomach."

Cheryl started crying. My mom gestured for her to come to her and she did.

"They need to run some more tests," he continued. "We'll know more in a few days. So, nothing to worry about until then, okay?"

We were all shocked and stunned.

"All righty, then," he finished, got up, and walked out through the dining room and into the backyard.

We all stared at each other, then at our mother. She comforted my sister, who hadn't stopped crying.

I got up and walked into the dining room. I saw him through the French doors, standing with his head down under the patio.

I went back into the living room, then veered left for the front door. As I opened the door, my mom asked, "Where are you going?"

"For a ride," I said.

I ended up at Gary's. As always. We played a game to distract me. APBA Baseball was a simulation board game that used cards to represent each major league player, boards to represent different on-base scenarios like bases loaded, and dice to generate random numbers. The game could be played against another person, or alone. We always kept track of the results so we could see how our players' performances compared to their real-life stats. Sometimes, we'd play in his room and sometimes we'd play on the kitchen table because Gary's parents had a really nice console stereo, the one with the radio and turntable built into it and big, cloth-covered speakers. You had to slide the top cover open to access all the fancy dials. Gary loved music, a love he inherited from his dad, who enjoyed singing gospels and Tennessee Ernie Ford songs. Gary would pick out tunes on an old upright piano that sat against a wall near the front door entrance. I remembered him playing "Moody River" by Pat Boone. He didn't have sheet music and didn't take lessons. He just played it by ear. He somehow heard the music. It always amazed me. And made me jealous.

We had both taken music lessons in elementary school. He took the saxophone. I took the clarinet. He stayed with it. I quit when the music teacher hit me with her music book because I was talking too much to Gary. We both took chorus from Mr. Leach and Mrs. Allen, the other fifth grade teacher and co-director of the school chorus. Each year, the two teachers would stage a musical for the school. When I was in fifth grade, it was *HMS Pinafore*. When I was in sixth grade, it was *Tom Sawyer*. We auditioned for all the parts, just like a real musical. We helped build sets, we wore costumes, and got made-up. The productions were usually staged at the Downey High School or Modesto High auditoriums. If we didn't love music before that experience, we definitely did following it.

When Gary wasn't noodling around on the piano, the stereo was on. As we took our turns rolling the dice, me the Yankees, him the Giants, because he loved them a little more than I did, we listened to "Twistin' the Night Away" by Sam Cooke and "I Can't Stop Loving You" by Ray Charles. I borrowed a copy of "Surfin'" by the Beach Boys from Roy because Gary didn't like surf music. He liked good old rock 'n roll by Elvis, the Everly Brothers, and Ricky Nelson. I liked the Beach Boys, Jan and Dean, and some of the new folksingers like Peter, Paul and Mary and Bob Dylan.

Elvis was still big, but he wasn't as popular as he once was. He was doing more movies, like *Follow that Dream*. Instead of being a pop singer, he was now a movie star who happened to sing. "The Twist" by Chubby Checker was a hit again, after first being released in 1960. There were a lot of other dance songs, like "Mashed Potato Time" by Dee Dee Sharp, "Loco-Motion" by Little Eva, and "Peppermint Twist" by Joey Dee and the Starlighters. Singers that had been around for a while, like Ray Charles and Nat King Cole, were being replaced by new artists like Tommy Roe, Gene Pitney, and Brian Hyland.

Gary was crazy about music, so he was a little more on top of it than me. He could afford to buy records and fan magazines. He had a second or third cousin who lived in London and had been listening a bit to a new group from England called The Beatles. The "Fab Four," as they were known, had released a song called "Please, Please Me" back in February and had made their broadcasting debut on BBC radio in March.

Popular music was going through a transition from the old, two-minute simple pop love song to longer, more controversial and thought-provoking folk songs. From Buddy Holly to the Beach Boys to Bob Dylan. The "older" generation, like Gary's big sister Lucy and her boyfriend, Joey, didn't like it. "Rock 'n' roll's been going downhill ever since Buddy Holly died," he used to always grumble. He loved the good old music and the good old days. He still wore a greasy ducktail haircut, a tight, white T-shirt with a cigarette pack rolled up in the sleeves, and blue jeans. And every car he ever owned was candy apple red with tuck-and-roll interior. He didn't much like change.

I couldn't afford to buy 45s or LPs like my friends, but that didn't stop me from devouring the music. On the radio, at home or in the car, on the transistor riding my bike or doing my homework, or down at the listening booths at Records, or just hanging out at Harley's Records or Records by Twilight in McHenry Village, our music was everywhere.

We kept up with what was current in popular music and dances thanks to Dick Clark and *American Bandstand.* Every weekday, we'd watch the kids from Philadelphia dance to all the latest tunes on ABC-TV. During each show, they'd do the "Top Ten" and rate a record. Kids in the audience would be the judges. They always seemed to say the same thing about their favorites: "It's got a good beat and you can dance to it." Dick would go up into the bleachers to introduce whoever was on the show that day to sing their latest hit. Only, they never sang. The record would be played and they'd move their lips and act like they were singing. It was pretty obvious, especially when they forgot the words. It was called "lip-synching." That's what another guy did all the time on his show. Lloyd Thaxton did a Los Angeles version of *Bandstand*, only he performed more than Dick Clark, including singing and playing along with hit records. He also had a lot of popular groups perform. But, he was known for his "lip-synching."

For my parents and all the people who grew up in the thirties and forties, it was movies that were important. They marked the significant events in their lives by the movies and the stars in those movies. For me, it was always music. I could remember exactly what I was doing by certain songs. Every time I heard one, I'd be back to what I was then, at that moment. In the late fifties and early sixties, that would be especially true. All the events, all the experiences, all the memories from that time were, at least for me, linked forever to a melody or chord, a lyric or chorus. The Sixties would be a time *for* change and a time *of* change. And rock 'n roll would provide our anthems.

My family loved music almost as much as Gary's. My dad had played saxophone and clarinet in school. He'd picked up the harmonica while in the Marines. My mom enjoyed singing. We always listened to music, on the radio or records. Every time we'd take a road trip, we'd all sing songs like "Harrigan," "Mairzy Doats," "Down by the Old Mill Stream," and "Let the Rest of the World Go By." Mom sang melody, Dad sang high harmony, and us kids filled in wherever we could.

"How sick is he?" Gary asked, as I rolled the dice.

"Dunno. They're gonna do some more tests."

"That's bad."

"Tell me about it."

"I'm really sorry."

"Me, too. Man, I'd do anything to make my father better."

"What would make him feel good?"

"Not to have it."

"What else?"

"Who knows?"

"You can't think of anything?"

"Not really."

"How 'bout this?" he went on. "He's a big fan of Mickey Mantle, right?"

"Lives and dies."

"Maybe we could figure out a way for them to meet?"

"What, you nuts? We live here in Modesto right smack dab in the middle of the big old Central Valley. He lives all the way back east in New York City."

"The Yankees play on the West Coast, right?"

"Yeah, they play the Angels in Anaheim."

"So, go to LA."

"On what? Our good looks? We don't have that kind of money. And," I clenched the dice and waited a moment before saying, "he may not have that kind of time."

We didn't. Plus, the doctor wasn't about to let my dad travel. We couldn't even afford things like fancy cookies or ice cream, let alone vacations. It was always cookies in big bags and ice milk. I used to sneak cookies from Gary's food drawer because he had all the good ones. I'd eat them real fast so he wouldn't see. I think he knew, but he never said anything. I was so ashamed of our family car, a beat-up old blue 1948 Chevy, that I would duck down and pretend to be looking for something on the floorboard when my mom dropped me off at junior high. It hurt my mom. She never said anything, though.

"Great idea," I told Gary, "but I don't know how it's going to happen."

"Don't give up, man. We'll figure something out."

"Thanks. I appreciate it."

As I rode my bike home, I was thinking to myself, it was all my fault. I knew that now. If I hadn't broken my brother's collar bone, if I hadn't thrown dog poop in the neighbor's pool, if I hadn't hit Floyd with that rock, Dad wouldn't have gotten upset and he'd be okay. Then I realized, I couldn't save my father from being sick, or… I couldn't even say the word. Even if I behaved. Even if I didn't hit my brothers, or didn't tease my sisters. Even if I never did another stupid thing. But, there was one thing I might be able to do.

CHAPTER 11

The second half of eighth grade was tough enough, since you could almost see the end. But once the good weather hit, it was impossible. I had block in the afternoon. Social Studies and English. I was doodling, which I never did, because I loved anything even remotely related to history. Mrs. Lang was lecturing, but I wasn't listening. I was thinking about the human body and why it does what it does. I was thinking I had known this bag of flesh for almost fourteen years and I still didn't know it. I recognized the scars and the contours and how it reacted when I got sick. But, I didn't really know it-know it.

Suddenly, I was aware of giggling. I stopped scribbling and looked around. Everyone was staring at me, including Mrs. Lang.

"Are you with us, Mr. Wright?" she asked.

"Yes," I responded.

"Well, then you must need to clean your ears out because I asked you a question."

"You did?"

"I did. I asked if you could explain the Monroe Doctrine."

"I'm sorry, Mrs. Lang, but I didn't read last night's assignment."

"And why not?"

"My dad's not feeling too well."

"I'm sorry to hear that, but that doesn't change things here at school. Be sure to read the assignments."

"Yes, ma'am."

Gym was my last class of the day. That's because anyone who participated in after-school sports was put in the last period. Since I had planned to play baseball, I had seventh period gym. Of course, that was before Ernie planted his knee in my gut. For most of the rest of that winter, I didn't do any of the exercises and activities, but I still had to dress. And watch the rest of the guys while standing around in my gym clothes. I had to shower, even though I hadn't done anything. Although I'd been showering naked in front of my peers for almost two years, I still hadn't gotten used to it. Some guys handled it better than others. I wasn't participating in eighth grade baseball practice, either. I was still healing and the doctor didn't want me to do anything strenuous. I was feeling a lot stronger and not as shaky, but I wasn't there yet. I was bummed about not being able to play, but I was more upset because that meant I wouldn't be in the team picture in the yearbook.

I was standing by my locker. Coaches Nard and Deaver were drinking coffee behind the metal mesh cage in their glass-windowed office. My embarrassed, naked-body reverie was interrupted when someone whispered the word, "karma." I wasn't sure I heard it correctly, so I kept toweling off. I heard it again, more clearly. It was definitely "karma." I turned around and saw Teddy and two of his cronies, Lamar and Max, at the end of the row of lockers. They walked toward me.

It didn't take long for a crowd to gather. Things like this must have a scent because it traveled fast, just like each time there was an after-school fight off campus and half the school showed up.

"You know about previous lives, don't you, boys?" Teddy asked his pals. "Some cultures and religions believe we all live multiple lives. Maybe in one, you were a bird. In another, a horse. In another, a cockroach. How well you live your life determines how high up in the animal kingdom you'll be in your next life. What you do also affects the rest of your family. Well, Mikey here must have done something bad when he was a bug in his last life because, you see, his dad has cancer. Just appeared. Came out of nowhere. And, there must be a good reason for it. If I were a betting man, which I'm not, I'd bet it had to do with our old pal Mikey here. People with good kids never get sick."

I dove at Teddy and caught him around the neck, dragging him to the ground. We wrestled, like two naked Greek warriors. I wasn't thinking about my tender stomach, or the stitches that were still healing. I should have been, but I wasn't. I felt someone grab me hard by the neck and yank me to my feet. It was Coach Nard. Coach Deaver did the same to Teddy. They both held us by the scruff of the neck until we stopped swinging and kicking.

"Get dressed, both of you," Nard shouted. "And get to the principal's office."

"Use your head, son," Mr. Deaver said to me. "You could rip your insides open." I always liked Deaver and I think he liked me, especially after the accident.

I sat staring at my feet in Mr. Maley's office. I had only been here once before. That was when the Block R, the campus club of guys who earned their letter in athletics, got into some trouble. During our annual fund-raiser, some money had disappeared. We had to be grilled by Mr. Maley and Mr. Palsgrove, the boys' counselor. They never did find out what happened to the money, although most of us knew Teddy had had a hand in it.

Mr. Maley stared at me, hands clasped, looking very serious and concerned.

"This isn't like you, Michael."

"Yes, sir."

"This is the first time you've ever been in my office. By yourself, that is."

"Yes, sir."

"I'd like to keep it that way."

"Yes, sir."

"Look, Michael, don't pay attention to what Teddy said. There's no such thing as karma and you're not responsible for anything or anyone but yourself. You understand?"

"I do."

"Excellent. When you leave, please tell Teddy to come in."

"Yes, sir."

"Unlike you, he and I have done this before."

"Thank you, sir."

Mr. Leach was a competitive guy, which made him a great teacher and even better coach. He always started practicing early for the baseball season. After school, a week or so following my encounter with Teddy, I rode my bike to Garrison to watch the A team practice. I had played with most of the guys last year since I was young for my age. If you were born late in the year, like October, November, or December, you could play one more year of Little League. So, as a seventh grader, I had been able to play one more year with a couple of the kids who had been fifth graders then and were now sixth graders. We had been competitive, but not as good as the team that had won the championship the summer before in 1960. Plus, Tim was playing for the A team this year, so I could watch him practice.

Coach and I were standing in back of the backstop behind home plate, watching Tim take some cuts. He kept tugging on the protective headgear we were all supposed to wear, trying to get it to fit right. The helmet was winning. It made me chuckle.

I understood why we had to wear them, but I never liked those plastic, elastic-banded, wrap-around helmets. They felt and looked like hard plastic clamshells. The wind was always blowing through the earholes as you ran, making it almost impossible to hear. It felt like it slowed you down, almost like the parachute that pops out behind a dragster at the end of a race to help it come to a stop. Some of the helmets were too tight, so they squeezed your brain, left half-moon indentations on the side of your face, and gave you a headache. Some were too loose, so they drooped onto your neck. They were never just right. But, the first time you got your bell rung leaning into a high, hard one, or got pegged by a throw while legging out a grounder to first, you were happy to be wearing the clams.

"I hear you saw Mr. Maley last week," Coach Leach said.

"Who told you that?"

"It's a small world, Mike. We teachers talk. Especially when it involves a student who nearly died."

"No big deal," I replied, as I shifted from foot to foot.

"It is for someone who's never been there."

"Teddy Jensen said some things he shouldn't have."

"Ah, Teddy. I had hoped he'd grow out of that."

"He hasn't."

"What'd he say?"

"Nothing."

"Come on, Mike. You're an excellent student who never gets into trouble about anything, so what was it?"

"My dad's having some problems."

"Really, I hadn't heard anything at school."

I gave him a look like "how would you know?"

"It's a little town, Mike."

"My folks haven't told anybody yet."

"What sort of problems?"

"Some health things."

"He okay?"

"I don't know. He and my mom aren't telling me much."

"What's that got to do with Teddy?"

"He kind of hinted it might be my fault. 'Cause I'm kind of selfish and all."

"That little punk. He's bad news. Always has been."

"It's okay. I'll figure it out."

"You doing all right?"

"Sure, I suppose."

"You know, if there's anything I can do, all you have to do is ask."

"I know that. I just wish I knew what to do."

"There's not much you can do. Unless you become a doctor overnight."

"No, I mean, something to make him feel better."

"Not getting in trouble would be a good start."

"I know. I'm pretty sure that stressed him out."

"Take care of your mom. And your brothers and sisters. Help out where you can."

"I pretty much do that already."

"Well, you could always talk baseball. You know he loves it."

"Yes, I do."

"Keep his mind off what's going on."

"That could work."

"Anything he loves, that's what you need to do for him."

Mickey Mantle had four boys. Mickey Elvin Mantle Jr. was nine, William "Billy" Giles was seven, David was five, and Daniel was two. One more boy than our family. No girls. His first son was born on April 12, 1953. Mickey wasn't there because he was on his way to an opening day game against the Philadelphia Athletics. He didn't see his first-born until June, when the baby was old enough to travel and Mickey had an off day. That was the way it would be for all his kids. Baseball came first.

It must have been lonely not having his wife and family around. In the early days, he couldn't afford to have Merlyn living in New York. Half the season, he was on the road. To him and his family, it must have felt like he was gone all the time. Deep down, he must have wanted to be there for them, unlike his dad was for him. I couldn't imagine what it would be like to not have Dad around every day. I was spoiled, I guess. And lucky.

CHAPTER 12

You could always tell what time of the year it was and what sport was in season by the game we were playing at Pike Park. We were out there as soon as school let out until the sun went down and all day long on weekends. Lob baseball with screwed-up, taped-up, salvaged wooden bats, flag or tackle football, one-on-one basketball, dodgeball, whiffle ball, kickball, three flies up, pitch-and-putt golf, even soccer. If we had the time and the gear and enough guys, we had a game. If it was just me, I'd throw the tennis ball against the cinder block bathroom wall and get my infield practice. We also played a lot of our Little League games there, since it was the closest city park to Garrison and was sort of our home field.

Modesto wasn't a big town. But, it was big enough to have car clubs and gangs. It wasn't the Jets and the Sharks, but we had some tough guys who didn't mind pulling out the tire chains and knives. The Toledo brothers lived across from the park and were in a gang mostly made up of Mexican kids called "The Monarchs," who used to wear bright yellow sweatshirts with the sleeves cut off. Alex Austin and Felix Berbena were part of that gang. When they'd see us playing lob ball in the park, they'd get their buddies and challenge us to a hardball game. We almost always beat them, even though they were older, bigger, and stronger. We were faster and knew how to play the game. Plus, they'd sometimes be drinking a little wine, which didn't help the old hand-eye coordination. Someone once said that a kid would rather steal second base than a car. I really think that was true of the Monarchs. They were good guys who did some bad things. Knowing them saved my bacon a few times around town, at the bowling alley, and definitely at football games. Some punks would be picking on us and the Monarchs would show up. It would take a minute, but they would recognize us from the park and the guys who had been bothering us were very quickly re-thinking their decision to mess with us.

Like every park in every city, people came and went. Some familiar, some not. There always seemed to be one old guy who was always there and always seemed to have nothing to do, except watch the neighborhood kids play ball, and offer advice on how to play the game right. He knew a lot about baseball and had an opinion on everything else. We never listened to him. Until the day we found out he played for the Chicago Cubs and had caught the legendary pitcher, Lefty Gomez.

Our local fixture was named Lowney. Calvin Lowney. He was tall with bandy legs and a barrel chest, slicked-back hair, big teeth, and glasses. He had macular degeneration, so his sight wasn't as good as it had been. But, his memory was sharp as a cut fastball. He liked me and Gary and our group of ballplayers, so he was always watching our games and offering advice. He always wore an ancient Chicago Cubs ball cap and a thread-bare Cubs warm-up jacket. Pinned to the jacket was a tiny wood baseball bat encrusted with tiny stones that looked like diamonds, but couldn't be because he didn't look all that well-to-do.

Whatever the problem, Mr. Lowney could always solve it with baseball, or the blues. He played both. I hung around one day after a game with the Monarchs so I could get some of his free advice.

"You've been around," I said. "You've done some things in your time, right, Mr. Lowney?"

"I have indeed."

"My coach says do what my dad loves," I told Mr. Lowney.

"What does he love?"

"Baseball. His family. His work. His hometown. My mom."

"If there was one thing he could do before he…," he stopped, looked up in the sky, and continued, "…what would it be?"

"Play catch with Mickey Mantle."

"Well, there you go."

"I already had this talk with him," I jerked a thumb at Gary, who had joined us. "Mickey plays for the Yankees. They're in New York. We live here in Modesto. In California."

"If it's important enough, you'll figure it out, slugger." He called everyone "slugger." He tapped the tin of tobacco, opened it up, sniffed it, and closed it again. "Ah, those were the days," he exhaled. "Mantle's a good kid. I was moving on when he was starting out. No telling how good he could be if the Dago hadn't called him off that fly ball."

"The Dago?" I asked.

"Old Joltin' Joe DiMaggio," he replied. "'Course, lovin' the nightlife like Mickey did and does might have contributed some. And hangin' out with some good guys with bad habits didn't and doesn't help any."

My dad and I had talked about Mickey tearing up his knee, but he never talked about "nightlife." What the heck was "nightlife?" I couldn't imagine how liking life better at night had anything to do with how good a ballplayer he was, or wasn't, during the day. I guess I still had a lot to learn. Mr. Lowney was a willing teacher.

"You know, son, there's an old saying, 'You can't win the game when you're sitting in the bleachers.'"

"Nothing ventured, nothing gained?"

He just smiled. "I remember a speech Teddy Roosevelt made at the Sorbonne way back in 1910. That's a university in Paris,

France. He wasn't president anymore and had just wrapped up a big game safari in east and central Africa. Here's what he said, 'It is not the critic who counts, not the man who points out how the strong man stumbles or where the doer of deeds could have done better. The credit belongs to the man who is actually in the arena, whose face is marred by dust and sweat and blood, who strives valiantly, who errs and comes up short again and again, because there is no effort without error or shortcoming, but who knows the great enthusiasms, the great devotions, who spends himself for a worthy cause; who, at the best, knows, in the end, the triumph of high achievement, and who, at the worst, if he fails, at least he fails while daring greatly, so that his place shall never be with those cold and timid souls who knew neither victory nor defeat.'"

Boy, he liked to talk. But, of course, he was right. It was time to get into the game. Time to do something. But, what?

CHAPTER 13

Our May days in 1962 were sunny and full. So was the calendar. In his fourth start, Bo Belinsky of the Los Angeles Angels pitched a no-hitter. Jockey Bill Hartack won the 88th running of the Kentucky Derby aboard Decidedly. The soundtrack to the movie, *West Side Story*, went to number one. Author Theodore H. White won the Pulitzer Prize for his book, *The Making of the President, 1960.* A laser beam was successfully bounced off the moon. Princess Sophia of Greece married Don Juan Carlos of Spain. U.S. Marines entered Laos. At the 14th annual Primetime Emmy awards, the *Bob Newhart Show* won for best comedy and *The Defenders* won for best drama. M. Scott Carpenter circled the earth three times in Aurora 7. *Wide World of Sports* with Chris Schenkel premiered on ABC.

One Saturday afternoon in early May, my brothers and I were pulling weeds as part of our weekly chores. Well, I was pulling weeds. They were chasing ants and butterflies and grasshoppers. I stopped hoeing and looked at them both. Tim finally noticed the quiet and turned around. Willy did, too.

"What?" Tim said.

"Look," I replied, "sometimes, uh, a lot of times, you guys bug me and I don't like you. You're always following me and getting in my stuff and telling Mom or Dad about something that I did and not doing your chores so I have to do them for you. Stuff like that, you know."

"Yeah, I know," they both said and giggled.

"So, even though you do all that and it makes me mad, I like having you around, okay."

"Sure, okay," Tim replied.

"So, don't go anywhere."

"Where we gonna go?" Willy asked.

"Just be careful, got it?"

"Got it," they both said again.

I went back to trying to control my little bit of the world, just as a dirt clod exploded at my feet.

We all had images of who we thought we were, or who we thought we wanted to be. It might have been based on an athlete, a movie star, a musician, an historical figure, a family member, or someone completely unknown. It may have been restricted to one person, or a montage of many. It could have been positive or negative, high or low, good or bad. I saw myself as Spin, the Tim Considine character in "Spin and Marty," the Walt Disney TV show. Kind of smart and athletic, a little bit quiet, sort of cool, and funny, and someone you could always count on. In contrast to the image we had of ourselves, there was the image others had of us. It wasn't always the same. I was pretty sure my dad saw himself as Glen Miller, while I saw him as Jimmy Stewart. My mom saw Lucille Ball, while I saw Vivian Vance. Gary saw Jerry Lewis, while I saw Spin's buddy Marty. Who we thought we were determined how we spoke, the clothes we wore, how we cut our hair, the gestures we used, and the values we tried to live.

That's why honesty, dependability, flexibility, modesty, loyalty, and consistency were all important to me.

I considered myself a pretty decent writer. Mr. Leach, Mr. Giddings, Mr. Peterson, and all the other teachers at Garrison Elementary School had taught us composition. We had even drafted real letters to our local government officials. And, of course, a few to Santa Claus. Mr. Thompson and Mrs. Lang continued the instruction in seventh and eighth grade. I also read a lot, so I was exposed to different styles of writing. I had written letters to DC Comics, requesting information on my favorite super heroes. I had written to Willie Mays. I had written to President Kennedy. He replied with a form letter and what looked like a real signature, as well as a signed photograph that didn't look quite as real. I had also written some of my own comic books and had even helped a classmate write a stage play featuring The Three Stooges, which I also performed in. I was originally cast as Shemp until I cut my hair short, then I became Curly Joe. I had written a few short stories in the style of Edgar Allen Poe and H.P. Lovecraft. I liked to write and I was a bit of a perfectionist.

My letter to Mr. Mantle had to be just right. After all, my father's life depended on it. I addressed it simply: "Mickey Mantle, Center Field, New York Yankees, Yankee Stadium, New York, New York." I had no doubt it would find him. In the letter, I explained that, although I was a San Francisco Giants fan, I thought he was one of the best players in baseball. I said I had his rookie baseball card, along with the cards of many of his teammates, and that I hoped some day I could see him play. But, I went on to write, the reason for this letter had nothing to do with me. It had to do with my father. I wrote that he was one of Mickey's biggest fans. I told him that my dad had played semi-pro ball, was a shortstop like Mickey was when he started out, and a switch-hitter, just like Mickey. That he had to give it up when he got married and had a kid. Me. I added that my dad had even tried to name me after him, but my mom had nixed the idea. I then added, and it wasn't easy, that my father was very sick. And the one thing that would make him really happy would be to play catch with his hero. I continued on to say I understood that Mickey lived way out on the East Coast and only visited California a few times a year. But, I continued, if there was any way he could make it to Modesto to play catch with my dad, I would be eternally grateful. I signed it, the son of your biggest fan, Michael "Mikey" Wright. P.S., "I hope you heal real soon."

I added that P.S. because Mantle had been ripping through American League pitching in April and May. He was leading his team in all offensive categories. It had all changed on one play, just like it had in October of 1951.

May 18 was a miserably cold and damp Friday night. In the last inning of an opening game against the Twins at Yankee Stadium, the Yankees were down to their last out. Tom Tresh was on second. Mickey was hitting. Lefty Dick Stigman was on the mound, summoned from the bullpen by Minnesota manager Sam Mele just to pitch to Mantle. Tresh took off with the pitch. Mickey crushed a high, hanging curve ball, shooting a nasty one-hopper to shortstop Zoilo Versalles. It looked like an easy out. But, it was hit so hard it almost knocked Zoilo out into left field. The ball handcuffed Versalles, came up, blasted him in the shoulder, and popped up in the air. Mantle saw the bobble out of the corner of his eye and kicked it into another gear. At least his brain did. Unfortunately, his body didn't get the message. Mantle was exhausted. He'd been playing tired. It had been a long, tough week with a lot of time spent on buses and planes and much less time spent sleeping. They'd played two night games and a day game against Boston and had returned to take on the Twins. Just feet from first base, it all came apart, like a dragster with a blown tire. Some of the infielders later recalled hearing a loud pop. Mantle went down in a heap. Gamer that he was, he still tried to stretch out and touch the bag with his hand. He didn't make it.

Tresh streaked across the infield and got there first. It was 10:23 p.m. Mantle had torn the adductor muscle in his right hip, strained the ligaments, and tore some cartilage in his good, left knee, as well as tearing his groin muscle. He refused to ride on the stretcher they brought out and limped off the field with the support of his teammates. Manager Ralph Houk, who played with Mickey in Mantle's rookie year in '51, later admitted thinking that it was the start of the end. "Well, we'll miss him," Houk was later quoted as saying. "But, we'll just have to play the best we can."

I licked the envelope, sealed it, put a stamp on it, and rode my bike to the new post office on Kearney Avenue, where I dropped it into the mailbox, but not before whispering a short prayer to make sure it found its way to New York City.

I was a glass half-empty kind of kid. I preferred Ralph Cramden to Norman Vincent Peale. I was cautious about the power of positive thinking. Although I was basically an upbeat and optimistic person, most of the time, I had convinced myself, either by reading about it or talking with others, that if you thought in negative terms – if you convinced yourself that something you really wanted wouldn't happen – then you increased the odds of it actually happening. In other words, being negative would result in something positive. So, I never wished for anything, because I knew that would lessen the chances of it happening. I never dreamed of having something, because I knew that would jinx it. If and when I did get what I wanted, I would be pleasantly surprised and confident it had happened because I had convinced myself it wouldn't. It was an odd kind of reverse psychology, but it determined how I lived my life.

I'm still not sure where, or how, this philosophy was born and developed. I suspect it had been the result of so many times wanting something and acknowledging that I wanted it, only to be disappointed when I didn't get it, or it didn't happen. I probably figured I should do just the opposite to change my luck and had enough positive reinforcement that I kept riding that negative train of thought.

Right now, I was overwhelmed by stinking thinking, having convinced myself Mickey was never going to come through.

CHAPTER 14

Girls grow up faster than guys. In all kinds of ways. They get taller faster, they're smarter, and they like us sooner than we like them. Throughout eighth grade, there was one group of girls that had my attention, when I wasn't thinking about baseball. They were all daughters of doctors and dentists. They were all very cute and very smart. And, they constantly passed notes around between them and wrote what they were thinking on their Pee Chee notebooks. You always knew who was dating who by whose name was added to any one of their names with a plus sign. They all had listed each other's names and their boyfriends on their folders. Us, boys, were always sneaking a peek to see who was with whom. As a guy, even though you really didn't like girls, you wanted to be on that folder. You definitely didn't want your name crossed out. And, you always wanted to get invited to their boy-girl parties.

That Saturday, one of the girls had an almost-out-of-school party to celebrate the final days of eighth grade and the beginning of high school. It was a good excuse for those girls who already had steadies to hang out with their beaus and for those who weren't going out, to meet some new guys so they'd have someone to hang out with during the summer and when school re-convened in the fall. For some reason, it was important for these girls that they have a boyfriend at all times. That's why I got invited. I guess I had suddenly become better looking or more interesting since seventh grade. Whatever the reason, I was definitely intrigued. Gary hadn't been invited, but he was okay with that. He was a little slower that way than me, although I was the original slow mover.

The party was at Joleen Murphy's house. Her parents lived in the College Neighborhood. Joleen and most of her friends had all gone to Enslen Elementary School, which was where I went after going to Washington and before going to Beard and then Garrison when it opened. There were a lot of elementary schools opening up in those days.

Joleen's parents had decorated the patio near their pool for the festivities. Everything was dimly lit. The pool light was on, giving the whole yard the look of a tropical grotto, which was reinforced by the balmy night. A portable stereo with speakers had been set up next to a table filled with iced soft drinks, chips and dips, and cookies. A stack of 45s was perched above the turntable, dropping one-by-one in a pre-arranged order selected by the girls and alternating between fast and slow songs. I was a pretty good dancer, so I wasn't worried about that like most guys. I had decent rhythm for a teenaged boy, and my mom and dad had taught me how to jitterbug.

I was standing by the snack table, which was my usual spot because I loved chips and dip and it was just far enough away from the dancing. I was talking with Roy, who had been invited since he was actually good-looking and a real jock, although he was even less experienced with all this than Gary and me. I scanned the rest of the guests and saw Teddy standing with some of the other kids from Del Rio and the rest of the Eights. He lifted his plastic cup in a toast and smiled. There was no telling what he had filled it with besides punch.

When the fast song ended and the next 45 dropped into place, Joleen suddenly materialized in front of me and I realized that I was the guy she was going to zero in on for the night. And maybe the summer. I gulped.

"You wanna dance," I said. She just smiled. She took my hand and led me out onto the patio. "The Way You Look Tonight" by The Lettermen filled the night air. My legs suddenly got all rubbery. I was prepared to do the waltz, just like I had been taught in elementary school. I raised my left hand and waited for her to take it and slide into place so I could place my right hand on the small of her back. She had other ideas. She stepped in close, yanked my left hand down, put it around her waist, put both her hands on my shoulders, and waited for me to place my right hand on her hips, which I promptly did. She moved close and we danced, or shuffled, since I wasn't thinking too clearly, thanks to the moon, the night, her perfume, and her lacquered hair roughing up my cheek. In spite of all that, it was pretty neat.

We danced like that for a few songs. Joleen kept pulling me closer, practically embedding her fingernails into my back. I checked for scars the next day. Our reverie was halted when her mother called from the sliding glass door, asking her to refill the bowl of chips. Joleen excused herself and I croaked "Okay," since my mouth and throat were totally parched. I made a beeline for the snacks and downed a Teem. As soon as I finished, I abruptly turned around. Unfortunately, someone was already occupying that space. It wasn't Roy. It was a girl. A girl I didn't know. A girl who hadn't gone to Roosevelt. And I had just knocked her Coke out of her hand, spilling its entire contents all over her pretty yellow dress. She just stood there, surveying the damage. I froze. She started to laugh. She had kind of a throaty horse-laugh. One of the guys I played baseball against passed by just then and whispered, "Smooth move, Ex-lax." I was embarrassed, but transfixed. I picked up the empty cup and held it out to her.

"What am I supposed to do with that?" she asked.

"Get a refill," I said.

"You're funny," she said. "And kind of cute." She giggled.

I was in love. It was that fast. "How about I get you another one? Or some chips?"

"Sure, uh…what's your name, klutz?"

"Mikey," I replied.

"Mine's Kelly," and she held out her hand. I just stared at it.

"What, you don't shake hands with girls? You afraid I have cooties?"

"Oh sure, I mean, no," I stammered, reaching out and touching her hand. I suddenly felt all warm inside. It got very quiet, except for the muffled buzzing in my ears.

"Tell you what; you can make it up by dancing with me. I don't know that many people here and I love to dance."

"Where you from?"

"Modesto," she smirked.

"No, I mean what school? I don't remember seeing you at Roosevelt."

"That's because I went to James Marshall then Mark Twain and now I go to Modesto High. I live in the middle of a vineyard near the Tuolumne River. My parents grow almonds, walnuts, and grapes. I like Bobby Vee, the color blue, and horses. I want to be a teacher when I grow up and maybe have a family. But, I want to travel the world first. Maybe start world peace. Now, how about you?"

I was thunderstruck. I didn't know where to begin. That's when "Sealed with a Kiss" started playing. Saved by Brian Hyland.

"Never mind," she said. "We'll get to that later." She took my hand and pulled me out onto the dance floor. I felt like a lamb led to slaughter. She held out her arms, waiting. I took them and we started a slow waltz.

"You're a good dancer," I said.

"Thanks. I learned in school, from watching my folks, and 'Beaus and Belles.'"

"Some of my friends do that."

"You're a lot better than all the guys I danced with there." I immediately stepped on one of her feet, then the other.

"Easy, Trigger," she said. "They're the only feet I've got."

"Sorry," I said. "I'm really sorry."

I recovered and we got back into rhythm. I have to admit, we danced well together. It was easy and effortless and natural. Until I felt one hard tap on my shoulder. I turned to see Teddy.

"Cuts," he said and pushed me out of the way. He wrapped both arms around Kelly, buried his chin in her shoulder, and whisked her away. Confusion, helplessness, and anger washed across her face as she receded across the concrete. I turned and walked over to sit on one of the benches rimming the patio. I watched, partly mad and partly resigned.

When the song ended, Kelly immediately, and in not a very lady-like fashion, disengaged from Teddy and left the dance floor without a backward glance. He was shocked. And I was thrilled. Because she was heading straight for me.

"Sorry about that," she said.

"It's okay."

She sat down next to me, opened the small purse dangling around her neck, grabbed a daisy-topped pen and piece of pink paper, and wrote a phone number down.

"Call me," she said. "So I can tell you how much you owe me to get this clean," she pulled on her stained blouse.

I just grinned.

In addition to being a little negative, I was kind of judgmental. I never appreciated the upside of things. I always seemed to think the worst of other people, whether it was the kids I hung out with, their parents, my family, teachers, someone on TV or in the movies, or people on the street. My first impression never gave anyone a second chance. I'd walk by someone, watch them on TV, see their picture in a magazine, and I would immediately think they were scary, fat, ugly, stupid, weird, mean, or stuck-up. Or, that they wore hats, coats, clothes, glasses, or shoes that didn't fit or were worn out or the wrong color or just plain dumb. Or, that they ate funny or talked weird or had a strange face. I never thought they might actually have a problem, or there might be something going on in their life that may have been the cause of what I perceived them to be. That first impression was often brutal and it was fairly permanent. I'd always fight the thought and tell myself not to think it, because "good" people didn't do things like that, but it would still worm its way into my brain and make me wonder what kind of person I really was. I wanted to be thought of as a nice, considerate, and kind guy. I wanted to be liked. I didn't want to be thought of as someone mean and selfish. It was hard, especially with all those negative thoughts I was sending out into the world.

The first time I saw Gary, I thought he was conceited and some kind of spoiled, rich kid. He wasn't. He was middle-class, just like me. His folks were blue-collar and white-collar workers. The family car wasn't all that fancy, although it was new. Their house was new, too, but it wasn't that big a deal. Once Gary and I started hanging around, all those first impressions were turned inside out and upside down. Of course, that didn't stop me from continuing to make snap judgments of others. Thank goodness, my first impression of Kelly was a good one.

Gary and I sat in the wooden bleachers in the activity court at Roosevelt eating lunch. I had traded my Twinkies to my buddy Billy for the fantastic roast beef sandwich his father made for him every day. Compared to my boring PB&J sandwich, it was *haute cuisine*. Miracle Whip, shredded lettuce, lean beef, and dill pickles on a sweet roll. Yum-yum. The bleachers were filled to overflowing with chattering kids, all trying to get the latest gossip of the day. Like who had broken up with who, who was interested in who, who had started their period, who had finally sprouted pubic hair. All that really important stuff to hormonal pre-teens and teenagers. Not that all that much had happened since we had first seen each other that morning at the bike racks.

I opened the slip of paper and gazed at the number.

"That's so cool," Gary said. "When you gonna call?"

"I don't know," I said.

"You're not gonna chicken out, are you?"

"What am I gonna say?"

"I don't know. Talk about the weather or baseball or almonds. Or music. She said she liked Bobby Vee, didn't she?"

I was overwhelmed. This really cute girl actually seemed interested in me. And I didn't know what to do. I sniffed the paper and it smelled like her. All sweet and clean, like Ivory soap. I was stuck in neutral the rest of the school day.

CHAPTER 15

My hands were clammy and trembled as I unfolded the piece of paper. *Did she really want me to call*, I thought, *or was she just being nice, or taking pity on me because I was such a dip?* I thought about what Mr. Lowney had said. "You can't win the game when you're sitting in the bleachers, slugger." How would I know if I didn't try? We had our own phone in the bedroom my brothers and I shared, thanks to the fact that my dad worked for the phone company and could get phones cheap, as well as being able to install extra lines in the house. At least no one could hear me blow it. I picked up the Princess phone my dad was able to get before anyone else did and dialed. It rang once, twice, and on the third ring, she picked up.

"Hello."

I froze. *This is a mistake*, I thought.

"Hello…Is anybody there?"

I was pouring sweat.

"I know somebody is there, I can hear you thinking."

"Uh, hello," I replied. "Is this Kelly?"

"It is. And who's this?"

"It's Mikey Wright. You know, from the party."

"The boy who mistook my feet for the floor."

"That's right. Mr. Two Left Feet. You remembered."

"How could I forget? My feet are still numb."

"I'm really sorry about that. I'm actually a pretty good dancer. Most of the time."

"Says who?"

"My mom."

"Really. Well, if Mom says so, then it must be so."

"Um, I liked dancing with you, even though I didn't do very well."

"You did fine. It was fun."

"It was. Joleen had some good food."

"I love clam dip and Lay's BBQ potato chips."

"Me, too." And I wasn't saying that because she did. I really liked clam dip and Lay's BBQ chips.

"The music was pretty neat, too. She's got a lot of 45s. I really liked 'Sealed with a Kiss' and all those slow songs."

She liked slow songs, I thought. Did that mean she liked dancing slow songs with me and that maybe she liked me?

"I really like the Everly Brothers," I said, seeking more common ground.

"Me, too. And Ricky Nelson."

"He's really good, too. I like his TV show, especially when he sings a song at the end."

"He's cute," she said.

What does that mean? I wondered. Does she think I'm cute, too? Or, is she just saying that because she wants me to know she thinks he's cuter than me? I finally answered, "Yeah, for a guy, I guess."

"I can't talk much longer," she explained. "I've got tons of homework and I'm not doing so well in algebra."

Darn, she wants to get off the phone and I haven't asked her what I wanted to ask her, I thought, feeling panic in my stomach.

"Uh, look, I was wondering…"

It was silent on her end. She's not making this easy, I agonized.

"Would you maybe like to meet somewhere and get a Coke or something?"

"Are you asking me out?"

"Well, sort of, I guess."

"Well, are you or aren't you? Don't be a fence-sitter, Humpty."

"Uh, yeah, I am."

"Okay, then. I work part-time at Penny's downtown on Saturdays. Maybe we could meet when I take my lunch break?"

"Sure, that would be great."

"Good, then meet me at the Kress's lunch counter at ten after twelve this Saturday. Can you remember that without me writing it on your hand?"

"I can."

"Great. See you Saturday, two-foot-dance-as-one."

"See you Saturday, Kelly."

She giggled and hung up.

I put the phone down and finally breathed. I tucked the paper into my wallet. I turned and saw Mom standing in the doorway.

"Well, well, seems my little boy is becoming a grown man."

"Mom, you didn't."

"I couldn't help myself. I just listened in for a little while."

"Mom…"

"Do you need any money for your big date?"

"Tony and Irma will pay me when I get off on Saturday. I've got enough."

"They giving you the day off?"

"I'm only working a half-day. Just stocking, so I'm going in early. I'll be done at noon."

"That's my boy," she said, smiled, and walked off down the hallway.

CHAPTER 16

I checked the mail every day after I sent the letter to Mickey, beating my mom to the mailbox, until she finally surrendered. After a couple weeks, I gave up. I was lying on my bed listening to the Giants one warm Tuesday afternoon when my mother walked into our bedroom and dropped an envelope on the bed. The first thing I noticed was the red, white, and blue Yankee logo then the New York address and then my name. I looked up at my mom and smiled.

"I thought you were a Giants fan and hated the Yankees."

"I am and I do."

She waited for clarification.

"I wanted to get an autographed card of Mickey for Dad. I was thinking maybe it would help."

My mom leaned down and kissed the top of my head.

"You're a good son."

She left me to my letter.

I carefully unpried the glued flap and gently removed the letter. It was on Yankees stationery. The bright red "New York Yankees, Inc." at the top, with the address in blue below, and the following typewritten note:

May 20, 1962
Mr. Mikey Wright
1500 Del Vista
Modesto, California

Dear Mikey,

Thanks very much for writing. It is nice to know that you and other fans like you are pulling for the Yankees. Also your personal interest in me is greatly appreciated.

I hope that both I and the Yankees will play the kind of ball that will merit your continued support and interest.

I am pleased to give you an autographed baseball card.

I am truly sorry to hear about your father. It is very sad. I lost my daddy to cancer just about ten years ago. It is very hard. We used to play catch, too.

I would like to grant your wish of playing catch with your dad. Unfortunately, our schedule makes that difficult. We have a series coming up against Los Angeles and we travel out there a couple times a year, but I do not see how I could travel all the way up to Modesto. I hope you understand.

Sincerely yours, Mickey Mantle

P.S. Sorry your mom won on the name. I like my name. And, the leg feels better. I should be ready to go by the time we open against the Angels in June.

He had signed both the letter and the card, which was encased in a wallet-sized plastic sleeve.

I was ecstatic and I was crushed. Mickey Mantle had written back. But, he couldn't help my dad. I laid the envelope and letter next to the plastic Hartland figurine of Mickey my father had given me, right beside my figurine of Willie.

Gary couldn't believe his eyes when I showed him the letter and the card.

"Did you show your dad?"

"Not yet."

"Why not? He'll love it."

"'Cause I don't want him to know what I'm doing. Yet. I want it to be a surprise."

"He'll be surprised all right. Shocked, more like. Probably scare him to death."

I punched Gary. Pretty hard.

"Sorry."

"If it all happens."

"Don't give up now, guy. You got a letter from big number seven."

"What else can I do?"

"Call him."

"Call who?"

"Mickey."

"How?" I asked.

"Pick up the phone, dial the number, and ask for him. See, the number's right here." He pointed at the letterhead. "Cypress 3-4300."

"He doesn't live at Yankee stadium."

"But, he plays there almost every day. And, if he's not there, they can get him a message."

"But, he's hurt."

"Letter said he was getting better. He probably goes to the clubhouse to at least get worked on."

"I don't know."

"What have you got to lose?"

"Nothin', I guess."

"That's right. Nothin'."

"Won't it be expensive? It's clear across the country."

"Will you stop coming up with reasons not to?"

"Sure, I just – "

"Look, we can use my phone. My mom and pop don't check the phone bill. We can call from here."

And we did.

On Wednesday morning, May 23, just as soon as his parents left for work and his sisters went wherever they went for the day, we made the call. We knew we had to phone early because of the three-hour time difference. It had to be a game day so the team, and Mickey, would all be there.

Gary dialed "0" for the operator.

"This is the long distance operator. May I help you?" a distant voice asked.

"Yes," Gary said, adopting a manly tone to his voice. "We would like a long distance connection to New York City. Cypress 3-4300."

"I'll be happy to make that connection, sir. Just one moment, please."

Gary handed the phone over to me and I heard a series of taps and clicks and buzzes until, very faintly, I heard a phone ringing. On the second ring, a pleasant female voice answered: "New York Yankees Baseball Club, how may I help you?"

I froze. I didn't know what to say. Until Gary slapped me in the back of the head and pointed at the phone. He flapped his thumb and fingers, mimicking lips talking.

"Hello, is anyone there?" the receptionist asked. "Hello, may I help you?"

"Yes," I replied, my voice cracking as I tried to make it sound grown-up. "I'd like to speak with Mr. Mickey Mantle."

"I'm sorry, sir, but Mr. Mantle isn't here today."

"But, they're playing the Kansas City A's, aren't they?"

"Yes, but Mr. Mantle is still hurt and won't be playing today."

"He never misses a game," I replied.

"He will today, I'm afraid. Is there anyone else you would like to speak with?"

"No, no thanks. Good-bye." And I hung up.

"Why didn't you leave him a message?"

"I forgot, I guess."

"Dumb. Really lame."

"This is crazy. He would never call me back."

"How you going to know without leaving a message?"

"It was dumb."

"Glad you agree."

We tried again the next day. This time, when the receptionist asked if I would like to speak with someone else, I said, "No, just tell Mr. Mantle that Mikey Wright called."

"Will he know who you are?"

"Yes," I replied, "I just got a letter from him."

"He writes a lot of letters, son," she said, obviously figuring out my charade.

"He'll remember this one."

"I'll give him the message. Is there anything else?"

"No, and thank you."

"You're welcome. Good-bye." And she clicked off.

Gary and I hung around the house as long as we could each morning for another week. Mickey never called back.

"I bet he never got the message," I said.

"You're probably right, slugger," said the old veteran Mr. Lowney.

We were watching Fremont play Orville Wright. I was rooting for Wright because Fremont was a rival and I didn't like them much, and because one of the first houses I remember living in when we moved to Modesto was just down the street from Orville Wright.

"They protect their stars, you know," Mr. Lowney added.

"He's just a guy. No different than my dad."

"Except he makes a lot of money for the Yankees. And they want to protect that."

"I'm not going to do anything."

"They don't know that. He's a celebrity. People like that get pestered by other people all the time."

"My dad's not doing so well," I said.

"Sorry to hear that."

"They're doing some more tests and trying some other things."

"That's encouraging."

"I can tell it's not helping. His eyes don't look good and they don't lie."

"Best thing you could probably do right now is be around and help your mom. She's probably getting lost in the shuffle."

"She is."

"I've read a lot of books in my time," he went on. "You can learn a lot from books. One of my favorite writers is Jack Kerouac. He wrote a book called, *On the Road.* You got me thinking about a passage from the book." The old man recited, "I was standing on the hot road underneath an arc-lamp with the summer moths smashing into it when I heard the sound of footsteps from the darkness beyond, and lo, a tall old man with flowing white hair came clomping by with a pack on his back, and when he saw me as he passed, he said, 'Go moan for man,' and clomped on back to his dark. Did this mean that I should at last go on my pilgrimage on foot on the dark roads around America?"

Mr. Lowney stopped reciting and watched the game for a moment. "Kerouac was on the road his entire life, moaning for man."

"Where does he live?"

"All over the country. He grew up in Lowell, Massachusetts. Then New York. Now, I think he's down in Florida. For him, there was no "there" there. He was always traveling."

"Did he figure it out? Did he get it right?"

"I don't know. Maybe. I guess we never know unless we try, right?"

"Right."

"I'm an old man, son. Old men are plagued with regrets. With all those things we were going to do some day. It's kind of sad."

Just then, a player for Orville Wright hit one past the third baseman to score the winning run. The kids from the Airport District went home the victors.

"Don't wait for some day," he said.

CHAPTER 17

One of my dad's part-time jobs had been as a checker at Bi-Rite Market, which was a "mom-and-pop" grocery store, located across from Modesto Junior College. The market was owned and operated by Tony and Irma Reese. When I started seventh grade, my dad turned the job over to me. Every Saturday, I'd ride my bike to Tully and Coldwell, park my bike in the shed beside the market, put on my green apron, and go to work. I worked first as a bagger, then I stocked shelves, dusted and cleaned cans and bottles, culled out the bad produce, did inventory, and eventually learned to be a checker. I took pride in my work and the fact that I was always on time and took the initiative, which meant I would find work to do instead of sitting around reading comics, which is what Tony and Irma's grandson did when he worked there. Their grandson's name was Micah. In one of those small world things, it turned out he was good friends with Teddy and part of the Eights.

Each May, Modesto Junior College would host the California Invitational Relays and State JC Championships, a track and field event that attracted some of the best athletes in the world. The 21st Annual "Cal Relays" were held in 1962 on Saturday, May 26. The official competition didn't start until six thirty at night, to beat the valley heat. This year, they were more worried about rain. It had been threatening all week. The state junior college track and field championships, which were traditionally held at the same time, started a little earlier in the day, so it was an all-day affair.

The first Relays were staged in 1942. They were initiated because Tom Mellis and Fred Earle Jr. decided to present a major track meet in their hometown. Mellis was a member of the Modesto Junior Chamber of Commerce. Earle was the athletic director at MJC. Mellis talked the junior chamber into supporting it and Earle got the city schools to join in. That first meet was put on with a budget of $500 and no big stars. In 1944, Tom Moore, a one-time world record holder in the high hurdles, got involved. With help from his friends and contacts in the sports world, the meet started to get better. It wasn't long before the Cal Relays were competing with many of the other major amateur track meets around the country.

The big star at this year's event was expected to be sprinter Robert Hayes of Florida a.m. He was attempting to become the "world's fastest human" at the Relays, which had become known for the number of track records broken each year. That's why a lot of athletes made the long trek to the valley. Hayes was hoping to run a nine-flat hundred. Ralph Boston was going to be back to compete in the broad jump and Al Oerter was aiming to set another record in the discus. According to the *Modesto Bee*, it was one of the most balanced and competitive fields ever. The meet organizers expected some records to fall.

When the Relays were on, things got crazy at Bi-Rite. People from out of town were always trying to park in our parking lot, which was just down the street from the main entrance to the stadium. It was my job to keep the parking lot open to our regular customers, in addition to working the register when the store was overflowing with people trying to buy snacks to take inside the event. It was nuts. It didn't happen very often, but sometimes people would shoplift. I never caught anyone, but I could always tell when something had been lifted. If I hadn't checked it out and it was gone, it had likely been stolen.

Micah blew through the front door, tailed by Teddy, who was shadowed by the rest of their "gang," Modesto's own Rat Pack.

Teddy smirked as he held up a fistful of tickets. "Best seats in the house, Mikey," he gloated. "Too bad you gotta work. 'Course, I guess it wouldn't matter, you couldn't afford them anyway." His cronies got a good laugh. Micah went right to the soda cooler and yanked out several bottles, like he always did. He grabbed some Fritos, Twinkies, and assorted boxes of candy. He reached behind the counter, grabbed a couple paper bags, and dumped the booty into it.

"Put it on my tab," he said to me.

When I turned to write it all down on the pad of receipts next to the cash register we used to track purchases by our regular customers, I looked up into the concave mirror hanging above the front door that allowed us to see everything that was happening in the store. I noticed Teddy by the bottles of wine we stocked on one group of shelves. It looked like he was stuffing a bottle of Thunderbird down the back of his pants and covering it with his long trench coat. I couldn't tell for sure because Micah grabbed the pad out of my hands and signed it with a flourish. When I looked back up, Teddy was gone.

"Let's go," Micah said. "We've got some races to watch."

Just then, Teddy came around the corner of the aisle where the alcohol was located and headed for the rest of the guys and the exit. I stepped out from behind the counter and blocked his way.

"Wait a second," I said.

"Sorry, we're in kind of a rush," Teddy replied.

"It can wait."

"What's the deal, banana peel," and he laughed, then the others laughed.

"Let's see what you've got hidden in your pants," I said.

"Whoa, Mikey, I'm not that kind of guy," he replied, laughing again, and held up his hands like he was being searched. "Go ahead, frisk me."

I spun him around, lifted his coat, and grabbed the back of his pants. There was nothing there.

"Sorry to disappoint you, friend," Teddy said. "Maybe next time." He put his arm around Micah and they pushed their way out the front door, followed closely by the rest of the guys. "See you in the papers, pal," he shouted over his shoulder.

That night, while I was cleaning up and getting ready to shut the store, Tony was counting up the day's receipts. He kept counting and counting. "This just doesn't make sense," he said. He'd count again and say the same thing. He did that two or three times. "We're about $100 short, Michael," he said to me. "You didn't drop any money, or give too much change back today, did you?"

"No, sir, I didn't. At least not that I know of."

"Well, I'm sure it will show up."

"I am, too."

"Well, we survived another one, didn't we?" He said this every year, too.

"We did," I replied.

"I'll finish up. You go on home."

"Okay, thanks. I'll be right back." I went to the back of the store, hung up my apron, got my jacket off the hook, and headed back up front. I went down a different aisle. The aisle where the wine was located. When I got there, I noticed a very expensive bottle of wine was missing from the shelf. In its place was one of the Cal Relay tickets that had been torn in half.

CHAPTER 18

"I've got to do something," I said. "Something, anything."

Gary and I were playing APBA Baseball in his bedroom again, sprawled out on the narrow double bed he slept in. As always, he was the Giants and I was the Yankees. As usual, we had the Giants' game on KBEE 970-AM.

"What can you do?" Gary asked. "You're just a kid."

"I don't know. Something."

"Forget about it. Your dad won't care."

"You really think so?"

"I know so."

"Aren't people who feel better supposed to be healthier? Least, that's what my mom says Jack LaLanne says."

"He's a fruit. He's always talking and saying nothing. And eating that gross yogurt stuff."

"He does talk a lot. But, he's in pretty good shape. For an old guy. And that yogurt doesn't taste half bad."

"My dad says be happy with who you are and where you are and what you got. I don't know how many times he's said that to me and my sisters. Usually after he's had a couple Burgie beers. In the winter, we want it to be summer. In the summer, we want it to be winter. Or, something like that. Sounds goofy to me."

"I can see that with my mom. She never seems too happy with what she's got," I said

"You ever thought you might make things worse by doing something?"

"No, not really."

"Well, think about it."

I rolled the dice and Moose Skowron cleared the bases with a double.

You're probably thinking I spent a lot of time at Gary's. I did. Almost every day. And nearly every waking hour during the summer. And I left my imprint. Gary's mom was a meticulous housekeeper. Everything was clean and in its right place. The hardwood floor was buffed to a high gloss. The floor was so slick, we used to practice our sliding in the living room. In our stocking feet, to make it extra slippery. We'd start by the front door, or at the entrance to the hallway that led to the back of the house and the bedrooms. We'd take off running, tuck our left leg under our right, drop down into the slide, and pop up onto both feet before we crashed into the stereo. We'd usually have some music playing on the stereo to get us pumped up. "Shout" or "Alley Oop" or "Runaway." I miscalculated once. I decided to get fancy and try a hook slide. I started right in front of the front door and took off. As I leaned to my left to start my slide, I lost my footing, stumbled, and fell right into Gary's mother's beautiful, mahogany coffee table. Face first. The front tooth I had accidentally chipped years ago went through the bottom of the skin of my chin, just below my lower lip, and hit the edge of the coffee table. It took a chunk out of the wood table. Of course, I started bleeding like a stuck pig. I dripped blood all the way to the bathroom. Gary's sister, Carol, who had stopped by the house to pick up some mail, tried to stop the bleeding. I filled the bathroom sink with blood. It was surprising I didn't pass out. Carol kept pressing a wet washrag to my chin until the bleeding stopped. She put a Band-Aid on it and I was as good as new. Gary's mom never repaired the table or replaced it. For years after that, I'd see that little white nick in the dark coffee table and think of that crazy hook slide. I definitely left my mark.

Of course, my chipped front tooth was another story. I got that in third grade when a buddy of mine and I were goofing around in the dry canal bed out behind our elementary school. When it was still functional, there were metal gates to control the flow of water. One of the doors had rusted off its hinges and was lying flat on the dirt bottom of the canal. John Hart, a school friend and fellow Cub Scout, whose dad also worked for the phone company, and I were playing "King of the Mountain," or something silly like that. He was bigger than me, so he pretty much always won. I was quicker, so I could usually get around him. As I was trying to scoot around him to climb up the canal bank, he grabbed me in a bear hug. I started squirming and he finally let go. And I went down. Yelling, mouth open, teeth first. I hit the metal door hard. When I rolled over, I felt my front teeth. An inside chunk of the left one was gone. I jumped to my feet and tackled John, driving him into the ground. I got up and pointed at my tooth.

"Look what you did, you dumbo," I yelled. It hurt as the wind whistled through my mouth and across the newly exposed nerves. "My mom is gonna kill me. And you."

John was sorry, I could tell, but that wasn't going to make it any easier at home, especially since we didn't have any money to fix the tooth. So, we never did. And I never did. It eventually became a part of who I was. As much a part of my body as the scar I had on my stomach from the ruptured spleen, the scar on my forehead from another friend's two teeth, the scar on my leg where a chunk of granite hit it when I fell off a rock at Buck Lake, the flabby scar on my right elbow where I'd sliced it open falling on a metal sprinkler head at my cousin's house in Tuolumne. So, it stayed. I always thought it would be fun to send out a Christmas card, or birthday card, with all the injuries I've had noted on various parts of my body. It would be encyclopedic.

Memorial Day was Wednesday, May 30. It was a national holiday, so nobody went to school and nobody worked. As usual, my dad was up early listening to the 46th Indianapolis 500. The temperature in Indiana was in the nineties. The track was a burning 140 degrees. Dad stood quietly as the radio crackled, "Gentlemen, start your engines." And the thirty-three racecars roared to life. They followed the pace car – a Studebaker Lark Daytona – for the pace lap. It was supposed to be Studebaker's brand new, very sleek Avanti, but it wasn't out of production in time. When the green flag dropped, they were off. During the time trials, Parnelli Jones had set a track record by averaging a blistering 150 mph. It was pretty exciting to hear them roar around the track. The field chased Parnelli for most of the race, until Roger Ward overtook Jones and held on to win the fastest Indy ever. Only fifteen racers finished. My dad tracked the entire race, meticulously writing down who was in what place, lap by lap, savoring every moment.

I never knew where my father developed his love for stock car racing. What I do remember is going to lots of races when we were growing up. Especially when it was just us three boys and our parents. Every Friday or Saturday night in the spring and summer, we'd be at a dirt track somewhere along Highway 99. My dad's barber owned a car and raced it locally, so we always had someone to root for when Charley was in the race. Eventually, with a fourth child on the way, my mom finally put a stop to the family night races. So, my dad turned his full attention to the annual race at the Brickyard in Indianapolis.

I made up my mind not too long after that day at Gary's. It was the middle of the night. I had had a dream about my father. He was playing baseball. He hit a shot in the gap in right-center. It wasn't that deep. He rounded first and decided to stretch it into a double. He just went for it. It was a bang-bang play. When the dust settled, he was out. He hadn't made it. He just lay there, staring up at the sky.

With the Wednesday holiday thanks to Memorial Day, I began quietly collecting a few things and getting organized. This wasn't easy since we lived in a 1,400-square-foot house and there were seven of us. But, I was able to tuck away a few things. I used my Cub Scout and Webelos training as a guide. I never made it all the way to Boy Scouts, so I hadn't learned all they had learned. I squirreled away some clothes, mostly things I could layer to stay warm. Several good pairs of socks. A windbreaker and sweatshirt. A second pair of shoes. A small pocket knife, some matches, a length of light rope. A canteen and flashlight with extra batteries. Toothbrush, toothpaste, soap, shampoo, and deodorant. My mom would have been very proud. Some hydrogen peroxide and Band-Aids. A rain-proof slicker. A pencil and some paper. A map of the U.S. and a list of phone numbers and addresses of friends and relatives. A small sheet of dark green plastic and a blanket. And my Giants hat. It was a tight fit, but it all made it inside my tan, canvas Boy Scout backpack, with the blanket rolled up and tied underneath, the canteen and flashlight dangling from the straps, and the sheet of plastic covering it all.

I went to school the next day and kind of kept to myself. I came directly home. I double-checked everything, had a quiet dinner, and went to bed early without griping the way I usually did.

It was a full-moon Thursday night. It was a travel day for the Yankees, who had just split four games in Minnesota. The Yankees were visiting Anaheim for a three-game, weekend series starting Friday, June 1. Mickey as much as promised me in his letter that he'd be playing. I figured I'd only be gone until Sunday, so I'd just miss one day of school.

It was past midnight and the house was finally quiet. I sat up and looked at my brothers. They were both lightly snoring in the bunk bed and trundle bed below me. I slipped out from under the covers. I was already fully clothed. Blue Levi's, my favorite blue windbreaker with my name "M. Wright" stenciled on the back, and my black-and-white striped Puma running shoes. I wadded up the sheet and blanket just like they did in the movies to make it look like someone was still lying in my bed. I quietly climbed down the back frame of the bunk bed. I crept out our bedroom door and crossed the hall into the bathroom. I turned on the light and ceiling fan to make it seem like I was taking a midnight pee. I flushed the toilet, turned off the light and fan, and waited by the door. When I was sure no one was moving, I walked quietly through the dining room, into the kitchen, and out the back door into the garage. One of our stupid cats slid by me and into the house. I tried to grab it, but it was too quick. It was gone and I didn't have time to chase it.

I closed the back door, went into the garage, out the back garage door, and tiptoed across the patio over to the side yard. I found my backpack tucked under the plastic tarp below the honeysuckle bush. I pulled it out, removed the plastic, rolled it up, and tied it to the bottom, threw the bag on my back, and headed for the back gate.

Ring caught up with me. He licked my hand like he always did. His collar jangled like it always did, which was how he got his name. I squatted down, gave him a hug, patted the top of his head, said good-bye, opened the back gate, and stepped into the alley. I looked around, crossed into the park, and headed for the highway.

CHAPTER 19

It was 342 miles to Anaheim. I had a map, but no real plan. I knew I would have to rely on the kindness of strangers to get there. I figured I'd hitchhike Highway 99 all the way to Los Angeles, then connect with Highway 5 – The Golden State Freeway – on the other side of the Grapevine, which crossed over the Tehachapi Mountains through Tejon Pass. I wanted to avoid the highway through Modesto in case anyone I knew saw me. It was still a small town and everyone kind of knew everyone. So, I headed for Yosemite Boulevard, which would take me to Santa Fe Avenue, which ran parallel to the highway. It would take me to East Keyes Road, which ran perpendicular to the highway. I'd head east past the Starlite Drive-In and back to 99. From there, I shouldn't run into too many familiar faces. I hoped.

I walked through town until I reached Yosemite Boulevard. The downtown was eerily quiet for a summer's night. It reminded me of the movie, *On the Beach*, which took place following a fictional World War III and nuclear annihilation. I remembered the scene in San Francisco when Gregory Peck's submarine surfaced and the sailors wandered around the empty city. One guy, who was born there, decided to stay, even though he knew he would die from the nuclear fallout. Gregory Peck tried to talk him out of it, but the guy wouldn't budge. The crewman was last seen fishing off a pier and waiting to die as the sub dove beneath the waves, never to return. That's how Modesto felt that night. Empty. And I felt utterly alone.

Once I hit Yosemite, I stuck out my thumb and kept walking. There wasn't a lot of traffic at that hour. Mostly trucks heading to, or coming from, the Gallo Winery or one of the canneries. I kept an eye out for Modesto Police or Highway Patrol. I knew they'd stop me since I was underage.

I stopped at a gas station at the edge of town between Modesto and Empire to use the restroom and buy an Orange Crush. I did both, guzzled the Crush, stepped back out onto Yosemite, and stuck out my thumb. Just then, a squat-looking, yellow convertible with a roll bar zipped by me, then slowed, and pulled over. The driver pumped his brakes a couple times to let me know he was waiting for me. I couldn't believe it. A ride. I ran like mad. I reached the passenger door and looked in to see a big-eared, geeky-looking guy with hair slicked down with Vaseline on top and undulating waves in front and on the sides, wearing an ivory jacket with a patch on it that read "Ecurie AWOL Sports Car Club." Blue jeans, low-top Converse tennies, and a flannel shirt completed his outfit. Pinned to his shirt was a big button that read: "Question Authority."

"How far you going?" the driver asked.

"Los Angeles," I replied.

"I can get you to Highway 99. You're on your own after that."

"Cool."

"Hop in."

And I did.

The driver gunned his car and pulled back onto the avenue. The car was quick and he was a good driver.

"What's your name?" he asked.

"Mikey," I said.

"Mouse or Mantle?"

"No, Mikey. But, it's Mantle, not mouse."

He held up his left arm, which had a Mickey Mouse watch strapped to it, with the face on the inside of his wrist.

"Mine's George. Where do you live?"

"On Del Vista near Pike Park."

"I'm out on Sylvan. On a walnut ranch."

"Cool, a ranch. You got horses?"

"No and not really. Moved there when I was fifteen. Had to leave all my buds."

"Bummer."

"I wasn't real jazzed. All I'd do is come home from school, go to my room, listen to Elvis records, read comics, *Mad Magazine*, and *National Geographic*, eat Hershey bars, and drink Cokes."

"Sounds pretty good to me."

"I grew up over on Ramona near T.B. Scott Park. I'm a senior at Downey."

"Wow, you going to college?"

"If I graduate. Grades aren't great."

"Where?"

"Not sure yet. Maybe somewhere in S.F. or L.A."

"What are you studying?"

"I like art. And movies."

"Very cool. Like *The Man Who Shot Liberty Valance*?"

"No, smaller. Much smaller. Art films. Kind of European. Maybe documentaries."

"My dad always said find something you really love and make it your career."

"He's a smart man."

I looked around the inside of the car. "What kind of car is this? I've never seen anything like it. It's kind of, um, funny looking." I had insulted him.

"It's an Autobianchi. Fiat owns it. When they bought the company, they changed the name to Bianchina. I customized it myself. When my dad first bought it, it was kinda dumb. And real slow. Sorta had this sewing machine engine. I souped it up a bit."

"It's fast?"

"Fast enough. I've won my fair share of trophies at some autocrosses. I rolled it once driving too fast. Smashed the top, so I took it off and added a windscreen and roll bar."

He opened the glove box, pulled out a handful of paper, and dumped it in my lap. I looked at the one on top and realized it was a speeding ticket.

"The local fuzz love busting us. It's like a sport to them. They used to be one of us. They changed and went over to the other side."

"Like white hats and black hats, or light and dark?"

"Yeah, kinda like that."

"There's a bunch of 'em."

"Too many. I thought about joining the Air Force. Wanted to fly jet planes. Recruiter said I had too many tickets. They wouldn't take me."

I stuffed the tickets back in the glove box.

"First time we went to traffic court, my dad made me cut my hair and wear a suit and tie. Man, I hate suits."

"My dad only wears one at weddings and funerals."

"That's when they should be worn."

"He pretty much agrees."

"You should see this baby take the turns."

With that, he hit the accelerator and we fishtailed down the boulevard.

We didn't talk much as we cruised Yosemite then Santa Fe and, finally, Keyes Road before hitting Highway 99. I finally fell asleep. I woke up as he pulled out of a gas station in Merced.

"You in a car club?" I asked.

"Yep. The Central Valley Esquire AWOL Racing Club." He pulled his left jacket sleeve up so I could see the patch better.

"You get in fights and stuff?"

"No, we just race cars. Drive around town."

"Look for girls?"

"You bet. You ever been cruising?" he asked.

"What's that?"

"It's the best. We drag downtown."

"Drag?"

"Race from street light to street light. We loop around Tenth and Eleventh Streets. Looking for fun. Start at three in the afternoon, go home at one in the morning."

As we zoomed along Santa Fe, we passed a luminous white '56 Thunderbird. Driving the T-bird was a knockout blonde. She was almost too beautiful to be real. She accelerated into the moonlight. We cruised into the night thinking about blondes in white cars.

Girls. Ah, girls. Chicks, babes, skirts, foxes, Betty and Veronica. This whole experience with Kelly had changed my view toward the opposite sex. I was like a moth drawn to a flame when it came to girls. They scared me, they intrigued me, they confused me, they teased me. I wanted to be with them, but didn't know what to do with them when I was. I was kind of slow in the opposite sex department, but was catching up sloooowly thanks to Kelly. Although I'd gone to a few parties in seventh and eighth grade, including the one where I'd met her, I'd never really gone on a date and had never gone steady. Some of my buddies were way ahead of me on that one, probably because they had older sisters and knew a little bit more about things. I wanted to be more like them, so I could see if I was missing anything, but was too chicken to ask. I had gotten better since being around them all day in class, at lunch, and before and after school. It was getting to a point where they, and now one in particular, were on my mind almost as much as baseball. It was confusing and kind of cool. I thought about them – and her. I dreamed about them – and her. I went out of my way to be near them – and her. I tried not to let them, or her, know I was too interested. Rumor in the locker room was to never give them the upper hand because it never ended well. I'm not sure I believed that, but that's what the guys said. I wish my folks had told me more, but I'm pretty sure they were happy keeping me a kid as long as possible. Man, I sure loved those skin-tight skirts.

CHAPTER 20

George pulled off Keyes Road at the Starlite Drive-In before the road ran into U.S. Route 99. He was thinking. Real hard. He looked at his Mickey watch.

"You know," he said. "I might just take you all the way to L.A."

"Really?"

"Sure, why not? Would sure piss off my old man."

"What about graduation?"

"My dad can get my diploma if it's so important to him. 'Sides, I'll be back before that."

"When is it?"

"Couple weeks. I got a lot of schoolwork to get done first."

"I don't want to cause any trouble with your dad."

"Don't worry about it."

"Okay."

"You got gas money?"

"How much you think we'll need?"

"Gas is twenty-two cents a gallon."

"That's a lot."

"Probably take ten bucks for me to get there and back."

"I got some."

"Let's rock 'n roll."

As we zoomed through Fresno, he explained why he changed his mind. "I might meet a couple of buddies and then tour USC. Check out the film school. Maybe check out UCLA, too. Me and my friend John are looking for a college with a creative side. Unless we go to Europe. My folks already said they'd pay for a trip to Europe. If I graduate."

"You going to work in Hollywood when you grow up?"

"Maybe, maybe not. I like Northern California better, but there's not much going on up here. We'll see."

"Is that what you've been studying in high school?"

"No, they don't offer stuff like that. I thought about studying to be an architect."

"My dad wanted to be an architect."

"Cool."

"They have classes for that in high school?"

"Not really. They had some drafting classes. I was really more into art and drawing anyway."

"Like comic books?" I asked.

"I love comic books."

"Me, too."

"I've got a pretty big collection. I had so many, my dad had to build some shelves in his backyard shed to hold them all."

"You watch much TV?"

"All the time. Especially Saturday afternoon serials, Westerns, and mysteries. My friend John got the first TV in our neighborhood. It was this little old brown Bakelite Champion. His dad put it in the garage and built bleachers because there were so many people who wanted to see it. It only got one station. KRON-TV in San Francisco. Showed mostly boxing and wrestling. I'd go over every day. We got our own in 1954. I sat in front of that thing so long, my mom thought my eyes were going to drop out. Used to watch cartoons, *Adventure Time*, and *Don Winslow of the Navy* with my little sister Wendy. Lots of cliffhanger-type serials."

"How about movies?"

"I don't go that much. Get too antsy. When I do go, it's to meet girls."

"Very cool."

"In school, I used to draw these elaborate panoramas and war scenes and hand-crafted greeting cards. My teachers didn't think it was such a good idea. One art teacher told me one day, when I was drawing some pictures of hot rods, 'Oh, George, get serious.'"

"That'd make me mad."

"I don't get mad. I get even," he said.

"Still, what they said wasn't very nice."

"No kidding. I was thinking about maybe becoming an illustrator. I applied to the Pasadena Art Center College of Design. And I've been accepted to San Francisco State University. They've got a really good TV and film department there, too. Bummer is if I do that, my dad won't pay for it."

"Why not?"

"He thinks it's a waste. He thinks I'm not living up to my potential. Thinks I'm going to turn into some kind of beatnik. He's kind of written me off. Believes L.A. is Sin City."

"That's kind of mean."

"Not really. It's just the way he thinks. Different generation and all that. You see, he kind of wants me to take over for him and run the family business."

"What's he do?"

"He owns a stationery store downtown. Pens, pencils, letterhead, paper clips, office supplies. All that stuff. I used to work there summers. Re-stocking and taking inventory. Cleaning the bathrooms. Delivering stuff."

"Now that sounds boring."

"After doing that all summer for a few summers, I vowed I'd never work in a job where I had to do the same thing over and over again every day."

"Don't blame you."

"The last big fight we had, I told him, 'There are two things I know for sure. One is that I will end up doing something with cars … and two, that I will never be president of a company.' I also told him I'd be a millionaire before I turned thirty."

"Guess you told him."

"I suppose. You see, I really enjoy working on cars. I used to work as an assistant on the pit crew for Allen Grant, a guy I know who raced cars. That was fun."

"I like riding in cars. Especially a '57 Chevy."

"I like music a lot, but I'm not real talented. I'd love to play drums or something, but I can't play a lick."

"I listen to the radio all the time. KFIV and KFRC."

"Me, too. When I was a kid, I listened to radio dramas. *The Whistler*, *The Lone Ranger*, *The Shadow*. There's something about radio that's always been radical. I love to listen and imagine what the images would look like. Kind of play it back like a movie or TV show in my mind."

"Never thought of it that way."

"I never liked the real classes I had to take. I daydreamed a lot, 'cause I was kind of bored. I was pretty much getting nothing but Ds. Guess I was kind of a hell-raiser. Excuse the French."

"All Ds is pretty close to flunking."

"Yeah. It's been rough on my dad. He's a good guy. We agree on most things, like hard work and the difference between right and wrong. But, we just don't see eye-to-eye on a lot of other things."

"I guess I'll get there with my dad some day."

"Maybe, maybe not. My dad and I fighting all the time has been really bad on my mom. She's been kind of sick and I've been kind of a butt ever since we moved out of town. How about you? What's life like around your place?"

I gave him the *Reader's Digest* version of my family, mom, my friends, the kid brothers and sisters. I told him what was going on with my dad and what I hoped to accomplish.

"That's a great thing you're doing."

"You'd do the same."

"I suppose. Yeah, sure, I would." He didn't sound convincing.

The sun was coming up as we hit Bakersfield. A new day and a new month. Even though George loved music, he also liked knowing what was going on, so at the top of every hour, he'd switch over to any all-news station we could pick up. We heard the usual collection of national, world, local, entertainment, and sports headlines for the month of June. Dinah Shore was about to end her variety show on NBC after ten years. Larry Doby retired from the Cleveland Indians to play in Japan. Three men escaped from Alcatraz and were never seen again. Brazil beat Czechoslovakia in the seventh World Cup of Soccer, played in Santiago, Chile. Jack Reed hit a home run in the twenty-second inning to win the Yankee's longest game in history. The Supreme Court ruled that there could be no prayer in schools.

It was time for a bathroom break. And a phone call. I wanted my folks to know I was okay.

"Where are you?" my mom asked, panic in her voice.

"I'm okay. Don't worry."

"How can I not worry? You're not here."

"I'm with a friend."

"Who?"

"George."

"George? Your teammate, George?"

"Not that George, another George."

"Son, this is crazy." It was my dad, on one of the other phones. "Tell us where you are and we'll come get you."

"I've got something to do first. Then I'll be home."

"The police have been out all night looking for you. We've been worried sick," Mom said and she started to cry.

I went cold and felt like I'd been punched in the stomach. "Stop, Mom. I hate it when you cry."

"Then come home. Right now."

"Stop worrying. I'm fine."

"Where are you, Michael?" my father asked.

"I can't tell you right now. I'll be back soon. And I'll call again. Don't worry. I can take care of myself. I've got to do this, okay?"

"Don't do anything foolish. And be careful."

"I will, Dad. You, too."

"Call us. And get home soon."

"Okay. Bye."

"Bye."

CHAPTER 21

We dropped down into the Los Angeles basin around nine o'clock. The traffic was kind of nuts. I remember it being bad from previous visits, but this was a little overwhelming. My family used to drive to Disneyland almost every summer. All seven of us crammed into our old 1948 Chevy. We'd stack blankets and pillows on the floor in the back to create a makeshift bed. Since they were smaller, one of my sisters would sleep in the flat storage spot below the back window. We'd always check into a hotel somewhere near Disneyland so we could walk to the park. We'd bring our own food, mostly sandwich fixings, because it was too expensive to take all seven of us out to dinner. Instead, we'd picnic by the pool, or up in our room. The hotel always had a pool and we'd spend hours swimming. I remembered the smell of chlorine and the muggy, smoggy Los Angeles days. I loved it. Every time I smelled chlorine on a hot day, I'd think of Disneyland.

George insisted on taking me all the way to Anaheim, even though it meant he would have to double-back to the USC campus, which was just off the Santa Monica freeway southwest of downtown Los Angeles.

"I love to drive," he explained. "As long as I've got gas, I could just keep driving. Right off the edge of the earth."

We stopped at the Jolly Roger Inn across the street from Disneyland. George signed for the room since I wasn't old enough. He had a fake ID that said he was twenty-one.

"This is one of my most favorite places on earth," he said, as he stared across the shimmering asphalt road and parking lot toward the Magic Kingdom. "I came here with my buddy Frank when it first opened, back in 1955. Stayed a week. I wrote about it in a neighborhood newspaper I started with Melvin, a kid from the neighborhood, that we called the *Daily Bugle*. It's okay to dream and have fantasies inside those walls. To dream about what might be instead of what has to be."

"Some day," I said.

"Yep, some day," he replied. "Good luck," he added, as he shook my hand.

"Thanks. And thanks for the ride," I replied. "Good luck to you, too. I'll keep an eye out for your first building or comic book or movie or whatever."

"You do that." With that, he jumped in, buckled up, gunned it, and burned rubber out of the parking lot.

Once checked in, the first thing I did was change clothes, put on my swimsuit, and dive into the pool. It was fantastic. Just like I remembered. And it smelled exactly the same. I rolled over and floated on my back, staring at the blue sky streaked with brown. It was a smoggy day, but not bad for Los Angeles. It made me think of my family. I wished they were here. But, I had more important things to do.

The Yankees were playing today and the next day, which was Saturday, June 2, and Sunday. I had the rest of Friday to myself, so I decided to go to the "Happiest Place on Earth."

Disneyland was absolutely the best. Dressed in my new Madras shirt, tan Bermuda shorts, Puma tennies, and my Giants hat, I bought an "E" ticket, walked under the monorail, around the large flower image of Mickey, through a tunnel under the railroad station, and into the park. A small sign above the east tunnel entrance read: "Here you leave today and enter the world of yesterday, tomorrow and fantasy." I was determined to ride every ride, which I had never done before. There were so many of us of different ages in my family that my parents had to split up to keep everybody satisfied and budget the money so everyone got to ride their favorite ride and eat their favorite food. This time, I didn't have any younger brothers or sisters to keep me from doing what I wanted to do. And, my pockets were full with work, birthday, and Christmas money. I knew I'd get frazzled trying to get to everything, but I figured this was my only chance. So, I went for it.

There was just one way to get into the park and back out again. You had to walk down Main Street U.S.A., before entering a central plaza with avenues that spoked out to each of the four different lands.

I started at Town Square. I stopped for a moment at the flagpole and scanned the brass plaque at its base. It read: "To all who come to this happy place… WELCOME. Disneyland is your land. Here age relives fond memories of the past…and here youth may savor the challenge and promise of the future. Disneyland is dedicated to the ideals, the dreams, and the hard facts that have created America…with the hope that it will be a source of joy and inspiration to all the world. July 17, 1955."

It wasn't called the "Happiest Place on Earth" without good reason and I was about to remember why.

I continued down Main Street U.S.A., where Disney had turned back the clock to days gone by and recreated the hometown feel of America at the turn of the twentieth century which, for Walt, was the town he grew up in – Marceline, Missouri. The apothecary, the ice cream parlor, the fire department, the penny arcade, and all the buildings looked like an old movie set of a small town. The street was crawling with people, costumed Disney characters, and vendors. Horse-drawn surreys clip-clopped up and down the street, while double-decked Omnibuses, horseless carriages, and fire engines wheeled through town. A red-coated marching band, led by a white-coated band leader, strutted their stuff.

Everything was clean and perfect. Maybe a little too perfect. I saw a guy armed with a putty knife down on his hands and knees scraping up chewing gum. What a lousy job.

Walt Disney's private apartment was located above the Disneyland Fire Department. It was a cute, jewel box kind of looking place. All red and gold and stuffed with gaslight-era antiques. It was from here that Uncle Walt surveyed his domain any time he visited.

George had told me he had read about the design of Main Street, which used a kind of forced perspective to create an illusion of height. All the buildings along the street were built at 3/4-scale on the first level, then 5/8-scale on the second story, and 1/2-scale on the third. Sort of made it like a doll house. I guess Mr. Disney wanted to feel a little bigger than the real world waiting outside his walls.

I hopped onto the Santa Fe & Disneyland train to take a ride around the entire park. Just to get familiar with it all over again. Our first stop was the Grand Canyon Diorama. Located inside a dark tunnel, it looked so real, you could swear you were standing on the rim of the canyon. All kinds of wild animals, including mule deer, mountain lion, desert bighorn sheep, golden eagle, wild turkeys, striped skunk, and porcupine, were frozen in time as the *Grand Canyon Suite* by Ferde Grofé played on the sound system.

Disney had always loved to combine his animated films with classical music. One of my favorites was *Fantasia*. When it originally came out in 1940, it included eight animated segments set to pieces of classical music conducted by Leopold Stokowski and performed by the Philadelphia Orchestra. It was re-released several times, including in 1956 in SuperScope, which was when I first saw it. My favorite sequences were *The Sorcerer's Apprentice*, which featured Mickey Mouse trying to control broomsticks carrying water buckets, and *Night on Bald Mountain*, which showed a devil summoning spirits from the grave. They used to show both of them every Halloween on *Walt Disney's Wonderful World of Color*, which aired on NBC on Sunday nights starting in 1961.

When we returned full circle to the station, I stepped off the train and, being the rebel that I was, decided to tour the park in a counter-clockwise direction. First, for old time's sake, I bought a felt Mickey Mouse hat with big plastic ears. I carefully folded my ball cap the way Coach Leach taught us, tucked it into my back pocket, and jammed the ears on my head. I was now officially a Mouseketeer.

I left Main Street and headed for the heart of Disneyland. I crossed the moat and drawbridge of Sleeping Beauty's Castle and entered Fantasyland. For an amusement park located in a part of the world that was semi-arid and had a desert climate, water was a key element of Disneyland. It was everywhere.

CHAPTER 22

Fantasyland was inspired by the lyrics to the song, "When You Wish Upon a Star" from the film *Pinocchio*, and was designed to be a place where dreams could actually come true. Here, in "the happiest kingdom of them all," I journeyed with Snow White through the dark forests to the home and diamond mine of the Seven Dwarfs. I flew with Peter Pan in a pirate galleon over Moonlit London to visit Never-Never Land, where Peter escaped the clutches of Mr. Smee and Captain Hook. I raced with Mr. Toad on his crazy auto ride through Old London Town. I absolutely loved Mr. Toad's Wild Ride, no matter how old I was. I followed Alice on the Through the Rabbit Hole ride into the nonsensical world of Wonderland and careened madly on spinning cups and twirling saucers on the Mad Tea Party ride. Dumbo, the elephant with aerodynamic ears, carried me on a flight high above Fantasyland. I rode colorful Dutch canal boats on a journey through Storybook Land and viewed the homes of the Three Little Pigs, Pinocchio's Village, and Cinderella's Dream Castle. I rode Casey Jr.'s train, which puffed up and down hills around Storybook Land, and the King Arthur Carrousel. Finally, I steered a speedboat through white-water rapids and swift currents on the Motor Boat Cruise.

The Mickey Mouse Club Theatre showed Disney's cartoon movies, as well as clips from the Mickey Mouse Club, which premiered on TV on October 3, 1955. I had watched it from the beginning, every day after school. It only lasted until 1959. But, we had re-runs each night at six o'clock on Channel 13. Jimmy Dodd was the Head Mouseketeer and Roy was the Big Mooseketeer. Once I heard the theme song, I couldn't get it out of my head. It was like a bad ice cream truck jingle. All my buddies liked Annette for obvious reasons. Me, I liked Darlene. Outside the theatre, a beautiful Cinderella and Snow White book-ended a dazed boy about my age. I was thinking how much I'd like to be the icing in that Princess Oreo.

It was Little League day at the park, so it swarmed with kids in ball caps and uniforms of all colors, sponsored by a variety of Southern California businesses. Disneyland always hosted days like this so organizations could sell discounted tickets. It was all about getting people into the park.

I pitied the poor boys and girls wearing the character costumes. There was no getting away from the horde and no protecting themselves. Every time I turned a corner, I'd see a pack of Little Leaguers hassling one of the Three Little Pigs, or one of the Seven Dwarfs. Since Dopey was the smallest and always stayed at the back of the character Conga line, he was usually the easiest victim. The kids would somehow separate him from the group, which wasn't so hard considering he could only see out a small screen in his large plastic forehead. But, Dopey had a weapon. If one of his attackers got too close, he started twirling, which turned his lifeless arms and hard rubber hands into lethal, propeller-like weapons. As soon as he conked the first kid, the rest scattered to hunt safer prey.

Although I wouldn't be able to stay to see it, each night during the summer, Disneyland's brilliant "Fantasy in the Sky" fireworks burst over Sleeping Beauty's Fantasyland Castle. It was during that spectacular performance that Tinker Bell would fly through the sky, zooming from the Matterhorn to a forest behind the castle. At the appointed time, a voice from the sky would boom out into the sultry Southern California night. "A long time ago, in a far away land, lived a sparkling little spirit named Tinker Bell...who sometimes, to this day, returns to fly above the magic land of fantasy. And the story is told for children of all ages, that if you wish hard enough, and believe strong enough, Tinker Bell may appear to light – fantasy in the sky!" With that cue, Tinker Bell flashed from the top of the Matterhorn, down a wire, waving her pixie dust wand, while the night sky burst into fireworks and "Zip-a-dee-doo-dah" crackled from speakers in the trees. I had heard that she'd gotten stuck a few times and had to be rescued at least once by a hook-and-ladder fire engine.

With that image of Tink still fresh in my mind, I boarded the Skyway Ride and soared over the Coral Lagoon and glided through the Matterhorn into Tomorrowland.

CHAPTER 23

In Tomorrowland, Disney had asked many of America's foremost men of science and industry to predict the world of tomorrow. I saw the future of city mass transportation as I rode the noiseless, smooth Disneyland-Alweg Monorail System. The monorail carried passengers to and from the Disneyland Hotel at speeds of up to forty-five miles per hour. Following that, I piloted my own flying saucer, which was almost as fun as the bumper cars at the Santa Cruz Boardwalk. I explored liquid space aboard the Nautilus, an authentic submarine which cruised the Seven Seas, passing through the Lost Continent of Atlantis, the Mermaid Lagoon, and the Polar Ice Cap. I got a little claustrophobic as I watched the water bubble above my porthole. As we torpedoed through the water, we glided past a mermaid. She was kind of cute. Real and unreal. That was the Disney way.

I boarded a rocket ship and blasted off into outer space inside the cavernous Space Chamber. I broke the sound barrier on the fast-flying AstroJet ride. I couldn't wait to climb into a real, gasoline-powered "Mark V" automobile on the Super Autopia Freeway. I jumped in and gunned it. Almost immediately, one of the park employees – the "people specialists" or "cast members" as they were officially known inside the park – jumped on the running board and forced me to throttle back. He was as clean and well-manicured as the park. He smiled a frozen smile, wagged his finger at me, leapt off, and disappeared. I hit it again. Of course, there was a concrete divider down the middle of the highway to keep the destruction derby types from banging into each other.

That brief encounter with the Disneyland "police" made me look a little closer at all the smiling faces working there. Although they all looked different, they all looked the same. The chicks were mostly blonde, blue-eyed, healthy-looking types. The dudes were All-American airline-pilot types; the kind of guy your mother would love to have as a son-in-law. The D-Land cops all looked like gym teachers and ROTC recruits.

At the end of Autopia, I stood facing the snow-capped Matterhorn. The fake mountain had two, high-speed bobsled runs that carried you down the slopes and through Glacier Grotto inside the mountain. It was the best roller coaster ride ever, especially when Big Foot lunged at you. I splashed into Glacier Lake at the end of the run. Rubber-legged, I left the Matterhorn. Every time I think of the Matterhorn, I think of an older high school buddy named Chuck Horne. Every time we'd see him, we'd ask, "What's it matter, Horne?" We thought we were so clever.

To get another glimpse of the immediate future, I toured Monsanto Corporation's House of the Future, which was manufactured entirely of plastic. Right next to that was the Circarama, a pioneering 360-degree motion picture experience that took me on a film tour of the United States entitled, "America the Beautiful." I spent a little time in the Art of Animation, which showed how Disney artists created their famous animated motion pictures, as well as the *20,000 Leagues Under the Sea* exhibit, which included Captain Nemo's submarine and sets from the film. The movie version starred Kirk Douglas, James Mason, and Peter Lorre. I still remember how funky and fake looking the gigantic octopus was. And Kirk Douglas singing. Badly. The movie had a little bit of over-acting by both man and beast. Walt Disney films always included somebody singing a song. Some were better than others. I skipped the Color Gallery and Hall of Chemistry. Too much like school.

Each night, Tomorrowland would host "Disney After Dark," which showcased music for the parents, like Woody Herman and the Herd and the Duke Ellington Band, as well as new pop stars for us, usually somebody whose first name ended in "y," like Bobby Rydell or Ricky Nelson. They'd let all the kids hang out and dance. But, they had a strict dress code. You couldn't get in unless you were wearing at least a sport coat and tie for the guys and a skirt for the girls. Anyone who didn't fit the mold was turned away. Anyone with hair over their ears or collar, were watched closely. Security frisked the guys for booze and drugs. They were very old school in trying to weed out the juvenile delinquents. I guess they didn't want anyone who was different to contaminate the rest of the park. A lot of high schools held their graduation night party at Disneyland. They'd rent one section of the park just for their class. You could ride everything for free. It was a neat idea. I hoped our senior class would consider it.

I walked out the entrance along the colorful Avenue of Flags. Circled around Town Square and galloped toward Frontierland, my favorite part of the park.

CHAPTER 24

I clomped over the slatted, wooden bridge that crossed the murky green creek, through the stockade gate, and stepped back in time. Frontierland was dedicated to our country's history and the pioneering spirit of our forefathers. In this part of the park, we could return to Frontier America, which spanned the Revolutionary War era to the final taming of the Great Southwest.

I was getting a little hungry, so I had some Mexican food at the Casa de Fritos, which was housed in a building made of fake adobe. The Frito Kid greeted me as I walked in. What could be better? Fritos and Mexican food.

I enjoyed Slue Foot Sue's floor show with the Can-Can girls at the Golden Horseshoe Saloon. I boarded the three-masted schooner Columbia Sailing Ship, which was an exact replica of the first American ship to sail around the world, and traveled the Rivers of America. The smell of the brown-green water that hid the tracks, along which the Columbia and the steam-powered Mark Twain Sternwheel Riverboat glided, reminded me of all the rivers and lakes I had ever played in. All around us, Mike Fink keel boats and Indian war canoes, poled and paddled by park guests, moved along the Rivers' winding courses. Each time I saw a keel boat, I thought of Fess Parker as Davey Crockett and Buddy Ebsen as George Russel, racing Mike Fink down the Mississippi to New Orleans and getting attacked by river pirates masquerading as Indians. I waved back at the war-bonneted chief on his painted pony.

The only way to get to Tom Sawyer's island was via Huck Finn's raft. As I waited for my turn to board, the Disneyland Stage Lines stagecoach clattered by. The island had everything an adventurous boy like me could want, including old Fort Wilderness, Injun Joe's Cave, and the Tree House. I wandered around the barracks, headquarters, parapets, and block houses of the fort. In the distance, I could see a settler's cabin burning. It wasn't real, but it sure looked it. I took the secret tunnel down to the river and back. I climbed like a little monkey into Tom and Huck's Tree House. I really missed having my brothers and sisters and parents with me. You could also do a little fishing off a small pier nearby if you wanted. I'm not sure I'd eat what was caught, but it looked like fun.

Being on the island reminded me again of the school play about Tom Sawyer we'd done in sixth grade, and my solo as Ben Rogers, the kid who talked all his friends into helping whitewash a fence, singing "A Captain on the Mississippi." Gary won the role of Dr. Robinson, who was killed by Injun Joe, who was played by Jeff, Gary's across-the-alley neighbor. Jeff kind of looked like an Indian. The play really made me appreciate the story a lot more. It was a very professional production for an elementary school, and I was proud to be a part of it. Mr. Leach and Mrs. Allen put a bunch of time and energy into making it happen and they did it because they believed in us and believed in the importance of things like music and art and dancing and singing.

Back in the present, I raced through the dark caves and climbed to the top of Castle Rock, touching the American flag that flapped in the gentle breeze. On the distant shores of the rivers, I saw the Old Mill, the Indian settlement and burial ground, and watched full-blooded, native Indians perform tribal dances. At Fort Wilderness, a cavalry man allowed me to hold his rifle, as I sighted through the logs at an imaginary enemy.

Security patrolled the island disguised as United States Cavalry. They wore boots, bandanas, ribboned hats, suspenders, and blue uniforms with yellow stripes. They were straight out of a John Wayne western, except instead of six-shooters in their holsters, they carried intercoms for radioing the Mainland Headquarters.

One of my friends, who had been to D-Land the summer before, said he'd hidden on the island until dusk, hoping to hide out overnight. He was tucked inside one of the teepees when he heard voices. He peaked out and saw a couple of the cavalrymen escorting two handcuffed, long-haired teenagers along a path toward the fort. One cavalryman, who was trailing the others, was carrying a plastic bag filled with what looked like dead grass. He held up a white cylinder that looked like an unfiltered cigarette, only the ends were pinched and twisted together. The cavalryman ran the cigarette under his nose, inhaled, and said, "Good stuff."

"Farm out," said one of the other cavalrymen.

My buddy said they had confiscated some marijuana from the other kids, who they were taking to an Anaheim Police Department jail located somewhere in the park. He said they were busting kids all the time because the island was a great place to "smoke dope." I had no idea what marijuana was, or what "smoking dope" meant, but it all sounded too weird. And, if it meant going to jail, I didn't want any part of it.

Frontierland included one of the park's newest attractions – a seven-acre wildlife preserve inspired by Disney's True-Life Adventure films. It was called Nature's Wonderland and it represented the great North American wilderness before the coming of man. In the ghost town of Rainbow Ridge, I climbed aboard the Mule Pack and rode past all kinds of animated, lifelike, mechanical animals. I especially enjoyed Beaver Island. Once we got back to the town, which also served as the train depot, I then boarded the Western Mine Train and traveled through the Painted

Desert, with its teetering rocks and "Old Unfaithful" geyser and bubbling Devil's paint pots, on its journey to the spectacular Rainbow Caverns, which had all kinds of breathtaking waterfalls, multi-colored, almost neon-looking stalactites and stalagmites. It sort of reminded me of what you'd see in the beatnik bookstores in San Francisco, where they shined some kind of black light onto some bizarre posters. It kind of made my eyes burn. I saw Sheriff Lucky win a shootout with Black Bart in the streets of Frontierland, while the Gonzalez Trio played traditional *mariachi* songs in the gazebo. On my way out, I tested my sharpshooting skills at the Frontier Shooting Gallery.

Then it was on to the heart of deepest, darkest Africa. I plunged beneath the crossed ivory tusks and into the jungle wonder world of Adventureland.

CHAPTER 25

Adventureland was dedicated to those who dreamed of traveling to mysterious, far-off places, or exotic tropical regions of the world. The Disney Imagineers envisioned a place far from civilization, in the remote jungles of Asia and Africa. In this "wonderland of nature's own design," I saw bright orchids, colorful flowers, tropical plants, and trees imported from the four corners of the world. It was also filled with "wild" animals and "savage" natives. It was pretty incredible.

I boarded the Jungle River Boat Safari, which carried me away from civilization on an exciting trip down mysterious jungle rivers. The winding waterways included the Irrawaddy and Mekong rivers of Southeast Asia, bordered by the ancient lost city of Ganesha. I watched giant Indian elephants and "little squirts" bathe and play in the Sacred Elephant Pool. As we entered the rivers of Africa, we steamed past cascading Schweitzer Falls and turned down the Nile River. Beyond a den of lions, we saw an angry rhino trying to impale the backside of the bottom man of a safari party the beast had chased up a tree. When the skipper piloted the craft onto the Congo River, a charging hippo nearly capsized us before our boat guide stopped him with a pistol shot fired point-blank at the monster. As we entered headhunter country, I heard the natives chanting their war cries. The last river we journeyed was the Amazon.

All the tour guides in all the lands of Disney had a set spiel they delivered on each ride. They were all pretty corny. The Wild River Ride narrative was the worst, filled with bad puns and wordplays. Here's what our guide said as we were ending our tour and passing a fake guy holding some shrunken human heads: "As we near our home port…there's old Trader Sam, head salesman of the jungle. Business has been shrinking lately, so this week only, Sam's offering a two for one special, to cut his overhead. That's two of his… for only one of yours! He's just trying to get ahead in life. At least he knows where he is headed. And now, we come to the most dangerous part of our journey…the return to civilization." Ouch.

As I shook off my river legs and stretched, I noticed a tall man with a moustache, kind face, and twinkly eyes surrounded by children and grown-ups, all thrusting slips of paper, brochures, photographs, napkins, and whatever was at hand in his face. Mr. Walt Disney himself just smiled and patiently signed each one. As I moved closer, I saw one plump woman take her Disneyland map as he handed it back, look closely at it, and frown.

"This doesn't look like your signature," she said, and shoved it back at him. "Do it again."

He smiled, took the map, signed it again, and handed it back.

"It's still not right," the woman said in her thick Texas drawl.

"It's the best I can do," he apologized. "Now, I need to run. We're getting ready to open a new exhibit in Adventureland and they're waiting for me."

"What is it? What is it?" the excited children of all ages chirped.

"Well, the Tahitian Terrace will feature dancers from Polynesia. And we'll be opening the Big Game Safari Shooting Gallery, which allows our guests to stalk big game with a high-powered elephant gun. And, the Swiss Family Robinson Tree House, well, it will be the largest in the world and you can view the entire park from there. We're awfully excited."

"Can we see? Can we see?" they all clamored.

"Next month," he replied and walked off up Main Street. Alone, which surprised me. No bodyguards, no security personnel. Nobody.

I fell into step behind him. He curved left at the plaza and headed for Fantasyland.

"I thought your autograph looked like the real thing," I said.

He stopped suddenly and I almost banged into him. He turned around. "Really?" he asked. "You really thought it looked the same?"

"I did."

"People don't believe me anymore. They look at my autograph and compare it to ones on signs and in books and in the movies and it really doesn't look the same. It started out as my signature, then we turned it into kind of a logo. You know what a logo is?"

"No, not really."

"It's an image, or a symbol, that represents a company. They usually put it on all their products and business cards and letterhead. Like the little blue bell that the phone company uses. Or the Pepsi logo. Or Volkswagen. Or Johnson & Johnson."

"Okay, I sorta see what you mean."

"We tried to do what Coca-Cola did. They used a very fancy, stylized, calligraphy-type text for their logo for the longest time, before they added the red background and that white wave. That's what we did, too. We started with my signature, then my artists enhanced it. Um, made it fancier. And that's what we put on everything now. The problem is, I can't sign my name exactly that way anymore. They made it so fancy, I can't get it right, partly, I guess, because the way I sign my name has changed over the years. I can't draw Mickey, either. And that upsets people. I can still do his voice. Most days."

"They need to chill out," I said.

And he laughed. A great, big laugh. Then he spoke in a high, squeaky voice, "Hello, my name is Mickey Mouse, what's yours, son?"

"Mikey."

"Mouse or Mantle?" he said in his normal voice.

"No, Mikey, not Mickey, although my dad wanted to call me that. After Mantle, not your mouse. But, that's another story."

"Well, Mikey, I would've been surprised, but flattered, if you had been named after my creation. Why don't you walk with me and tell me the rest of the story? I really need to get going. Lots to check up on."

"Sure," I said, and tried to keep up with his big strides.

"Where you from, Mikey?"

"Modesto, in the Central Valley."

"I know exactly where it is. Been through there countless times. Nice town. A lot like our Main Street."

"I agree."

"Is this your first time here?"

"No, I've been here a lot. Almost every summer since I was eight, or so."

"Well, welcome back."

"Thanks."

"You here with your family?"

"Not this time. It's just me."

"You have any brothers and sisters?"

"Two each."

"Very symmetrical. I like that kind of symmetry."

"Me, too."

"You all get along."

"As well as most."

"That's the way it is with my big brother, Roy. We do pretty well. Most of the time. My two older brothers, Herbert and Ray, weren't around much when I was growing up. And I was too busy working to spend much time with my little sister, Ruth. It all kind of flew by. That's another story, too."

"I'm the big brother, so I'm expected to take care of them."

"That's what you're supposed to do. That's what Roy did for me."

"I don't always want to, but I do."

"How about your mom and dad?"

"Mom's a mom. Dad works for the phone company."

"Is he good to you?" he asked.

"The best."

"Is he a good man?"

"I think so."

"What's wrong?" he asked, noticing the frown.

"Oh, nothing, my dad's been kinda sick."

He stopped and looked at me. "Well, I'm truly sorry to hear that."

"Thanks."

"He going to be okay?"

"I hope so."

"How serious is it?"

"Pretty serious, I think. In fact, that's why I'm here."

"At Disneyland? I know we're the Magic Kingdom, but I'm not sure how strong our healing powers are."

"No, here in Los Angeles."

I proceeded to tell him the *TV Guide* version of my story, which I'd gotten pretty good at.

"What you're doing is pretty amazing, Mikey. It reminds me of a saying. 'When a father gives to his son, they both laugh. When a son gives to his father, they both cry.'"

"That's nice, but I don't like to cry."

"It's really okay, even for a young man."

"That's what my mom says."

"Family is all we've got, you know. Having a place to go is a home. Having someone to love is a family. Having both is a blessing. A man can travel the whole world over in search of what he needs, and he'll return home to find it. Home really is where the heart is. And family is the compass that guides us, that inspires us to be the best, and comforts us when we fail. That's why I created this place. I wanted a family park where parents and children could have fun. Together."

"We always enjoyed coming here. Even when it was too hot and the lines were too long and we weren't in a good mood. This place made it all better. It was kind of like Shangri-La."

"That's what we were dreaming of. I'm sorry your family's not here. Maybe you'll consider coming back when your father gets better? You can be my guest."

"That would be great. Really great."

Then he started to sing. Not very well, but a nice, clear baritone. Almost as good as the guy who played Jiminy Cricket in *Pinocchio*, where the song was first sung; his name was Cliff Richards, and he was also known as "Ukulele Ike."

Just hearing "When You Wish Upon a Star" made me feel better. I truly wanted to believe that doing that would really make my dreams come true.

"I grew up listening to that song," I said. "It's still one of my favorites."

"Believe in what it says, Mikey. Good luck."

"Thanks."

"Here."

He wrote something inside the Disneyland brochure he was carrying and handed it to me. He patted my shoulder, turned, and walked across the moat into Snow White's castle, which was where my tour had begun. I looked at what he had written: "One free pass for Mikey Wright and his entire family. Any time, any day. No expiration date. Miracles do come true." He signed it and it looked exactly like it was supposed to.

It had been an exhausting day, but a good one.

CHAPTER 26

Game time the next day was eight o'clock, so I had some time to kill. I decided to go to the ocean. I hadn't been in the ocean since the last time we had visited my Aunt Cat.

Aunt Cat was my dad's older sister, Catherine. She lived in Poway, near San Diego, with her husband, Uncle Jim Monroe, and her three kids, my cousins Rod, Robbie, and Susan. We used to visit them at least once a year. We'd go dune-buggy riding, eat the best homemade tacos, and go to the beach. We'd pack a lunch and take truck tire inner tubes to float on the waves. We were all wrinkly after being in the water all day. We'd go home, barbeque hot dogs and hamburgers, and play a little baseball before dropping exhausted into bed. Ready to go another round the next day.

My Aunt Cat was my favorite relative. She had been a Marine like my dad. My Uncle Jim was a Navy man. She had a great, hearty horse laugh and loved life. So did he. She took good care of her little brother, my dad. A lot of people said we looked alike. I thought we did. We had the same high cheekbones and eyes that went up a bit at the ends, which prompted some of my friends to nickname me, "Chink Eyes." Not very nice, but still kind of funny.

My family loved nicknames. We gave them to each other, to relatives, to friends, even strangers. My dad was known as "Tooter," for his clarinet and saxophone playing in high school. My mom was known as "Dynamite," for being who she was. My brother Tim was "T" and "Bone Sights Jr." Willy was "Spindle Fibers," and "Harry Joe Brown." Diane was "Dee Dee," "Tooter Jr.," and "Dion." Cheryl was "Cheri" and "Little Dynamite." Aunt Cat was sometimes called "Bob," but nobody knew why. If we gave you a nickname, that meant you were accepted into the clan. I guess it was our way of controlling our world. If we could name it, we could own it. My other nicknames included "Pinky" and "Kenji," which was homage to Japanese-American big-time wrestler, Kenji Shibuya, and my pointy eyes.

I came by that name logically because we all used to watch *Big-Time Wrestling* on Channel 2, KTVU in Oakland. The live wrestling matches were sponsored by Gateway Chevrolet, "top of the hill, Daly City." That phrase was burned into my brain each time Jim Westman would say it, as he stood perched on a ladder, selling cars in between bouts. The show featured wrestlers like Pat Patterson, Ray Stevens, who called everybody "Pencil Neck," the Sheik, Mitsu Arakawa, with his "Stomach Claw," Pepper Gomez, Haystack Calhoun, and Andre the Giant. There were also bouts broadcast out of the studio at Channel 13 in Stockton, with announcer Bob Fouts, and at the Uptown Arena in Modesto. I never got to go to any of the matches in town because Mom thought they were too violent, even though we all knew they were fake. We even tried a few of the moves on each other, usually with Tim or Willy ending up crying before we were done. It was all good, clean fun for us kids.

I caught a bus to Manhattan Beach, since that was the closest beach to Hawthorne, the town where the Beach Boys grew up. Their song "Surfin'" had come out in February and my buddy John, of the chipped tooth incident, and his two older brothers had turned into land-locked valley surfers all because of that song.

Every weekend, they'd drive to Santa Cruz, which had the best surfing beaches nearest to Modesto. They grew their hair long and swept it across their foreheads in a wave like the Beach Boys. They wore white Levi's, Pendleton shirts, and no shoes, just like the Beach Boys. They learned how to do the Surfer's Stomp, just like the Beach Boys. Another friend's oldest brother even bought a Woodie Wagon, which was a wood-paneled station wagon, to carry his surfboards around, just like the Beach Boys. I loved the song and the music, but I wasn't ready to start surfing, although I thought the Pacific was pretty stoked. I wanted to see where it all began.

The bus dropped me at the corner of Manhattan Beach Boulevard and Manhattan Avenue. I exited the bus and headed toward the ocean. I passed a magic shop. Through the storefront window, I could see a man I recognized from newspapers and television shows, like *The Tonight Show.* It was The Great Blackstone, a magician known around the world. There was another shorter and rounder man wearing black glasses standing next to him. They were in the middle of an animated conversation. Like my mother, who was fascinated by any kind of celebrity, I wanted to get a closer view of the magician and maybe find out what they were talking about. I pushed open the door and walked in. The tiny bell above the door announced my arrival. Both men turned to see who it was and, when they realized it wasn't anybody they knew, they went back to their discussion.

"It was the Genesee Theatre in Waukegan, Illinois," the man in glasses said. "After seeing all your shows, I vowed to be the world's greatest magician. It didn't quite work out."

"No, instead you became the greatest writer of science fiction and fantasy. One of the world's most respected storytellers."

"You're too generous, Mr. Blackstone," said the man in glasses.

"You're too modest, Mr. Bradbury," said the magician.

"I began by putting on shows in my hometown," Mr. Bradbury continued. "Oh, my poor family. My parents would give me magic sets on my birthday and for Christmas. I got good enough, or thought I was, that I recruited two school chums, who were twins and amateur magicians, and took my show on the road. We played Oddfellows Hall, the Elks Club, the Moose Lodge, and the VFW Hall. I loved the sense of power and control that performing magic gave me. I think that's why so many boys become interested in it as a hobby. Plus, I liked being in the limelight."

I realized that the man in glasses was Ray Bradbury. I knew that because I had read some of his books. I recognized his photo from the dust jacket and remembered from his biography that he was born in Illinois and was an amateur magician.

"You came back to the Genesee in the last week of 1931," Mr. Bradbury went on. "You invited audience members to come on stage to help. I was one of the ones you selected. A horse was brought on stage and a curtain was draped in front of it. I helped you fire a gun and, when the curtain went up, the horse had vanished. Before I left the stage, you gave me a rabbit to take home. I couldn't believe that you had actually given me a gift. I kept it until it started leaving droppings all over the house and my mother made me give it away."

"That was a wonderful trick. I'm sorry the rabbit was such a bother."

"Many years later, our paths crossed again. This time, up in Los Angeles. I was seventeen, so it must have been 1937. You were performing and you asked for volunteers again. And, this time, I didn't wait to be picked. I bolted onto the stage. As you began your trick, you leaned closer to me. I smelled whiskey on your breath."

"I drank a bit back then."

"I was disappointed," Bradbury said.

"Can't say as I blame you."

"And felt sorry for you."

"Why?"

"I realized you were bored. All those performances, day after day, doing the same thing. It must have gotten to you."

"It did."

"From that moment onward, I made a promise to myself that I would never do the same thing. I would never be bored."

"That's hard to do."

"Writing made it easy. No day was ever the same as the day before. I realized that I could capture an audience through words, rather than illusions. But, my stage props were different. As a writer, I could use language and metaphor, but the outcome was much the same. Storytelling allowed me to enrapture an audience, oftentimes tricking them with literary bedevilment and, in the end, entertaining them."

"People like being fooled," Mr. Blackstone said.

"But, not being tricked," Mr. Bradbury said.

I slipped quietly back out the door and into the street.

I continued down Manhattan and crossed Ocean Drive until I reached the Strand. I took off my tennies, stepped across and onto the soft beach. The beautiful white sand stretched away to my left and right. I dug my toes into the sand and wriggled them around. People were swimming, laying in the sun, playing volleyball, reading books, running with their dogs, snoozing, or just walking – simply doing all those summertime beach things. Straight ahead was the Pacific Ocean.

There was something about the ocean that mesmerized Central Valley kids, something about its vastness and it marking the edge of the continent and land's end. The Native Americans up around Santa Cruz were the Ohlones. The Spanish called them the Costeños, or coast people. The English-speaking settlers renamed them the Coastanoans. When they danced along the ocean's edge, they said they were dancing on the brink of the world. And, that's what it looked like. The edge of the world. I could see why the early explorers were afraid they would sail off the end of the planet. And yet, the ocean seemed to also symbolize infinite possibilities. The smell of wet salt air was so exotic. In the valley, the landscape was wide open, too, but it was so different. There was always something blocking the horizon, like a building or trees or foothills or cars. As spacious as it was, it could sometimes feel claustrophobic. Standing there staring out at the Pacific, I realized you wouldn't run into anything until you hit Hawaii. If you missed that, the next stop was Japan or Australia. It was pretty awesome.

Off to my right was the pier and, at its very tip, the six-sided Roundhouse, which was built in 1922. Below the Roundhouse, surfers were darting in and out of the barnacle-encrusted pylons that supported the pier. The Roundhouse opened as a pavilion on July 4, 1922, and featured a bait shop, tackle rental business, and cafe. Over the years, various cafes and restaurants operated there, including a teen canteen, which was what it was now. A lot of kids hung out there and I had seen a couple headlines and news stories that indicated the city fathers weren't real happy about it because there was always trouble. I figured it was worth checking out.

I slipped my tennis shoes back on and headed for the pier. As I stepped onto the asphalt pathway leading out to the end of the pier, I heard this high, sweet voice rising above the crashing waves. Then, a second voice came in just a little lower. It sounded like a hymn. The two voices and the waves seemed entwined, somehow complementary, inseparable. I crossed over to the other side of the path, stepped back down onto the beach, and peered through the cool shadows beneath the pier. Sitting cross-legged in the sand at the base of a pylon near the edge of the ocean was a dark-haired, skinny kid. He was wearing a light-blue Pendleton shirt over a white T-shirt, white Levi's, and no shoes. Squatting next to him was a blonde-haired guy wearing a red and white striped surfer shirt, cut-off Levi's, and huarache sandals. I ducked into the shadows under the pier so I could hear better and they wouldn't see me.

They stopped singing. The dark-haired kid grabbed a handful of sand and let the grains sift slowly out the bottom of his fist. "He's at it again," he said.

"Man, what'd he do this time?"

"Slapped Carl."

"That sucks. Carl won't fight back."

"I know."

"Uncle Murry's a bully," the blonde guy said.

"I hate fighting with him all the time."

"That's how you become a man."

"Then I'm superman."

The dark-haired kid opened his fist and clapped his hands together to shake the damp sand loose from his palms. "You don't have to live with him, you know," he said.

"Neither do you, Brian. You're twenty. That's old enough to light out for the territories. Like Huck Finn, dude."

"Look, Mike, there's no way I can leave Mom and my little brothers. They need me."

"Dennis can take care of himself. Unc better be careful. Your brother's going to pop him one of these days."

"Thank God he's got surfing. It's the only life for him. The only thing he lives for."

They both looked out at the end of the pier.

"And he won't be doing that for long if he doesn't stop playing chicken with those pylons," Mike said. "He'll end up in Davy Jones's Locker. Twenty-thousand leagues down."

I looked where they were looking and saw a bushy-blonde-haired, muscled kid darting in and out of the pylons on his surfboard.

"It was the same old song, cuz," Brian said. "He was telling us to 'Kick some a—.' Always got to 'kick some a—.'"

"He just wants you to be tough. How many times have I heard Unc say, 'You think the world owes you a living? You think the world is going to be fair? You've got to get in there and kick a—!'"

"And that's when he hit Carl. To make his point."

"He's just frustrated."

"And jealous," Brian replied. "We're doing what he wanted to do. All he ever dreamed about was being a songwriter. Write a few hits. He couldn't, but we could. He should be proud, but he's not. He's pissed off."

"He can still sing pretty well. And he plays a mean piano. I can't believe he never sold any of those songs of his."

"He did. A couple. Back in the fifties. They never made much of a splash."

"We're gonna have big hits. Huge," Mike said. "Banzai Pipeline big."

"Then I can tell him where to shove it."

"Can't do that. He's counting on you. He's got expectations. And mistakes to make up for."

"Screw that."

"You'll do it. You'll hate it, but you'll do it."

"You know I love him," Brian said and smiled a crooked smile out of the left side of his mouth. "But, he scares me. He's competitive, you know, and I respect that. He's kind of like one of our coaches. He scares us into doing well."

"And he totally digs the music we make."

"It's, like, the only time we get close, the only time he seems human, is around music. You know, me and Dennis and Carl used to lie in bed and sing some of the old hymns, like 'Come Down from Your Ivory Tower' or 'Good News.' I knew the sound of our voices would draw him to the door. He never came in. He'd just stand there and listen."

"And Aunt Audree said he'd always cry."

"I've never seen it," Brian said.

Neither had I. I don't think I ever saw my dad cry. I sat down on the cool sand.

"Man, I'm so tired," Brian said. "He's been working us pretty hard."

"That's one of the problems with having your old man as your manager. There's no time off."

"We're always practicing. When we're not practicing, I'm writing. He wants us to be ready to record. And then tour. We've never toured. Can you imagine what it will be like to be on tour with your dad? It'll suck."

"Naw, it'll be cool. Wait and see. You think we got some cute California girls, wait'll you see those east coast girls, the Midwest farmer's daughters, and the southern girls with the way they talk. Oh, man, oh, man. Cowabunga, dude."

I had to agree. There were probably a lot of beautiful girls out there, but the California girls were the cutest girls in the world.

"I'm afraid," Brian went on.

"Why? Dude, you're young. You're talented. The world is our oyster. Let's suck it up. Let's kick out the jams," Mike said, jumping to his feet, spinning around, and hanging ten on an imaginary surfboard.

"I don't know what's ahead. All those expectations, the loneliness, the change. It's all so unreal, absolute, and inevitable."

"Then you've got to keep laughing, man. Laughter is a necessity. Without it, we'd go insane. So, chill, Brian, it'll all work out."

"I already got kids around here treating me like I'm some kind of god. I'm no god. I'm no role model. People shouldn't look up to me. I just wish they would leave me alone."

"Too late, cuz."

"Everyone around the world wants to be a Beach Boy. They want to live a life filled with girls, sunshine, surf, and fast cars."

"Hell, I want to be us," Mike said and chuckled.

"I don't want to do that fizzy, pop stuff. I don't want to write what Dad wants me to write. I want to try stuff. There's big changes coming in music and I want to be part of it. Two verses and a chorus of 'June-Moon' won't cut it anymore. I dunno, maybe I just wasn't made for these times."

"Well, things had better work out here, Brian," Mike said. He nodded toward the ocean and said, "Because this here's the end of the continent. We got no place left to go."

I realized they were right. We were sitting at the edge of things. The wind shifted and I could hear the song "Surfin'" floating on the air. I looked toward the horizon and saw a boy and girl doing the Surfer's Stomp. It looked like they were dancing on the brink of the world.

Then it was game time and I had to scoot.

CHAPTER 27

1961 had been an expansion year for baseball. The American League added the Washington Senators and Los Angeles Angels. Owned by entertainer Gene Autry, the latter was named for the city of Los Angeles, which meant "City of Angels." The Halos finished 70-91, which wasn't bad for a new team. It was a motley crew. Chunky Steve Bilko had played for years with the Pacific Coast League Angels. Another fan favorite was the little guy, El Monte native Albie Pearson. Other players of note included outfielder Leon Wagner, infielders Jim Fregosi and Eddie Yost, as well as pitchers Dean Chance, Art Fowler, and Ryne Duren, the ex-Yankee who was known for his blazing fastball and Coke-bottle-thick glasses. Of Duren, Casey Stengel once said, "I would not admire hitting against Ryne Duren, because if he ever hit you in the head you might be in the past tense." Bill Rigney, the ex-Giants manager, was the skipper. The Angels played their first year at Wrigley Field in South Los Angeles, which had been the home field of the PCL Angels, as well as the location of the TV show, *Home Run Derby*.

Home Run Derby had only lasted one year, from January 9 to June 2, 1960. In this made-for-TV show, two major league sluggers would go head-to-head to see who could hit the most runs. Any ball not hit fair and over the fence was an out. Each player was given three outs. Whoever had the most home runs after nine innings, won.

The pitcher for each contest was a former major-leaguer named Tom Saffell. The catcher was a minor leaguer named John Van Ornum. The man calling strikes was a major league umpire, Art Passarella. There were also umps in the outfield to judge any close calls. If the pitcher, who was basically throwing batting practice-type pitches, threw a strike and the batter didn't swing, Passarella would call it a strike, which was an automatic out. While one player batted, his opponent would sit down with the host, actor/producer Mark Scott, and talk about the contest, or how it was going that season.

The winner received a check for $2,000 and was invited back for the next week's episode against a new opponent. The runner-up received a check for $1,000. If a batter hit three home runs in a row, he would receive a $500 bonus check. A fourth home run in a row would be worth another $500 bonus check. Any consecutive home runs hit beyond that would each be worth $1,000. A guy could make pretty good money in one day, especially if he kept hitting them out.

In the first contest, the competitors were no surprise. Mickey Mantle beat Willie Mays 9-8. Even though he was a switch-hitter and the right field fence was closer, Mickey batted right-handed because he had hit his longest home runs as a righty. Over the course of the season, Hank Aaron won the most contests with six in a row, which earned him $13,500.

On opening day in 1962, the Dodgers had unveiled their new, state-of-the-art facility at Chavez Ravine, which looked out over downtown Los Angeles. When Commissioner Ford Frick wouldn't allow the Angels to play at the Los Angeles Coliseum because he felt the left field fence was too short, Angel owner Autry worked out a deal with fellow owner Walter O'Malley to rent Dodger Stadium for their home games, which the Angels would always refer to as Chavez Ravine, so they wouldn't be reminded of their landlords.

For most of the '62 season, the Halos were actually in the pennant race. They took over first place on July 4 and finished the season in third, ten games behind the Yanks. One of the better-known misfits on the team was a pretty decent country pitcher. Bo Belinsky, who was as well-known for his fast cars, fancy clothes, two-fisted drinking, and starlet girlfriends, including Mamie Van Doren, pitched the first no-hitter in the history of Dodger Stadium on May 5, blanking the Orioles 5-0.

I had to catch a couple cross-town buses to get to the stadium from Hawthorne. I got there early so I could see the players as they came in. I was hoping to catch Mickey's eye so I could slip him the note I had carefully hand-written. It was a shortened version of my original letter and read: "Dear Mr. Mantle: My dad is your biggest fan. He is dying of cancer. Could you play a game of catch with him? He lives in Modesto. LAMBERT-20441. His son, Mikey."

I got a good spot right near where the players got off the bus and headed toward the visitor locker room. When the bus pulled into the lot, I clutched the note even tighter in my hand.

The first to exit the bus were some serious looking people in suits and ties I didn't recognize. One of them was probably what they called the "traveling secretary." Of course, that didn't make any sense because I didn't see any ladies traveling with the team. Then, the players stepped off. Yogi Berra, "Moose" Skowron, Roger Maris, Clete Boyer, Whitey Ford. I couldn't believe I was actually seeing these Titans of Baseball in the flesh. But, no Mickey. The bus looked empty. I nudged the kid next to me, who'd been busy running around getting autographs.

"Where's Mickey?" I asked.

"Don't you read the papers, dumb?" he replied.

"I've been kind of busy," I responded.

"He tore a hamstring legging out an infield single against the Twins back on May 18. Been out ever since."

"I knew about that. Man, that's old news. I got a letter from him a couple weeks back and he said he'd be ready to go."

"No way you got a letter."

"Sure did. Just wrote him and he wrote me back."

"Neat."

"Yep, pretty neat."

"Well, all's I know is the injury was pretty bad. Worse than they thought. He's still trying to get back in shape."

"I thought manager Houk told the papers he'd be ready to play by now. That's the last I read."

"Well, managers are always ready before their players are."

"And fans."

"Ain't that the truth?"

"When's he coming back?" I asked.

"Nobody knows."

I was thunderstruck. I thought for sure he'd be playing by now, and he'd be here. He said as much in his letter. The team needed him. He had never stayed out this long before, never any longer than he had to. The Yankees were in the thick of the pennant race and they couldn't win without him.

Mickey Mantle was a team player. He always said he wanted to be remembered as a great teammate. As good as he was, he wasn't a showboat. For him, it wasn't about individual stats, although his were pretty good. It was about winning games. Whether it was laying down a sacrifice bunt, stealing second, running down a fly ball, breaking up a double play, legging out a ground ball, or hitting a dinger, it was all about the team. A home run that won a game was better than a home run that added to his season total. He always circled the bases with his head down, so he wouldn't show up the pitcher. He figured the other guy was feeling bad already, so why add to his misery. No matter how much his body was aching, or how much trouble he got into off the field, he never let the team down and always gave his teammates everything he had to help them win. When his teammates had a good game, Mickey rooted for them and patted them on the butt. When they couldn't hit the broad side of a barn, he took them out for dinner and drinks, then picked up the check. If they were down, he'd pull some kind of prank to get them to laugh. Mickey played hard and he played hurt. He never complained, or made excuses. He just did his job. He didn't like letting people down, especially his teammates and the fans. He played every day, even when he shouldn't, because he was afraid some kid might come to the game that day just to see him and he'd be sitting on his brains in the dugout. He just couldn't do that.

Mickey loved and respected the game. He trusted his fellow players and they counted on him. It was always about the other guy and never about him. He always put his teammates ahead of himself. The stats backed him up. Between 1951 and 1961, Mickey's Yankees made nine trips to the World Series and won six.

Mickey never let his team down. Except this time. I'd traveled all this way for nothing.

Just then, a young man exited the bus and headed for the locker room. As he passed, I pulled the note out of my pocket and held it out to him desperately.

"Sir?"

He stopped.

"You want an autograph?" he asked.

"Well, sure, but – Well, no," I blurted out. "Do you know Mickey Mantle?"

"I sure do," he said. "Why?"

"I'd like to get him a note." I held out the note, looking pretty pathetic. He took it and read it.

"Wow, that's tough, kid. How's your dad doing?"

"Not very well," I said.

"I'll see what I can do, okay?"

"That would be swell."

"How about that autograph?"

"Sure."

He took a baseball card from the side pocket of his duffel, signed it, and handed it over.

"Good luck, kid," he said and walked off.

I looked at the card. It was the rookie card for Tom Tresh.

Dejected, I went inside to watch the game, but I didn't pay much attention. Ken McBride and the Angels beat Whitey Ford and the Yankees 6-1.

I found out later that Mickey had gone home to Dallas when he left the hospital in May to start rehabbing with Wayne Rudy, the trainer for the Dallas Cowboys of the National Football League. While he was out, the Yankees had lost fourteen out of twenty-eight games and had fallen into second place behind the Indians. Old Whitey Ford sent Mickey a bouquet of eight tired-looking daisies and a note saying that that's what the line-up was like without him in it. Roy Hamey, the Yankees' General Manager, figured he'd better do something to snap the team out of its slump. He asked Mickey to fly out to Los Angeles to buck the team up, which he did. Hamey didn't tell any of the reporters, or the team.

Mickey had snuck into the stadium, dressed, and slipped quietly into the dugout just to buck up his teammates because that's the kind of guy he was. Hamey's plan worked. The Yankees ended up winning two out of three and moved back into first place. Mantle told his teammates, "I got you into first place. Now you're on your own." He had never left the clubhouse. He had been there after all. And I had missed my chance.

CHAPTER 28

When the game was over, I caught my buses back to Anaheim. I stepped off the bus and started walking the dark street toward my hotel. It was pretty late by then. I really wasn't paying much attention to anything, still thinking about what I could have done differently, how I could've known. I turned a corner and, suddenly, some stinky wino stepped in front of me.

"Got a quarter for some coffee, mate?" he asked.

I mumbled, "No," and tried to step around him.

"Not so fast, friend," he said and blocked my way. "I'm sure you can help a veteran out."

"Sorry, I don't have anything. Except this card," and I held up the Tresh rookie card.

He snatched it out of my hand. When he did that, I took off. I was fast, so there was no way this old drunk was going to catch me. As I raced into the night, I heard him yell, "Thanks! I'm a big Yankees fan!"

When I got to my room, I was huffing and puffing and completely bummed out. It was all falling apart. My best intentions had gone bad. I called home and told mom and dad what had just happened. I could barely say anything I was so pissed at myself and determined not to cry.

"Where are you?" my father asked quietly.

"Anaheim. At the Jolly Roger Inn. You know, we stayed here the last time."

"Stay there. I'm going to have your Aunt Cat come get you and bring you home."

"Okay," was all I could say.

In her time, my Aunt Cat was a heck of a ball player. She had played hardball with a women's semi-pro team right after the war and then played softball with some of the women she worked with driving bus for the local school district. She always said I was her favorite nephew, probably because we did resemble each other a bit and were both very competitive and a little selfish. She didn't like me that late Saturday night, though. She didn't say anything as she navigated her Ford Econoline van through the traffic. It was so new it still had that new-car smell.

"What were you thinking?" she finally asked as we pulled out of the Los Angeles basin and headed for the Grapevine. "You could've got hurt, or worse. There are some nasty people in this town."

"I thought it would make the cancer better."

"Only doctors can help him, not thirteen-year-old boys with silly ideas."

"I'm sorry."

"This isn't helping your father. Stress makes it worse."

"I said I'm sorry."

"All right, I am, too. Climb in the back and get some sleep. You look exhausted."

I was and I did.

When we finally rolled into my driveway a little before sunrise on Sunday, you'd have thought I had died. My mom was wailing and kissing me. My brothers and sisters actually looked like they felt sorry for me. And, my dad. Well, he just smiled. As my mom hugged me and wouldn't let go, I thought to myself, *I should disappear more often*.

That afternoon, I called Kelly and told her what happened. I explained everything. She was a great listener. It really helped to have someone besides Gary to talk to.

Then I went looking for Mr. Lowney. I found him in his usual spot. He looked very happy to see me. I told him about my big adventure and how good my family had treated me when I got back.

"Pretty grown-up of you," he said. "And kind of dumb, slugger. You could have gotten seriously hurt, even killed. Los Angeles is a big city."

"Yeah, I suppose so," I mumbled. "I guess I thought it was no different than here."

"There's a very big difference."

"I know that now."

"Lesson learned."

"Right."

"Well, you're home safe and you've got a story to tell."

"I do," I said.

"They say a journey without a story told is a journey incomplete. A traveler is never truly home until he tells his story."

"I made it."

"One thing," he said.

"What's that?"

"You haven't finished the job."

His saying it caught me a little off-guard, but it wasn't like I hadn't been thinking about it, because I had. A lot.

"I know. I was kind of hoping there would be a letter or a phone message when I got home. There was nothing."

Mr. Lowney pulled a sheaf of folded newspapers out of his inside coat pocket.

"I've been doing a little research." He unfolded and fanned the paper out on his knees. It was a dog-eared copy of the *Chicago Tribune* with the entire season's baseball schedule printed out. He flipped to the section with the Yankees' schedule. He ran his finger down the column. "The second All-Star Game is in Chicago on July 30. The Yankees play a single game with the Senators the next day and a double-header on Wednesday. They've got Thursday off, then they're back to Chicago to play the White Sox on Friday, August 3. That's perfect."

"For what?"

"For us to take a little trip."

"Us?"

"You and me."

"Where?"

"Chicago. The Windy City. Chi-town. The Hawk. Sweet home Chicago. That's where I was born, you know?"

"I didn't."

"That's why I get the *Trib*. Have to keep up with the old stomping grounds."

"There's no way – "

"Now, don't be so negative, slugger."

"But, my folks will be watching me."

"You just need a chaperone."

"They don't even know you."

"Wasn't thinking about just me."

"Who? My dad can't go. Mom, neither."

"Maybe your aunt would consider it?"

"Wow, I don't know. She's done enough already. And she's been gone a few days now."

"Didn't you say she was a bus driver for the school district down in Poway?"

"I did."

"And didn't you say she had that nice, new Ford Econoline van with the camper conversion?"

"Yes, but –"

"If you're her favorite nephew, like you said, and she's a baseball fan, a player even – "

"I am and she was – is."

"– well, that should just about do it."

"I guess all's I could do is ask."

"I guess."

"If they decide to let me go and my aunt is okay with it, which is not real likely, why don't we go sooner and try to catch him at the All-Star game? If we miss him, we could wait until the Chicago series, right?"

"Because I suspect your aunt has some organizing to do. Plus, Mickey has been known to miss a few of the mid-season classics. And, they won't be hanging around town 'cause the Yanks got to leave the next day for the series in Washington before turning right around and heading back to Chicago. 'Sides, none of us have enough money to stay in Chicago for that long. Let's hedge our bets. We know he'll be there when the rest of the Yankees come to town 'cause he should be healthy by then. And ready for some real competition."

"Sure, that makes sense. I guess." I really didn't think it did, but I was always taught to respect my elders, which I did. This time.

CHAPTER 29

That night, my dad barbequed his signature dish. Chicken slathered in Woody's Cook-In Sauce, green salad, and corn on the cob. Nothing said summer like those foods. After dinner, while everyone was digesting, I asked my dad to play a little catch. We went out the back gate, crossed the alley, and went into the park. Tim and Willy grabbed their gloves and a bat and followed us.

Right away, I could tell it hurt my dad to throw, but that didn't stop him. We tossed the ball back-and-forth for a few minutes. As we tossed, we talked. Tim and Willy wrestled more than they played catch. When I could tell Dad was getting tired, I stopped and we headed back. He put his arm around my shoulder, partly as a pal and partly so he could lean on me a bit. That surprised me.

The night was warm and muggy. Too hot to sleep. After settling us kids onto mattresses laid out in the living room, which was cooler than the rest of the house, my folks and Aunt Cat went out on the patio for cigarettes and coffee. Once my sisters and brothers started to snore, I snuck into the back bedroom, which was my parent's room. It had two corner windows that opened out onto the backyard and patio. I could feel just the slightest breeze and could smell the smoke and coffee. I slumped down below the windows.

"How you doing, Tooter," my aunt asked.

"I went through the entire war and all I got was some dysentery. And now this. Makes you wonder."

My dad didn't enjoy his time in the military. While we were still young, he burned anything having to do with his service. Unfortunately, he also burned his high school yearbooks, letterman sweaters, and other high school memorabilia. One thing he couldn't burn was the "Devil Dog."

It got to the point where we didn't see it anymore. I supposed that's the way it was with tattoos. My father's arms and my arms were pretty much the same. I recalled sitting on his lap and staring at the bulldog with the spiked collar and the furled banner that read: "United States Marine Corps." It took some serious prodding, or a little alcohol, to get him to tell stories about the war in the Pacific. He didn't like talking about it. He went in at seventeen and came out much older. Grampa Owl accepted his high school diploma while he was in a foxhole in Saipan.

"This is my rifle, this is my gun," he would repeat the chant he learned in basic training to distinguish between the two. "This is for shooting, this is for fun." He chuckled as he recalled his fellow recruits were forced to walk through camp holding their private parts when they forgot and called their rifle their gun. He didn't smile as much when he would talk about going out on patrol with men, kids like him actually, who were in his squad and wanted to scrounge up some souvenirs. My dad was a natural leader and was quickly called upon to take charge of others. He would frown when he told us about one of his men puking his guts out when the bloated corpse of a Japanese soldier, who had been burned alive by a flamethrower, cracked open and oozed yellow goo, as the peach-fuzzed grunt tried to remove the dead man's samurai sword.

My father was one of the young men of his generation who were called upon to do things that were often less than great in order to save the world. The tattoo was cool, but not what it represented. He wasn't always proud of what he had done. He was reminded of it every day as he stared at the fading ink of the Devil Dog.

It's amazing how little we knew about our parents. Their hopes and dreams at the various stages of their lives. One time, as I was going through some of the papers my dad missed when he burned everything, I had found a copy of his U.S. Marine Corps Report of Separation – Form N a.m. 78-PD. It was basically his discharge papers, a snapshot of my father the gyrene just before he transitioned back into the real world. Nicely typed out on a manual typewriter with the requisite carbon paper copy.

As I scanned the document, I wondered who came up with the titles for each section and the required data for each. It listed all the usual facts: name, address, date and place of birth, race, sex, citizenry, marriage status, rank, pay grade, and serial number. Where and when he entered and exited service, and type of discharge. Then it got into more interesting territory.

His *Record of Marine Corps Service* held the first new information for me. His military specialty was "Guard duty." Did that mean that was what he volunteered for, what he was ordered to do, what he was interested in, or what fell to him by default?

His principal military duty was "Machine Gun crueman" which, I assumed, was a misspelling of crewman. Or not. I remembered him telling us that's what he did, when he chose to talk about the service, which wasn't often. I wondered what kind of machine gun? How many men were in the "crue"? How many men did he kill? He would never say. We never pressed.

His *Employment and Non-Service Educational Data* offered many additional surprises. His civilian occupation before he enlisted was "Student (H.S.)." He had enlisted at age seventeen and a half before graduating from high school. My dad had no secondary occupation listed. He had no last employer. He was a kid caught up in the patriotic fever infecting his country at the time. He and most of his buddies signed up to kill some bad guys. And that's what they did. After he'd been in the service for a short while, Dad called one of his buddies, who I was named after, and told him to forget the Marines and join the Navy, which his friend promptly did.

Under Trade Courses, nothing was listed. Under Courses of Greatest Interest was listed "Physical Ed." Did that mean he was a jock, or that phys ed came easily? Did he want to become a PE teacher? Why does one pick PE as a course of interest? Or, was it because he was a good baseball player and someone – a teacher, a coach, or a scout – thought he could make a career of it?

Preferences was the most revealing because it gave me a glimpse of his dreams, as well as the most frustrating because it raised so many questions. Under Preference for Additional Training, he listed "University." I knew he had always wanted to go to college under the G.I. Bill, but marriage and a family quickly derailed that and forced him to abandon his young boy ways. He always said he wanted to be an architect, which reminded me of George Bailey in *It's a Wonderful Life* and all those who lived "lives of quiet desperation," waiting for some day to arrive when they could do all those things they had daily dreamed of doing, all those "some days" that many people never cross off their to-do list.

Under Job Preference, my father listed "FBI" I had never known that, or didn't recall knowing that. What was it about the FBI that had interested him? Had he been inspired by G-Men movies? By J. Edgar Hoover and Elliot Ness taking down Capone and Nitti? Guns, I doubt it. Forensics, probably not because he didn't like death. Investigation, perhaps, because it was a puzzle and a challenge. Maybe it was just exotic. Perhaps he was really just ready to do something as far removed as possible from Manteca and the Central Valley.

As I looked at the simple document, I wondered what happened to the young man sitting in a wooden chair beside the uniformed clerk who asked him the questions and meticulously typed in his responses. What turns in life changed what he wanted to be to what he finally became? Then I realized I better ask him. Before it was too late.

Another link to his military past was one of his favorite Saturday morning rituals. When it was time for us sleepyheads to roll out of the sack, Dad would come into our room and start playing a home-grown version of reveille by tooting his lips through his closed fist and then yelling, "Rise and shine." We hated it. He loved it. It was a memory for him of what had been and a reminder for us of what might be.

"He's nothing if not persistent," my dad said, snapping me back to reality, as I sat half-dozing below the bedroom windows.

"He's obviously serious about doing something," he continued.

"Hon, this is crazier than what he already did," my mother pleaded.

"Why don't you just call Mr. Mantle?" my aunt suggested. "It's not all that expensive these days. And that might do the trick."

"He already tried that. And writing letters. That's not the point," my father replied. "Besides, that would be the easy way, wouldn't it? Easy isn't always the best, or right way. This is something he wants to do. Needs to do. For me. I feel I've got to let him do it. He's growing up, becoming a man. He's getting independent, taking responsibility. I guess this is one way to do that. He's thinking about someone other than himself. For a change. He's trying to figure things out. Trying to figure this world out. It's my job – our job – to help him."

"Maybe he just needs to grow up a bit," Aunt Cat said.

"He's growing up too fast as it is," Mom replied.

"He was born older," Dad added."

"Comes naturally when you're the eldest son," Mom said.

"Growing up means letting go," Dad answered. "For both of us. All of us."

The coffee must have been strong because my dad was on a caffeine roll and there was no stopping him.

"I've always told him to use his own good judgment. Now, he is. What kind of message would I be sending if I said he was wrong, or it was a bad decision, or he shouldn't do it? This may not necessarily be good judgment on my part, but he's taking the initiative. He's trying. I need to reward him for that. They say fathers never listen to their kids. Well, I don't believe that. He may think it's for me, but it's really for him. He has to do this. More for him than me. He really needs it more than I do. It's been a rough summer. He's got to get away from the face and smell of…death."

"Sweetie, don't talk like that," Mom pleaded.

"It's the truth. I wish they all could go. And get away from here. And me."

"There's no changing your mind?" my mom asked.

"No."

"Now what?"

My dad looked at Aunt Cat. "I guess it's kind of up to my sister."

"That's not fair," Mom replied.

"I guess that's what families are for and what they do," my aunt said. "School doesn't start for a few more weeks. I've just been driving around some of our senior citizens until it does. They've got plenty of other drivers. 'Sides, I haven't been to Chicago since I was in the service. Would love to see the city and Wrigley Field again."

"What about that old man he wants to take along?" my mom asked.

"Mr. Lowney? He's harmless," my dad replied. "He knows his baseball. Could make the ride seem a lot shorter. Plays a little blues, I hear."

"Could be fun," my aunt said.

"We'll get out the maps tomorrow and plan a route," my dad said.

"Why don't you come?" my aunt asked her little brother.

My dad just stared at his sister, sadness in his eyes. "I wish I could."

"You both are crazy," my mom said. "It's just not going to happen."

"Miracles do happen, hon," my dad said.

I grinned like the Cheshire Cat as I crept away from the window and went to bed.

That night, I dreamed I was flying over the sea. My arms were covered with wings of feathers and wax. As I glided and swooped, I could hear my father's voice warning me not to fly too close to the sun. I heard him, but I was having too much fun seeing the world the way the birds see it. Each time I would dive earthward, I would pull out and climb a little higher. Finally, I wanted to see how high my wings would take me, so I flew in ever-tighter circles closer and closer to the sun. I did loop-de-loops and barrel rolls, just like Von Richthofen and Rickenbacker and the other World War I dog-fighting aces. As I climbed straight for *El Sol*, my feathers began molting and streaming away behind me. At the height of my climb, my wings would no longer support me. I flapped and flapped, but soon realized I had no feathers left and was only waving my bare arms. And I plummeted. Just as I was about to hit the ocean, I woke up, sweating. Sitting there in the middle of the night, I hoped I would never fly too close to the sun.

Monday morning, Aunt Cat took off bright and early to get things organized at home so we could start the next leg of our journey. After she left, things went back to normal for a while. School, baseball, my dad's illness, approaching summer, and thoughts of a certain girl.

CHAPTER 30

Playland was Modesto's first outdoor public swimming pool. Originally called Modesto Plunge, it was located south of the tracks by the Borden's dairy. It had been built there to take advantage of a supply of warm water that was piped in from the Pacific Fruit Express Company, which sat on the north side of Highway 99 at Tully Avenue. The warm water was a by-product of the ice the company produced to cool all the fruits and vegetables they shipped around the state and throughout the country. The heated water was supplied until the 1940s. Frank Russo, who originally managed the Plunge, also started Modesto Baseball for Boys in April 1956. In 1946, Clyda and Al Basmajian bought Playland and renovated it. They built clubrooms, a large kitchen, a steakhouse, lounge, and dance pavilion. They held dances with big bands, dancing classes, swimming aquacades, service club meetings, fashion shows, and private meetings. There was also a go-cart track nearby. A few years later, Mr. Basmajian was killed by a jealous husband. After that, a couple of local businessmen bought the facility.

The heart of Playland was a large, 50x150-foot pool bordered by grass with a slide and three diving boards, including one that was pretty high. There were changing rooms with coarse, uneven concrete floors that always seemed wet and slimy. The men's room had racks of wire mesh baskets to put your clothes and valuables in. You'd fill it up, give it to an attendant, and pin the metal safety pin with the basket's number on your swimsuit, so you could get everything back later. There was always music playing, usually KFIV, spinning all the hits. There was also a concession stand, with a small apartment above it, which sold soft drinks, hot dogs, candy bars, and really big sno-cones. My favorite was the frozen Zero candy bar. Sometimes, I'd buy the Payday because you got a lot for your money. Plus, I liked the combination of sweet and salty. There was lots of chlorine in the water, so we always came home with blood-shot eyes.

The Saturday after I got back, summer arrived with a vengeance. Gary and I rode our bikes to Playland to cool off. We hurried to get into our suits and get everything stowed away, so we could be the first in the pool. He won. We floated around the edge of the deep end of the pool instead of the shallow end because all the little kids were at the shallow end, yelling and peeing in the pool. We liked the deep end, especially since that was the end where all the older girls hung out in their beach chairs getting a tan. It was beautiful scenery.

Gary and I were so competitive, we had to do something to challenge each other. We were never content to just sit around and relax. Sometimes, we'd throw a penny in the pool and let it sink as close to the drain as possible. Of course, we did it quietly so the lifeguards wouldn't see us. They were stationed on both sides of the pool in their red swim trunks, sunglasses, chlorine-bleached hair, sunblocked nose and ears, and whistle-mouthed. I have to admit, they were pretty cool. All the chicks were always checking them out. Anyway, back to the challenge. Gary and I would both dive in and see who could get to the bottom of the pool and grab the penny first. It was pretty deep and it took all your breath and your ears were popping like mad. But, if you did it, it was so cool.

I had just got to the penny before Gary did and broke the surface, my eyes burning from the chlorine. When I wiped the water out of my eyes, I saw Kelly sitting on a lounge chair. She was reading *Something Wicked This Way Comes* by Ray Bradbury. She stared at me over the top of the book and smiled.

"Holy crap," I whispered.

"What?"

"Kelly's here."

"So."

"So, I'm all wet."

"So's everyone else."

"I look terrible."

"Man, you're so vain."

I waved back to Kelly, dove under the water, and shot toward the shallow end. Gary followed. I darted through the brats, clambered out of the pool, grabbed my towel, and shot for the men's changing room. I dried my hair, combed it, tried to hide the flecks of dead skin, wrapped the towel casually around my shoulder, checked my bathing suit to make sure nothing was showing, and took one last look in the mirror.

"You look beautiful," Gary teased.

"Loan me a couple of bucks."

"For what?"

"I got to buy her something. A Coke or a Zero or something."

Gary dug into the little pocket inside his suit and dug out a couple sopping dollar bills.

I took them and headed for the concession stand. I ordered a Diet Rite, which was a new low-calorie cola that Royal Crown Cola had just started selling. I thought she might like it since girls were always worrying about their weight. At least, that's what I heard and saw on TV. I got me a RC Cola and a Snickers bar for both of us.

I turned and headed her way. Before I could get there, Teddy appeared out of nowhere, with two cherry-flavored sno-cones. I hurried, shuffling as quickly as I could since we weren't supposed to run on the wet concrete. I was picking up speed when a shrill whistle blasted.

"No running!" the lifeguard nearest me shouted.

I slowed to a fast duck-walk.

"Here's something sweet for someone sweet," I heard Teddy say.

"That's nice, Teddy. I was getting thirsty."

"Here, this is better if you're dry," I said, thrusting out the Diet Rite. "It's a diet coke."

"Diet? What, Mikey, are you saying I'm fat," she said, with a little tease in her voice.

"No, I thought all girls liked this stuff. I don't think it tastes all that great, but RC Cola makes it and that's my favorite."

"Well, if you don't like it, what makes you think she'll like it?" Teddy asked.

"I don't know," I stammered. "Just thought she might."

"Doesn't sound like she does to me," he replied.

"Okay, well, here's a Snickers bar."

When I held it out, I could feel that the sun had made it a gooey mess. I hadn't noticed before because I was in such a hurry to get to her before Teddy did.

"It's kind of melted," she said.

"You're a real cool dude there, Wright. You offer the lady a drink you wouldn't drink and a candy bar you wouldn't eat. Real classy."

"I'll take them anyway," Kelly said.

I held them out and she took them. She placed the Diet Rite beside her chair and put the candy bar in the shade beneath her chair.

"Let's let it cool off a little," she said, as she started sucking on the straw of the sno-cone.

I decided to kneel down in a catcher's squat, just to show that I knew how and could, to wait. Teddy did the same.

Just then, Gary strolled up behind me.

"Looks like all the gang's here," Teddy said.

"One too many if you ask me," Gary said.

"Well, nobody did."

"You much of a diver, Teddy?" Gary asked.

"I've done a little with the swim team at the country club."

"How about you show us your form," Gary said. "Up there." He pointed at the high dive, silhouetted in the sun.

"Only if he does," Teddy said, pointing at me.

"Now, don't be stupid you two," Kelly said.

"We're doing it for Gary," I said. "You first," I said to Teddy and waved my hand toward the diving board.

"With pleasure," he replied. He tossed his untouched sno-cone in the trash, walked over to the diving board, and confidently climbed each rung.

"Sorry about this," I said to Kelly.

"You should be. Both of you. This is stupid. I'm not some damsel-in-distress you two are fighting over."

"I know."

When Teddy reached the top of the diving board, he walked out to the edge, looked down, turned around, walked back, and saluted Kelly. He spun around, walked to the edge of the board, turned, and positioned himself to do a back flip, his toes perched on the tip of the board, his arms at his side. He bounced once, sprung up and out, lifted his arms and put them together to form a point, and plunged headfirst toward the water. He sliced into the pool, barely making a splash. He quickly came to the surface, swam to the ladder beneath the board, and clambered out, shaking the water off him like a dog. Kelly applauded quietly.

"I forgot to mention," he said as he rejoined us, brushing the hair out of his eyes, "I've won a few ribbons diving for the club."

I'm in deep trouble. I thought, as I shot Gary a dagger stare, thrust my warm RC into his hands, laid the towel down, walked to the ladder, slowly climbed up, and out onto the board. I stepped to the end and looked all the way down to the surface of the water. It was a long way down and the water looked hard. I took a deep breath, inched my feet back until my toes were curled over the edge, clinging to the front edge of the board. I figured I needed to do something memorable.

I kicked my feet out in front of me, landed on my butt on the edge of the board, bounced up in the air, shot my arms out front and my legs back, and dove for the pool. Unfortunately, I hit the pool before I could get my hands fully extended into a pointed dive. When my body slammed into the pool, it made a very loud slapping sound. I had belly-flopped. I came to the surface coughing and fighting for breath. Kelly and Gary rushed to the edge of the pool and dove in. Teddy waltzed up to watch.

Before either could get to me, the lifeguard was in the pool, had me under the armpits, and was dragging me to the ladder. I was fighting him now because I had my breath back and was totally embarrassed. But, that was his job and he was very good at his job. He got to the ladder at the side of the pool, let me go, and rotated me around so I could grab the ladder. I stepped onto the lower rung and stepped up and he gave me a little shove, probably more than he needed to. I climbed out and stood by the ladder, breathing deeply. Kelly and Gary clambered out right behind us and stepped next to me.

"You okay?" Gary asked.

"I'm fine," I said.

"You sure?" Kelly asked.

"I am."

"Look a little shaken up," Teddy said, as he sauntered up to join us.

"Okay, you two," the lifeguard interrupted. "You're off the board the rest of the day. You can swim, or you can sit. But, no more going for the gold, got it?"

"Yes, sir," I said immediately.

"Whatever you say, Mr. Lifeguard," Teddy replied.

The lifeguard was a couple years older than us. He went to Downey High. I had seen his picture and name in the sports section of the paper. He was bigger than Teddy and in pretty good shape. The lifeguards were always lean and muscular.

"Give me any more lip, pal, and you're out of here. For good."

"My daddy won't like that."

"Well, I don't know who your daddy is and I don't care."

"You should. He's your boss. He's one of the owners."

"What's your name?"

"Teddy Jensen."

"Dr. Jensen's your father?"

"He is."

"Well…um…I'm sorry…um…no harm, no foul, okay kid?"

"Sure," and Teddy gave him a look that said, "Until next time."

"Just stay off the board. You obviously know what you're doing, but he doesn't," he pointed to me. "I don't want anybody hurt."

"Absolutely," Teddy replied.

"I thought your old man was a surgeon," Gary said.

"He is, but he makes investments. This is a pretty good one, wouldn't you say?"

"I guess," Gary replied.

My face was as red as my belly. The backs of my legs were scraped raw where the rough surface of the diving board had scratched them. My bathing suit had a hole in it. My pride felt like it had been hit with grapeshot.

"I'm not feeling so good," I said to Kelly. "I'm going to take off."

Teddy smiled in triumph.

"Sorry," was all she could say.

"Me, too," I replied. I turned and headed for the changing room.

"You're giving up too easily, man," Gary said, as we changed into our dry clothes. "You can't let him win."

"I can't compete with that," I replied. "I'll never be able to compete with that. He's rich, he's good-looking, and he can offer her everything I can't. It's over. I quit."

I glanced back over my shoulder at Kelly. She stared at me, before reluctantly turning around and following Teddy back to her chair.

CHAPTER 31

For me, spring and summer were nothing but baseball and I devoured it all. Even the College World Series. Held each June and broadcast on TV, the series crowned the NCAA Division I college baseball champion. Eight teams would qualify each year in regional playoffs. Those teams would then play a double-elimination round robin until two undefeated teams were left, who would then play for the championship. Since 1950, the CWS had been held in Omaha, Nebraska at Rosenblatt Stadium. In 1962, the series was held from June 11 to June 16. The Michigan Wolverines team, coached by Don Lund, defeated the Santa Clara University Broncos. The MVP of the series was pitcher Bob Garibaldi of Santa Clara. A Stockton native, Garibaldi would sign a contract with the Giants on Independence Day, bringing youth, a live arm, and a local boy to the hometown team. I always dreamed of playing in the series someday, on my way to the bigs. There were plenty of California schools that had played over the years, including Stanford and UC Berkeley, who won the very first series in 1947, the year before I was born. Of course, I'd need to be good enough and then I'd need to get a scholarship since my parents couldn't afford to send me to expensive schools like those two. But, I could dream.

After school one Wednesday afternoon, Mom asked me to go to our neighborhood market to get a few things before dinner. When I asked her why Tim couldn't do it, she said because she needed some "feminine products," and, because I was the oldest, she didn't need to write a note so the store manager would let me buy whatever it was she needed. I wasn't happy, but I went. I figured maybe I could store up some of that "karma" that Teddy had threatened me with.

As I was coming out of the store, loaded down with a bag of groceries, the *Modesto Bee* delivery guy was loading the newspaper box in front of the store with the afternoon paper. The top paper on the stack he had unbound to take inside the store was rippling in the breeze. A stronger gust blew it open to page D1 of the local section. As I walked by, a front page photo caught my eye. I leaned closer. A car was wrapped around a tree. It looked pretty bad.

The headline read: "DHS Student is Injured Seriously in Car Crash." I looked at the photo of the mangled car and wondered how anyone could have survived. The article's first sentence hit me right between the eyes. "Eighteen-year-old George Walton Lucas…" I looked closer at the picture and recognized the car club symbol on the front fender just above the wheel. The photo caption read: "Youth Survives Crash." The caption went on to say: "Just what part in saving his life the roll bar (arrow) and a safety belt played is not known, but George W. Lucas Jr., survived this crash yesterday. The highway patrol said the safety belt snapped and Lucas was thrown from the car, which was slammed into the tree by another vehicle in the collision."

It was my friend George. The kid with the Fiat Bianchina. And the roll bar. The article reported that "George was heading home, traveling east on Sylvan Road when he was about to turn toward his house. Attempting to pass him at high speeds, seventeen-year-old Frank Ferreira smashed into Lucas's small Fiat Bianchina, flipping the car several times before it crashed into a tree. Lucas was thrown from the car, helping save his life, although he was injured badly. He had minor fractures but his lungs were hemorrhaging. Soon thereafter, he awoke and began recovering."

George was at City Hospital, which was the same hospital I stayed at when I had ruptured my spleen. I jumped on my bike, raced home, dropped the bag of groceries on the kitchen counter, and flew out the front door with an "I'll be right back" thrown over my shoulder. I hopped back on my bike and rode downtown to the hospital.

I peeked through the door of his room. The privacy curtain was pulled back. George was staring out the window at the park and water tower across the street. He looked terrible. He was all bandaged up and was pretty black and blue, with all kinds of tubes stuck in, and coiled around, him. I quietly edged closer. He must have heard me, or seen something out of the corner of his eye, because he slowly turned to look in my direction, groaning as he did.

"Hey, Mikey, how you doin', pal?" he asked through clenched teeth.

"Better than you," I replied.

He tried to laugh, but couldn't. "Come closer," he said. "I won't break."

"Tell that to that walnut tree," I said.

He laughed again, but stopped, grimacing. "It only hurts when I laugh," he joked.

"Well, like the doctor always says, if it hurts, don't do it."

"Good advice," he said. "So, how'd your trip go? Did you get what you went for?"

"Not really. Mickey was hurt and didn't play. He was there, but I didn't know it."

"That's too bad. But, hey, you gave it the old college try. When did you get back?"

"Sunday, June third."

"A little over a week before all this happened," he gestured to the bandages.

"I saw the article when I was getting some stuff at the store. Kind of by accident."

"I'm surprised you didn't read it when it happened. They made a big enough deal out of it."

"I only read the sports section. The rest is too depressing."

"Tell me about it. That's why I only read the comics."

"What the heck happened?"

"Aw, I was coming back from the library. I had three incompletes to turn in, or I wouldn't graduate. I think I told you about it."

"You did."

"Seems like an awfully long time ago. Anyway, it's what I get for tryin' to live up to my potential. Usually I'd take my little sis to help, but my mom had just gotten back from the hospital, so Wendy wanted to keep an eye on her. And lay by the pool since it was so hot. It was getting late, around 4:50, so the light wasn't all that good. As I hung a left onto the road to my house, this kid from Downey named Ferreira tried to pass in his Impala. He musta been doin' ninety. Show-off. I never saw him. Sun was in my rear view. Or heard him. I mighta had the radio too loud. He hit me broadside. I flipped about three times and ended up wrapped around a big old walnut tree. Shifted the whole tree, roots and all, about two feet."

"Paper said that roll bar saved your life. And the seat belt."

"By not doing its job. It didn't hold. On about the third roll, it snapped and I was tossed out of the way. If it hadn't broken, we wouldn't be talking right now. I fell hard on my chest and stomach. They found me unconscious, with no pulse. Ferreira didn't get a scratch. The spaz. Crushed my lungs and broke a bunch of ribs and bones. Gashed my forehead. Seat belt bruised my shoulders. Had hematomas on my lungs, which were bleeding."

"Darn."

"Our neighbor across the road heard the crash and came running out. He called the ambulance. On the way here, I turned blue and started puking blood. I was in a coma for forty-eight hours. Then they put me here in intensive care. I woke up the next morning and didn't know where the heck I was. There was a nurse there, and she immediately said, 'You're okay. All your arms and legs are fine, and you'll be all right.' I was glad to hear that because I had no idea what parts of me were there, or not. Almost became the hero of one of those songs."

"What songs?"

"You know, those sappy love songs, like 'Tell Laura I Love Her' or 'Ebony Eyes.'"

"You're real lucky."

"You could say that. Guess somebody up there likes me. They figured they'd thump me in the head to get my attention." He lifted his bandaged arm and pointed heavenward. "When my mom got here, I asked her, 'Did I do something wrong?' Boy, she lost it. Wendy just stared at me, probably thinking she woulda been dead if she'd been riding with me."

"The way the car looked in the picture, she woulda been."

"To top it off, the police gave me a ticket for making an illegal left turn. You believe that?"

"Add to your collection."

"Yep." George got kind of serious looking. "The fact that I'm still alive is a miracle. Tell you one thing. Lying here all this time got me to thinking. About there being some kind of force out there that's bigger than we are. Surviving something like that makes you wonder maybe you're here for a reason. And now maybe it's time for me to figure out what that is. Then I've got to trust my instincts to get done whatever it is I'm supposed to do. Time for me to be myself and do what I do best, I guess. I realized that I've been living my life so close to the edge for so long that it's way past time to make something of myself. Every day now is an extra day, you know. I've tapped into some kind of force and I need to do something with it."

"When they going to let you out?"

"Couple more days. They want to make sure my lungs are clear."

"Then what?"

"Probably some rehab. No more cars for a while, that's for sure. I went over the edge and didn't like what I saw on the other side."

"This mean you won't be going away to school?"

"Probably not. Think I'll go to JC and see how it goes."

"Bitchin'."

"Time to buckle down and show my dad I can take care of business."

"That should make him happy."

"I hope. I can't pay for it all by myself."

"He'll come around."

"I suppose. He knows I'll pay him back."

"Then it's just a loan, right?"

"Right. One thing I've learned watching him. Working hard to make good money buys freedom. I'm not going to forget that. How 'bout you? What's next?"

"My aunt's going to take me to Chicago. I'm hoping to catch Mickey there."

"Your family know about that?

"Yep."

"And they're okay with it?"

"Sure enough. In fact, my dad thinks it's a good idea. He thinks it will help me be more … independent."

"Wow, he must have a lot of confidence in you."

"I guess."

"Wish I could say the same about my dad."

"He will. Once you let all those great ideas loose and show him what you can do."

"I sure hope so. I should have you talk to him. You're a pretty good salesman."

"Yeah, 'cept there's one deal I can't seem to close."

"Maybe Chicago will change that."

I looked around the room. "This place is kind of depressing. What do you do for fun?" I teased, trying to lighten things up.

He pointed at a small black-and-white TV in the corner of the room. "Watch that," he said. "Not much on. Mostly reruns. A lot of sports, which I don't care that much about. Sorry. Been watching *The Tonight Show*."

"There's been some pretty good movies this summer," I said. "I've caught a couple at the Starlite or Ceres Drive-Ins with my family."

"Like what?"

"*Cape Fear*. Kind of a scary drama with that weird actor, Robert Mitchum. *Lolita*. My folks won't let me see that, but some of the guys I know had a copy of the book, so I borrowed it. Kind of racy. Then there's *The Music Man*. A musical about trombones, I guess. A lot of foreign films have been playing at The Strand. I don't get to those, either."

"I still mostly listen to that," he said, pointing at a black transistor radio perched on the window sill with its antenna sticking straight up. "Late at night, when I can't sleep, I been picking up this wild guy out of Shreveport, Louisiana. He's on a station called KCIJ-AM. Don't know how it reaches clear across the country, but it does. His name is Bob Smith. Goes by 'Wolfman Jack.' He's got this really deep, growly kind of voice. And he howls a lot, just like a wolf. And plays all the old rock 'n roll and rhythm 'n blues. The good stuff. Kind of an outlaw of the airwaves."

"I've never heard of him," I said. "I'll have to stay up tonight and see if I can pick him up."

"He's everywhere. He can reach anyone, anywhere in the world."

"I wish he could help me and my dad, maybe get the word to Mickey."

"All you can do is ask, right?"

"If I could find him."

"Try KFIV. I heard they sometimes replay his show. He's been known to drop in and spin a few tunes. Maybe they can help."

George reached over and gingerly picked up something from the tray table.

"Check it out." He handed me what looked like a piece of blue cardboard.

"What is it?"

"Open it up and look."

I did. It was his high school diploma.

"It was delivered this morning. Teachers must have felt sorry for me. Or, didn't want me to come back. Just forgot all about those incompletes. Principal Olson dropped it by."

"Congratulations."

"Thanks. About time, I guess. 'Course, now I'm eligible for the draft."

"Army might not be so bad. Got no real wars going on right now. Might be a good time to go. Could learn some stuff, I guess."

"Still wouldn't mind doing the Air Force, but that's probably out of the question now. Maybe I can get a student deferment. But, that means I gotta get serious about the books."

I handed the diploma back to him and he carefully placed it on the table, visibly proud to have it.

"You look tired," I said.

"I am, kinda."

"I think I'll take off."

"Don't be a stranger. Check in once in a while."

"I will."

"Go with the flow, Mikey."

"Sure, uh, sounds good. Whatever it means."

"It's about the energy or force that's all around us. It comes from mythology. It's kinda spiritual, you know, which I been thinking a lot about lately. I'm still working on it."

"I get it. I mean, you almost…"

"Died. Yep, I can say it."

"Glad you can."

"Well, enough of the serious stuff."

"Sure enough."

"See you later alligator."

"After 'while crocodile."

George was laid up there for another two weeks. The doctors sent him home to recuperate for the rest of the summer. He was driven in each day for physical therapy. The Europe trip with his friend John was canceled, and they hauled his Fiat off to the junkyard. It was not a good summer.

George wasn't able to attend his graduation, but I was able to go to mine. June 14 was a warm Thursday evening. At seven o'clock, the Roosevelt Orchestra played "March of the Graduates" by Merle Isaac, then "Piano Concerto No. 1" by Peter Ilyich Tchaikovsky. We proceeded into the activity court to the "March from Athalia" by Felix Mendelssohn. We pledged the flag, heard the invocation, and received our diplomas from Principal Maley and Robert Bienvenu, a member of the Board of Education and the father of one of our classmates, as our parents watched from those hard and splintery wooden bleachers and several rows of folding chairs placed on the asphalt in front of the small, concrete pavilion. I felt pretty proud, considering all that had happened so far that year.

After the graduation, Gary and his parents came over for cake, ice cream, and gifts. I got a new Rawlings baseball mitt and more homemade cards. It was really good.

CHAPTER 32

School was out. I was free and alive. I could pack away all those school clothes until September. I ran out through the back gate, took off my tennis shoes, and raced barefoot through the park, being extra careful not to step on any bees. It felt good. Except for one thing.

There were days, a lot like this one, when you'd wake up feeling good. Optimistic. Glass filled to overflowing. Everything seemed to be lined up and going your way. There were days when that feeling lasted all day. Then there were days when that feeling was spoiled by the nagging feeling that something wasn't right, a remembrance in the back of your mind that something unpleasant had happened, that something had taken place that meant the good feeling was an illusion. You would scan your thoughts and memories in search of what it was. Was it something minor, like something you forgot to do, or something major, like your father had cancer? That was the feeling I was feeling today. My sunny disposition and the prospect of a brand new day had just been darkened by the realization that my father was sick and that it wasn't a bad dream I had finally awakened from. It was still happening. I was still dealing with it. It wasn't going away.

I was running out of options. And getting desperate. I kept thinking about what George had said about the Wolfman. Maybe he could help after all. I had finally been able to tune him in late last night, the Friday after my graduation, the night George should've graduated. The signal was faint, but I could definitely hear the howling.

The next day, after a full day stocking and checking at Bi-Rite, I rode my bike down to Burge's Drive-In at Ninth and O Streets. KFIV had set up a small, portable studio inside the drive-in so disc jockeys could sit at a booth, play records, and do song dedications. The booth was fitted out with a microphone, a tiny record player that could only play 45s, a little combo amplifier, and soundboard, a machine that played audiotape cartridges, and a set of headphones for the DJ. George said the Wolfman sometimes made a guest appearance when he was in town, or was doing shows somewhere in the valley, so I thought I'd check it out myself.

It was a busy night downtown. All the cool kids were out dragging Tenth. The cruisers would start at Burge's and drive up Tenth Street to the Modesto Fire Station at F and G, then turn around and drive back down Eleventh Street to Burge's. Tenth and Eleventh used to be two-way streets, which made it easy for the cruisers to bust each other's chops as they rolled along. It caused such a traffic jam that the city turned Tenth Street into a one-way street heading south and Eleventh Street into a one-way street heading north. That didn't stop anyone from cruising and yakking.

Burge's was always filled with cars and kids. The drive-in was the place to be and be seen. It was where the action was. It was where my friend, Autobianchi George, went to hang out, meet friends, and talk about cars and girls.

Owned by Edward Burge, Burge's was opened at 1514 Ninth Street in 1948, the year I was born. It was primarily a Highway 99 stopping point and a Modesto High hangout through the forties and fifties and into 1962. Its unique, round design was a magnet for young cruisers. It was part of the cruise because the kids needed to eat, just like their cars needed gas. There was always a roar of tailpipes as cars came in from the hop or the movies, and other cars went out to the canal for the submarine races or back out to cruise. The drive-in featured car hops, both on foot and skates. Hamburgers were thirty cents, cheeseburgers were forty cents, and Cokes were a dime. The most expensive item on the menu was a New York Cut Steak with salad and shoestring potatoes for $1.90. Burge's also served breakfast.

There were many tales told about the cruisers and their pranks, like pouring oil on the downtown streets and setting it afire, or hooking a chain to the rear axle of a police car and yanking it loose when the cop tore out to chase down a speeder. I never saw any of it, so I'm not sure any of it ever really happened, although George swore it did. Whatever the reality was, they were still great stories.

I rode my bike through the parking lot. I swerved to avoid a low-slung Mercury on its way out, bumped up onto the sidewalk, careened off a cigarette machine, and finally stopped right next to the side entrance door. I hopped off, checked the front tire and, judging everything to be okay, leaned my bike against the cigarette machine. I tucked my shirt in, sniffed my armpits to make sure I wasn't too offensive, pulled my Giants cap down tight on my head, and pushed through the door and into the drive-in. It smelled great. Grease and salt, burgers and fries, pickle juice and ketchup. This must be heaven. I took a deep breath, closed my eyes, exhaled, opened my eyes, and nearly got run over by a tall, red-headed girl on roller skates wearing a round maroon cap bobby-pinned to her hair and carrying a silver-colored tray overflowing with packaged burgers, fries, milkshakes, and Cokes.

"Look out, son," she said, as she opened the door and skated through. I was amazed at how graceful she was. I watched her skate out and attach the tray to the side of a black '55 Chevy driven by a guy in a cowboy hat with a gum-chewing girl sitting next to him.

I turned back and started scanning the inside of the drive-in. It wasn't all that big, so it didn't take long. The booths were filled to overflowing and every swivel chair at the counter had a body in it. I finally saw a big, barrel-chested man sitting in a booth at the back. He had big, greasy hair and a short goatee. He was wearing a too-tight T-shirt with a tuxedo printed on the front and headphones.

I worked my way back to his booth. I stopped next to the table, as he laid the arm of the record player gently onto the spinning 45. He flipped a switch, twisted a couple knobs, and the inside speakers of the drive-in launched into "Twist and Shout" by the Isley Brothers. I could hear hoots in the parking lot and looked out to see kids jump out of their cars and start twisting. It all looked like some kind of ancient, tribal ritual. I turned back and the man in the booth was staring at me, the headphones now dangling around his neck.

"Are you him?" I asked.

"Him who?" he answered

"The Wolfman."

"Naw, I ain't him," he answered.

"I need some help," I stuttered.

"Don't we all," he said.

"I want to talk to him."

"He ain't here."

"I know, he lives in Louisiana."

"Not really."

"Look, he's got to do something before—"

"Like I said, he ain't here. You got to come back some other time," the disc jockey said.

"It can't wait. The Wolfman sounds like a good guy. I know he'd try to help me if he could—"

The DJ held up his hand and I stopped jabbering. He picked up an audiotape cartridge, checked it, and put it into the cartridge machine. The 45 was about to end. I could see the needle inching closer to the center. As it did, he flipped another switch, punched some buttons, and the record was drowned out by a howl and a gravelly voice.

"Who dat callin' the Wolfman?" I heard over the speakers.

"Judy," a voice replied.

"How's your ding-a-ling doin' tonight, Judy?"

"Wouldn't you like to know, Mr. Wolfman, wouldn't you like to know."

"I would, Judy, I would."

The man smiled at me, as I watched the tape spin inside the cartridge. He pointed at the tape and said, "That's him."

"He's a recording? You telling me he's not real?"

"Am I your favorite Wolfman, Judy?" the Wolfman-on-the-tape asked.

"You are and always will be."

And the Wolfman howled.

"He's real enough," the DJ said.

"Where is he?"

"He's everywhere and nowhere, man. He's been around the world. Me, I'm stuck in this turkey town."

"It's not that bad."

"No, but wanting to get out is. A great writer once wrote, 'When you're safe at home, you wish you were having an adventure; when you're having an adventure, you wish you were safe at home.' That's me, man. Never happy with where I am."

"I'm sorry."

"That's okay for now. You're just a kid. It ain't so great when you're my age. All those things I missed. All that stuff I coulda done and coulda been."

"Well, since the Wolfman isn't here," I said, "maybe you could give him this?" I held up a neatly folded piece of paper. "I gotta get it to him. It's a matter of life and death."

"Nothin's ever that bad, son."

"It is, though."

"Here, let me see it," he said, as he gently took the note from me. It was the same letter I had written to Mickey back in May.

He read it. "Son, that ain't no dedication. That's a letter. The Wolfman only does dedications." He handed the note back to me.

"Couldn't he make an exception just this once?"

"Son, I'm sorry about your old man, but the Wolfman won't do it. 'Sides, how do you know Mr. Mantle will even be listening?"

"Everybody listens to the Wolfman, don't they?"

"Well, he'd sure like to think so."

"And he's on late at night?"

"After midnight. All the better to reach you, my dear."

"And I've read Mickey sometimes stays up late?"

"That's what they say."

"So, the odds are good."

"If you're a bettin' man."

"This is really important. I don't know how much longer—" I choked on the words. "—he's going to be around. If you or he – whoever he is or wherever he is – can't help me, I guess, there's nothing else I can do. Sorry to waste your time, mister."

"Now, just hold on," he said. "Have a seat," he added, pulling a chair up from the next table.

And I did.

"Here's the deal. The Wolfman is in a different time zone and I don't want to put words in his mouth. But, if he was here, he'd probably say, this is a great thing you're doing. Heck, I think it's a great thing you're doing. There's not many people in this world would do what you're doing. It reminds me of something I read once."

"You read a lot."

"All the better to understand the world, my dear. Anyways, the quote goes somethin' like this. 'Most men lead lives of quiet desperation and go to the grave with the song still in them.' Henry David Thoreau wrote that. Heard of him?"

"Yeah, I read something of his in government or social studies. Something about a lake or a river or some kind of water."

"Walden Pond."

"That's it."

"Well, that's not you, son. You're doing something grand. Me, I'm just sitting here playing what people tell me to play. I should know better. Shoot, I'm a DJ. I live for music. He's talking about me."

"You could do something about it," I said.

"Too late."

"It's never too late to be who you were supposed to be."

That stopped him for a second. But only a second. "Easy for you to say. You got your whole life ahead of you. Not me. So, I gotta make the best of what I got, you see."

I nodded and stood. He held up a finger so I'd wait a minute, pulled a 45 out of its sleeve, placed it on the turntable, set the needle down, started it up, flipped the switch, twisted the knobs, and "Things" by Bobby Darin poured from the speakers. He looked up and motioned for me to give him the note. I did.

"Look, I'll see what I can do to get it to the Wolfman. No promises, okay?"

"Okay."

"You're my hero, you know that," he said.

"I'm no hero."

"Sure you are. A hero is a man who does what he can and the best he can for others and the common good."

"I'm just a kid."

"Tell you what. I'll do what I can do. If the Wolfman can get it on the air, he'll get it on the air. If Mickey hears it, all the better. We'll give it a shot. Put it out there on the air waves and see what comes back. Kind of like a boomerang, you see."

"I really appreciate it."

"My pleasure."

"There's something else."

"Now, don't push it, son. I'm doin' the best I can do."

"No, this is a dedication. A real dedication. Right up the Wolfman's alley."

"Okay, lay it on me."

"Could you play 'Oh, My Papa' by Eddie Fisher? And dedicate it to, 'The greatest dad in the world. Hang in there. Love, Mikey.'"

"Now, that's more like it. Piece of cake."

"Thanks."

"*No problemo.*"

"See ya 'round."

"See ya."

I went out the side door of the drive-in, grabbed my bike, and pointed it toward home. I was about to hop on when the Wolfman's raspy voice blew out of the drive-in speakers. The Wolfman howled and I looked back inside. Through the drive-in's glass-paned window, shifting like a prism, I saw the big man in the tuxedo T-shirt sitting in his booth hunched over the microphone. He was howling. Laughing and howling. He was mouthing the words along with Bobby and thumping along in time on the table-top.

"Wolfman," I whispered, and looked away, hopping on my bike and heading for Del Vista and home, leaving the Wolfman alone, dancing the night away and keeping all those lonely listeners company.

Mickey came off the disabled list that same Saturday, June 16, just under a month after the injury. He returned in style, hitting a three-run homer off Gus Bell of Cleveland. He immediately went on a hitting binge, knocking homers and boosting his average.

I don't know if the Wolfman ever put my letter on the air. And, if he did, whether or not Mickey heard it. Since I didn't get a call or a letter, I figured it didn't happen. I kept my fingers crossed anyway.

CHAPTER 33

Robert Irving Christopher Nard was born in San Francisco in 1929. He was a right-handed second baseman who played four years in the minor leagues for the Class C Twin Falls Cowboys (1950), Stockton Ports (1951), and Modesto Reds (1954). He ended his career with the Class B Yakima Bears (1955). He served two years (1952 and 1953) in the military. He settled in Modesto, working for the city school district. He was our eighth grade gym teacher and baseball coach. In 1958, he started "Bob Nard's Baseball School for Boys." For a fee, he taught boys aged eight to thirteen the fundamentals of baseball. If you were serious about getting good at baseball, you tried to talk your folks into paying for it. It was a good school, but it wasn't cheap.

Coach Nard was also secretary of the local Babe Ruth league. When he found out about my accident and realized I wouldn't be able to play eighth grade baseball, he offered to let me go to his school. For free. He also promised to help me get on a Babe Ruth team. But, I had to prove I was healthy enough to play.

The baseball school lasted one week and was always held in the summer, right after school was out, at the Modesto Junior College varsity baseball diamond. You could sign up for a second consecutive week if you had the time and money. Each participant got a hat, T-shirt, and commemorative patch. Class was always first thing in the morning, nine to noon, before it got too hot. We'd start with warm-ups, then break into pitchers, catchers, infielders, and outfielders to work on fundamentals, followed by batting practice and situations, which allowed us to apply our skills immediately in a real game environment. We also learned about the game itself, strategy, and thinking baseball. Each player received lots of individual attention. Every coach had his favorite players – kids he'd heard about from other coaches, or seen play, or coached. Guys that were good ball players. So did Coach Nard, and he let a lot of those kids go to the camp for free. He usually had some of his former favorites help out. They had been his junior high and Babe Ruth players and were now juniors and seniors in high school and playing Legion ball or Pony League. Guys like Kim Normoyle, Dick Lawrence, Jerry Bird, and Dave Mello. In addition to helping with fundamentals, they'd also ump our scrimmages. Some also umped Little League games. On the last day of camp, Coach Nard would have a skills contest with players competing to see who was the best bunter, thrower, slider, and hitter. The winner of each received a small trophy. He'd then divide the attendees into two evenly matched squads. A seven-inning game would then be played for bragging rights. When camp was over, Coach Nard would give out a certificate of participation. The final day always ended with an ice-cold bottle of Coca-Cola.

Since it was time to play ball again, I decided to shave the head and go back to the butch haircut look. It made wearing a wool cap in summer a lot more bearable. Plus, Kelly kind of liked it.

On the first day of baseball school, I walked around the corner to sit in the dugout, trying to go unnoticed. I stopped dead in my tracks. Down at the opposite end was Teddy. When he saw me, he smiled and flipped me a bird behind his catcher's mitt. That's pretty much how the rest of the school went. Teddy dogged me the whole time. Every mistake I made, he'd make sure Coach Nard saw it. He also went to great lengths to let everyone know that he, like them, had paid for the camp, while I had gotten a free ride because I'd had a little operation on a body part nobody had ever heard of. I put up with it because I wanted to get in shape and I wanted to impress the Coach, so he'd find me a good Babe Ruth team to play for.

In the scrimmage on the last day of school, I was ready to show everyone I could play again. I was playing second for the red team, Teddy was catching for the blue team. It was the bottom of the seventh. We were ahead 2-1. It had been a real pitcher's duel. One of the pitchers was Mark Norman, a lefty I went to elementary school with, who had a great curve ball and a fantastic pick-off move to first. The pitcher for the other team was Peter Abbott, a big, burly kid from Enslen School we had played against in the Little League championship a couple years before. He had a blazing fastball and not a lot of control.

Teddy came to bat with one out. He took a couple close pitches, then barely got the bat on the ball and looped a Texas leaguer to right field for a single. Rounding first, he watched me very closely as I fielded the ball and tossed it to the shortstop covering second. The next batter settled into the batter's box. Teddy inched off first and got a pretty good lead. Mark tossed a few over to keep him close. He got Teddy leaning on one and almost got him. Teddy had to eat a little dirt. To add insult, our first baseman lightly slapped Teddy in the face as he dove back. I had to laugh. Teddy didn't. When he got up, he glared at me and pointed a finger. The batter tried to lay down a bunt, but fouled two off, which gave him a 0-2 count. He had to swing away. Teddy was off with the next pitch. The batter slapped one in the hole between short and third. As soon as he hit the ball, I was sprinting to cover second, hoping for a double play, just like Coach Leach, Coach Nard, and my dad had all taught us. I stood a little behind and to the left of the base so I could take the throw, tag the base, and use my momentum to carry me across the bag out to the runner's path and make the throw to first. All in one continuous motion.

Our third baseman cut the ball off in front of short. As I stood there, I looked from the third baseman to Teddy barreling down the base path. Teddy wasn't even looking at the bag. He was focused on nothing but me. I had a strange feeling. Like I'd done this before. And I had. Last February. In the fog. For a moment, I froze. I realized the team was counting on me, like every team counted on its players. I looked back to the third baseman. He wound up and fired a seed to second. Just as Teddy reached the bag. I took the throw, but instead of pivoting on the bag and throwing, I lightly touched the bag, jumped in the air, and threw, like Y.A. Title or John Brodie. Teddy slid under me, grabbed the bag with his left hand as he slid by, and stopped. The ball slapped into the first baseman's glove just ahead of the runner. I plummeted to earth, slamming down on top of Teddy. Double-play. Game over.

Teddy immediately shoved me off him and jumped to his feet. I rolled away and got to my feet. He doubled up his fists and started after me. Before he could reach me, the rest of my team roared past him and started slapping me on the back, on the head, and on the butt. They shoved Teddy out of the way and surrounded me.

"I'll get even, Wright," he shouted at the backs of my teammates. "You'll get yours." He shook his fist at me.

Coach Nard grabbed Teddy's fist and yanked it out of the air. "Jensen," he shouted. "Get off my field. And never come back. That kid just had surgery on his gut and you're trying to take him out."

"He shouldn't be out here if he can't take it," Teddy shouted back.

"Get out of here," Coach Nard yelled, pushing Teddy toward the exit gate.

I was back. I was ready. Now, I just needed a team.

Modesto's Babe Ruth teams were organized by high school, just like its American Legion teams. If I had been healthy, I would've been drafted by a Davis team. I wasn't and I wasn't. Once I finished Coach Nard's baseball school and he saw that I was okay to play, he made arrangements to put me on a team.

E.D. Blakeley & Son, a local fuel and oil distributor, sponsored a team made up of guys from Modesto High School. They needed another thirteen-year-old, since each team had to have five each of kids aged thirteen, fourteen, and fifteen. You could have more thirteen-year-olds, but not more fifteen-year-olds. The team had been working out since shortly after the draft in May and had started league play the first week in June. I had some catching up to do.

After I had moved up to "A" ball back in sixth grade, my dad had started coaching my younger brothers. He had pretty much chosen to keep doing that instead of coaching me again when I was old enough to shift from Little League to Babe Ruth. After I'd ruptured my spleen, he decided to do both, which had to have been rough on him. Once I was cleared to play, and Coach Nard had put me on a team, Dad volunteered to be an assistant. I think he did that to make sure I'd have a team to play for and to make sure I had healed and really could finally play. I always thought he did it just because he loved the game. I guess that was only a small part of it.

At the first practice, I was scared to death. I almost talked my dad into turning around and going home. He talked me out of it. The other players were all so big. And knew what they were doing. There were two brothers on the team. Delbert and Jack Hill. Delbert was older and real friendly. He was kind of a goofy jokester. He took me under his wing. Jack was a lot more intense. I wasn't sure what to wear, so I wore jeans and one of my old

Modesto Baseball for Boys T-shirts. I had my Roosevelt baseball cap, my Rawlings glove, and my metal spikes from junior high. Seventh grade baseball was the first time I had ever worn metal spikes. We always wore tennis shoes in Little League, or rubber spikes, if we could afford them. The metal cleats took some getting used to. The first couple times I wore them, I cut myself running when the spikes nicked my ankles. Injuries I gladly endured to be able to wear what the pros wore.

On that first day, I took some infield practice at second. The catcher was named Vern Zorn. He was a fifteen-year-old with a cannon for an arm. Or, at least it seemed that way to me. The first time he threw down to second, he nearly knocked me over. My hand stung and was bruised for days.

I took some swings at the plate and was amazed by how hard these guys could throw. Both Delbert and Jack were pitchers. Good pitchers. Good enough to play varsity for Modesto High. Delbert was really tall and looked even taller standing on the mound. He took it easy on me by throwing a few lob pitches I could handle. Then he started messing with me. He threw a couple of blazers and then some junk. I didn't touch any of it.

Our biggest fan was Delbert and Jack's mom. She was a large lady and loud and she knew the game. She'd sit under her umbrella each game and keep the scorebook. She didn't let the umps, or the other team, get away with anything. She reminded me a lot of my mom.

CHAPTER 34

July was a busy month in the valley and around the world. Algeria gained its independence after 132 years of French rule. Rod Laver beat Martin Mulligan, while Karen Susman beat Vera Sukova, at the 76th Wimbledon Tennis Championship. Martin Luther King Jr. was arrested during a demonstration to desegregate government buildings in Albany, Georgia. Telstar was launched from Cape Canaveral to beam live television from Europe to America. The U.S. performed several nuclear tests in Nevada. A new band named The Rolling Stones played their first show at the Marquee Club in London. Arnold Palmer won the 91st British Open at Royal Troon, while Gary Player won the 44th PGA Championship at Aronimink Golf Club in Pennsylvania. The House of Representatives passed a bill requiring equal pay for equal work regardless of sex.

Next to Christmas and Thanksgiving, the Fourth of July was my favorite holiday. Knowing me and how much I loved summer and American history, it probably should've been number one. But, it wasn't. Gifts and turkey outweighed patriotism.

Modesto held its first Independence Day parade in 1874. We'd been having parades here in town for eighty-eight years. This year, the route followed the same path it usually did, winding its way from Tenth and F Streets to J and then up to Eleventh and onto I Street, until it ended at Seventeenth Street.

The judges' stand was located in front of the county courthouse. The announcer was Cal Purviance, a disc jockey at radio station KTRB, who would call out the name of the parade entrant and try to say something funny or clever or informative about the theme or the sponsors or the participants. He always knew somebody on each float, so he'd usually be in a running conversation with someone.

My family would traditionally go down the night before to park the car in our favorite spot, along with half the town. We'd pick a location in front of the downtown post office, which was across the street and a little north of the reviewing stand. The parade would start around 9:30 a.m., so we'd be down there by nine. Mom never wanted to miss anything. I inherited that trait of being early to be on time from her. Once we'd parked, we'd throw some old army blankets on the fenders, put a few lawn chairs down in front of the car, and settle in. My little sisters usually sat on top of the car. As they got older, they stopped doing that because they were denting the roof.

Then the fun and pageantry would begin. Following the parade, usually around two o'clock, there would be events on the court house lawn, like a fiddling competition, hog calling, and a talent show. We'd hang around and watch for a bit, then we'd go home, barbeque hot dogs or hamburgers, and wait for it to get dark enough to start blowing things up. We'd buy a big box of "safe and sane" fireworks from the Red Devil stand in the parking lot in the Ulrich Shopping Center on Roseburg. We'd set off the cones, fountains, snakes, spinners, and Piccolo Petes in the street in front of our house, while dancing around with one or two sparklers in each hand. The snakes would always leave little rings like black eyes on the concrete sidewalk. I was usually barefoot and, once in a while, would step on the hot stem of a discarded sparkler, which resulted in a pretty bad burn and blister. I only did that a couple times. I was a quick learner.

Occasionally, we'd go to the Modesto Municipal Golf Course, which was next to Del Webb Field. The city always hosted a fireworks show starting at eight fifteen. We'd take our blankets and sit under the stars on the fairways and watch the sky burst into a kaleidoscope of dazzling and shimmering fountains of color. We'd bring some snacks to nibble on and a few sparklers so we could join in.

This year was a little different. I now had a sort-of girlfriend, so Kelly and I decided to go together. Although she really got along with my mom and dad and brothers and sisters, I wanted to be alone with her. We agreed to find a spot in front of the J.C. Penney store on Eleventh Street, which was celebrating its sixtieth anniversary in 1962. Mom and Dad dropped me off in front of the Covell Theater and Kelly's mom and dad dropped her off there a few minutes later. I had two lawn chairs and a small cooler with some Cokes. It was going to be a hot one, between ninety-three and ninety-eight degrees the forecaster had predicted, so I figured we'd better have something to wet our whistles.

I took Kelly by the hand and headed up J Street toward Tenth.

"I thought we were going to sit back there?" Kelly said, as she glanced over her shoulder. "By Penney's?"

"I came up with a better spot," I replied and plowed forward.

We walked to Tenth and H Streets, which was located near the middle of the first part of the parade route. There was an abandoned building there that used to house the old Tack Room. I thought it would be a good vantage point. I opened up the lawn chairs, placed them on the sidewalk, and we sat down. I flipped open the cooler, took out the bottle opener, and popped open one bottle of ice-cold Coca-Cola. I dropped two flex-straws into it and we both took a few sips.

"You're such a romantic," Kelly said, touching her straw.

"It's all your fault," I said and gave her a quick kiss, so we wouldn't draw any attention. This was all still very new and I wasn't at all sure what I was doing. It seemed kind of forbidden and I was digging it.

Off in the distance, we could hear the national anthem being sung, so we knew it was almost time. The first thing we saw was a brand-new, Modesto Police Department Ford Galaxy, followed by a veteran's group carrying the United States, California, and VFW Post 3199 flags. Everyone saluted and applauded. Then there was a long string of marching bands like the Modesto Band of Stanislaus County, mounted posses like the Tuolumne County Sheriff's Posse, drill teams, ropers and rodeoers, politicians and office-holders in brand new cars provided by the local auto dealers, dance troupes throwing Tootsie Rolls, the Estanislao chapter of *E Clampus Vitus*, car clubs featuring old cars like the Modesto Area As Car Club and new, customized cars like the Modesto Throttlers Car Club, Cub Scout and Boy Scout troops, an old cowboy riding a big bull, a really ancient car carrying a thrift-store family and pulling a trailer with all their worldly possessions that had a sign on the door that read: "Grapes of Wrath," and the Shriners, with their motorcycle troop, mounted posse, clown troupe, and mini Tin Lizzies. There were over 200 entries and they were all enthusiastically red, white, and blue. Even the sponsor of my Babe Ruth team, E.D. Blakeley & Son, had a float. So did my friend George's car club, the Ecurie AWOL Sports Car Competition Club. I'm sure he would have been driving his Autobianchi in the parade if he had been in better shape and the car wasn't rusting in the junkyard. We knew the parade was over when the two street sweepers came along to clean up all the horse and cow droppings. They were always preceded by the smell of warm water and steaming dung.

"That was fun," I said, as the last sweeper brushed past us.

"It was," Kelly replied. "I really liked the Shriners. They're so funny."

"Well, I guess we better go. Your mom and dad said they'd be back at the Covell at 12:45. It's 12:30 right now."

"Time to go, then," she said.

I folded the chairs and grabbed the cooler. I heard a scream. We both turned and saw a car coming right toward us. There was a boy caught on the hood of the car, which I thought was odd. He was trying to get off, but couldn't. The car struck an older woman, as it roared through the crosswalk and headed directly at us, picking up speed. There were two little girls next to us. I pushed them off to the side. There were two other young girls standing next to them. *Sisters*, I thought, in a flash. I tried to grab them, but they slipped away, running to stand next to the brick wall behind us, figuring they'd be safe there. I heard the car accelerating and was wondering what the driver was doing. I just had time to grab Kelly and the both of us dove to the sidewalk, as the car hurtled forward and crunched into the building, pinning the two little girls to the wall. The car engine kept racing, like it was trying to bust through the brick, but it couldn't go anywhere. The spinning tires sent plumes of black, stinky smoke into the air. I looked at the driver and he stared back at me with a blank look in his eye. He was an older Mexican man. A Mexican woman about the same age sat next to him, holding her head. There were two small kids crying in the back seat. A tall man in a short-sleeved white shirt and straw fedora suddenly appeared, reached in, and turned off the ignition. I looked back at where the little girls had stood and all I could see was a patch of blood. The young boy was lying face down on the hood of the car. I thought I was going to throw up. Kelly tried to look, but I stepped in front of her. She looked me in the eye, then wrapped both arms around me and held on for dear life. I thought she'd never let go.

It was our last league game of the Babe Ruth Season. We were playing Marathon Corporation, one of the toughest teams in our league, at the Modesto Junior College varsity diamond. They were in second with a record of six wins and three losses. We were in third with five wins, two losses, and two ties. We couldn't move past them into second with a win, but we could keep them from taking over first if we could beat them.

The score was tied 3-3 in the bottom of the seventh. I was on second, after bunting for a single and stealing second. I was still adjusting to the pitching, so I relied on what I knew I could do, which was drag bunt and walk. Our left-handed first baseman, Rick, another junior high buddy of mine, was at the plate. I had wheels, so I knew if he got it in a gap or in the outfield, I would score. He connected with a 2-2 fastball and laced the ball down the right field line. I was off at the crack of the bat. I headed toward third as the right fielder cleanly fielded the ball and pegged it to the second baseman in short right. I wheeled around third, took a quick look over my left shoulder, and saw the second baseman wind up. I accelerated, barreling down on the plate. The ball and I arrived at the same time. Butt-head Teddy, who was catching that day, caught the ball just as I slammed into him, kicking up a cloud of dust and knocking him ass-over-teakettle. Everyone in the stands jumped to their feet to see what the call was. The ump waited until Teddy held up his glove. The ball was still in it.

"You're out!" the ump cried.

I saw my father flash by out of the corner of my eye. Not to pick me up, but to help Teddy to his feet. Teddy's father, who was one of the assistant coaches for the opposing team, was there by then. They both helped Teddy up. Teddy smiled, rolled the ball out to the mound, and headed for the opposing dugout.

I leapt to my feet, dusted myself off, and glared at the umpire. I kicked dirt onto the plate, said, "I was safe," turned around, and moved toward our dugout. The other team's fans booed.

My father caught up with me halfway to the dugout. He grabbed my arm, then grimaced, and exhaled, like he'd been gut-punched. He sucked it up, then dragged me back to the dugout, spun me to the bench, and barked, "You're benched. We don't play that way. And I don't ever want you to show up an umpire again. You hear me?" I nodded. "I can't hear you," he yelled.

"Yes, sir," I replied, looking down and sulking. He glared at me.

Kelly had come to watch the game. I saw her out of the corner of my eye, standing hands clasped together. I was too angry and embarrassed to make eye contact, as I leaned back in the dugout.

Our pitcher fell apart in extra innings and we lost by one. Marathon finished second, which qualified them for the playoffs. Teddy was in the post-season. I was done for the year.

We drove home in silence. My dad and brother in the front. Me in the back. When we pulled into the driveway, I jumped out of the car, slammed the door, and raced into the house. As I walked by my mother, who was setting the dinner table, I yelled, "It's not fair," and stomped off to our bedroom.

It was a quiet supper. As soon as it was over, I cleared my dishes, put them in the sink, and went back to my room, muttering over my shoulder, "I'm going to shower."

That season, we ended up being a middle-of-the-pack team. Our final record was 5-3-2. Delbert Hill and Vern Zorn were selected for the All-Star team, which would play in the second annual Modesto Elks Babe Ruth League All-Star Carnival at Del Webb. The winners would play in the District Four Tourney at Billy Hebert Field in Stockton. I only got to play a little bit that season. I mostly walked, bunted, or struck out. I never could hit the curve. I finished the season batting .200. I didn't even reach the Mendoza Line. But, I got to play.

CHAPTER 35

Minor league baseball in Modesto was the best ticket in town. It was cheap and you got to watch the pros play, some of who would someday end up in the Big Show. As Little Leaguers, and now Babe Ruthers, we got discounted tickets. Plus, Roy's dad, who worked for the *Modesto Bee*, sometimes got tickets from guys in the sales department, who used the tickets to convince local companies to buy advertising in the *Bee*. They were box seats right behind home plate, although we hardly appreciated what good seats they were because we were chasing foul balls, playing grab-ass, or getting something at the concession stands.

I only went to a handful of games, but there was one guy who was at every one. He sat in the box seats behind home all the way to the left, as you faced the field. He had a cowbell that he would clang every time our team was up and would yell, "Load the bases," in kind of a low, droning voice. He was loud and he never gave up. Every time we batted, he would clang that bell and yell. Sometimes it worked. Probably because it bugged the opposing pitcher as much as it bugged the rest of us.

Watching the ballplayers hit and run and field, I dreamed about being out there playing in front of a hometown crowd and hitting a game-winning home run. Of course, I never thought about all the long practices, hot bus rides, lousy food, crippling injuries, crazy fans, and seedy hotel rooms you had to endure to get there. The dream loves company, but it never pays the bill.

The Colts opened the second half of the season with a 5-2 win over their archrivals, the Stockton Ports. Jack Lane, who had just joined the team, won his first game as a Colt. Ken McCain's grand salami over the right field fence in the bottom of the second was all Lane would need to chalk up his inaugural victory. A merchants' night crowd of 1,627 watched the contest.

Mickey was getting blistering hot just when it was time for the league to take its yearly break. The Major League Baseball All-Star Game, also known as the "Midsummer Classic," was an annual game between players from the National Legue and the American League, selected by a combination of players, coaches, and managers. The fans had been given the chance to vote on the eight starting positions from 1947 to 1957. However, when fans of the Cincinnati Reds stuffed the ballot box and nearly elected a Red for every position but first base (and batboy), Commissioner Frick stepped up to the plate and removed two Reds from the starting lineup and discontinued fan voting.

The All-Star Game usually took place on the second Tuesday in July and marked the symbolic halfway point of the season. The venue for each All-Star Game was chosen by a league selection committee. The reason for choosing a particular location might be based on the opening of a new field, an historical occasion, or to commemorate a significant year. The game's site traditionally alternated between the two leagues every year.

The first Major League Baseball All-Star Game had been held as part of the 1933 World's Fair in Chicago on July 6 at Comiskey Park. It was the idea of Arch Ward, who was sports editor for the *Chicago Tribune*. Ward thought it would be a unique way to celebrate the city's Century of Progress Exposition. The game was originally designed to be a one-time event. But, it was so popular and successful that the league decided to hold one every year. Ward's contribution was recognized by Major League Baseball in 1962 with the creation of the "Arch Ward Trophy," which was to be given each year to the All-Star Game's most valuable player.

The managers of the game were the managers who faced each other during the previous year's World Series. The coaching staff for each team was selected by its manager. For the first game, Connie Mack and John McGraw, who were both regarded as baseball's greatest living managers, were asked to lead the American and National League teams respectively. McGraw came out of retirement just to manage the one game.

In that first All-Star Game, American League players wore their team uniforms instead of wearing uniforms made specifically for the game. On the other side, the National League players wore uniforms made just for the game with the lettering "NATIONAL LEAGUE" across the front of the shirt. For the second game, they all reverted to wearing their team uniform. Both teams kept it that way from then on.

The game had been played at night for the first time in 1942, at the Polo Grounds in New York. In 1945, as a result of travel restrictions caused by the world war, the All-Star Game to be played at Boston's Fenway Park was postponed until the next season. From 1959 to 1962, two All-Star Games were held each season. The second game was added to raise money for a variety of causes, including the players' pension fund, as well as to increase interest in the game.

In '62, the first of the two games was played on July 10 at one o'clock at D.C. Stadium in Washington D.C. No regular season games were scheduled on the day before or the day after, so it provided a nice break for those who didn't play. 45,480 attended. President John F. Kennedy threw out the first pitch. Ralph Houk of the Yankees managed and right-handed pitcher Jim Bunning of the Tigers started for the American League. Fred Hutchinson of the Reds managed and Don Drysdale of the Dodgers started for the National League. The Nationals won 3-1. Juan Marichal, a pitcher for the Giants, was the winning pitcher, and Camilo Pascual, a pitcher for the Twins, was the loser. The game was broadcast by NBC, with Mel Allen of the Yankees and Joe Garagiola, the retired Cardinal/Pirate/Cub/Giant catcher, doing the play-by-play and color commentary, while Lindsey Nelson, broadcaster for the New York Mets, and John MacLean, announcer for the Washington Senators, were on the radio side.

The Giants had five players selected, including Felipe Alou (OF), Orlando Cepeda (starting 1B), Jim Davenport (3B), Juan Marichal (P), and Willie Mays (starting CF). The Yankees contributed Elston Howard (catcher), Mickey Mantle (starting CF), Roger Maris (starting RF), Bobby Richardson (2B), Ralph Terry (P), and rookie Tom Tresh (SS).

It was a game of the best-of-the-best, but the day belonged to Maury Wills, who showed what speed could do to change a game. He entered the game in the sixth inning to pinch-run for Stan Musial. He stole second and scored the first run of the game when Dick Groat of Pittsburgh singled. In the eighth, Wills singled, moved to second on Jimmie Davenport's single to left, zoomed into third when the ball was cut off, and scored when the next batter fouled out to right field. He could thank his legs for helping him win the very first MVP award.

President Kennedy was later quoted as saying to Stan Musial, "A couple years ago they told me I was too young to be president and you were too old to be playing baseball. But, we fooled them."

Mickey played right and struck out his first time up. He walked his second time and Rocky Colavito went in to run for him.

CHAPTER 36

There was no full moon, so it was a dark night. Perfect for what we needed to do. Roy, Gary, and me waited in the shadows by the back fence of my old house on Grinnell, which was adjacent to the raised bed of the Tidewater Southern Railway Company tracks. We heard the train before we saw it. The singing vibration on the metal track, then the slow rumbling and clanking of the steel wheels of the railroad cars.

The Tidewater Southern, which was part of Western Pacific Railroad Company, traveled from downtown along Ninth Street and then due north out of town, where it high-balled it to Stockton, connecting Modesto to points in California, the West, and the rest of the country.

The train always moved slowly through the commercial downtown and residential areas. So, it was easy to hop. We'd been doing it for years. Catching a ride to friends' houses that lived on the edge of town. The reason we wanted to hop this train was that it went past Del Rio Country Club. Within spitting distance of Teddy's house.

I pulled the straps of my Boy Scout backpack a little tighter. I bounced on my toes and shook my hands to get ready, like a long-jumper determined to break his personal best. As soon as the engine passed, we dashed out to the edge of the track bed and squatted, scanning the oncoming boxcars for any open doors. The first one wasn't long in coming. As it approached, rocking and swaying along the tracks, we stood up. When it reached us, we stepped up on the graveled crossties and took a few steps parallel to the tracks to gauge how fast it was going, which was slower than a Hoyt Wilhelm knuckleball. The bed of the boxcar was low, reaching to about our waist, so it would be slow and low enough for us to jump in without getting killed. We'd heard stories for years, especially from our parents, about kids hopping freight trains and falling on the tracks and having both legs cut off. We were dumb, but not stupid.

Roy hopped on first, then Gary. I slung the pack off my shoulder and gently handed it up. I didn't want to ruin the surprise inside. I placed both hands flat on the bed and prepared to hop in, simply planning to flip my right leg over the edge, just the way a gymnast would straddle the pommel horse, or a high-jumper would vault over the bar. When I stepped into a low spot on the track and stumbled, the image flashed through my mind of me in a wheel chair with bandaged stumps where my legs used to be. Before it became a reality, the ground leveled out, I got my balance, and didn't hesitate. I steadied my hands on the bed, pushed up, and dove, face-first, into the boxcar. I planted my nose, rolled over, got to my feet, and let out a strangled breath. "Dang!" I wheezed.

As our eyes adjusted to the even darker inside of the car, we looked on either side of the open door into the coal-black corners to see if there were any hobos. Nobody. We had it all to ourselves.

Roy handed me my pack, I peeked inside then closed it up. We stepped into the shadows and watched north Modesto slowly glide by. We rolled past Roosevelt School and Roosevelt Park, then Beard Brook Elementary School, as well as endless fences of different designs and materials, churches, apartments, and office buildings. It didn't take long for us to leave the city limits and enter miles and miles of peach, walnut, and almond orchards and vineyards. Everything had recently been flood irrigated. I loved the smell of the wet earth. It smelled like the valley. The three of us sat on the boxcar floor with our legs dangling out the open door, the warm summer night blowing in our faces. Flatland Huck Finns.

When we crossed Kiernan Avenue, we stood up and got ready. Once we passed Ladd Road, we knew we were close. We also realized we'd have to get off quickly because, once the train reached this part of town, it started accelerating. We'd never be able to get off. Next stop – Stockton. The tracks hugged the rail-bed paralleling Saint John Road. As we approached Country Club Drive, we got in position. Roy first again, then Gary, then me. Roy jumped, landed flat-footed, stumbled slightly in the powdery dust, caught himself, turned around, and moved slightly right to trot parallel with the open door, in case we needed help. Gary hopped out and immediately went down. He rolled in the dirt, jumped to his feet, and hustled to catch up, following in Roy's wake. I handed the pack down carefully to Roy. I sat down on my butt, pushed off with both hands, and leaped to the ground. Just then, the train whistle blew and we heard the clacking start to accelerate. We jogged for a few feet, slowed to a stop, stepped back, and watched the train pull away into the night. When the caboose passed us, the flagman shook his head and waved at us. We tipped our hats. We crossed over the tracks, dashed into the almond orchard, and ducked behind a tree.

"Everything okay?" Gary asked.

I opened the backpack, poked around, and said, "Peachy keen."

"Let's go then," Roy said, checking his watch. "The southbound train is due in about an hour." Roy always wore a watch, and it was a nice one that still looked brand-new and never lost time. It was meticulous, just like him.

We scanned Saint John and Country Club for cars. No headlights. It was pitch black, because there were still no street lights, since this was part of the county. We left the protection of the trees, scurried over the tracks again, scampered across Saint John, and hid behind a clump of trees at the end of the first hole of the golf course. We could see the bright lights of the Del Rio clubhouse just north of us. We needed to move quickly because people would be leaving soon from a late dinner, cocktails, or a game of gin rummy.

Teddy's house was dark. It was located just south of the green on the first hole. Teddy was always bragging about how much putting practice he did on this hole. For free. We were going to give him a few hazards to deal with.

Still hidden by the trees at the edge of the course, we kneeled down. I opened the pack. I handed Gary six rolls of toilet paper. I gave Roy the hand trowel and five CO2 cartridges filled with black powder, each with a small length of fuse. The last thing in the pack was the carton of a dozen eggs. I pulled it out, opened it up, carefully checked the eggs, and closed the container. We put our hands together, palms down, in front of us.

"Revenge," we whisper-shouted and took off in three separate directions.

Roy headed for the green. He carved out the letters "T-E-D-D-Y" in the beautifully manicured grass of the green. At the bottom of each letter, he buried a cartridge, making sure the fuse was still visible. When he was done, he waited.

Gary made a beeline for the front of the house. He started TP-ing trees, bushes, and the empty, sunken carport. He tossed some rolls high into the tops of the surrounding trees. When a car's headlights flashed down the road from the clubhouse, we all three flattened out on the ground. The car paused at the stop sign, waited a moment, and then went straight. As soon as it was gone, we went back to work. Gary threw another roll over the top of the house, hoping it would keep going and end up in the pool out back. After that, he joined me.

I opened the carton. We each took six eggs and pegged the house like we were Juan Marichal trying to whiff Frank Howard. The soft smoosh told us the eggs had exploded on target. We tossed the empty carton in the pack, hustled around the corner of the house, and back to the shelter of the stand of trees by the first hole.

Seeing that we were in position, Roy flicked open his Zippo lighter, quickly lit each fuse, and ran for the trees where we waited. We didn't stick around to enjoy the fireworks. We flew across Saint John, over the tracks, and back into the orchard. As we ran away south from the scene of the crime, keeping parallel to the tracks and hidden by the almond trees, we heard a deafening series of five explosions, as the bombs went off. We couldn't help but grin and whoop and holler and slap each other on the back, which made it difficult to run. We didn't stop until we reached Ladd Road. We crossed and slipped into the peach orchard. We sat down in the soft, cool dirt, and waited for the freight train.

"That'll teach the butt to try to steal my girl," I hissed.

"I hope they make him clean it all up," Gary said.

"His old man will pay some Mexican to do it, I bet," Roy added.

"As long as he gets the blame," I said.

We hopped aboard the southbound train, reversed our journey, and got home before the folks started wondering where we were.

CHAPTER 37

For as long as I could remember, the Modesto Band of Stanislaus County had been presenting free concerts every summer at Mancini Bowl in Graceada Park. There were usually six concerts, each starting at a quarter after eight. The first one this year was scheduled for the Friday right after Independence Day.

The Modesto Band had a long and illustrious history, being one of the oldest, continuously performing bands in the United States. It started way back in 1919 as the Modesto Boys' Band. When the founder, Professor W.W. Higgins, unexpectedly died two years later, the band was taken over by Frank Mancini, a world-renowned clarinetist, who had purchased a farm on River Road outside Modesto just around that time. Mancini, whose nickname was "Proof," was the band director at Modesto High School and founded the Modesto Symphony Orchestra. He was still conducting the county band in 1962 at the ripe old age of seventy-six. He had announced earlier in the year that he would be retiring, so this would be his curtain call season.

Under Mancini's baton, the band grew and got really good – good enough to win the state championship five times in a row, as well as being named the official band of the California State Fair for nine consecutive years. In 1927, the band changed its name to the Stanislaus County Boys' Band. When women were allowed to join the band in the early 1950s, it changed again to the Modesto Band of Stanislaus County. From the very beginning, the band had performed around town, usually in parades and at concerts held at local parks, such as the Fourth Street Park, Beard Brook Park, and Court House Park. On May 15, 1949, thanks to money raised by a group called "The Band Mothers," which had been started by Mancini's wife, 3,200 Modestans celebrated the dedication of the Mancini Music Bowl in Graceada Park, which would become the permanent home of the band.

My mom and dad used to go to the concerts when we first moved to Modesto and the only kids were Tim and I. We were living at the corner of Santa Cruz and Monterey, across from the Gallo Glass plant, which had been built in 1957, and down the street from Orville Wright Elementary School, which had opened in 1948. We'd pack some soft drinks and things to munch on, throw some folding chairs and an old army blanket into the car, drive downtown, park on Magnolia, walk a couple blocks to the park, and find a nice, cool spot on the lawn under the trees. A lot of people preferred sitting in the permanent amphitheater seats that formed a half-circle in front of the bowl. My folks liked sitting off to the east side, near Sycamore. Now that there were five of us and it was the middle of summer, with temps hovering in the nineties, Mom would rather stay home where it was cool and watch TV. I still tried to go as often as I could, even if it meant riding my bike down there by myself.

The second concert was on lucky Friday the Thirteenth. Kelly and I planned to meet at the park and take in the performance. It was going to be another hot one, likely hitting ninety, which wasn't all that bad considering we usually had one hundred plus degree days this time of the year. I rode my bike and her folks dropped her off and then decided to stay for the concert. Kelly met me in the sand box behind the cinder block bathrooms, where I sat waiting in one of the rubber-seated swings. She was standing in front of me. I took both her hands and pulled her closer. I looked around.

"It's okay," she said. "They're sitting on the grass behind the seats. Mom promised she wouldn't come snooping."

And then I kissed her.

"How long will you be gone?" she asked, after I filled her in on my plan to go to Chicago.

"If it all works out, probably seven to ten days. It takes about three days to get there and another three or so to get back and then a couple days in Chicago. Why? You going to miss me?"

She smiled and pushed me and I swung away.

With much fanfare, the band started playing. It sounded like a piece of classical music, or a popular Broadway show tune. As I swung back, I hopped out of the swing and into her arms. We began to dance, cheek to cheek.

"You've gotten better," she said.

"I was good before," I said. "Now I'm not afraid of you anymore."

"Did I scare you that badly?"

"You did."

"I'm sorry."

"It was worth it," I said, and dipped her.

"Fred and Ginger," a voice said from the edge of the sand box. "How sweet."

I looked up and saw Teddy and company, arrayed in a line and decked out in their purple sweatshirts. I lifted Kelly up and she stepped beside me.

"This is a private party," she said.

"Well, we're crashing it," Teddy replied, as he stepped down into the sand box, followed closely by his boys. "Me and your beau have some things to settle."

"Glad to," I said. "When she's not around."

"Hiding behind skirts?"

"At least I fight my own fights," I said, looking past him to his friends.

Teddy took a few menacing steps toward us. "I don't need them. I don't need anyone or anything," he said.

"Sure you do, *amigo*," said a low, gravelly voice off to my right.

Felix Berbena, Alex Austin, and the rest of the Monarchs stepped out of the summer darkness and into the light illuminating the play area. Their yellow sweatshirts flashed in the light. "Sure you do. 'Cause you're messin' with my *compadre*. You hurt him and we got nobody to play ball with. *Comprendo*?"

"Look, I got no beef with you dudes," Teddy said.

"Now you do."

"We were just having some fun."

"Didn't look like it to me."

"Tell him, Mikey, we were just fooling around," Teddy pleaded.

"I don't know what you're talking about, old friend," I replied.

"Tell you what, Mikey," Felix said. "Why don't you and your *chiquita* go enjoy the music and we'll take care of your friends. Show them a real nice time."

"Sounds good to me," I said. "See you all around." Kelly and I turned and walked out of the light. I looked back in time to see the Monarchs surround the Eights. As they moved closer, I thought of a hangman's noose.

Another showcase for the best players in the game of baseball was scheduled to take place in between the two All-Star games. The annual Hall of Fame Game was set for Monday, July 23. Played at Doubleday Field in Cooperstown, New York, it would pit the Milwaukee Braves against the defending World Champion New York Yankees.

Doubleday Field was named for Abner Doubleday and was located two blocks from the National Baseball Hall of Fame and Museum. The grounds were built on what was Elihu Phinney's farm, which had been used as a baseball field since 1920. In 1924, a wooden grandstand was erected and was replaced in 1939 by a steel and concrete grandstand, erected by the federal Works Project Administration (WPA).

In 1940, the Hall of Fame hosted its first game. It was initially a contest between two old-timers teams. Later, it changed to an exhibition game between two major league squads. The game was held on the same weekend that the Hall held its annual induction ceremony. Later, it was moved to May or June to accommodate the participating teams' travel schedules. Because it was an in-season exhibition game, the results didn't count in the official standings. A lot of substitutes were used to keep the starters healthy for the rest of the season. The game drew well because it was the only game, except for those played in Spring Training or the World Series, which featured two teams from the two separate leagues competing against each other.

On that July day in 1962, Bob Feller and Jackie Robinson were inducted into the Hall. Unfortunately, the game itself was rained out.

CHAPTER 38

To avoid the blistering valley heat, me, my aunt, and Mr. Lowney left just before midnight a couple weeks later, on Sunday, July 29. My brothers and sisters didn't bother to get up to say goodbye. My mom gave me a hug and wouldn't let go. Finally, dad took her by the shoulders and she released me. She sobbed and turned into his shoulder. He smiled at us and waved us on our way.

I rode shotgun and Mr. Lowney rested in the back noodling quietly on his harmonica.

"My dad has a harmonica," I said.

"He play much?"

"A little. He plays one song really well," I said.

"What's that?"

"The Marine Corps hymn."

My aunt smiled as Mr. Lowney played it.

I was asleep before we reached the stink of Manteca. Whenever we used to visit family or take road trips, I'd always know we were almost home when I smelled the Spreckles processing plant in Manteca. The odor was a combination of rotting sugar cane waste, as well as the methane the cows in the adjacent feedlot produced when they ate the cane. It was pretty nasty. Someone said John Steinbeck worked at the plant a summer or two before he became a famous author.

My aunt followed Highway 99 north to Sacramento then northeast on Interstate 80 out of Sacramento to U.S. Route 40 east to Reno. We made it as far as Elko before the sun came up. We had a quick breakfast at a local diner and got back on the road. This time, Mr. Lowney drove, my aunt took the passenger seat, and I curled up in the back with *The Sun Also Rises* and my *Mad* magazines.

Aunt Cat and old Mr. Lowney talked baseball and the blues until it was time for a quick lunch break in Salt Lake City at the original Kentucky Fried Chicken. At least, that's what the plaque said. We didn't make real good time since the speed limit was sixty during the day and fifty at night, but we would make it up once we hit Wyoming, which was seventy; Nebraska, which was seventy-five; and Iowa, which was seventy-five and sixty-five, respectively.

Back on the road, I took over in the front seat for my aunt to keep Mr. Lowney entertained and awake. He didn't need any help. He was going home and he was non-stop remembering the men who played ball and sang the blues. That's all he needed. My aunt slept contentedly in the back. The road alternated between Interstate 80 and U.S. Routes 40 and 30 – the Lincoln Highway – across the rest of Utah, into Wyoming, and through Nebraska.

My aunt had a CB radio, so we had fun connecting with our fellow travelers. We also listened to the radio broadcast of the All-Star game when we could pick it up.

The two major league All-Star teams battled again in the second game at Wrigley Field in Chicago on Monday, July 30, at one o'clock in the Central Time Zone. 38,359 fans attended the classic. Dave Stenhouse of the Senators started for the Americans and Johnny Podres of the Dodgers for the Nationals. The American League won 9-4 and Leon Wagner, left fielder for the Los Angeles Angels, was named MVP. Ray Herbert, a pitcher for the White Sox, was the winner, and Art Mahaffey, a pitcher for the Phillies, was the loser. The game was broadcast by NBC, with Vin Sculley of the Dodgers and Russ Hodges of the Giants doing the play-by-play and color, while Jack Quinlan, sportscaster for the Chicago Cubs, and George Kell, the retired third sacker and baseball broadcaster for the Detroit Tigers, handled the radio broadcast.

There was no two-game break this time. The Yankees had played a double-header at Yankee Stadium against the Chicago White Sox the day before, winning 7-4 in the first game and losing 6-2 in the nightcap. That might have been the reason Mickey didn't play in the second midsummer classic. The left knee and right thigh injuries he'd suffered in May had been giving him some trouble in late July. He was still nursing them and probably didn't want to take a chance making it worse in a game that didn't really mean anything. Maris took his spot in center. It was a good thing I didn't talk Aunt Cat and Mr. Lowney into going early.

As we motored east, I picked up bits and pieces about Mr. Lowney. He was born in Chicago in 1905. His family moved to Modesto in 1909. He went to Modesto High from 1921 to 1925, where he lettered in football, basketball, baseball, and track. He was quarterback and team captain in football and was offered a scholarship to play at the University of Santa Clara. In basketball, he helped the Panthers win league championships and reach their first-ever post-season playoffs. On the diamond, he played third and then switched to catcher and led Modesto to the Stanislaus County and Central California championships in his senior year in 1925.

Mr. Lowney decided to keep playing ball instead of going to college. He played in Kalamazoo, Michigan and York,

Pennsylvania, before joining the Salt Lake City Bees in 1928, where he caught Lefty Gomez, while winning the league title. Gomez went on to be a twenty-game winner and all-star for the Yankees and Senators. In 1929, Mr. Lowney moved on to the San Francisco Seals. The next season, he signed with the Chicago Cubs. An injury and family responsibilities brought him back home to Modesto in 1933, where he worked as an electrician for the city of Modesto. But, he wasn't done playing ball. He was a member of the Modesto Reds' semi-pro team from 1933 to 1945, including a championship season in 1940. He later played for the Modesto Rangers and the Green Frog Inn team from Stockton. That was on the weekends. On weeknights, he played softball for as many as three different teams starting in 1929.

In 1937, he was a member of the Helm Chevrolet team that won the state championship and went to the national tournament. The next season, he helped the Merchants reach the state finals. In 1939, the Merchants won the state title and played in the national tournament at Soldier Field in Chicago. The Modestans finished second and Lowney was named the catcher for the all-star team. He switched from player to umpire in 1947, but came out of retirement to play on a city league team in '52 and '53. He took an early retirement from his city job because of an industrial accident and, soon after, his wife died. He never had any children. So, he started spending time at our park. As he told me his life story, I realized he was only fifty-seven, which wasn't all that old. I guess he just looked it.

When he was done giving us the lowdown on his baseball career, he turned to the blues. He punctuated each pronouncement with a note or two on the harp. Happy and sad, upbeat and downbeat, fast and slow, cool and hot, and all the colors and flavors in between.

"There's nothing more American than baseball and the blues," he said. "Both were born on the backroads and in the backwaters and at the crossroads of the American continent. If you want to understand the heart and mind and soul of America, who we are as Americans, you need to know both." He gave a rapid-fire rundown of the long road they'd traveled together.

"Baseball and the blues were born to break your heart.

Baseball ain't nothin' but a good player tryin' not to be bad. The blues ain't nothin' but a good man feelin' bad.

Baseball opens in the spring, when everything begins again. The blues have always been about new beginnings.

Baseball ends when the chill rains of fall come. The blues never end.

Baseball blossoms in the summer air and light. The blues are in full bloom just 'round midnight.

Baseball and the blues celebrate all the curves that life throws you.

We play baseball to lift our souls. We play the blues to bare our souls.

We play baseball to heal our hearts. We play the blues because our hearts have been hurt.

We play baseball to get home safe. We play the blues because we have no safe home to get to.

Baseball and the blues have a long memory.

In baseball and the blues, you fail more than you succeed. One for three gets you into the Hall of Fame.

In baseball, many are best remembered for their failures, not their successes. The blues celebrates that.

Baseball and the blues reflect our triumphs and defeats. When we're good, we're very good. When we're bad, there's nothing worse.

Baseball and the blues both make you suffer.

Baseball and the blues tell a lot of the same stories. About race, playing it straight and cheating, immigration, the tension between fathers and sons, acceptance, class warfare, alienation, labor and management, pop culture, myth, the individual and the crowd, and heroes.

In baseball and the blues, you can feel good and bad. Up and down. In and out. Fair and foul. Like a winner and a loser. Sometimes all at the same time.

We see our own daily lives reflected in the wins and losses, trials and tribulations, of our baseball heroes. The blues sings songs about it.

Baseball and the blues are haunted by ghosts of who and what have gone before. Of past heroes and moments, of present successes, of future dreams.

Baseball and the blues are all about hope. Of a brighter day and a better tomorrow.

For baseball and the blues, practice sometimes makes perfect.

Baseball looks easy when it's done right. So does the blues. They both fool us into thinking we've got it all figured out. Just before it all falls apart.

No one beats baseball or the blues for long.

In baseball and the blues, trouble happens.

And I love them both as dearly as the Valley loves the rain."

By the time we reached Cheyenne, after a couple of detours since Highway 80 wasn't done yet, everyone was ready for a good night's sleep. We filled up with gas and the attendant sent us to a trailer park on the edge of town. We parked and unloaded. Me and Mr. Lowney started a fire while my aunt popped up the top of the van and opened her up. We cooked some hot dogs over the coals, heated up a can of beans, opened a bag of chips, and had one of the best meals of our lives. Boy, were we tired. We spread out our sleeping bags and drifted into sleep.

I woke up to the smell of coffee, bacon, and eggs. My aunt and Mr. Lowney had been up for a while and figured I should get my beauty sleep. We ate, packed up, and got back on the road.

We continued rolling down Route 30 and made a pit stop in North Platte, Nebraska, grabbed something quick and easy, and kept rolling. We made it to Omaha by dinner. We got gas, bought a bag of White Castle burgers, found the trailer park, unloaded, ate a quiet meal, and settled in. We were all pretty tired and the excitement of the road had started to fade.

Exhausted as we were, Mr. Lowney wasn't done yet. "I have a theory," he started, and I knew we were in for a long lecture. He had a lot of wild and crazy theories, especially about baseball. I battled to stay awake and wished I had a couple toothpicks to prop my eyes open. "Ty Cobb is a zombie. You know, like the living dead, or maybe an alien," he added. "He's just too good to come by it naturally. He has to be the undead, or from a different planet, with super-human powers, to get on base as often as he does and to be as mean as he is. He's got an edge. I'm not sure how he got it, but he's got it. I know some of the modern ballplayers drink and smoke and take uppers to enhance their performance, but Cobb, he came by it supernaturally."

"Uppers?" I asked.

"Pills that wake you up, give you energy, and make you feel good. Like when you drink coffee, or eat too much sugar."

"I don't drink coffee."

"Good for you. As I was saying, back in those days, the players drank and smoked and chewed, too. Heck, old Babe Ruth was a drunk and ate too much and chased skirts and look what he accomplished."

"Chased skirts?"

"He liked the ladies," my aunt chimed in.

"Anyways, it's like that slogan DuPont uses in their commercials: 'Better Things for Better Living…Through Chemistry.' Some of these guys will do anything to get the advantage. Even if it means cheating."

"Sort of like spitballs?"

"A lot like spitballs."

"Yuk."

"Or, that cyclist who died in Rome during the Olympics two years ago. His trainer injected him with something prior to the race. Never finished."

"Do athletes still do things like that, like, you know, 'uppers'?" I asked.

"Well, your hero, Mickey, he supposedly gets injections of vitamin B to keep his energy up, especially on day games after night games. That's usually when players need something, so they can bounce back."

"Doesn't sound fair."

"It's not. And you can really do some damage to your body. He got one injection that put him in the hospital for five days last year."

I didn't know whether to believe him, or not. Mickey was too All-American-Kid-Next-Door to be doing anything that sounded that bad. 'Course, I only knew what I read in the papers, or magazines, or heard. I figured I'd check with Dad since he knew everything, especially about Mickey and baseball. I wasn't sure I really wanted to know. I liked my heroes heroic.

We were all up with the roosters and the sun the next morning. It didn't take long to pack up now that we'd been travelling together for a while. We were getting close and I could feel it.

At the Nebraska-Iowa border, Interstate 80 switched from following State Route 30 to U.S. Route 6. We stayed on that highway through Des Moines and Davenport, where we stopped for a quick lunch and a look at the mighty Mi-ss-iss-ippi, which marked the border between Iowa and Illinois. We continued into Illinois past Moline and through La Salle until we hit historic Route 66, just west of Joliet, following it northeast into the Windy City.

Mr. Lowney serenaded us with a spirited version of the song, "Route 66," singing and playing harmonica.

"That's a Chuck Berry song," I said. "I heard it on the radio."

"He did a cover of it, slugger," he replied. "It was written by Bobby Troup and Nat King Cole made it a hit."

My aunt and I joined in, harmonizing as we rolled along. We sang about getting our kicks on Route 66 as it wound two thousand miles from Chicago to LA.

We made it to Chicago around five o'clock. We decided to get a hotel room somewhere near Comiskey Park, since my aunt didn't want to be driving in and out of city traffic. That way we could also walk to the park.

CHAPTER 39

August was a bleak month in 1962. Almost nothing but bad news. Marilyn Monroe died in Los Angeles from an overdose of sleeping pills. Jamaica became independent after 300 years of British rule. Nobel Prize-winning author Hermann Hesse died in Switzerland. The Beach Boys released "Surfin' Safari" on Capitol Records. A young East Berlin man named Peter Fechter was shot while attempting to escape to West Berlin, bleeding to death in the no-man's land between the two cities. Peter, Paul, and Mary had their first hit with "If I Had a Hammer." And Dodger coach Leo Durocher almost died from an allergic reaction to a penicillin injection.

The All-Star game was history and all the players had scattered to re-join their teams and kick off the second half of the season. The Yankees were headed to Washington for three games and then back to Chicago on Thursday for a weekend series starting Friday, August 3. We had tickets for the Saturday game starting at 1:30 p.m. The second game in D.C. went eleven innings, so the Bronx Bombers got a late start for Chicago. The Yanks were in first, Chicago was in seventh, and the Senators were in dead last. The powerful Yankees were feasting on the lower division teams.

Unfortunately, Mr. Lowney's old team, the Cubbies, were in San Francisco playing the Giants, so we couldn't catch one of their games. We went to the park anyway and just walked around. It was so cool to see the old apartment houses surrounding the park with makeshift bleachers and seats set up to watch the game, and to realize how small it was compared to Candlestick. It really was cozy. We had lunch at a small tavern right across the street. We sat by the window so I could stare at all the comings and goings.

Built on the grounds of an abandoned seminary in 1914, Wrigley Field was once known as Weeghman Park and could hold 14,000 fans. In 1920, when the Wrigley family, owners of the chewing gum company, purchased the team from owner Charles Weeghman, they changed the name to Cubs Park. It was named Wrigley Field in 1926, in honor of William Wrigley Jr., the club's owner. The Wrigley Field bleachers and scoreboard were constructed in 1937, when the outfield area was renovated to provide more seating. The original scoreboard remained intact. The outfield walls were covered with ivy vines by Bill Veeck in 1937.

A lot of things had happened there over the years. Babe Ruth called his shot during game three of the 1932 World Series, supposedly pointing to a spot in the outfield bleachers and then hitting a home run off pitcher Charlie Root. On May 2, 1917, pitchers Jim "Hippo" Vaughn of the Cubs and Fred Toney of the Reds both had no-hitters going through nine innings before Olympian and pro football player Jim Thorpe of the Reds drove in the only run in the tenth inning. And, the second of the two '62 All-Star games had just been held there.

Although it was a Thursday in August, it felt like October. All smoky and cool with an orange sky. It made me think of school, which wasn't a welcome thought. I hadn't seen any new clothes in the department store windows, or Ticonderoga pencils and spiral tablets and Pee Chee folders in the stationery store displays, but

I knew it wasn't far away. What happened to June, when school was light-years away?

My aunt wanted us to visit the Adler Planetarium, but Mr. Lowney had other plans. He showed me a flyer for "Cooger and Dark's Combined Shadow Show."

"They're set up in a field on the edge of town," he explained. "Pulled in last night on a coal-black freight train. It's waiting."

"Wow," was all I could say, as I stared at the handbill. "A thousand and one wonders," I read. "Mephistopheles, the Lava Drinker. The Illustrated Man. Egyptian Mirror Maze. See Yourself Ten Thousand Times!"

"Think your aunt will mind if just us boys go check it out?"

"No, she'll be fine."

"This is what I want to see," Mr. Lowney said, as he pointed at the calligraphy that read: "Mr. Electrico's Time Machine. Far Travel to the Immediate Past and Future! Re-Live Past Lives!"

"A time machine. Man, oh man," I said.

"Just my style," Mr. Lowney replied.

I had really wanted to go to the planetarium with my aunt, but this was too good to pass up. My aunt was disappointed, but she understood. Mr. Lowney and I caught the "El" and headed north out to the edge of the big city along Lake Michigan.

The carnival was gigantic. The tents were kaleidoscopic. Multi-colored flags and banners flapped above the canvas. Cotton-candy-colored booths of all sizes stretched away to forever. The sideshow paintings proclaimed the monstrous wonders of the world. The calliope played mind-numbing tunes over and over again. The midway was jammed with people and carnies were flirting with the ladies and challenging the manhood of their boyfriends or husbands.

We walked goggle-eyed through the labyrinthine maze.

"'By the pricking of my thumbs, Something wicked this way comes,'" Mr. Lowney recited. "William Shakespeare wrote that about MacBeth, but he could have written it about this place."

"I just saw a book with that title. A friend of mine was reading it the other day," I said. "Ray Bradbury wrote it. I think I saw him while I was down in Anaheim."

"Truly?"

"Yes, in a magic store."

"That fits. He is an amateur magician. And a great author. You ever read *Dandelion Wine*?"

"Not yet."

"His best in my opinion. About a boy a lot like you. A year or two younger. The summer of his growing up. It's magical. Could be about boys growing up anywhere. Your friend know that one?"

"I don't know. I'll have to ask her."

"Her? Mikey, my boy, do you have a girlfriend?"

"No, she's just a friend. I think."

"Well, isn't that something you should find out, slugger?"

"I suppose. Maybe when we get back."

"I should think so. I should think so," and he smiled. "Ah, to be a young man again. You know, they say youth is wasted on the young. I've thought that for a long time now."

We stopped in front of a large, dusty, dark tent filled with a collection of penny arcade machines. And an ancient fortune teller encased in glass.

"I think I'll check this out," I said.

"Fine," said Mr. Lowney. "I'll see if I can find Mr. Electrico."

"See you in a bit," I said, as I stepped inside.

She had seen better days. The wood frame was faded and dinged. The glass case was chipped and so badly scratched, you could barely see her. Her being "Madame Fortuna," the gypsy fortune teller. She was also in pretty bad shape. Her clothes were threadbare. She was blanketed in dust. Cobwebs stretched from the top of her silk cap to a corner of the case. The threads that stitched her eyes shut were frayed. The slight smile that toyed around her lips revealed badly discolored, wooden teeth. The crystal ball she cradled in both hands was smudged and filled with moldy, green liquid. But, there was still something about her. Something magical. Something a little too real, not unlike the figures I once saw at a wax museum in San Francisco. Were they alive, or did they just exist?

I dropped the copper coin into the slot and heard it rattle home.

"A penny for your thoughts," I said, my breath fogging the glass.

When the glass cleared, I heard a slight whispering sound. I looked down to see a small, red business card lying flat at the end of the dispensing chute. I gently picked it up. The front of the card read: "Madame Fortuna, Psychic and Fortune Teller to the Crowned Heads of Europe." I turned it over. The message read: "There is no 'I' in team."

"Wow, a baseball fan, no less," I said to myself. I pocketed the card, touched the bill of my hat, and moved deeper into the arcade.

A young guy sat on a milk crate and whittled on a piece of wood. He had an apron filled with change wrapped around his waist. I handed him a dollar.

"Some quarters and dimes," I said.

Without speaking, he took my money, fished inside his apron, counted out the change, dropped it in my left palm, and went back to whittling. Some old rock 'n roll played through small, cob-webbed speakers hung in the corners. "Palisades Park" by Freddy Cannon.

"Appropriate," I said.

"Say what," he said, not looking up.

"The music is appropriate. It's about an amusement park."

"I wouldn't know," he said. "Gets so you don't hear it anymore."

I stuck out my right hand, just like a grown-up. "Mikey's my name."

He finally stopped carving and looked up. "Mouse or Mantle?" he asked.

"Actually, it's Mikey, not Mickey."

"My ears are bad thanks to all this white noise. Bet you hear that a lot?"

"I do, but that's okay."

He stuck the knife in the ground, wiped his hand on his jeans, shook my hand, and said, "They call me Leroy."

"You live around here?" I asked.

"No, I travel with the carnival. We move around a lot."

"Your parents work here, too."

"They're not here," he replied, picking up the knife and resuming his carving.

"Where are they?"

"Dead, gone, disappeared. Shoot, I don't know. They left me when I was born."

"Wow, that's horrible."

"Tell me about it."

"How old are you?"

He squinted up at me. "Probably about the same as you. How old are you?"

"Thirteen, going on fourteen."

"I turned fourteen on July fourth. A real Yankee Doodle Dandy, I am."

He looked a lot older.

"So, you travel all over the country?"

"Pretty much."

"You like it?"

"Got no choice."

"I think it would be pretty exciting."

"You ain't done it."

"No, maybe someday."

"You got parents?" he asked.

"I do."

"They alive?"

I hesitated a moment, then said, "They are."

"You're a lucky kid," he said, then got up, folded the knife, tucked it away, and gave me the carving. It was a baseball bat. "Go home and never look back," he said, and then he left me alone in the middle of the arcade.

CHAPTER 40

I found Mr. Lowney sitting on a bench across from the entrance to a large, red canvas façade that read: "Mr. Electrico's Time Machine." He was staring at the open door.

"Hey, Mr. Lowney," I said.

He jumped, startled from his reverie.

"Oh, hey, Michael. How was the arcade?"

"It was okay."

"Just okay?"

"Yeah, just okay. You been in yet?"

"Nope, getting up the courage."

"For what?"

"The unknown. No telling what will happen once I step inside that Wayback Machine. Not sure I want to know what's out there, you know. What's next and all that."

"Sherman and Mr. Peabody always change history and get in trouble when they time travel."

"That's what I'm kinda afraid of."

"Where do you want to go? Forward or back?"

"Old people always want to go back, Mikey. There's nothing for them in the future."

"That's not true, Mr. Lowney. You've got a lot of road ahead of you."

"I wish, don't I wish."

"My dad always tells me to be careful what I wish for 'cause it might just come true. He usually says that when I say I wish my brother was dead."

"You should never wish that."

"I know that. Now. I guess I've been kind of mean to them over the years. Need to work on that."

"Good for you."

"Won't be easy. Hard to change old habits."

"I've got a few things left undone that I hope this machine can help me with. I left some things unfinished. A few of those 'some day' kind of things."

"Some day things?"

"Yep, like 'some day I'll learn how to play piano, or some day I'll write that book, or some day I'll get re-married.'"

"You going to learn how to play piano?"

"Something like that, Michael. Something like that." He stood up. "Wish me luck."

"Good luck, Mr. Lowney."

"Save my seat?" he smiled.

"Sure thing."

"Yeah, what's that?"

He slowly shuffled toward the ticket booth, bought a ticket, turned around and held it up, then passed through the turnstiles, and entered the scarlet tent.

I guess I must've fallen asleep on the bench because I suddenly snapped awake. I looked around. It took a moment to remember where I was. I turned to gaze at the entrance. Just then, a young man wearing an old-timey Cubs cap and warm-up jacket stepped out of the doorway and walked toward me, smiling.

"I got what I wished for," the young man said.

"I'm sorry, sir, but—" I stammered.

"I'm playing for the Cubs tomorrow," he said. "I've got to get to Los Angeles. We're facing Drysdale."

"I don't understand," I yammered. "Who are you?"

"A man who's been given a second chance."

"What happened to Mr. Lowney? What'd you do with him?"

"Don't worry, he's fine."

"Where is he?" "Gone home."

"I'm confused."

"Don't be. Just remember, Michael. Don't ever give up. On your dreams. On what makes you happy. On your family. On your friends. On anything that's important to you. Someone told me once, just like I'm telling you now, 'Life is too short to wake up angry, or with regrets. So, love the people who treat you right. Forget about the ones who don't. Believe things happen for a reason. Do one thing well, not a lot of things halfway. If you get a second chance, grab it with both hands. If it changes your life, let it. Nobody said life would be easy, they just promised it would be worth it.'"

I looked closer at the young man. He sort of looked like Mr. Lowney, especially the eyes.

"I'll miss you," I said.

"No regrets, slugger. No tears goodbye."

"Good luck."

"Luck is the residue of design, my boy. Old Branch Rickey said that." He touched the bill of his cap. "I've got a plane to catch." He took something out of his pocket, handed it to me, and walked into the night. It was Mr. Lowney's harmonica.

As I walked down the dusty aisles heading for the exit, I passed a wax museum housed in a lemon-yellow-colored tent. I saw effigies of Napoleon, Lincoln, Hitler, and Marilyn Monroe. Something odd caught the corner of my eye. I stepped closer and peered through the forest of waxen bodies. At the very back of the tent, a shriveled old woman was putting the finishing touches on a new display that looked disturbingly like the old Mr. Lowney. I blinked my eyes a couple of times and strained to see better in the dusky half-light. She placed an old fedora on the pomaded head of the dummy. She swiveled around and saw me. She motioned to someone at the front of the tent and the entrance flaps slapped shut.

"I'm happy he made it home safely," Aunt Cat said.

"Me, too," I replied, half-heartedly.

"The trip back home won't be the same."

"No, it won't."

"Maybe you can learn to play that?" she said, pointing at the harmonica.

"I'll sure try."

We spent all day Friday getting to know Chicago. We did the Architecture Cruise, which travelled by boat along all three branches of the Chicago River. We cruised past dozens of landmark buildings, including the Tribune Tower and the Wrigley Building. Our guides told the story of Chicago's rise from the Great Fire of 1871 to become "the home of the skyscraper and the cradle of modern American architecture."

Then we went to the Field Museum of Natural History, which was located on Lake Shore Drive right next to Lake Michigan and near Navy Pier. The museum included all kinds of exhibits about our history as humans. I saw artifacts from ancient Egypt, the Pacific Northwest, the Pacific Islands, and Tibet. It had a huge taxidermy collection with all kinds of large animals, as well as an impressive exhibit of dinosaurs. It was a little overwhelming, even for a history buff like me.

We took a short drive out to Oak Park to visit the birthplace of Ernest Hemingway. Next to Thomas Hinkle, who wrote stories about dogs and horses, Hemingway was my favorite writer. My dad's, too, when he had time to read. I think the fact that Hemingway had been to war was appealing to a veteran like my father. Or, maybe he just envied Hemingway's need to embrace and experience the world, his need to consume it whole. I had read many of Hemingway's short stories in junior high and graduated to novels like *For Whom the Bell Tolls* and *The Old Man and the Sea*. There was something about his stark, spare style that I really enjoyed. He was all about things being real and true. He was living in Ketchum, Idaho, when he blew his brains out just before the Fourth of July in 1961. I sometimes wondered these days if my dad ever thought about doing what his hero had done.

Another Oak Park resident was architect Frank Lloyd Wright, who had moved there in 1889, shortly after his first marriage. He was another of my father's heroes, since he had once hoped to be an architect. When Dad got out of the Marines, he had decided to see a little more of the country, since he'd seen more of Asia than he had America. He bought a used Indian motorcycle and hit the road. He saw as many of Wright's works as possible during his pilgrimage.

My dad had a book about Wright that had been on a bookshelf somewhere in our house for pretty much all my life. We kids loved going through it and looking at the exotic buildings, so the book was a little beaten up. Like Hemingway, Wright's work seemed so American. I don't exactly know how it happened, but there was a house designed by Wright in Modesto. It was way out in the country on Hogue Road off McHenry, near the Stanislaus River. It was designed in 1957 and completed in 1961 for a local doctor named Dr. Robert Walton and was one of Wright's largest single-story homes. It was a small world.

That Friday was a big day for Chicago sports fans. The annual College All-Star Game would kick off at 9:00 p.m. at Soldier Field, pitting the world champion Green Bay Packers against the College All-Stars. And the Yankees were playing a day game against the Sox. We listened to the game on the radio in between sightseeing. Mickey only played three innings. It was his first appearance since hurting his knee again the previous Sunday. He hit into a double play his first time up, struck out in the top of the third, and called it a day. He told the reporters his knee wasn't strong enough yet. Something still wasn't right.

My aunt suggested we camp out at the Bismarck Hotel, which was where the Yankees usually stayed, to see if we could catch Mickey coming back after their game against the Sox. I thought it was a great idea. We had dinner at a diner and got to the hotel about eight o'clock and waited. And waited. And waited. We saw many of the players come in, including Tom Tresh. He stopped when he saw me.

"Hey, bad penny," he said. "You just keep showing up."

"Hello, Mr. Tresh. This is my Aunt Catherine."

They shook hands.

"You waiting for Mickey?" he asked.

"Yep," I replied.

"Could be a while."

"We've got nothing else to do," Aunt Cat answered.

"Going to the game tomorrow?"

"We are."

"I hope we have a good one."

"Is Mr. Mantle going to play?" my aunt asked.

"He's scheduled to."

"Great. That's great," I said.

"See you," he said. He tapped my shoulder and bowed slightly to my aunt. A real gentleman.

We nibbled on chips, ate some chocolate-chip cookies, and sipped some soft drinks we got from a mom-and-pop store down the street. On a small black-and-white TV snuggled in the corner over the Garden Lounge bar, we watched the Packers dominate the All-Stars. The game was broadcast on *ABC's Wide World of Sports.* The Packers won forty-two to twenty. The final score didn't reflect what a tough game it was for the pros. I always wondered how the college kids could play with the pros without getting creamed, but they always seemed to do pretty good. In the game of youth and enthusiasm against age and experience, the latter usually won.

65,000 fans saw one of the more competitive games in recent years. Otto Graham, coach of the All-Stars, had several talented players that year, including QB John Hadl of Kansas, who was named MVP. Other players included Lance Alworth of Arkansas, Merlin Olsen of Utah, Curtis McLinton of Kansas, and Bob Ferguson of Ohio State. The 1961 Heisman Trophy winner, Ernie Davis of Syracuse, didn't play because he was sick. The score was fourteen to ten in favor of Green Bay at the half. In the second half, the World Champion Packers bombarded the college kids. With the win, the pros extended their lead in the series nineteen to eight with two ties.

At some point before the game ended, I nodded out. It was around midnight when I startled myself awake. I'd had a bad dream about my dad getting beaned in the head during one of his semi-pro games. I woke up just as he hit the ground. My aunt was gone. I looked around, a little panicked. I saw her standing at the reception desk talking with the night clerk. I walked over and stood next to her.

"Hello, sleepyhead," she said, and stroked the top of my head like she always did.

"They're night owls, miss," the clerk said. "No telling when they'll get in. I wouldn't wait up."

"Thanks," we both said and trudged off toward the lobby exit.

"This isn't good," I said. "He needs his rest. His leg is still messed up. This won't help."

"He'll be fine," my aunt said, without much conviction in her voice.

CHAPTER 41

Game time the next day was 1:30 p.m. Frank Baumann (4-3) of the Sox was facing Bill Stafford (9-7). According to the Tribune sports section, everyone was scheduled to be in the line-up. Tresh, Richardson, Maris, Mantle, Reed, Lopez, Howard, Skowron, and Boyer. Only old Yogi was missing, but he was available to pinch-hit.

We decided to swing by the Bismarck again, just in case we could catch them before the bus left. The clerk had told us last night that the team usually left about four hours before the first pitch, around nine or half-past for a day game. Unfortunately, thanks to a late city bus and a lot of traffic, we got there too late. The team bus was long gone and we were running out of time.

"Let's get a cab," my aunt declared.

"Isn't that expensive?"

"Yes, but this is important."

She hailed a cab with a shrill whistle, just like my dad's, that would bring a pack of dogs running. Anytime my dad used that whistle, we knew we were in trouble and it was time to high-tail it home. Must've worked the same way with cabbies because a taxi stopped immediately, we piled in, and off we raced for the ballpark.

We pulled up at the corner of Thirty-fifth and Shields and jumped out. My aunt paid the cabbie as I stared at the concrete-and-steel monster. The façade above the bunting-layered entrance read: "Comiskey Park. Home of the Chicago White Sox." I couldn't wait to see thc field where Luke Appling played. Where Ty Cobb terrorized his White Sox opponents. Where "Shoeless" Joe gripped Black Betty and the infamous "Black Sox" threw the 1919 World Series. And, now, where Luis Aparicio and Nellie Fox protected the middle.

The Black Sox Scandal was one of the darkest chapters in professional baseball history. The White Sox had won the pennant in 1919, but they weren't happy. Not with their teammates, or their penny-pincher owner, "The Old Roman" Charles Comiskey. Some gamblers decided to use the players' anger to make a little money. The ringleader was first baseman Arnold "Chick" Gandil, who convinced some of the local gangsters that his teammates would throw the Series against the Cincinnati Reds.

Starting pitchers Eddie Cicotte and Claude "Lefty" Williams, outfielder Oscar "Happy" Felsch, and shortstop Charles "Swede" Risberg were all part of the fix. Third baseman Buck Weaver was asked to join, but he refused. And didn't tell anyone, which would cause him some problems later. Utility infielder Fred McMullin found out about it and threatened to blow the whistle unless he got some of the action. "Shoeless" Joe Jackson was implicated, although his participation was never confirmed.

Two years after the Series, the truth was revealed and the players were dragged into court. They were found innocent by a jury. The baseball owners felt the need to clean up their league and restore the public's confidence in the game, so they hired federal judge Kenesaw Mountain Landis to be their first commissioner. His inaugural act was to suspend all eight players for life.

Baseball and gambling had always had a complicated relationship.

Comiskey Park opened on July 1, 1910, on the South Side of Chicago. It was built over an old city dump. During one game, shortstop Luke Appling, "Old Aches and Pains," tripped over an ancient teapot that had worked its way up from the dump into the base-paths. The roofed, double-decked stadium had a catwalk that ran behind the scoreboard. Like Candlestick Park in San Francisco, Comiskey Park was plagued by a cold north wind coming off a body of water. Instead of San Francisco Bay, it was Lake Michigan. In 1960, owner Bill Veeck installed the Monster Scoreboard, the first of its kind in the majors. It was so popular, even baseball purists predicted it wouldn't be the last. It was the world's first scoreboard that put on its own show. It featured foghorns, a cavalry charge bugle, crashing trains, fire engine sirens, the "William Tell Overture," a chorus whistling "Dixie," flashing strobe lights, and fireworks. In one game in that first year of operation, the Yankees made fun of what they considered a monstrous distraction by lighting sparklers after one of their teammates hit a home run.

My aunt and I picked up our tickets from Will Call, which was located in one of the round, red-topped, conical ticket booths in front of the stadium entrance, and headed inside. We had tickets in the front row at the far edge of the upper deck of the right field grandstand, as close to center field as possible, so we could get a good view of Mickey.

Before we went up to our seats, we stopped by the picnic area in left field, which gave us a great field-level view of the park. Anybody could sit there anytime, as long as there were seats available. They were fantastic. We watched a little of batting practice and some of the warm-ups. I looked for Mickey, but couldn't see him.

"He's probably getting taped up, or sitting in a Whirlpool bathtub to loosen up," my aunt said. She knew what she was talking about, since she had played a few innings in her time.

"Let's go up and find our seats," she said, sensing my rising level of panic.

"Sure," I said, clutching my program tightly.

Mickey didn't play that day. Without him in the lineup, the White Sox won 2-1. The evening newspaper said his leg was still acting up from wrenching it the past Sunday. He dressed, but never left the dugout. I overhead some knucklehead in our hotel lobby say, "Bad leg, my foot. He probably stayed out too late last night."

"Nah, he was likely alley-cat'n around with some floozy," another yokel added.

I whirled around and shouted at them, "He's married!"

They both laughed. "What's that got to do with the price of beans, kid?" the first one said.

My aunt gently took my arm and escorted me to the elevator. "Don't listen to people like that," she said. "They're rude and they don't know what they're talking about."

The Yankees were playing another day game on that Sunday. My mind was spinning. I wasn't ready to give up.

Then we got the one-two punch. It knocked us down, but not out. Uncle Jim had telephoned after the game. I could tell it wasn't good news because my aunt's face looked down, which never happened. She was always smiling and joking around. When she got off the phone, she told me he was being called back to the Navy. Things were heating up all over the world, but especially in Vietnam, and that's where he was going. As some kind of advisor. My mom had also called. She was crying, so I knew it was bad. My dad was getting worse. As much as my aunt and I wanted to try one more time to see Mickey, we had to go. My aunt wouldn't say anything, but I knew she was running out of money. I felt bad. It was definitely time to go. I said we should drive straight through. She said that was silly. I offered to help with the driving. "Now, that's just plain dumb," was all she said. "But, thanks," she offered. "We've got some time."

We picked up a Chicago-style pizza from a neighborhood pizzeria and stayed in that Saturday night. I didn't eat much. Another missed opportunity and I didn't know what I was going to do.

"We'll figure something out when we get home," my aunt said.

"Like what?"

"I don't know." She flipped from the *Tribune* crossword puzzle to the sports section. "Let's see. Well, the Yankees are in first in the American League. The Giants are in second in the National. If the Yankees stay in first and the Giants can beat the Dodgers, which I wouldn't be happy about since the Bums are my team, maybe the Yankees will play the Giants in the World Series? Stranger things have happened. That means the Yankees would play at Candlestick. In San Francisco. In California. Just over the Altamont Pass from Modesto."

"But," I thought to myself, "there's no way my parents are going to let me go anywhere, or get anywhere near the Yankees, after what's already happened."

And I was right. But, that reality would have to wait until we got back.

CHAPTER 42

We got up at five a.m. on Sunday, August 5, and pointed the Econoline toward California. We decided to return a different way. Mr. Lowney wasn't there, but his spirit had inspired us.

"Get our kicks on Route 66," Aunt Cat exclaimed. "Haven't been on that stretch of highway in a long time. Can't wait." And we harmonized on another verse about getting hip to a timely tip on our California trip.

Route 66 was a more direct and faster way home for my aunt. And, it just happened to run through Commerce, Oklahoma, the town where Mickey was born and raised. We hoped to kill a couple yardbirds with one stone.

I had always wanted to travel this road and it was all thanks to a TV show. In the fall of 1960, CBS-TV launched a weekly show called *Route 66*. It was about two young guys, played by actors Martin Milner and George Maharis, traveling around the country in a hot Chevy Corvette getting their kicks. The whole thing was filmed, literally, on the road.

Opened on November 11, 1926, U.S. Route 66 was one of the original U.S. highways. The highway started in Chicago, ran through Missouri, Kansas, Oklahoma, Texas, New Mexico, Arizona, and California, and ended in Santa Monica, covering a total of 2,448 miles. Route 66 served as a major path for those who migrated west, especially during the Dust Bowl of the 1930s.

Over the years, Route 66 had been called by many names. When it was first commissioned, it was known as "The Great Diagonal Way" because the Chicago-to-Oklahoma City stretch ran northeast to southwest. Later, it was advertised as "The Main Street of America." In 1952, the highway was unofficially designated "The Will Rogers Highway." I read all this to my aunt from the travel guide book I'd bought at the hotel lobby store.

We sat poised at the intersection of Lake Shore Drive and Jackson Drive in downtown Chicago, by the shore of Lake Michigan, which is where it all began.

"'They come into 66 from the tributary side roads, from the wagon tracks and the rutted country roads. 66 is the mother road, the road of flight,'" my aunt recited.

"What's that?" I asked.

"*The Grapes of Wrath* by Mr. John Steinbeck."

"The Mother Road. Very cool," I replied.

"Very 'cool.'"

I played a few bars of the Bobby Troup song on my harmonica, one of the few tunes I'd learned thanks to Mr. Lowney. Then the Marine Corps hymn. And, we were on our way.

We followed the signs out of Chicago, retracing our route through Cicero, Berwyn, and Joliet, the home of the first Dairy Queen. We passed the Statesville Prison. We left the city behind and entered small town America. In the town of Wilmington, we passed a giant green guy off to our right. The "Gemini Giant" was now part of the Launching Pad Drive-In. Originally, the statue had been an advertisement for a chain of muffler shops. When the shops closed down, the locals kept the statues and personalized them. With this dude, they replaced the muffler in his hands with a rocket and put a space helmet on his head. Pretty clever.

We continued west until we hit Springfield, birthplace of Abraham Lincoln and site of the state capitol. We stopped to stretch our legs and toured Lincoln's home and the capitol building. Down the road, we learned from our tour book that the Union Miners Cemetery in Mount Olive was the final resting place of Mary Harris, better known as Mother Jones, who fought for the rights of miners and children. We made a little detour out of Edwardsville to see the World's Largest Ketchup Bottle, which stood seventy feet tall with a hundred-foot base. Rumor had it that if a pregnant woman drove too close to the bottle, she would have a red-headed baby. Past Edwardsville, we crossed the Chain of Rocks Bridge, the longest bicycle and pedestrian bridge in the world. It spanned the Mississippi, which also doubled as the state line.

Around noon, we crossed into Missouri and entered St. Louis, which straddled the border. It was a travel day for the Cardinals, who just happened to be Mickey's favorite team growing up. And Stan Musial was his all-time favorite player, not Joe DiMaggio, even though that's what the Yankees' front office always wanted him to tell reporters. The Cards had just split a double-header with the Houston Colt 45s and were on their way to Pittsburgh to play the Pirates. We drove by Busch Stadium just to say we did, then stopped at Ted Drewes Frozen Custard for a little lunch.

Passing through Pacific, St. Clair, and Stanton, we made a short stop at the Antique Toy Museum, which had thousands of collectible toys. We also did a quick tour of the Jesse James Museum. The people who founded the museum claimed that Jesse didn't die in 1881 at the hands of Robert Ford, but had lived under another name until he died of old age in 1952. We moved on to explore the Meramec Caverns. It was the first cave discovered in North America and had more than twenty-six miles of underground caverns. It was also one of Jesse's hideouts.

The road from Rolla to Springfield followed the Cherokee Trail of Tears. The Cherokee Indians were forced to leave their ancestral homes in Georgia and were marched to a reservation in Oklahoma. Many of them died along the way. I just could never understand how people could do things like that to other people. I guess if you looked different, or had something someone wanted, it was somehow okay. It made me sad.

Route 66 was where the fast-food industry was born. It allowed travelers to make a quick stop and get back on the road without wasting too much time. Red's Giant Hamburg in Springfield was the site of the first drive-through restaurant. The sign was supposed to read "hamburger" instead of "hamburg," but Red didn't measure the sign right. It was too short, so he dropped the "er." We continued on and entered the Ozark Mountain Range, one of the oldest mountain ranges in North America. As we moved west, the steep hills changed into a more rolling landscape. We kept going until we hit Joplin. Beyond Joplin, we passed through the southeast corner of Kansas for a little while. We left Galena and headed west towards Riverton. We crossed the Spring River on a classic old Marsh Rainbow Arch Bridge. We motored across the border into Oklahoma and the Great American West.

CHAPTER 43

We drove through Quapaw, which had some pretty neat historical murals. The next stop was the stop. Commerce, Oklahoma, the birthplace of Mickey Mantle, the "Commerce Comet."

Once upon a time, Commerce sat right in the middle of the biggest deposit of lead and zinc in the world. The first shaft dug was called the Turkey Fat mine and it was just a few blocks from where Mickey grew up. We passed through several man-made mountains of chat, left over from the mining days. Chat was fragments of rock and limestone waste created during lead-zinc milling operations. It was pretty ugly. We hit the main street of Commerce around five o'clock.

In this part of the country, they did without and made do. Except for baseball. They loved round ball around here, as well as drinking and fighting. Baseball was an escape from the hard work and rough life. Mickey's grandfather, Charles, had played semi-pro ball and so had Mickey's dad, Elvin "Mutt" Mantle, who suited up every weekend. He was pretty good and probably could have played pro, but none of the scouts ever saw him because he competed in too many backwater towns.

Mickey's mom was named Lovell Thelma Richardson Davis. When she and Mutt met, she was divorced with a daughter and a son, which didn't happen very often back in those days. Mutt and Lovell were polar opposites. Mutt was a get-along, go-along kind of guy, but Lovell was tough, determined, and Mutt did what she told him to do. So'd everybody in the family. She was a big woman and didn't mind mixing it up, especially if it meant protecting her brood. Reminded me of a few mothers I'd known, including my mom and Mrs. Hill.

Mickey was born in Spavinaw in 1931. It was the Depression and Oklahoma was a Dust Bowl. Mickey was raised in a mining shack on 319 South Quincy Street, provided by the Eagle-Picher Zinc and Lead Company. It was a small, four-room white house with a front porch. There was no foundation. It sat right on the dirt. There was a cellar dug below ground. It was pretty cramped for such a big family. In addition to him and his parents, it housed Mickey's grandfather, Lovell's children Ted and Anna Bea Davis, Mickey's twin brothers Ray and Roy, little brother Larry, who was known as "Butch," and a sister, Barbara, who they called "Bob," for a reason known only to the family.

There was an old, sagging, corrugated metal shed that leaned close to the house. Mickey used it as a backstop when his dad and grandfather started pitching tennis balls to him, when he was around four years old. That's where he learned to be a switch-hitter. His dad would pitch right-handed and he'd bat left-handed. His grandfather would pitch lefty and Mick would turn around and bat righty. He'd blast shots over the house and Roy and Ray would chase the balls down.

Both buildings were still there as we pulled up. I got out and poked around a bit. It was all in pretty bad shape. I walked over and stood in front of the tin shed, trying to figure out where Mickey might have dug in when he was swinging the broken wooden bats his dad had whittled down to his size. I took a few imaginary cuts from both sides of a phantom home plate. I felt the hairs on my neck stand up just a little.

With the money he got for the 1951 World Series, Mickey moved his folks to a new house he bought at 317 South River Street. Mickey and Merlyn lived in Commerce until 1958, when they moved to Dallas. Mickey's father died in 1952 from cancer. Non-Hodgkin's lymphoma to be exact. Very similar to what I think my dad had. Like my dad, his disease was organic, not mechanical like a bad ticker.

We drove out to the ballpark in Baxter Springs, where Mickey had played for the Baxter Springs Whiz Kids. That's where he'd met Tom Greenwade, a scout for the New York Yankees. The rest was baseball history.

Mickey's mother had never remarried after Mutt passed. And had never left. She was still living in the last house Mickey had purchased for her. Religion and education weren't all that important to Mickey's parents. And they weren't ones to express, or show, their feelings. That was pretty obvious as soon as I laid eyes on Mrs. Mantle. She glared at me through the screen door. I had just finished telling her my story, about how I thought since my dad was dying of cancer, too, maybe she could help me out. She stared at me like I was some kind of Yankee carpetbagger down from the north to steal everything that wasn't nailed down.

"I don't see much of Mighty Mouse," she drawled. "That's my nickname for my son," she said to my confused face.

"Maybe the next time he calls…" I suggested.

"We'll have more important things to talk about," she cut me off.

"Well, anything you can do…"

"I'll do, son," she said, ending the conversation.

"I don't suppose his wife's in town now?" I asked.

"No, and don't go bothering her none, neither. She's got enough to worry about raising those four grandsons of mine."

"Could you at least give him this," and I held up a small envelope, which contained a copy of the original letter I had sent Mickey, plus the shorter note I had tried to get to him in Anaheim.

"What's that?"

"A short letter."

She opened the screen just wide enough for me to slide the envelope through, which she took with the tips of her thumb and forefinger like it was contaminated.

"Well, thanks," I said, grateful.

"Have a safe trip, y'all," and she closed the door.

Turns out Merlyn – Mrs. Mantle – had just passed through a week or so earlier and had gone back to New Jersey. Another strikeout for me.

My encounter with Mickey's mom made me think of my family. We weren't a particularly affectionate bunch, either. We didn't hug like some of my friends' families did. We didn't kiss like other families did. We didn't touch like people we knew touched. We poked, prodded, and punched, all in good fun. It was just something we didn't do. I'm not sure why. I guess it started with my parents. I know my dad's family wasn't big huggers or kissers, although Aunt Cat became one thanks to Uncle Jim. My mom's side of the family shook a lot of hands. When we encountered a relative, or friend, who liked to lay on hands and lips, we didn't know what to do, except cringe a little and make sure we avoided them the next time.

CHAPTER 44

We spent the night in a small motor inn in Commerce. We had a quick breakfast at a local diner and pulled back out onto the road at dawn on Monday.

We passed through Miami, pronounced "my-am-uh" in honor of the Indian tribe of the same name, where Mickey took Merlyn Louise Johnson on their first date to the Coleman Theater. They would later marry and raise four boys. South of town, we drove along the Sidewalk Highway, which was only nine feet wide. It was fun deciding which car would go first each time a vehicle approached. It was kind of like medieval jousting. We finally made it through the gauntlet. Past Foyil, we took a side trip to see the Totem Pole Park, which included the world's largest totem pole, a ninety-foot monster made of brightly-colored concrete. A little farther down the road was Claremore, the hometown of Will Rogers. We stopped and toured his home and the museum.

We cruised through Tulsa, the oil capital of the world, and drove on to Chandler then Stroud, where we passed the Rock Café, which was built from rocks left over when Route 66 was built. In Arcadia, we saw a huge Round Barn. Next stop was Oklahoma City. We took a quick tour of the National Cowboy Hall of Fame and Western Heritage Center. Moving west, it was nothing but green fields and blue skies. The American Prairie. We crossed the Pony Bridge over the Canadian River. In Hydro, we saw Lucille's, a gas stop and restaurant that looked like it had been born where it stood. The main street of Sayre was used in the film, *The Grapes of Wrath*, which was released in 1940.

It seemed like we were in Oklahoma a long time. When I looked at the road map, it proved I was right. The longest stretch of Route 66 was located in the Sooner State. The last stop was Texola, named that because it pretty much sat right on top of the border. Then it was across the border and into the Texas panhandle.

The first town we hit was Shamrock and the Tower Station and U-Drop Inn. The sign outside said "Delicious Food Courteously Served." It must have been true because it was surrounded by cars and buses. We decided to give it a try since the hands on my old Timex watch had just clicked to one o'clock. It was tasty and well-mannered. Back out on the road and cruising through the town of Groom, we saw the American version of the leaning tower of Pisa. It was the leaning water tower, erected by the Britten U.S.A. Truck Stop. The next stop was Amarillo. We kept moving. When we got to Adrian, we knew we were half-way there. The Mid-Point Tower and signs indicated that it was 1139 miles back to Chicago and 1139 miles forward to Los Angeles.

The little town of Glenrio sat right on top of the Texas-New Mexico border. Four lanes shot right through the heart of the business district, which featured the First in Texas/Last in Texas Motel and the Longhorn Café. Travelers would always stop here when the weather got dicey. From Glenrio, we cruised to Tucumcari. I read in the guide book that the town was once said to be "two blocks wide and five miles long." It was filled with motels. In Santa Rosa, we saw the Club Café, with a really funny neon sign of a smiling fat man. We decided to grab a bite to eat because we had a choice to make. West of Santa Rosa, Route 66 split in two, one road heading to Santa Fe, the other heading to

Albuquerque. It was just past five o'clock so we figured we should sit down, have an iced tea, and talk it over.

We chose Santa Fe. We crossed beautiful, grass-covered plains and climbed to the Glorieta Pass, the highest point on the route. The first settlement we hit was Las Vegas, New Mexico, located on the edge of the eastern plains of New Mexico, at the foot of the Sangre de Cristo Mountains. Though it wasn't as well-known as other Wild West towns, such as Dodge City, Deadwood, or Tombstone, Las Vegas was believed to have been the worst of the worst of the Old West towns. It was home to, or had been visited by, all kinds of outlaws, including Doc Holliday, Big-Nose Kate, Jesse James, Billy the Kid, Robert Ford, and Wyatt Earp. Because Santa Fe had so much history and was so incredibly beautiful – and we were dog tired – we decided to stay the night.

Santa Fe was the oldest capital city in the United States, as well as the second oldest city founded by European colonists in the United States. Only St. Augustine, Florida, founded in 1565, was older. The end of the Santa Fe Trail terminated at the La Fonda Hotel in the heart of old Santa Fe. A lot of famous people had come through Santa Fe, including Billy the Kid, Kit Carson, and D.H. Lawrence. Over the years, a number of artists called Santa Fe home, including Georgia O'Keeffe. The nearby San Miguel Church was the oldest church in the U.S.

We had a zesty Mexican dinner at a little place on the Plaza and decided to work it off by walking around and doing some people watching. I noticed this young guy standing next to an old jalopy alongside a diner. He was eyeing me pretty good. He looked like a young Gene Autry. He was wearing a three-piece, Western-style business suit, blue with pencil stripes, a white shirt and bolo tie, a watch and watch chain.

"Name's Jack," he said, fidgeting. "Yes! That's right! Just Jack." I could tell he liked to talk. Like his mind was going a mile-a-minute and his mouth couldn't keep up.

A canvas duffle bag and small wooden case stood at his feet. He saw me looking. "My typewriter," he explained. "I'm a writer."

"What do you write?"

"Anything and everything. About people that interest me. And the only people who interest me are the mad ones, the ones who are mad to live, mad to talk, desirous of everything at the same time, the ones that never yearn, or say a commonplace thing but burn, burn, burn like Roman candles across the night. Wow! Man! Phew!" he said, as he wiped his face with his red handkerchief. "It's exhausting."

"Where you going?" I asked.

"Heading for Frisco. You?"

"Los Angeles, and then home."

"Ah, home."

"Where's home for you?" Aunt Cat asked.

"America. But, I was born in Lowell, Massachusetts."

"Aren't you scared to be traveling alone?" I asked.

"I'm not alone and I'm not scared. I'm just somebody else, some stranger, and my whole life is a haunted life, the life of a ghost. I'm halfway across America, at the dividing line between the East of my youth and the West of my future."

"What are looking for?" I asked.

"The pearl," he said. "The pearl of great price."

He was too weird for me, so we moved along. Back to our motel and a nice, soft bed.

We awoke to the most incredibly blue sky I had ever seen. It was no wonder that artists and photographers loved this place. The light was fantastic. We filled up the car with gas, ourselves with flapjacks, our bottles with water, and hit the road around seven a.m. on Tuesday.

We wound through the small towns of Algodones, Bernalillo, and Alameda before rejoining the other branch of 66 headed toward Albuquerque. We didn't get to experience it, but I read that a trip down Central Avenue in that city at night was a trip back through time, with all the neon lights glowing, blinking, and throbbing. There were also some great places to stay, including the De Anza Motel, the Royal Motor Inn, the Town Lodge Motel, and the Aztec Motel, all built in the 1930s. We stopped to stretch our legs and checked out Nob Hill and the Lobo Theater.

We made a long run through Indian country. Just another couple miles brought us to the Villa de Cubero. This old stopover had a tourist court, café, and trading post. The tourist court was so popular that Ernest Hemingway stayed there when he was writing *The Old Man and the Sea*, and Lucy supposedly stayed there when she left Desi Arnez in 1960 because her TV co-star, Vivian Vance, lived nearby.

We continued our journey through some wide spots in the road called Milan, Bluewater, Prewitt, and Thoreau before reaching the Continental Divide, which was the backbone of the North American continent. If you didn't know what that meant, it meant that rainwater that fell on the west side of the Divide flowed to the Pacific Ocean, while rainwater that fell on the east flowed to the Atlantic via the Gulf of Mexico. There were all kinds of trading posts up there to serve the motorist, including the Great Divide Trading Company, the Continental Trading Post, and the Top O' The World Hotel and Café.

Our next stop was Gallup, one of the oldest towns in the U.S. In the nearby Canyon de Chelly, there were a lot of Indian ruins. We decided to take a short break to take a quick look. Back out on 66, we passed the Eagle Café, which was the oldest restaurant on New Mexico's portion of Route 66, and the El Rancho Hotel. Built by the brother of movie mogul, D.W. Griffith, the hotel quickly became the temporary home for many Hollywood stars when Gallup became sort of a Hollywood of the Southwest. All the rooms were named after Hollywood celebrities.

We crossed the border into Northern Arizona and the Navajo Nation, the largest reservation in the U.S. Our next stop was the Petrified Forest, where we saw millions of trees that had turned to stone. According to local Indian legend, when a goddess tried to light a fire using the logs, they were too wet, which made her mad and, in her anger, she turned them into stone. There was a better scientific explanation, but I liked the local version. Traveling in, through, and back out the park, we were able to experience the Painted Desert. It was pretty incredible. The colors just kept shifting as our perspective changed.

In Holbrook, we stopped to take a closer look at the Wigwam Village Motel. All the rooms looked like these big old Indian wigwams. In Joseph City, we pulled into the Jackrabbit Trading Post, which had a billboard announcing, "Here It Is!" Aunt Cat took a photo of me sitting on the back of a giant composition jackrabbit. Our next stop was Winslow, which was the headquarters of the Santa Fe Railway. We saw the famous La Posada, which was the last of the Harvey House hotels. We decided to check it out and get a little lunch since it was noon already. We took a quick walk around because we were both getting tired of "Eco," the nickname I'd given the Econoline. We probably should have called it "O-no," because it was smelling a little. We asked a local if they wouldn't mind taking a picture of us. He positioned us standing on a corner in downtown Winslow.

Six miles south of Meteor City, which wasn't really a city but a trading post, was the Meteor Crater. It was created approximately 50,000 years ago when a meteorite 150 feet across, weighing 300,000 tons, traveling at 40,000 miles an hour collided with the Earth. It created a crater about 4,000 feet wide and 570 feet deep. The air blast killed everything for miles around. The desert to and from the crater was filled with the debris of civilization, including rusted-out cars and old appliances riddled with bullet holes.

Back on the road, the land changed from grasslands to scrub juniper pretty quickly. We passed the old Twin Arrows Trading Post, where someone had disguised a couple of old leaning telephone poles by adding red plywood feathers and an arrow tip and painting the shaft a bright yellow. Two Guns had a gas station, a few places to stay, a café, a souvenir shop, and a zoo, which included mountain lions, panthers, and bobcats.

As we motored through Flagstaff, I couldn't believe the number of motels and mom-and-pop cafés, including Miz Zip's, which lined the main street. The town of Williams was the jumping-off point if you wanted to go to the Grand Canyon. We did, but we didn't have time. We needed to be – and were ready to be – back in California. We zoomed past the entrance to Dinosaur Caverns, which was marked by replicas of dinosaurs. It was all new, the caverns having just opened back in May.

It was a long run to Kingman and into the Black Mountains for the climb up Sitgreaves Pass. We drove by Cool Springs Camp and kept climbing. It was a wild ride thanks to the narrow road and hairpin turns. The scenery was spectacular, as we motored past Ed's Camp and the Kactus Kafé. Downhill, we passed through Oatman, where Clark Gable and Carole Lombard honeymooned after getting married in Kingman. We continued south through some dry desert lands. We followed along the Colorado River to the bridge that would take us back home into California. I was ready. The Trails Arch Bridge carried us over the Colorado River and dropped us down into the Golden State.

Around four o'clock, we hit Needles, home of the old El Garces, which was a Santa Fe Southern Railway depot and hotel. Then there was desert. Miles and miles of it. Although we were ready to be home, it had been a long day and Aunt Cat, who had driven the whole way, except for the few times she let me try, was bone-tired. I was a long way from having my permit, but my dad had let me drive a few times when we'd been out in the country, so we both felt I could handle driving a few miles so she could rest her eyes. Me and Aunt Cat figured we'd get up before the sun did and make the final push to the coast. That way, we could see the ocean in the daylight and say our final goodbyes. We had dinner at a small, greasy spoon, found a clean, inexpensive motel, and hit the rack.

We were up at cock's crow, filled up, grabbed some coffee and donuts, and headed out. We roared through Amboy and then Bagdad, with its little café. Someone was funning us when they named the next couple of towns Klondike and Siberia. In Daggett, we saw the Stone Hotel, which had hosted visitors like Tom Mix, Death Valley Scotty, and John Muir. The next town was Barstow and the vintage El Rancho Motel. Most of the towns we travelled through were created thanks to mining, or the Santa Fe Railroad, as it worked its way west. We crossed a bridge spanning the Mojave River and entered Victorville.

The Cajon Pass separated the San Gabriel Mountains from the San Bernardino Mountains. Once upon a time, it was the only way to get through the mountains to California. It was here that many of the overland trails – Mojave, Mormon, and Spanish – all converged, following an old path blazed by Indians, trappers, explorers, and scouts. At the top of the pass, we blew by the Summit Inn and crossed the Pacific Crest Trail, a rugged hiking trail that ran from the Mexican to the Canadian border. The pass then opened up to reveal the Inland Empire, a valley of almost 300 miles.

We stopped in San Bernadino around 10:30 that morning, so we could have a burger at the very first McDonald's. We still didn't have a McMuck's in Modesto, but we had a lot of other drive-ins, like Burge's, Al's and Felix's. The first Spanish mission was also built in San Bernadino. There was a sister Wigwam Village Motel in Rialto, a suburb of San Bernadino. There were originally seven of these villages, with the first one having been built in Horse Cave, Kentucky. We continued on through miles of orange groves, passing juice stands shaped like giant oranges, and many other small towns before entering Pasadena. We drove over the beautiful Colorado Street Bridge, not far from the Rose Bowl. We motored through Los Angeles and finally reached the end of the road at the intersection of Lincoln and Olympic Boulevards in Santa Monica. We parked, walked out to the end of the pier, and spit in the ocean. It was 11:00 a.m. Pacific Standard Time, Wednesday, August 8.

We hopped back into "Eco" and headed for Union Station in downtown Los Angeles. A short while later, Aunt Cat gave me a big old hug and sloppy kiss, put me on my train, and headed back to the van and home. The train ran me up to Bakersfield where Gary and his dad picked me up and took me home. As the old saying goes, there was no place like home.

CHAPTER 45

And I had been right. When I finally got home, it was my mom's turn to make the calls.

"This nonsense ends right now," she said, stamping her foot.

And that was that. At least that's what I thought. Of course, that didn't mean I didn't continue to hope for a letter or phone call or something. I followed the standings and read the paper every day like a slumping hitter desperate for his next hit, hoping that my aunt would be proven right and my dad's team and my team would finish the season on top.

I had promised Kelly before I left for Chicago that I'd take her to the Stanislaus County Fair if I got back in time. She loved the fair, partly because she had participated as a 4-Her when she was younger, exhibiting her pet bunny rabbits, but, mainly, because she loved her hometown and county. So did I. Plus, it was always fun to see the exhibits, ride the rides, eat fair food, try to win something at the carnival, enjoy the live performances, and just watch the people.

The fair had started on Monday, August 6, while Aunt Cat and I were walking the streets of Santa Fe. It would run for six days until August 11. I got off the train from Los Angeles to Bakersfield on Thursday afternoon. Gary and Mr. Rawlings picked me up and drove me the rest of the way home. We arrived Thursday night, which meant I still had Friday and Saturday to do the fair. I talked it over with my folks, who were a little disappointed I didn't want to spend time with them, so I could tell them the whole story of my big adventure. I explained that we could catch up over the weekend and that I really wanted to see Kelly. They understood and I called her right away. We decided to go on Friday, since there was a dance just for kids that night. Kent Whitt and the Downbeats, a popular local band, would be playing.Our parents dropped us off at noon on Friday at the main gate of the fairgrounds, located in neighboring Turlock. As soon as both cars were gone, I kissed her, grabbed her hand, and headed for the ticket booth. I paid for two tickets and we pushed through the turnstiles. It was going to be a beautiful day. The weather was cooler than normal. Only eighty-five degrees compared to the normal, sun-burning one hundred plus.

It was always hard to decide how to approach these kinds of events. I liked to do it logically and symmetrically because I was that kind of organized guy. Kelly was more of a pinball person, kind of bouncing from place to place and then circling back to whatever she skipped. If she missed something, it was no big deal. If I missed something, my well-ordered world was threatened. We started out my way and ended up her way.

There was something about symmetry that satisfied me. It could be straight lines that were exactly parallel, books on bookshelves lined up by height and thickness, buildings that were balanced, clothes that matched, or a baseball diamond. Any time I saw these kinds of perfectly-shaped, man-made, or natural objects, I knew that all was right with the world.

Preferring balance, being organized, and trying to control things was not a good recipe for contentment, because things never went as planned. If they didn't go as planned, I got anxious and then I got mad. My mother reminded me constantly to relax and not set myself up for failure and disappointment by expecting things to go a certain way, preferably my way. I understood what she was saying, but didn't believe it. I was convinced that with enough careful planning and solid organization and a little luck, I could orchestrate the world, or at least my world, to get it to do as I wanted it to do. I convinced myself it did, but very often it didn't.

To the left of the fair's main gate was the Arts and Crafts building, to the right was the Floriculture Building. We decided to start with arts and crafts. We walked through samples of needlework, cooking, and artwork that included oils, water colors, pen and ink. Outside was an event called "Artists in Action," which had local artists painting on the lawn in front of the building. We passed by a water colorist putting finishing touches on a valley landscape, then crossed over to the Floriculture Building, and toured the collection of fresh-cut flowers and feature gardens inside. It was nice and cool, dark and green, with a variety of water fountains and fragrant plants. It reminded me of a tropical grotto I had seen on TV, or in *National Geographic.* In another group of exhibit halls, we saw a wide variety of household gadgets, farm aids, and scientific products, as well as wood and metal projects done by local high school students. There were eight community booths scattered around the fair that were put together by the county Granges, showcasing the best of each part of the county.

We headed down the long avenue of food booths and bought a big lemonade and corn dogs. A corn dog was one of my favorite foods. I ate one every time I went to the fair, or the Boardwalk in Santa Cruz. I drenched mine in mustard. Kelly spritzed a little ketchup on hers. They were crunchy, greasy, and delicious.

We walked past the new outdoor stage, where they had live performances. This year's acts included the Wheeler Marimba Trio, clown act Tackle and Little Tic, and the juggling Carlssons. We continued on toward the livestock barns. We stopped for a moment to check out the rabbits and chickens and other small animals. Kelly looked kind of sad that she still wasn't exhibiting.

I squeezed her hand, she rubbed the fur of one of the bunnies through its cage, and we moved on.

There were more than 1,000 head of beef and dairy cattle, sheep, and hogs. Kids and their parents were busy with curry combs, brushes, soap and water, putting the final touches on their animals before they entered the show ring. Some of the kids had cots and sleeping bags so they could sleep next to their animals. The girls were giggling and checking their livestock, while the boys were smirking and checking the girls.

Then it was off to the carnival. I had decided I was going to do whatever it took to win Kelly a Yogi Bear stuffed animal at the milk can toss. She loved Yogi Bear and Boo Boo, the Hanna-Barbera TV cartoon bears. I was hoping my good right arm would be strong enough to knock down all three of the leaded milk cans. Everyone knew the games were rigged, but that didn't stop us from trying.

As we turned the corner of the Tilt-a-Whirl ride and headed for the milk can booth, I saw something I really didn't want to see. It was the Eights, with Teddy in the lead. I stopped in my tracks.

"What is it?" Kelly asked.

"Teddy and the seven little hoods."

"Just ignore them."

"I plan to," I replied, as I did a one-eighty to head in the opposite direction.

Just then, Teddy turned to look in our direction. He saw us and started walking after us, his posse in tow.

I hustled to the ticket booth of the Ferris wheel, bought two tickets, and we got in line. We were the last ones on. Once we were settled in and the safety bar was latched across our laps, the wheel started to ascend. We went up and up. As we crested and descended, I looked for the boys. I didn't see them and relaxed. I took Kelly's hand and held it tightly. She squeezed back and I put my arm around her. We went around again and again and... suddenly, the ride was over. At least, I thought it was because we had stopped. At the very top. It was pretty high up. We stared out across the parking lots, residential neighborhoods, and dry farmlands that surrounded the fairgrounds. I looked at Kelly. She was amazing. I kissed her. It felt great. In my head, I heard the song "Palisades Park" by Freddy "Boom Boom" Cannon playing back again. He was right. Nothing could feel as great as kissing a girl at the top of the Ferris wheel. We kissed again. It was like there was nobody else in the world at that moment but us.

Until I heard a buzz of angry voices and some shouts and cussing. Kelly and I disengaged and looked over the edge of the bucket. A bunch of carnies, and a slightly cleaner looking guy who must have been their boss, were standing around the machinery that ran the wheel. Something wasn't right. One of the carnies was yanking on what looked like a long bar of steel, like a crowbar. What it was wasn't budging. Out of the corner of my eye, I saw some movement. I swiveled my eyes to where the distraction was and saw Teddy and the seven other punks waving at me. Teddy pointed at the bar, pointed at himself, and started laughing. I realized he had jammed the works of the wheel, so I would be stuck at the top of the Ferris wheel. I was wondering what happened to the operator who had let us on and was supposed to be in charge. I saw him walking away in the distance counting some money. He folded the wad in half, kissed it, tucked it into his pocket, and disappeared behind the camp of trailers the carnies stayed in during the fair. I looked back at Teddy. He was holding his wallet up. He thought it was all so funny, but the joke was on him. I smiled, pointed at Kelly, pointed at me, pointed at my butt, pointed at him, turned my back on all of them, and kissed my girlfriend. While we were kissing, I stuck my left hand over my head and flipped him the bird. It was a good night, especially after I won Yogi.

While I was tracking the Yankees and Giants, I was also following stories about the 1962 Little League World Series, which took place between August 21 and August 25 in Williamsport, Pennsylvania. Moreland Little League of San Jose, California, defeated Jaycee Little League of Kankakec, Illinois, 3-0 in the championship game of the 16th series. San Jose had beaten Vienne, France, and Monterrey, Nuevo León, Mexico, to reach the championship game. Kankakee had beaten Stoney Creek, Ontario, Canada, and Pitman, New Jersey.

Big Ted Campbell, a six-foot, one-inch 210 pounder, pitched a no-hitter. Campbell, who was the largest twelve-year-old to ever appear in the playoff, gave up just one walk and fanned eleven. The Kankakee batters only got one ball out of the infield. I'm sure some of the parents were ready to look at his birth certificate. In the consolation game, Pitman, New Jersey, defeated Monterrey, Mexico. According to the paper, about 20,000 fans jammed the scaled down park and surrounding hillsides for the six-inning climax of the week-long, eight-team series. Jackie Robinson and Ted Williams were both on hand to work with the stars of tomorrow. It was the second consecutive victory for a California team. El Cajon had won the title last year. Kankaee had been in the series three times so far without winning a title.

Because it wasn't a big event and didn't have a lot of sponsors, the game wasn't usually on TV. This year, the entire game was re-broadcast the next day, which was a Sunday, on WPIX, an independent TV station owned by the Tribune Company in New York, which also owned the New York *Daily News*. The game was recorded in black-and-white on two-inch videotape, which was pretty new, and the station did what was called a "tape-delayed" re-broadcast. KOVR Channel 13 re-broadcast it on *Wide World of Sports* that same Sunday at five o'clock.

Carl Stotz had founded Little League Baseball in 1939. He lived in Williamsport, where he began working on the idea of an organized baseball league for children that would teach fair play and teamwork. He worked with his nephews and some neighborhood kids to figure out the best field layout and game rules. He launched the league the following summer. That first league only had three teams, each sponsored by a different local business, which included Jumbo Pretzel, Lycoming Dairy, and Lundy Lumber. The first League game took place on June 6, 1939. Lundy Lumber defeated Lycoming Dairy, 23-8. The following year a second league was formed. And the league grew from there.

In 1962, President Kennedy issued a proclamation naming the second week in June as "National Little League Baseball Week," echoing a similar proclamation made three years earlier by his predecessor, Dwight D. Eisenhower. Two of Kennedy's staff, including Secretary of State Dean Rusk and press secretary Pierre Salinger, had been involved with their local Little League programs.

In Modesto, our Little League organization was called Modesto Baseball for Boys. It wasn't part of the national group. It was founded by the Modesto Optimist Club in 1956, fielding six teams. In 1962, it had grown to sixty-four, divided into A, B, and PeeWee Divisions. Frank Russo was the man in charge, with a little help from Gil Prouty, who worked at Weeks, one of our local sporting goods stores. The Little Leaguers would start practicing as soon as the weather got good enough in April. We'd have practice games in May and early June. We played a six-week league with two games a week right after school got out near the middle of June. A round robin elimination tournament was then held near the last week in July to see who would play for the championship in the middle of August. An awards banquet would be held at the end of the season at Modesto High School. Every year, we would have a competition to see who could sell the most raffle tickets to help raise funds to support the league. Whoever sold the most would get a brand new glove. Near the end of the season, we would have a hot dog feed at Belle Nita

Park and then go watch the Modesto Reds and, sometimes, an Old-Timer Game.

I played Little League as soon as I was old enough, starting with PeeWee. Our "B" team won thirteen and lost one. Our "A" team won the championship in 1960, beating Enslen 5-2, on a cool Sunday night at Del Webb field. I played again the next year, but we didn't repeat as champions. We were competitive and had a lot of fun.

On the Sunday after Kelly and I went to the fair, Gary, Roy, and I had gone to the Little League championship game at Del Webb. For old times' sake, I guess, and to relive our glory of two years ago. There were a lot of people there, mostly family and friends of the teams that were playing.

In the championship game the night before, the Beard PeeWee 2 team had beaten the Garrison PeeWee 1 team 14-10 and the James Marshall B1 team had beaten the Beard B2 team 16-3.

Before the start of the "A" championship game, all the players for each participating team in the league were announced and certificates and trophies were handed out. The round robin tournament that led to the championship nights had started about a month earlier. In the "A" game, Bret Harte beat Our Lady of Fatima 11-10. A kid named Lonny Croslow hit a grand slam that was the big blow for the winners. It was a pretty good contest, but all three of us decided our championship game had been better.

CHAPTER 46

You know how people say that when you're around someone all the time, they never really change. It's only when you've been gone for a long while and haven't seen them, and then you see them again, that you notice how much they have changed. Well, when I got back home, my dad looked really different. Not in a good way. From then on, I was around him every day and I could still tell he was changing. He was getting thinner. He had a weird color in his face. He was always tired. He was always sick. My mom kept saying he was getting better, but I didn't believe it. He was getting worse. I didn't know what I was going to do. Time was running out. Every time my mom turned over the little hourglass she used to time how long to cook the hard-boiled eggs, I thought about my dad.

My aunt was an optimist. So was Gary. To a point. They both truly believed my dad would get better and they both really believed that it would all work out. But, they were having doubts, too.

Gary's sister, Carol, had a good friend who lived out in the country, surrounded by orchards her family farmed. More importantly, she had a built-in swimming pool. That's where Gary and I were headed. Not many of the kids in our neighborhood had pools. So, when it was really hot, we'd go to Playland, or we'd swim in the canals. We kids would usually swim at Nunes

Drop by Enslen Park. Even when my parents wanted to cool off, we'd head for the canals out past McHenry, or one of the lakes, Modesto or Turlock. I remember one big canal that had a sandy bottom. One time when I was a little kid, my dad put me on his shoulders and threatened to dive in. I was scared to death. He never did it. I should have just trusted him.

I once heard someone say that the two things that helped shape modern California were irrigated agriculture and the freeway. Our canals were part of the Modesto Irrigation District and carried water from rivers and reservoirs in the mountains to the valley farmers, which is what made Modesto and the rest of the Central Valley the most productive agricultural area in the world. Most cities in California had irrigation canals. We grew up with them, swam in them, fished in them, and threw stuff in them. We figured everybody had canals.

Gary's dad worked for MID, whose motto was: "Where the Land Owns the Water and Power." His livelihood depended on flowing water. It was his job to make sure the La Grange dam continued to feed the canals that channeled life-giving water to the farmlands of Stanislaus County. It was irrigation that turned the sky farmers of the county into year-round farmers. They transformed the Valley into a sea of wheat, the staff of life.

I remembered Gary's dad picking us up one day after we had finished mowing Gary's grandmother's lawn. We drove under the Iron Rainbow that spanned I Street. Spelled out in metal and light bulbs were the words: "Water, Wealth, Contentment, Health." That was the motto of our city, although it originally lost to "Modesto, nobody gets our goat," when citizens were asked to come up with some slogan suggestions in 1911. The arch was completed in 1912 to promote the city by the Modesto Business Men's Association, which later became the Chamber of Commerce. The original slogan was intended to read "water wealth" as one phrase meaning an abundance of water and then "contentment" and "health," implying one led to the other. Somehow that connection got lost in translation.

As we cruised, we sipped on our soft drinks while Gary Sr. pulled on a sixteen-ounce Burgermeister beer that he tucked into a small paper bag that looked like it had been designed just to disguise sixteen-ounce beers. Gary Sr. sang gospel songs, while Zeke, Gary's loco Airedale, howled in harmony in the bed of the truck. We pulled off the road, drawn by a collection of city police and sheriff county cruisers parked along the edge of a canal. We got out and walked up to the edge of the canal and looked over the steeped dirt banks. A young girl, about twelve, floated in the canal. Surrounded by water hyacinths, her amber hair was spread around her like Ophelia in her suicide dress. She was snagged in the grate that caught all the flotsam and jetsam that people tossed into the canal. Staring at her billowing hair, I thought of a field of wheat. And how dangerous canals could be.

I couldn't shake that image that hot afternoon as Gary and I zoomed our bikes over the bridge of a canal on our way out to his sister's friend's house. As we pedaled past the peach and walnut trees, I thought about a poem I had read in junior high. It was written by William Everson, who was born in Sacramento and raised in Selma near Fresno. He would later become one of the Beat poets in San Francisco in the mid-1950s.

This valley after the storms can be beautiful beyond the
telling,
Though our cityfolk scorn it, cursing heat in the summer
and drabness in winter,
And flee it: Yosemite and the sea.
They seek splendor; who would touch them must stun them;
The nerve that is dying needs thunder to rouse it.

I in the vineyard, in green-time and dead-time, come to
it dearly,
And take nature neither freaked nor amazing,
But the secret shining, the soft indeterminate wonder.
I watch it morning and noon, the unutterable sundowns,
And love as the leaf does the bough.

Everson was a valley refugee. He loved this valley. In all its kaleidoscopic glory. The familiar sight of the sun low on the flat horizon. The soft sound of rustling grapevines. The cool touch of flowing rivers. The sweet taste of a fresh peach. The memory-etching smell of irrigated soil. That beauty surrounded us and filled our senses as we raced for the cool swimming pool.

It was a strange feeling. It would come over me from time to time, completely out of the blue. A feeling like I'd been here before, done this before. It was almost always triggered by one of my senses – a smell, a sound, a sight, a taste, a touch. I was feeling it right now as Gary and I rode through the orchards. It was the smell of wet earth. It made me think of summer. I'd have the same sensation when I smelled a gardenia, heard the song "White Christmas," saw a swallowtail butterfly, ate a tuna sandwich, or ran barefoot through the park grass. It was weird. It made me wonder if there was something beneath the five senses – a world hidden from what we thought was real.

"Maybe I should just get on a train or a bus and go out to New York," I said, as we pedaled our bikes home side-by-side, bleary-eyed from the chlorine and pleasantly exhausted from the swim.

"Do you have that kind of time?" Gary replied.

That got my attention.

"I don't know," I said.

"You know your mom won't let it happen again. She'll be watching you like a dog watches a bone or a rooster watches the sunrise or – "

"I get it," I said. Gary was a poet at heart.

"And she'll call the police on you faster than old Walter Alston steals signs."

"I know."

"Even if you had the time, it's not cheap. Where would you get the money?"

"I've got some saved up."

"Not that much."

"Maybe Kelly could help me out. Her mom works part-time as a travel agent."

"Still can't afford it."

"Then I'll steal it," I yelled.

"Now you're being stupid. How would that make your dad feel? You get caught and go to jail. Why would you do that to him?"

"I'm at the end of my rope."

"Look, something will happen."

"That's what Aunt Cat said."

"I agree. Heck, maybe the Giants will win the pennant."

"She said that, too."

"And, if the Yankees win, too, they'll play in San Francisco. That's not that far away. You could almost ride your bike there," he smiled, veered in close, and punched me on the arm.

"Sure, something'll happen. I hope."

"That's the spirit," he said. Then he took off. "Last one home is Sandy Koufax's butt."

And I raced after him. He called me "Sandy" the rest of the day.

The Yankees had a mediocre August. They lost a few more than they won. They started the month 63-39 and finished it with a 79-57 record. They ended the month beating the Kansas City Athletics and were in first by three games.

The Giants tore up August. They started the month at 67-40 and ended with an 85-49 record. They closed out the month by shellacking Cincinnati and were trailing the Dodgers by only two-and-a-half games.

CHAPTER 47

Summer vacation was over. Fall was in the air. Everyone was getting back to their normal routine, including the news makers, the news reporters, and the news readers. September was a busy month in Modesto, America, and the World. Stan Musial got his 3,516th hit, which moved him past Tris Speaker into second place on the all-time National League list. Timothy Leary founded the International Foundation for Internal Freedom. The Beatles cut "Love Me Do" and "P.S. I Love You" at EMI Studios in London with producer George Martin. Governor Ross Barnett refused to admit James Meredith, a Negro student, to the University of Mississippi and President John Kennedy responded by authorizing the use of federal troops to integrate the university. Bob Dylan played Carnegie Hall. ABC television debuted its first color TV series, The Jetsons, from animation studio Hanna-Barbera Productions. Sonny Liston knocked out Floyd Patterson in round one to win the world heavyweight title at Comiskey Park in Chicago. Dodger Maury Wills became the first player to steal one hundred bases in a season. The Beverly Hillbillies premiered on CBS. "Green Onions" by Booker T. and the M.G.'s peaked at number three. The Roy Rogers and Dale Evans Show debuted on ABC. The Mets lost a record 120th game, as the Chicago Cubs turned a triple play and beat the New Yorkers 5-1.

With five children in the clan, my parents didn't always have the money to do the things a lot of my friends' families did, like the California State Fair. So, our friends and their parents would take up the slack. In this case, Gary's folks came through, as they almost always did, and invited me to join them to experience the annual showcase of our great, golden state.

The first California State Fair was held on October 4, 1854, in San Francisco, as part of the young state's attempts to promote California as a great place for farming and industry. Most of the fair was held just off Market Street at the Musical Hall on Bush Street near Montgomery. The livestock show was held at Mission Dolores, which was the heart of the Mission District in the city. Because it was difficult for people from around the state to get to San Francisco, the organizers decided to have different cities host the event each year in those early days. In 1855, it was hosted by Sacramento, then San Jose, then Stockton, and then Marysville in 1858. The fair returned to Sacramento in 1859 and 1860. In 1861, Sacramento was selected as the permanent home. As the fair became more popular, it outgrew its location in Capitol Park at Fifteenth and N Streets. The State Agricultural Society, which had been formed by legislators to initiate and oversee the exposition, sold the Capitol Park land and purchased property southeast of the city limits at the intersection of Broadway and Stockton Boulevard. The first fair was held there in 1909 and it has remained there ever since.

On fair day, the Rawlings family would hop in their Ford Fairlane and head for Sacramento, with me and Gary playing goofy travel games in the back, like the license plate game, where we'd try to spot the most cars from different states, or twenty questions, where we'd pick something to be – animal, vegetable, or mineral – and the other person would have to guess what it was in twenty questions or less, assuming we didn't lie about what we were. We'd also sing, since that's what Gary's dad did every time he got behind the wheel. This trip we got "Big Bad John" by Jimmy Dean stuck in our heads, as well as "Roses Are Red (My Love)" by Bobby Vinton.

The California State Fairgrounds covered a lot of territory, about 200 acres. It felt like it went on forever, especially on those asphalt-melting, 110-degree days, which we sometimes got in late August or early September when the fair was running. This year, we went the day the fair opened on Wednesday, August 29, which was Kid's Day, so we boys got in for free, along with what seemed like a million other brats.

Mr. Rawlings was a man of habit. When it came to the fair, he religiously followed the same routine each and every year. I knew because I'd gone with them more than once and Gary's mom always asked why we had to do it the same way every year and Mr. Rawlings would always reply, "Because it's tradition."

"It's a reason," she'd reply, "not a very good one, but a reason."

It was one of those routines every husband and wife and family had and repeated, year-in and year-out. The "Mr. Rawlings State Fair Routine" was to pass through the south entrance on Fifth Street and walk past the Governor's Hall, which was a big brick building on the left, and head up the broad, tree-lined avenue that ran through the middle of the fairgrounds, until we reached the outdoor theatre just north of the race track. Mr. Rawlings would buy a beer for himself, a lemonade for Mrs. Rawlings, a Coke for Gary and me, and a hot dog for each of us. We'd load up the dogs with mustard, onions, relish, and sauerkraut. We'd find a shady place to sit and enjoy this summer treat.

As we ate, Mr. and Mrs. Rawlings decided to get caught up on the latest news on the home front.

"How's the family?" Mrs. Rawlings asked.

"Good," I replied.

"Your mom?" she asked.

"Kind of tired. Doing okay, considering."

"How is your dad?" Mr. Rawlings asked.

"He doesn't joke around as much as he used to."

"He'll be fine," Mrs. Rawlings said.

"It'll all work out, Michael, it'll all work out," Mr. Rawlings added.

"How are the girls?" Mrs. Rawlings asked.

"Good. Getting bigger."

"They do that," Mr. Rawlings said.

"And the boys?" Mrs. Rawlings continued.

"Tim is good. He thinks he's in love."

"Oh, really, with who?"

"Laura, Vito's sister, you know, who lives around the corner from you guys."

"Sure, I know her. She's sweet."

"For a girl," Gary snickered.

"How about Willie?"

"Liking music a lot these days."

"Which you quit," Gary said.

"Really?" Mrs. Rawlings asked.

"No music for me this fall."

"You shouldn't have done that," Gary said. "The pep band needs all the players it can get."

"I know, but it was too much. I figured with just starting high school and all the schoolwork and sports and my dad and Kelly…"

"Mikey has a girlfriend," Gary teased, punching me playfully in the arm.

"Good for you," Mr. Rawlings chimed in.

"…so, it was just too much," I continued.

"Must have been a tough decision knowing how much you and your family love music. Almost as much as this man here," Mrs. Rawlings said, as she leaned against her husband.

"Yes, it was. I just didn't want to disappoint anyone."

"Yeah, like me," Gary chimed in.

It was my turn to punch him. And I did.

"You know, Michael," Mrs. Rawlings continued, "Maybe you try to control things too much? Maybe you should just pay attention to what's going on right here, right now, in the moment?"

"I know. I always want things to go my way. It's kind of selfish, I guess."

"It's more than being selfish, Michael. It's more about going along with things instead of swimming upstream, or trying to push that rock uphill."

"My wife has been listening to too many of those beatniks on TV and the radio. It's giving her some wild ideas," Mr. Rawlings said.

I nodded and ate the last bite of hot dog.

Once we were done and "had a full tank," as Mr. Rawlings commented, as he did every year, we retraced our steps, hitting each of the exhibition buildings that lined the avenue. Our first stop was the Hall of Flowers, which had been transported from the 1939 World's Fair at Treasure Island. It always provided a nice break from the heat because it was kept cool inside to protect the fresh-cut flowers. Thanks to a perpetual watery mist, it always felt humid inside and smelled similar to what I imagined some tropical place like Hawaii or Tahiti would smell.

Next in line was the Counties Building, another brick building, which showcased exhibits from every one of California's fifty-eight counties, arrayed on two floors. Each year, each county would pick a theme that reflected what was unique about them, usually having to do with a business or product (usually agricultural), or a physical landmark. Sonoma had apples, Placer, Amador, and Sierra had mining, Yolo had rice, Los Angeles had movies, and Monterey had seafood, while Stanislaus had wine, chickens, and wheat. Kind of boring, but it was still our county.

Then there was the Industrial Building, which allowed all kinds of companies to show off their products, new and old, all of which were guaranteed to make your life easier and better, faster and simpler. There were always vendors who offered samples of food and drinks, or cooked different kinds of meals with their amazing cookware, which we were encouraged to try. Many of the pitchmen wore a bulky microphone wrapped around their neck, so their hands would be free to sauté and fricassee. There were cleaning products, clothes, kitchen gadgets, artwork, political parties, and government officials, all trying to tell their story. Inside the hall, it was elbow-to-elbow and cheek-to-jowl, like worker bees inside a honeycomb.

When we'd had our fill of new gadgets and old information, we'd get back on the avenue until we reached Governor's Hall again, and head east. We'd pass the race track, which was a big oval set at an angle pointing northwest. It offered harness or quarter-horse racing for people who liked to watch horses run and people who liked to bet on running horses. We'd pass through the livestock barns, with its collection of dairy and beef cattle, sheep and swine, just like the county fair, only bigger. The same animals, the same 4-Hers and their families, the same ribbons, and the same smell and noise. Coming from a community filled with farms and dairies, it didn't bother me like I'm sure it did someone from San Francisco or Los Angeles or San Diego.

We'd stop to re-fuel at the Chuck Wagon restaurant, with its menu of cowboy chow like BBQ ribs, ranch beans, and cole slaw. Gary and I would gobble our food down as fast as humanly possible because we were ready for the next and last stop, which was always the carnival. We had brought our own money, but Mrs. Rawlings always gave us each an additional five dollars to blow on challenging games of chance and skill, thrilling rides, as well as mind-boggling, strange, and exotic exhibits. We rode the Hammer, the Tilt-a-Whirl, and the Sky Wheel. We played games like the Derby, which used pinball machines to simulate a horse race; the faster you could shoot your ball into the chutes, the faster your horse would run. If you won, you'd get a tiny plastic or metal horse. Each additional win would deliver a bigger horse. The top prize was a huge silver or bronze-plated horse with a clock in its belly. I always wanted to win that, so I'd spend most of my money on the ponies. In addition to the games, we peeked at the two-headed cow, the Siamese twins, the bearded lady, the monkey boy, and the sword swallower, although it was kind of creepy and gave me goose bumps.

Gary and me had a routine, too. First, we'd have Mr. Rawlings snap a photo (this year a Polaroid) of us sitting together on one of the four golden bears, as well as one of each of us on our own bear. The bears were located in front of the Counties Building. Whenever people planned to meet, or any time they got lost, they'd always say, "Meet me at the golden bears." Next, we'd slip into one of the photo booths scattered around the carnival so we could get four photos taken for a dollar. We'd compete to see who could do the silliest pose. Gary almost always won. Unfortunately, the photos came out a little dark this year, so we both looked like we were Sabu of India. They made us giggle. The first time we took our photo at the fair, we both wore the same buttoned-down, short and puffy-sleeved, back-to-school shirts. We both had butch haircuts with the front row of hair sticking straight up, thanks to Butch Wax. We thought we were pretty cool.

Each night, in an area next to the carnival, they'd put on dance concerts for the teenagers. They brought in popular bands like Dick Dale and the Del-tones, as well as local bands. They were always packed with kids doing the Twist, the Mashed Potato, and the Hully Gully. A day at the fair always ended at nine o'clock with a really boss fireworks show, shot out above the lake in the center of the race track. I never got tired of the fair.

CHAPTER 48

Modesto was growing, thanks to all us kids born after the war, and growing so fast they needed another high school. Grace M. Davis was the third. The school was supposed to open in Fall 1960 with its first freshman class, but construction problems delayed its opening until January 1961. Until then, a "school-within-a-school" was set up for 319 Davis students at Downey High. They had their own teachers and football team and elected their own class officers, while occupying rooms at Downey. When the Davis campus was finally ready, although still not complete, the entire class moved. A sophomore class was added in Fall 1961 and my class of freshmen in 1962. No seniors. The school still wasn't done when we started on Tuesday, September 11.

That same night, the California League playoffs began, with the Reno Silver Sox visiting the San Jose Bees. San Jose had won the first half, Reno the second. The Bees won it all in seven.

My first few months as a freshman were a blur. Dimpled concrete walls, Spanish, assemblies, home room in the gym, student body card, parallel bar dips and long distance runs, Harley's Records, game week butcher paper posters, Starlite Drive-In, "Mashed Potato Time," FFA, the Purple Onion, pleated skirts, punks, English, new kids and old friends, hoods, tiny bows in bouffant hairdos, Weeks Sport Shop, geeks, pom-poms, teachers' skinny ties, jocks, progress reports, Hi-Y and Tri-Y, cheerleaders, yell leaders, and song leaders, brains, KFIV, pegged pants and pointed shoes, Hob Nob Pizza, sock hops, hot cars, the school bus, Modesto Bowl, White Levi's, the Cousins, and the song "Sheila."

I remember feeling a little overwhelmed and a lot like the new kid on the block. The glory days of being the oldest kids at junior high were behind us. I felt so small. The upper class dudes seemed really huge. The upper class chicks looked like women, not girls. One girl in my Spanish class, who had a bit of a reputation, would always sit next to me and rub her well-endowed chest against my arm so I would let her cheat off my paper. I gladly obliged. I couldn't deny my hormones. She still failed.

Jennifer, Chris, Barbara, and all the sophomore and junior girls looked like Sandra Dee or Tuesday Weld. I was in love. Tight sweaters, tight skirts, bouffant hair-dos. It was mighty fine. The classes were tough, but I had good study habits, so I did all right. A lot of my friends had older brothers and sisters ahead of us and that made it a little easier. Plus, I had played sports against some of the upper classmen in Little League and in junior high, so it wasn't like I was walking into a brand new world. But, it was.

I had always been a behind-the-scenes kind of kid. I decided to mix that up a bit my freshman year, so I ran for freshman vice president. I'm not sure why, but it probably had something to do with impressing the girls. Running for class office meant launching a campaign. I did that, but it wasn't very organized or sophisticated. Gary and Roy helped me with posters and name tags. I made a few speeches, which was very painful for someone who was pathologically shy like me. I really didn't get out there and campaign. As a result, I lost to a guy named Stan Podesta. I never ran again. I disappeared backstage and never came out from behind the curtain.

It was amazing how cruel kids could be, especially if you looked different, dressed different, spoke different, or did anything different. I never understood it and I never did it. Too often, that is. It was just too cruel. I wasn't much of a joiner, so I never became part of any of the campus clubs. I had already decided to pass on band, chorus, and orchestra. I didn't do the Spanish Club, although I took Spanish. The only club I joined was the Hi-Y and that's because Gary did.

The Hi-Y was a club affiliated with the YMCA. High school boys organized the clubs with the purpose of doing things for the community and "promoting the high standards of Christian character." We named ourselves the "Vikings," so our emphasis was more on the former than the latter. The equivalent for high school girls was Tri-Y. We were the only boys' club, but there were a couple girls' clubs. We'd sell See's suckers at football games to raise money for our club. Other Hi-Ys sold fireworks.

A big fad in 1962 for guys was the black turtleneck. All the cool guys, particularly the Block "D" Lettermen, wore turtlenecks under their plaid shirts and letterman jackets. And white Levi's with pointy boots. It was kind of sharp, but I couldn't afford any of it.

One of the best parts of high school was the sock hops. I remember going into the boy's gym, taking off my shoes, stowing them in my gym locker, checking how I looked in the bathroom mirror, then stepping into the dimly lit gym ringed with basketball hoops. Walking onto the freshly-waxed hardwood, I heard the thumping sound of the bass and drums as the live band, often made up of classmates or upper classmen, played a popular instrumental. And stockinged feet doing the Twist or Mashed Potato. All the guys would be on one side of the gym, the girls on the other. Man, that was a long walk. Some of us never made it.

I had always been a good student. Like elementary school and junior high years, I was rarely sick, and never missed class. I got good grades and the teachers seemed to like me. When I got to high school, I started thinking real hard about the future. What would be next? Get a job with a local company? Get married and have a family? That was the traditional route. Join the military? A lot of guys were doing that to get out of town and maybe find a career. Go to Modesto Junior College and then on to a four-year school, or just go directly to a university? It was all pretty scary. I really wasn't ready to start thinking about it. Since none of my family had gone to college, even though my dad had wanted to, I decided it was time to knuckle down, so I could get accepted to college and maybe get some financial help, since Mom and Dad couldn't afford my tuition.

It was then that I decided to concentrate on studies over sports. I wasn't going to quit playing ball just yet, but it wouldn't be a priority anymore. I'd probably go out for the freshman team in the spring and see how it went; see how much time it would take away from my studies. I'd probably play Babe Ruth again next summer. Hopefully, Dad would be healthy enough to take over one of the teams, or help coach one. The future was about college, not baseball. It was a tough decision, but I was convinced it was the right one for me, right now.

The Yankees had a much better September. They started 80-57 and ended 96-66, a full five games ahead of the Twins. On September 11, at Detroit's Tiger Stadium, Mickey hit his 400th home run and moved into seventh place on the all-time list. Only Musial, Mantle's hero, had hit more home runs among active players. The Yankees clinched the American League pennant on September 25.

Sophomore manager Ralph Houk, who had been named Manager of the Year in 1961, had kept the Yankees in the race all the way, and in first place continuously from the first All-

Star break on. It hadn't been easy. A lot of players had been hurt, including Mantle and Cy Young winner, Whitey Ford. Shortstop Tony Kubek missed two-thirds of the season while serving in the Army. Somehow, Houk kept the team in the win column.

The Giants also kept winning in September. They improved from 85-50 to finish 101-61. The Dodgers lost ten of their final thirteen games. The Giants only lost six. With just seven games left, the Dodgers still led the league by four games. With three left, they had a two-game lead. They led by one when they faced St. Louis in the final game of the season. And lost, 1–0. The Giants beat the Houston Colt .45s 3-2, after an eighth-inning home run by Willie Mays. The two teams finished the season on September 30 in a dead heat. That meant, just as it did back in 1951, that the two teams would play a best two-out-of-three, tiebreaker playoff. During the regular season, they had split their eighteen games right down the middle. They were that evenly matched.

Houk was disappointed with the fact that there would be a National League playoff because of the effects the layoff might have on his club. "The playoff delayed the start of the World Series and could have taken away the sharpness the Yankees had at the completion of the American League race," he told *The Sporting News*. Houk pointed out that pitching, in particular, suffers from a break like that. "In any short series, there is no question that the important thing is pitching," he added. "If your pitching is bad for a week, your ball club is bad. The worst thing that can happen to a pitching staff is lack of work over an extended period."

He would have to wait and see if he was right for at least another two days, and maybe three.

With the long history they had, it was no surprise that Dodgers manager Walt Alston and Giants manager Alvin Dark couldn't agree on dates and sites for the tiebreaker. They ended up flipping a coin to decide home field advantage. Alston won the flip. He decided to play the first game in San Francisco and the remaining games in Los Angeles.

The 1962 pennant chase and the long-standing Dodger-Giant rivalry had been celebrated that year in a song by entertainer Danny Kaye, a good friend of Leo Durocher's, who was then a coach for the Dodgers. A resident of Los Angeles and a big follower of the game, with an almost encyclopedic knowledge of America's pastime, Kaye was a big fan of the Brooklyn then Los Angeles Dodgers, and sometimes travelled with the team. He wrote, recorded, and released a song about an imagined game against the Giants. He had some fun with the Northern and Southern California baseball siblings in "D-O-D-G-E-R-S SONG (Oh, Really? No, O'Malley)" and twisted tongues with the Hiller Miller Haller Hallelujah Twist.

My two little sisters loved that song. They memorized it and would perform it without a mistake at the drop of a hat. The song was a perfect reflection of the crazy end to this wild season.

CHAPTER 49

There was nothing like Friday night football, sitting in the stands on a fall night, while two sets of helmeted, padded, and cleated gladiators did battle for school pride. It was an opportunity to check out the cheerleaders, as well the rest of the girls at our school and the opposing school. It was a chance to show our school spirit and root for the home team. And try to stay out of fights. There were always hoods from our school and the rival school that were ready to pick on smaller kids and maybe each other, if they'd gotten enough liquid courage. Never a dull moment.

Kids, like schools of swarming fish, came together and separated in the autumn sunset, giggle-talking to one another, checking their hair and make-up while looking for the other, trying to find that special missing person and hoping they were looking for you, with waving banners of school spirit and wide-mouthed, laughing faces overwhelmed by everything drowned out by the uniformed pep band and short-skirted yell leaders under bright, white lights begging you to watch the game on the field instead of the game in the bleachers, but knowing they were a side-show not the main attraction as the announcer described the action and named names and the fans on the opposite side were a faint memory of hot dogs and See's suckers, cotton candy and cool evenings threatening rain, but you were packed so tight on hard, splintery, wooden benches that you were warm enough and hoped you wouldn't have to pee in a crowded bathroom before half-time when the drum major strutted onto the grassy field followed by a phalanx of uniforms, playing fight songs and Souza marches until the muddy combatants returned following a locker room pep talk, fired up and leaving it all on the dead brown field until the Zebra's gun sounded victory or defeat and everyone streamed away to their next rendezvous to do it all over again.

Even though we didn't have all four classes yet, we still had a homecoming game. Of sorts. For that big game, our Hi-Y club decided to team up with the freshman Tri-Y to build a float. For our theme, we picked the Trojan horse. I'm not sure why. Maybe we wanted to see if we could slip a veiled reference to rubbers past school administrators. Or, maybe we had just studied the Trojan War in freshman world history, so we knew it had something to do with Sparta and we were the Davis Spartans, after all. We spent a lot of days and nights fabricating a chicken-wire horse and then decorating it with white, green, and yellow Kleenex to resemble a horse. One of the girls in the Tri-Y had a little black-and-white Nash Metropolitan that we set the frame on and would serve as the heart of the horse. Since we were still too young to drive, her father was behind the wheel. The rest of us would wear togas and follow the horse, throwing flowers. We built it at one of the Tri-Y girl's friend's home, a ranch in Ripon. We were also going to parade our creation through downtown Modesto the next day.

The night of the game, Kelly couldn't stop laughing when she saw me in my white-sheet toga over cut-off Levi's, a green T-shirt, tennis shoes, and a laurel wreath.

"You're going to get cold," she said.

"I'll be fine. It's not that cold."

"We'll see."

"Will I see you after half-time?"

"I'll be right over there," she said, pointing to the visitor's side of the stadium. "At the very top on the fifty-yard-line." She kissed my cheek and sent me warm into the lion's den.

We were playing Kelly's school, Modesto High. Modesto High was the first high school in town. Over the years, as the town had grown and moved north, South Modesto – the part of town where the high school was located – got poorer and rougher. And segregated. All the black families lived in the old neighborhoods and tiny houses surrounding the school. All the really rough guys went to Modesto, including the Monarchs.

The MJC stadium felt like the Coliseum. As we paraded along the track in front of the home team bleachers, you could've sworn we were in ancient Rome. The crowd erupted in laughter, catcalls, hoots, and all styles of thumbs-down signs. And, they were on our side. They started throwing wads of gum, balls of paper, chunks of hard candy, even the See's suckers we had sold before half-time. We kept smiling and waving and urged the driver to drive a little faster. We navigated the gauntlet pretty much untouched.

Once we got the float safely out of harm's way and had changed into street clothes, I back-tracked, with Gary shadowing me, and found Kelly in enemy territory.

"Tough crowd," she said. "You're lucky they didn't let the lions out."

"Or the tigers," I replied.

She introduced her friends, I introduced Gary. He was almost as shy as I was, so it was a short conversation.

On the field, the lions had been let out. Because we didn't have any seniors, Modesto was beating us pretty badly. It wouldn't have mattered. I watched what was going on in the stands more than I watched was happening on the field. And, I watched Kelly watching.

Kelly and I left before the game ended. We wanted to get to the pizza place before the crowd did. I was in such a hurry to get her alone that I didn't even see Teddy, who was sitting with some slutty chick the next section over.

After the game, we always went to Hob Nob. It was a place and it was what we did. Hob Nob Pizza was a tiny pizza joint on McHenry Avenue near an irrigation canal. We'd go with our buddies or, if we were lucky, our girlfriends of the moment. It was always so packed you could hardly move. Sardines in a can. Forget trying to order a pizza. You had to submarine your way through the crowd and past two accordion doors to get to the counter to order and then hope you could hear when they called out your name to pick up your pizza.

The pizza wasn't great, but it was good enough on a cold, foggy Friday night. The cheese was always so darned hot it burned the roof of your mouth. But, it was the place to bc. If the Davis High Spartans had won the night, everyone was in a good mood. If we had lost, there was usually a fight. Especially if someone from a rival high school showed up. Hob Nob was our pizza place. We had pissed in the parking lot to mark it.

Kelly and I pushed through the fogged-window backdoor and into the press of flesh that had already gathered. We found an empty spot at one of the heavily-lacquered picnic tables near the misty windows that opened out on McHenry Avenue. We held hands and watched the room fill up. There wasn't any place else I wanted to be right then.

Ah, Friday night lights and fights. Football and pizza, young love and hormones. Confusing and exciting, gut-wrenching and heart-burning, comforting and reassuring. Some things mix better than others. Wouldn't it be nice to be that much in love again? And all the time.

There was always a fall day, usually in late September or early October, when you knew summer was over. The tenor of the light, the timbre of the air. Everything looked and smelled differently. Somehow thinner and a little more damp. The days were still warm, but the mornings were chilly. The sun was no longer a summer sun. Or a vacation sun. I knew it meant winter was just around the corner, short days just around the bend. I never liked being cold and wet. But, that's what the valley in winter was all about. Bare trees and gray skies. Although the end of summer meant football, Halloween, Thanksgiving, Christmas, and New Year's, I was never quite ready to see it go. It was about that time of the year that my brothers and I would trade in our ball caps and mitts for football helmets and pads. Yankees, Giants, and Dodgers for Colts, Niners, and Rams.

It was also grape harvest time in the valley. You could smell the grapes fermenting all the way from the Gallo Winery over by Dry Creek. Last fall, I had earned a little money cutting grapes at my friend Vito's small family vineyard in Salida. They were Italian, so they kept some of the grapes they'd grown to make their own wine and sold the rest to one of the local wineries, like Delicato, Pirrone, or Gallo. It was hard work. We were in the fields early to beat the heat of the Indian Summer. The ground was soft and sandy, which made walking very tough. The vines were usually wet from the morning dew or irrigation. There were flies, bugs, and spiders. The plastic tubs were back-breaking, once they were filled. I used a cutting knife with a short, curved blade and wooden handle. It was sharp. One morning, I cut the inside of one of my left fingers and nearly passed out before I could get the bleeding to stop. The work wasn't fun, but the money was good.

It was in these same fields that Vito, me, and Tim went hunting rabbits. Vito's grandfather wanted us to kill as many as we could because they were always nibbling on the plants or eating the new vines. Tim and I weren't big hunters, but we liked the idea of shooting a shotgun, even though our dad discouraged it.

I had never killed anything before. The morning of the shoot, I was given a twelve-gauge shotgun, some shells, and a few words of caution. Mainly to set the safety and know where everyone was. I started off down a row of vines. The sun was high and I was sweating. When the rabbit hopped into my row and stopped, I was as shocked to see him as he was to see me. I put the gun to my shoulder, aimed, flicked off the safety, and fired. When the blue haze and thunder cleared, I saw the rabbit lying there, twitching. Heart thumping, I raced to where it lay. I nudged it with my tennis shoe. It was dead. That was the last time I ever shot a living thing.

I was thinking of that day on the last Saturday in September when Kelly poked me in the ribs.

"You with us?" she asked.

"Yes, sorry," I answered.

She handed me the cutting knife. I took it very carefully, the finger on my left hand throbbing from the painful memory.

"Why don't you start on this row?" She pointed at an end row of vines.

I had agreed to help her and her family harvest their grapes and now I was holding the knife and remembering the cut.

"Be careful, it's kind of sharp," she cautioned.

"I know," I replied and trudged off toward the end of the row.

I wanted to show off, I guess. I cut as quickly as I could without losing a finger. By the time I got to the end of my row, I was grimy and sweat-stained. I took off my Giants cap, wiped my forehead with a blue Levi's handkerchief, and stared into the October sun.

"Pretty hot for October," a man's voice said behind me.

Startled, I jumped and swung around.

A round man, about fifty years old, stood next to a line of oak trees bordering the vineyard. He wore a broad-brimmed, sweat-stained straw hat, denim work shirt, and blue jeans. He was carrying a short-handled hoe I'd seen a lot of the local farmers and Mexican farm workers use to weed the vineyards.

"Yes, sir, pretty hot," I replied.

"Thank God for these trees."

"The shade helps."

"See that one over there," he pointed at a massive tree in the center of the vineyard.

"Yes, sir."

"I planted that myself. A long time ago."

"How old is it?"

"Pretty old."

"It's very impressive."

"It loves this valley almost as much as me."

"What kind is it? I don't know much about trees, except climbing them."

"It's a valley oak. They're native."

"It looks really old."

"I respect anything older than me," he chuckled. "I hope I live as long as it does."

"You live here?"

"My family and my brother all do. That's his house over there." He pointed and I saw a bit of a roof through the oleander bushes and palm trees. "I'm the next one over," he said as he pointed to a second roofline very near the first.

"You always lived here?" I asked.

"Born and raised."

"Me, too."

"A native. Not many of us around."

"You work here?" I asked.

"You could say that," he replied.

"You look like you've cut your hands almost as many times as me."

He opened his hand and looked at it. Every crease and crack was filled with valley silt. "I'm becoming the land," he said. As if his hand wasn't dirty enough, he reached down, grabbed a fistful of dirt, lifted it up to the sun, and let it cascade to the earth. "Richest soil on the planet. This valley was made by God for growing things. I love being outdoors and working the land."

"Seems like a lot of stuff grows around here."

"Take care of it and it will take care of you."

"The grapes taste pretty good."

"I'm glad you like them. They make an even better wine."

"I'm too young to drink."

"A little wine doesn't hurt anybody. Even somebody as young as you. My children have been drinking wine almost since the day they were born. In moderation. Everything in moderation."

"Maybe someday I'll give it a try."

"You do that," he said and walked off toward the overshadowing oak.

Kelly walked up and offered me a jug of ice cold water. I drained it. Water dribbled along my cheeks.

"Don't choke on it," she said.

I finished, handed the jug back, and wiped my lips with the back of my arm. "Who was that old farmer," I asked.

"Old farmer?" she chuckled. "You didn't recognize him?"

"Nope."

"You ever heard of the Gallo Winery?"

"Sure. We sell their stuff in the store."

"Well, that was Julio Gallo. The winemaker. He and his brother, Ernest, own the winery."

"All of it?"

"All of it."

"No kidding?"

"No kidding."

"Julio makes it. Ernest sells it. They make quite a team."

CHAPTER 50

October, my birthday month, was a busy one. Johnny Carson replaced Jack Paar as the regular host of NBC's Tonight Show with guests Joan Crawford, Rudy Vallee, Tony Bennett, Mel Brooks, and the Phoenix Singers. The Lucy Show premiered on CBS. Stop the World – I Want to Get Off opened at the Shubert Theatre in New York City. Wally Schirra was launched into earth orbit on Sigma 7. Dr. No, the first James Bond film starring Sean Connery and Ursula Andress, was released in Britain. Houston Oiler quarterback George Blanda threw six touchdown passes against the New York Titans in an American Football League game. President Kennedy addressed the nation about imposing a blockade when American U-2 planes discovered missile launchers in Cuba. Novelist John Steinbeck was awarded the Nobel Prize in Literature. Bobby "Boris" Pickett had a hit when "Monster Mash" reached number one on Halloween.

My mother got a real kick out of decorating for Halloween. As soon as the calendar ticked over to October 1, she was busy putting up jack-o-lanterns, ghosts, goblins, skeletons, black cats, and vampires. My dad used to fabricate a life-sized dummy that he placed in an old chair on our front porch. One year, we ran a speaker out to it that was hooked up to an audiotape recorder and microphone hidden in the house. As soon as some unsuspecting kids came up to knock on the door, one of us would yell into the microphone and scare the bejesus out of them. Another year, I dressed up in the very same outfit and sat in the very same chair, only to slowly rise as the neighborhood kids showed up. It was mean, but it was a hoot.

I trick-or-treated every year until 1962. Mom and Dad figured being a freshman made me too old. So, this year I figured I'd hang out with some of my old friends and new high school buddies to see what kind of good, clean fun we could get into, most of which had to do with egging the houses of guys we didn't like and TP-ing the houses of girls we did like. Maybe smashing a few pumpkins and tossing some firecrackers. All good, only-in-America, All Hallow's Eve hi-jinks.

Trick-or-treating became one of those things I used to do, like a walk in the park – things that I couldn't do now. Things like believing in Santa Claus, the Easter Bunny, and the Tooth Fairy; sleeping in late on Saturday; not having to work or do homework; not thinking about girls; not having chores to think about; not having to make school lunches for everyone; not worrying about making the team, any team; not taking the garbage out or feeding the dog or mowing the lawn; being able to run barefoot and play tag all summer long; staying up all night eating ice cream and watching scary movies. I'm sure there would be many more. I wondered how many of those things my parents wished they still could do.

The National League playoffs started on Monday, October 1. Game time was one o'clock. We were in school, but we snuck a radio in with us and listened when we could – in class, in the hallways, and out in the gray, concrete activity court. Students in every room sprouted ear buds snaking into their collar, down their shirt sleeve, and into a transistor. George Kell called the game for NBC-TV alongside Bob Wolff, the former broadcaster for the Washington Senators and then the Minnesota Twins when they moved to the Twin Cities in 1961, as well as the play-by-play man on NBC's *Baseball Game-of-the-Week* in 1962.

Gary and Roy bought their lunch at the cafeteria window. I had my sack lunch. We walked out to the edge of the disked-up tomato field beyond the Quonset huts, which served as temporary classrooms. We were sitting huddled over the transistor when Teddy sauntered up. Chewing on a dry weed, he had that smug look on his face I really hated. The "I'm-better-than-you-'cause-I'm-rich-and-you-got-nothin'" look.

"This town sucks," he muttered. "Flat, dusty, too hot or too cold, not enough to do, and too many okies."

"Love it or leave it," Gary said.

"I wish. They made my old man chief of surgery at City Hospital. We ain't goin' nowhere."

"The way I see it," I said, "you've got a couple choices. You can make it better, leave, or shut up."

"You ducks will never leave," he replied.

Teddy sucked on the weed, thinking and eyeing us. "They can't win, you know," he said.

"Who?" I asked.

"The Giants."

"Why's that?"

"Too many black and Mexican players."

"They're not Mexicans. They're from the Dominican Republic and Puerto Rico," Gary pointed out.

"Same diff."

"You're ignorant," Roy said.

"The Dodgers are a great team," Teddy went on. "Got a lot of great, white players. Too bad Koufax is a Jew."

"Jackie Robinson was a Negro."

"Old news."

"How about Maury Wills or Junior Gilliam or the Davis boys? They're all Negroes."

"You're not gonna win. Period."

"We'll see," I said.

Teddy squashed one of the many rotten, unharvested tomatoes still littering the flat, dry field. "A little birdie told me you wrote a letter to Mickey Mantle about your old man. Maybe I'll write Mickey and tell him my pops or moms is dying. I bet he gets back to me, especially since my dad's not a loser like somebody I know."

I tried to stand, but Gary put his arm around my shoulder and held me back.

"Hit the road, Jack," Roy hissed.

"I also heard that old bum that hangs out at the park looking at the little girls' underwear died up in Chicago."

"You heard wrong," I flared. "He's alive. Just changed. That's all."

"What's the deal?" Teddy asked. "Why do you care about that old geezer? He doesn't give a fig about you."

"You'll never get it."

"Get what?"

"That people can get along and even like each other. And help each other. And take care of each other without expecting anything in return."

"And that adults and parents can like their kids," Gary chimed in.

It took Teddy a minute, but he finally got it.

"How's your old man, anyway?" Teddy asked me. "My pops says he's not doing so well."

"He's fine. And it's none of your business."

"Sure it is. One less piece of white trash for me to take out with the rest of the garbage."

I jumped to my feet before Gary or Roy could grab and stop me.

"He'll be fine. Got it? He'll be fine," I yelled, clenching and un-clenching my fists.

Teddy took a step back and glanced around, looking for teachers. He caught the eye of Coach Laun, who was watching us as his noon gym class ran the track. Teddy looked back at me and smirked. "Be careful. You don't want to make a trip to the office. Might spoil your perfect record."

As I drew my arm back, Gary grabbed it and yanked me away.

"Clear out, Teddy, you fat jerk," Roy said.

"Whatever you say," Teddy replied. "See you 'round." He backed away, turned, and walked slowly back toward the school.

"What a spaz," Gary said.

"Yeah," I said.

Modesto didn't have a lot of Jewish or black people. I didn't even know what a Jew was until I got to high school. I remember adults talking about "Jewing" someone down, or being a "Jew" when they talked about being cheap, or, that the Jews killed Jesus Christ. I really didn't know what it all meant. A couple of the kids I grew up with were Jewish. Some of them had names like Seideman and Grossman, which could sometimes indicate their heritage. Being Jewish and what that signified wasn't anything I thought about, and it wasn't part of my day-to-day world. I guess if I had asked any of my Jewish friends, they might have had a different opinion since Modesto was the same, and probably worse, than the rest of the world about all this.

Teddy's comments reminded me of that, as well as of the day I was walking along Old Oakdale Road with my friend, Phil, who was Jewish. Back then, that part of Modesto was mostly peach orchards, grape vineyards, and flat, open fields. The side of the two-lane blacktop was dusty and debris-strewn. We kicked up plumes of dust as we trailed Phil's grandmother and grandfather. *Babushka* and *Dedushka*, as he called them, which was Russian for grandmother and grandfather, looked as if they'd just gotten off the boat from Kiev. Swaddled in dark, heavy, woolen clothes and thick shoes, she wearing a kerchief and he a peaked cap, they waddled along, heads down so as not to attract attention, which could be lethal for Jews where they came from.

Every so often, as they moved alongside the peach orchard, *Dedushka* would stop, stoop down, pick up a ripe peach, and tuck it into the voluminous pocket of his overcoat. He did this several times before we reached Scenic Drive, which was our route back into town and home.

"Why does he do that?" I asked. "That's kind of icky."

"The peaches are good," Phil replied.

"Is he hungry?"

"Not now."

"So, what's the point?"

"It's an old habit and a hard one to break. In the old country, he never knew where his next meal was coming from. This kind of bounty was enjoyed only by the wealthy. There was no food just lying around on the ground. Especially something as exotic as a peach. For him, America really is the land of milk and honey. You and me, we take a lot of things for granted. Not him."

I ran into the orchard, picked a particularly luscious peach, yanked it off the branch, caught up with *Dedushka*, and presented him with the golden fruit. The old man looked up and his eyes crinkled in a smile. He took the peach, wrapped it in his clean, white handkerchief, and tucked it carefully in the inside pocket of his coat. That kind of poverty was something I didn't understand. And didn't have to.

All the Negroes in town lived in South Modesto, or South Mo, on the other side of the tracks. We didn't have any black students in any of my schools when I was a kid, including high school. The only time I would see any black families was when I went shopping, or we played James Marshall in Little League or Mark Twain in seventh and eighth grade basketball or Modesto

High in football. I remember there were some great black athletes at Modesto. They always beat us. They had stars named Ard and Jenkins and Green. I finally got to play baseball with a couple of them when I played Babe Ruth for Blakeley's.

CHAPTER 51

National League Playoff Series

Game One – Monday, October 1, 1962 – 1:00 p.m. PST at Candlestick Park

In Game One, the Giants, behind left-hander Billy Pierce, who had been 12-0 at Candlestick Park during the season, shut out the Dodgers and Sandy Koufax 8-0. Mays went three for three, stealing a bag, and slugging two home runs, one off Koufax.

Koufax had missed two months of the season due to arm problems. In the three games he started just before the playoff series, he lost all three and only pitched seven and two-thirds innings. The night before the first game of the tiebreaker, manager Alston asked Koufax to start the game because Don Drysdale and Johnny Podres had pitched the last two games. Koufax agreed.

The Giants scored first when Felipe Alou doubled in the bottom of the first and Willie Mays followed with a home run, making it 2-0. Pierce set the Dodgers down in order for the second inning in a row. In the bottom of the second, Jimmie Davenport led off with a homer. When Ed Bailey followed with a single, Alston replaced Koufax with Ed Roebuck.

Roebuck got three straight batters out to end the inning. The Dodgers and the Giants each got one hit in the third. Neither Pierce nor Roebuck allowed a base runner in the fourth or fifth innings. The Giants added a run in the sixth. Ken McMullen pinch-hit for Roebuck in the top of the seventh. He got on with a single, but didn't score. Larry Sherry went out to pitch for Roebuck in the bottom half. He got the first out, but then gave up back-to-back homers to Mays and Orlando Cepeda to give the Giants a 5–0 lead. Davenport then singled and Sherry was relieved by Jack Smith, who got out of the inning without any more runs scored.

In the eighth, Doug Camili pinch-hit for Smith and got on, but couldn't score. Phil Ortega replaced Smith on the mound to face the Giants in the bottom of the eighth. Mays walked and stole second. Davenport and Bailey both walked to load the bases. José Pagán emptied the bases with a double, boosting the score to 8–0. Pierce closed out the ninth and earned a complete game shutout.

Game Two – Tuesday, October 2 – 1:00 p.m. PST at Dodger Stadium

Before the start of Game Two, the San Francisco Chronicle reported that manager Walter Alston had decided not to start pitching ace, Don Drysdale. Big Don was not happy with Alston's decision.

"What the hell," Drysdale snapped. "Are they saving me for the first spring intrasquad game?"

"I could take a chance and pitch Drysdale with two days' rest," Alston was quoted as replying. "Drysdale wants to pitch, and that's a good sign, but he would be going with only two days' rest for the third time lately." Drysdale had already pitched eight games in September. Drysdale prevailed and started the second game.

Once again, the Giants scored first when Orlando Cepeda came home with one out on a double by Felipe Alou. The Giants' Jack Sanford battled Drysdale, keeping the Dodgers scoreless through the first five innings. In the top of the sixth, Tom Haller walked and moved to third on a double by José Pagán. Haller scored and Pagán moved to third when Drysdale made a throwing error to first, which allowed Sanford to reach base. Chuck Hiller and Jimmie Davenport hit back-to-back singles, which scored Pagán and Sanford. The score was now 4–0. Ed Roebuck relieved Drysdale. The Dodgers forced Davenport at second on a grounder by Willie Mays. With runners at the corners and two outs, Willie McCovey singled, scoring Hiller before Cepeda made the final out.

Sanford walked Jim "Junior" Gilliam to start the bottom of the sixth. Giants manager Alvin Dark did a double-switch, bringing in Stu Miller to relieve Sanford and replacing McCovey in left field with Matty Alou. Dark later said he took out his pitcher, even though he was doing well, because "Sanford was suffering from a cold and he was pooped." Gilliam moved to third on a Duke Snider double. Tommy Davis then hit a sac fly to score Gilliam and advance Snider to third. It was now 5–1. It had been thirty-five innings since the Dodgers had scored last. Wally Moon walked and Frank Howard singled to score Snider. Dark brought in lefty Billy O'Dell to relieve Miller. Doug Camilli pinch-hit for catcher John Roseboro, singling to load the bases. Andy Carey then pinch-hit for Willie Davis. He was hit by a pitch, which forced in Moon. Lee Walls pinch-hit for reliever Roebuck and Larry Burright went in to run for Carey. Walls hit a double, clearing the bases, and giving the Dodgers a 6–5 lead. Walls made it to third on the throw. That hit made Walls thirteen-for-twenty-six with twelve RBIs for the season as a pinch-hitter.

Don Larsen relieved O'Dell, who had not gotten an out and blew the save opportunity. Maury Wills hit a ground ball to Cepeda, who threw home to get Walls. Walls slid hard into catcher Haller, knocking the ball loose. The slide cut Haller's arm deep enough to later require six stitches. The Dodgers led 7–5. John Orsino replaced the injured Haller. Wills then stole second. It was his 101st stolen base of the season. Orsino's throw got past second and into center field. Wills took off for third, but Mays gunned him down. Larsen got Gilliam to fly out to end the inning. In the sixth inning alone, the two teams had combined to score eleven runs, as well as use six pitchers, three pinch-hitters, two defensive substitutions, and a pinch-runner.

Ron Perranoski came in to pitch the top of the seventh, Camili stayed in to catch, and Ron Fairly took over at first base for Moon. Burright went in at second, Gilliam moved from second to third, and Tommy Davis moved from third to center field. Perranoski got Felipe Alou to ground out before giving up consecutive singles to Orsino and Pagán. Harvey Kuenn pinch-hit for Matty Alou and hit a grounder to Wills at short, which forced Pagán at second and moved Orsino to third. Bob Nieman pinch-hit for Hiller and flew out to center. In the top of the eighth, Davenport and Mays singled off Perranoski. Jack Smith relieved Perranoski and gave up a single to Ed Bailey, who was pinch-hitting for pitcher Larsen, driving in Davenport to cut the Dodgers' lead to 7–6. Mays tried for third, but Tommy Davis threw him out. Mays, Dark, and third base coach Whitey Lockman argued with third base umpire Jocko Conlan, who made a safe call before changing it to out. Carl Boles went in to run for Bailey. Cepeda reached on an error when Howard misplayed his fly ball, which allowed Boles to advance to third. Stan Williams relieved Smith and walked Felipe Alou to load the bases. Orsino hit a sacrifice fly, which scored Boles and tied the game 7-7, before Pagán grounded out to Gilliam at third to end the inning.

In the bottom of the eighth, Bobby Bolin relieved Larsen. Bolin kept the Dodgers from scoring, as did Williams in the top of ninth, by retiring the Giants' ninth, first, and second batters in order. Wills walked to lead off the bottom of the ninth. Dick LeMay went in for Bolin, and walked Gilliam, moving Wills to second. Daryl Spencer pinch-hit for Snider and the Giants brought in Gaylord Perry to relieve LeMay. Spencer bunted, moving Gilliam and Wills up a base. Later, some commentators thought Perry had a play on Wills at third, but Perry decided to throw to first instead. Mike McCormick relieved Perry and intentionally walked Tommy Davis. Ron Fairly then lined out to Mays in center, which drove in Wills with the game winner. Final score: Dodgers 8, Giants 7. Game Two lasted four hours and eighteen minutes, which broke the existing record of four hours and two minutes, for the longest nine-inning game in major league history. It was also Maury Wills' thirtieth birthday.

After Game Two, the *Chronicle* reported from Los Angeles: "'I have,' said portly Alfred Hitchcock, sitting erect and dignified at a table with his wife, 'the utmost confidence in the ultimate defeat of the Giants – the good guys always win in our fair city.'"

Game Three – Wednesday, October 3 – 1:00 p.m. PST at Dodger Stadium

Game Three pitted two aces against each other – Juan Marichal and Johnny Podres. Manager Alston had thought about starting reliever Larry Sherry, but went with one of the guys that had gotten them there. The game was scoreless through two. In the top of the third, José Pagán led off with a line-drive single to left. Marichal bunted and Podres threw the ball into the outfield trying to get Pagán at second. Harvey Kuenn's single scored Pagán and moved Marichal to second. John Roseboro made a throwing error trying to pick off Marichal, allowing him to move to third. Chuck Hiller lofted a fly to shallow left, forcing Marichal to hold. Left fielder Duke Snider threw home, but the ball was cut-off by Tommy Davis at third, who then threw to second, hoping to catch Kuenn, who tried to tag up, in a rundown between first and second. Gilliam's throw to first hit Kuenn in the back, which allowed Marichal to score and Kuenn to get back to first. It was now 2–0. Felipe Alou singled to center, Kuenn went to third, and Alou moved to second on Willie Davis's attempt to get Kuenn at third. Podres intentionally walked Willie Mays to load the bases with one out. Orlando Cepeda then hit into a double play to end the wild inning.

In the fourth, Snider led off with a double to right, moved to third on a Tommy Davis single to left, and scored when Jimmie Davenport forced Davis at second on a groundout by Frank Howard.

The Giants loaded the bases in the top of the sixth when Cepeda and catcher Ed Bailey singled and Davenport bunted safely. Ed Roebuck came in for Podres and retired the Giants without scoring. In the bottom of the inning, Snider singled, followed by a Tommy Davis homer, which made the score 3-2 in favor of the Dodgers. They added to their lead in their next at-bat. Maury Wills singled, stole second, then stole third, and scored when Bailey tried to throw him out. In the bottom of the eighth, Don Larsen relieved a struggling Marichal in the middle of a Tommy Davis at-bat. Larsen walked him anyway. Ron Fairly bunted Davis over to second. Davis stole third when Howard struck out. Larsen then walked Roseboro and Willie Davis to load the bases so he could pitch to Roebuck, the pitcher, who grounded to third to end the inning.

It was the Giants' turn in the ninth. Matty Alou pinch-hit for Larsen and singled to right to lead off. Kuenn forced Alou at second with a grounder to Wills at short. The Dodgers were two outs from going to the Series. Willie McCovey pinch-hit for Hiller and walked, moving Kuenn to second. Ernie Bowman went in to run for Big Mac. Felipe Alou walked to load the bases. Mays shot a line drive back at the pitcher, which Roebuck was barely able to knock down. Kuenn scored and Mays made it safely to first. Stan Williams relieved Roebuck. Cepeda hit a sac fly to deep right, scoring Bowman from third, which tied the game at 4–4. Alou advanced to third. Mays moved to second on a wild pitch to left-hand-hitting Bailey. Williams intentionally walked Bailey to reload the bases. Davenport worked a walk to give the Giants a 5–4 lead. Left-handed starter Ron Perranoski replaced Williams. Pagán reached on an error by Larry Burright, who had replaced Gilliam at second, that allowed Mays to score and extended the Giants lead to 6–4. Bob Nieman struck out to end the inning. The Dodgers still had a chance in their home half of the ninth inning. Lefty Billy Pierce replaced Larsen and set the Dodgers down in order, earning his only save of the season. And it was over.

When Mays caught Lee Walls's ball for the final out, Mays started dancing, threw the ball toward the right field stands, and everyone just went crazy. During the post-game celebration, Mays was quoted as saying: "This is my third World Series. I feel real good about the young fellows. I'm getting a big kick out of it. But, look at them – they're wild. It's wonderful. You know, we've got so many fine young ball players on this club, we should be up there fighting for the pennant for a long time. Me? Well, I hope to play for seven or eight years."

When asked about the ninth inning rally that beat the Dodgers, manager Alvin Dark said, "When the inning began, I wished for two things to happen. I was hoping we could get one of our first two hitters – pinch-hitter Matty Alou or Harvey Kuenn – on base so I could send Willie McCovey, our left-handed power hitter, up to hit against their pitcher, Ed Roebuck. Naturally, I was fully aware that a home run by McCovey in a spot like this would tie the score. My other wish was to somehow get the tying run to third base with Willie Mays at bat. Who else would any manager rather have up there? Fortunately, I got both wishes." McCovey, AKA Big Mac, added: "This is the greatest moment of my life."

The *San Francisco Chronicle* reported that, in the clubhouse, José Pagán was intrigued by the appearance of ex-Vice President Richard Nixon. After Nixon recited the life history of Billy Pierce to the press, including Billy's near-perfect game in 1957 against Washington, José muscled in and extended his hand. For the first time, Nixon fumbled. "Er … I beg your pardon, but I don't recognize you without your working clothes," said Nixon. "Who are you?"

"I am José Pagán. I am happy you are here."

Nixon was doing a little barnstorming, glad-handing, and baby-kissing because he was running for governor against Pat Brown. The election was in November and there were candidates popping up everywhere.

With the 6-4 win, the Giants claimed their first National League title and World Series spot since moving to San Francisco in 1958. They were also the first NL Champions of the 162-game schedule era. It was only fitting that they had beaten their old "borough mates" from Brooklyn to get there.

Because tiebreakers were considered regular season games, all statistics counted in the season totals. That meant Mays added to his league-leading home run total of forty-nine and Maury Wills raised his record-breaking stolen base total from 100 to 104, the most since 1900.

The World Series would start the next day – Thursday, October 4, at one o'clock at Candlestick Park in San Francisco. The day before my birthday. What a great birthday present. Now, I just had to figure out how to get there and get to Mickey.

CHAPTER 52

The weather was changing. The Season of the Witch was fast approaching. The sweet smell of maple trees turning filled the air, a smell I always associated with King Harvest. It was time to rake leaves, which I didn't mind because I loved seeing the pile of leaves in the street and the smell of leaves and fires burning. There was even a threat of rain. On the evening news, the local weather forecasters were talking about a tropical storm that was forming out in the Pacific near Wake Island. They called it Typhoon Freda. Cool weather or not, I was headed for Pike's before it got too dark to play catch with my brother Tim. Little brother Willy decided to hang with us. It was time to re-enact the Giants/Dodgers playoff games since Tim, somehow, had decided he was a Dodger fan. Willy was black and orange through-and-through just like me, although it was probably more Gary's influence than mine.

As we three approached the sand box, I saw a familiar, hunched figure sitting in his usual spot on the bench. It was Mr. Lowney. I ran around in front of him to make sure he wasn't a mirage. It was him all right.

"Mr. Lowney, when did you get back?" I asked, breathless from the sprint.

"In time to see the Giants beat the Dodgers," he said. "That was one for the ages."

Just then, Tim piled into me and Willy into him. I teetered, but didn't fall.

"You look different," I said. "A lot different than the last time I saw you."

"Yes, nothing lasts forever, does it?" he replied.

Mr. Lowney told us what happened to him that dusky August night in Chicago.

"I took a front-row seat on a bench sitting on the sawdust floor. Mr. Electrico perched in an electric chair. His assistant yelled, 'Here go ten million volts of pure fire, ten million bolts of electricity into the flesh of Mr. Electrico!' The assistant pulled a lever and a voltaic charge thundered and coursed through Mr. Electrico's body. Reaching out into the audience, his eyes flaming, his white hair standing on end, sparks leaping between his grimacing teeth, he brushed an Excalibur sword over the heads of the audience, knighting them with fire. The electricity coursed from his body through the heavy sword into all of us spectators, causing our hair to stand on end. Lightning surged through me, thumping in my eardrums. The blue fire swarmed into my brain and down my arms and out my fingertips like electric fountains. I must've passed out. I woke up and everyone was gone. Except him. Mr. Electrico stood up and walked right toward me. Holding the sword, he tapped me on each shoulder, then on the brow, and finally on the tip of my nose and whispered, 'Live forever!' There was an eye-popping flash of brightly-colored, multi-faceted light, like a stained-glass window blasted by the sun. It was blinding. I closed my eyes and covered my face with my arms. When the light faded away, I uncovered my face and opened my eyes. I looked at my hands. They were the hands of a twenty-one-year-old man. Smooth, strong, and ready to play. I stood up. My legs felt light, sinewy, and coiled. I touched my arms. I had muscles again. I looked around and he was gone. There was a mirror near the back entrance to the tent, so the performers could check their make-up and costumes one last time before stepping into the spotlight. A little frightened and very anxious, I walked up and stared into it. The face looking back was my face, but it was a face I hadn't seen in many, many years. I was a young man again. The same wet-behind-the-ears kid I had been when I had first been called up to play for the Cubbies. It was a miracle."

"What happened? Did you play?" I blurted out.

"I did. One game. I replaced Cuno Barragan at catcher in the bottom of the seventh and got to bat in the top of the ninth."

"And?"

"Flew out to deep right."

"Yay!" I shouted and started clapping. Tim and Willy did the same.

"It was something, slugger. Really something."

"How'd it feel?"

"Like home."

"Wow," I said.

"Yep, wow," he replied. "Couldn't have done it without you."

"Sure you could've."

"Nope. If you hadn't decided to go to Chicago, I wouldn't have gone. If we hadn't gone to the carnival, I would never have jumped on that time machine."

"Time machine? What time machine?" Tim asked.

"Quiet," I said. "Your elder is talking."

"I have you to thank for giving me a second chance."

"Pretty cool."

"Another thing."

"What's that?"

"Just shows to go you that you can never give up. Not with your dad and not with your life. Follow your dreams. Do what you love."

When the Giants flew home to San Francisco that night, "Baghdad-by-the-Bay" lost its cool. Police Chief Thomas Cahill said he had over 300 officers on Market Street alone, which was more than he'd ever used on a New Year's Eve. "They're really running wild," he said. "Fights all over town – in bars and on the streets." The real madhouse was at the airport, where the crowd forced the Giants' United Airlines jet to unload at the airline's maintenance terminal instead of at its regular unloading area. A lot of folks who got there late just left their cars on the Bayshore Freeway and walked to the airport to join the celebration.

Just after 9:00 p.m., the Giants were loaded onto a special bus and escorted along an airport taxiway by police cars and motorcycles. The crowd saw them and surrounded the caravan, forcing it to halt. Cahill, who estimated the crowd at 75,000, said he never would have had enough men to hold back the happy crowd. It was only the beginning of *loco*.

The Giants would be facing the Yankees. It would be a revival of the "Subway Series" that had happened many times before the Giants moved west.

Chronicle columnist Herb Caen had this to say to the Yankees: "I know there are lots of things you'd like to do besides play baseball, since you've never been here before, and we want you to do them. You're probably as sick of baseball as baseball is sick of – but no; politeness at all cost. On behalf of all San Franciscans, we bid you welcome, Yankees. Welcome to a city that has always been big league, and has made major leaguers out of a club that had bush league support in New York. The cry around here used to be 'Wait till next year!', but next year is here at last, and now all we're waiting for is you."

The Giants and Yankees would play two in San Francisco, then move to New York for three, before returning to San Francisco for the final two; assuming they played that many. The Yankees were 7-5 favorites, thanks to their past record and the fact that the Giants had just gone through a grueling playoff while the Yankees rested. The way the Yankees had been tearing up the National League in past World Series, there was a good chance it would be over in four. They were the defending World Champs, having beaten Cincinnati in five last year, to earn their nineteenth championship in thirty-nine seasons, and had won six titles prior to that, dating back to 1950. So, I had to get moving.

There was no way I was going to make it to the first game. My best bet was the game on Friday, October 5, which was my fourteenth birthday. Seemed like a sign. That's what I told Gary as we wandered around the student store before class on Thursday morning.

"I could catch the Greyhound," I said, as we looked at the collection of rally ribbons for sale.

"But, that drops you off downtown. That's a long way from Candlestick. Even if you caught a bus to San Bruno, you'd still have to get to the park. Not easy."

"Same with the train, I found out. It drops me in the south part of town, which is nowhere near the ballpark."

"Besides, it's never on time," Gary said.

"My mom would kill me if she knew I was even thinking about hitch-hiking again, or jumping on a freight train."

"Hey, I've got an idea," Gary said. "Jeff Bellotti's dad is a season ticket holder. I bet he's got tickets. Maybe you could ride up with them?"

Jeff lived across the alley behind Gary and had gone to Garrison with us, had played on our championship Little League team, and had been in "Tom Sawyer." His dad was a stock broker in town. His little brother, Bobby, had been our bat boy during our championship season.

"Sure, or somebody," I replied. "He's not the only one in town who's got tickets, I bet."

"I'll have my dad ask. They're always talking over the back fence when my dad feeds the pigeons. I'll have him check tonight when he gets home."

CHAPTER 53

World Series

Game One – Thursday, October 4, 1962 – 12:00 p.m. PST (3:00 p.m. EST) at Candlestick Park

We listened to bits and pieces of the game on the radio when we got a free moment. In between classes, at lunch, during gym. My Giants sounded a little shell-shocked. I knew I needed to be there to root my boys on and to do the one thing I knew would help my dad. Somehow.

In Game One, sophomore skipper Ralph Houk went with Yankees ace and Series veteran, Whitey Ford, while Alvin Dark, also in his second season as manager, countered with Giants lefty, Billy O'Dell. The Yankees jumped out in front in the first inning on a two-run double by Roger Maris. Willie Mays scored for the Giants in the second, ending Ford's record World Series consecutive scoreless inning streak at 33 2/3. Chuck Hiller's double and Felipe Alou's hit in the third tied the game. O'Dell kept pace with "The Chairman" through six. The Yankees broke the tie in the seventh on Clete Boyer's home run off the ageless Don Larsen. The Yanks scored three insurance runs in the final two innings. It was a complete game victory for Ford, who had been dominant for years in the post-season. Final score: Yankees 6, Giants 2.

Gary called right after dinner. He said his dad thought my plan was pretty great, having played a little ball himself once upon a time. Gary Sr. hadn't wasted any time. They went right over and asked Jeff's dad, Jeff Sr., and he agreed. There was plenty of room, he said. He didn't have an extra ticket because the game was sold out and Gary Jr. told him it was no big deal, explaining that I didn't need to see the game, I just needed to see Mickey Mantle.

"So, we need to get there early," Mr. Bellotti had said.

"I'll tell him. Thanks, Mr. Bellotti," Gary Jr. had replied.

"What's he going to do during the game?" Mr. Bellotti had asked.

"I don't know," Gary Sr. had answered. "Sit in the car, I guess."

"And sleep," Gary Jr. had added.

"There's no need to do that," Mr. Bellotti had said. "Let me make some calls."

And everything was set. Mr. Bellotti would pick me up at six in the morning and we'd be on our way. I couldn't wait. I was ready to go.

Until later that night when my dad got a call from Teddy's dad.

I was doing my homework when Mom and Dad came into the bedroom. They asked Tim and Willy to leave so they could talk with me. That's when I knew it was bad. It was never a good sign when they asked my brothers to clear out.

"I just got off the phone with Mr. Jensen," my dad said. Maybe this wasn't going to be too bad, I thought.

"After that," my father continued, "I called Mr. Bellotti."

My heart dropped.

"I told him you won't be needing a ride tomorrow after all."

I started looking for a hole to crawl into.

"Look, Michael, I appreciate what you're trying to do, but you need to stop. Now."

"But, Dad –"

"No 'buts,' Michael. It's done. No more foolishness." He started coughing. It was horrible.

My mom touched his hand and took over.

"You heard your father. You're not going anywhere except to school. Then straight home."

"But, it's my birthday."

"Yes, it is. All the more reason to be here. How about we go to putt-putt, or the bowling alley, for your birthday?"

"Sure, I suppose," I said, sounding less than enthusiastic. Then I looked at my father. "No, that sounds cool…uh, good."

"Great, then it's settled," my mom said. And they left.

I was pissed. Kick someone in the nuts pissed. I knew exactly who was going to feel it.

At lunch on Friday, I saw Teddy eating in the cafeteria at the usual table, with some of the Highway Village hard guys he gave money to so they'd hang out with him when the Eights got tired of his act. After he finished eating, I followed him out to the parking lot. He was headed for Micah's cherried-out '57 Chevy. Probably to take a puff or two on the cigarettes he and the boys kept out there. I found him crouched inside the passenger side door.

"Hey, asshole!" I shouted.

He turned.

"Glad you know your name."

"Guess my old man called your old man," he sneered

"How'd you find out about my wanting to go to the game?" I asked.

"You should be careful how loud you talk. Should never use your outside voice, inside. I have friends with really big ears. I slipped Jeff Jr. a little money and he spilled his guts. He'd like to be one of us, so he rolled over pretty quickly. Funny about coincidences, isn't it?" he smirked.

"Try this on for a coincidence."

I stepped up and kicked him square in the nuts. He crumpled. I quickly lifted him and rolled him onto the passenger side seat.

"Stop messing with me and my family," I said.

"I've only begun," he said, through gritted teeth.

I slammed the door on him.

Since I couldn't see it now in person, I was bound and determined to listen to the whole game on the radio. I tucked my transistor into my jacket, ran an earpiece up the back of my jacket, and into my ear. I pulled my jacket collar up and combed my hair down over my ears so it was hard to see.

Game Two – Friday, October 5 – 12:00 p.m. PST (3:00 p.m. EST) at Candlestick Park

I couldn't have asked for a better birthday present. Jack Sanford of the Giants got revenge by beating Ralph Terry and the Yanks, 2-0. With the Giants protecting a 1–0 lead in the seventh inning, Willie McCovey smashed a towering home run over the right field fence to back twenty-four-game winner Sanford, who only gave up three hits to the Yankees.

The Series was even and I was feeling good, although I hadn't done what I'd set out to do. It meant the Yankees wouldn't sweep and they'd have to come back to California. Saturday was a travel day, so both teams were headed to New York City to continue the Series.

I was now fourteen. Two years into my teens. I didn't feel any different. I guess I looked different. My hair was growing long again. The butch haircut was no longer cool. A lot of other kids would have had a boy-girl dance party on their birthday. I thought about it, but I still wasn't quite there yet, even though Kelly and I had been "going out" for almost five months now. Instead, we had cake and ice cream at home for just the family and Gary and Roy. Gary gave me a Beatles 45RPM. record with "Love Me Do" on the "A" side and "P.S. I Love You" on the "B." Roy gave me an autographed baseball from the old Modesto Reds. Mom and Dad gave me underwear and a new fuzzy blue sweater. Tim and Willy gave me candy. Diane and Cheryl gave me socks that Mom had bought and they had wrapped. With some of the money I had gotten in the mail from my relatives, I bought Bobby Vee's *Golden Greats* album.

Mom took Gary, Roy, and me to Modesto Bowl, where we rolled a few balls, played the pinball machines, drank cherry Cokes, ate French Fries, and talked baseball.

We ran into Doug Baldwin, one of the kids we had gone to elementary school, junior high, and high school with. He was our shortstop and the fastest kid on our Little League team, until he got some kind of bone cancer and they had to cut off his leg. I still remember when Mr. Leach told us and how sad he was. I don't think I had ever seen a teacher, or a coach, cry before. He would take the entire team down to City Hospital to cheer Doug up. It was tough.

Doug got an artificial leg and kept playing baseball, becoming one of the best pitchers on our "A" team. He hung out at Campus Inn by the JC and Modesto Bowl and played pinball. Nothing but pinball. He was a wizard. Sometimes, just to show off, he'd lift the machine up and place two ashtrays under the legs so it would be easier to hang the ball up and score points. He'd rack up all kinds of games that way, enough to stay there the entire day.

He'd invite one or two of us over to his house to play since he wasn't as mobile as he once was. We'd play board games, drink Cokes, and eat chips.

My dad had decided to take some time off work. He said he was kind of tired and thought a few days off might help him get his strength back. Besides, he wanted to watch the games. Dad said he planned to sit in front of the TV and relax, but I knew better. He was getting weaker. He barely left the bedroom. If he did, it was to lie on the living room couch and stare out the picture window at the passing traffic on Kearney.

CHAPTER 54

Travel Day – Saturday, October 6

My only distractions from what was happening at home were my classes, high school football, the World Series, Kelly, and Typhoon Freda. She was headed our way and getting bigger. Freda, not Kelly. The newscasters were now calling it "The Big Blow." The system became an extra-tropical cyclone as it moved into colder waters and interacted with the jet stream. It was shaping up to be a bad one.

That Saturday was a travel day for the Yankees and Giants. Since it was my birthday weekend, I asked Tony and Irma for the day off from working at the store so I could spend all day with Kelly.

Trying to date without a car was a hassle. If a guy wanted to be alone with a girl, he had to ask his parents to either drop him off someplace, with her doing the same. Or, ask them to take him to the girl's house and pick her up, then go wherever you planned to go. Or, pick someplace where you could both walk, or ride your bikes. I asked Kelly to meet me at the Putt-Putt Golf Course way out on McHenry. My folks drove me and hers drove her. Very romantic.

I paid for both of us, we grabbed our golf balls, putters, and score cards, and headed to the first tee. I was pretty competitive. So was Kelly. This was going to be fun. I let her go first. The hole was a straight shot and not very long. She made a hole-in-one. The pressure was on. I holed mine, as well. We got our balls out of the hole and moved onto the second hole.

"I'm really sorry about Teddy that day at Playland," she said. "I was just trying to be nice."

I had been avoiding the topic, but obviously she wanted to talk about it.

"I know. It's okay." We had never really talked about my diving exhibition. I was too embarrassed. She was too polite.

The next hole had a sharp right turn. You had to bounce the ball off an angled piece of wood positioned in the corner of the turn so the ball would ricochet toward the hole. She went first. She got the carom right, but didn't hit it hard enough. I hit mine a little harder, so I was closer to the pin.

"He's kind of hard to say no to," she said.

"Must be nice having that kind of money."

"It's not the money. He's just a little pushy, is all. And my parents know his folks from the country club."

"All one big happy family."

She hit her ball too hard and it slid past the hole and caromed off two of the wood borders. I sank my second shot.

"Let's forget Teddy, okay?" I said.

"Sorry, I won't say anything more."

She made her putt and we moved onto the third hole. It had a little bridge over a stream of water and a windmill that you had to shoot through without the blades stopping your ball. I timed my shot so it scooted over the bridge and through the tunnel cleanly. It didn't go in, but sailed to the left of the hole.

"Nice timing," Kelly said.

"Thanks."

She hit her ball a little too hard. It flew over the bridge and flew through the tunnel untouched. It hit the back edge of the cup, popped up in the air, and dropped down right in front of the back wooden border.

"Good shot," I said.

"Learned from the pro."

We walked around the windmill to where our balls lay. As we did, I took her hand. She let me.

We stopped beside our balls. I didn't want to let go of her hand.

"Happy birthday," she said, and kissed my cheek.

The whole side of my face got hot. I guess that's what happens when you blush.

I turned toward her and looked in her eyes. Everything was suddenly very quiet. I was beginning to understand what people meant when they said people who liked each other were kind of in their own world. At that moment, we were. I was debating what to do next. Keep the game going, or take the next step. I leaned toward her, closed my eyes, and brushed my lips against hers, ever so slightly. They were so soft. I pulled away, afraid I may have pushed it. Her eyes were still closed and she was smiling. She opened her eyes.

"Is that what you boys refer to as getting to first base?" she asked.

I blushed again. It felt like it went from the tips of my hair to the tips of my toes.

"Some guys do."

"You're not like other guys?" She teased.

"I'm not like Teddy, that's for sure," I said.

"That's so true," she said. She leaned in and kissed me. This time, the tip of her tongue touched my lips. I opened them. Our tongues touched and I thought I was going to explode. So, this was what they called a "French kiss." I really liked it. A bunch. So much that I dropped my putter. As it clattered to the ground, we both opened our eyes and stared at each other. We were still close and I could smell her perfume and her breath, warm and smelling slightly of spearmint toothpaste.

I took a long, deep breath and said, "This is the best birthday ever."

"You won't be saying that when we're done with this game," she said.

I let go of her hand. "It's your turn," I said.

I stepped away, she straddled her ball, and sunk it.

I was in love.

But, there was a snake in my Eden.

Game Three – Sunday, October 7 – 11:00 a.m. PST (2:00 p.m. EST) at Yankee Stadium

New York hosted Game Three. It was the twenty-seventh time in the modern era that the Yanks had represented the American League in the Series and it was the twenty-fifth Series played in historic Yankee Stadium. In the 1962 season, the Yankees broke all previous road attendance records, attracting a record total of 2,215,659 fans to the other nine parks in the league.

The Yankees' Bill Stafford and the Giants' Billy Pierce dueled through six scoreless innings. The Yankees ended the scoreless tie in the seventh with three runs. Roger Maris broke the deadlock by driving a two-run single off starter Pierce. Alert base-running allowed Maris to score the winning run in a 3–2 Yankee victory. Stafford almost blew it in the top of the ninth, after giving up a two-run dinger to Giants catcher Ed Bailey. The Yankees were up two games to one.

I watched the whole thing on Gary's parents' beautiful color TV, which they had just bought as part of a World Series special at Asbill's. I just couldn't stand being at home seeing the bad shape my dad was in.

The World Series was broadcast for the first time in 1947 to five cities, courtesy of the DuMont Network. Gillette sponsored the game, so they could introduce a new razor, and an estimated 3 million people watched. In those early days, everyone was trying something new every day. WPIX Channel 11 in New York went on the air in 1948. They landed the Yankees' broadcast rights because none of the other networks liked baseball, since there were no set time limits, which made it hard to schedule and run commercials. WPIX hired Mel Allen and Curt Gowdy to be their television team. The two broadcasters didn't say much different than they would have said on the radio.

In addition to Gillette, who promoted their new products each year during the Series, the beer companies were the first to sponsor regular season games, which made sense since a majority of the TV sets were in bars. The tavern owners were trying to lure patrons – who now drank at home thanks to beer in cans and new homes in the suburbs with refrigerators – back to the downtown bars. The Ballantine Brewing Company sponsored the Yankees in those early days.

Those who could see the writing on the wall knew TV could be a new home theater showing the best live entertainment, especially sports like baseball, the Friday Night Fights, or football. Many team owners saw TV and radio as competition with stadium attendance, so some fought it. The new medium won. Television made everyone richer and it turned everyone, from umpires to players to fans, into Shakespearean hambones.

In 1962, the Giants' games were broadcast in the Bay Area on KTVU-TV Channel 2 in Oakland and on KSFO- a.m. radio. Russ Hodges and Lon Simmons did the play-by-play and color. The Yankees were on WPIX-TV and WCBS-AM. Mel Allen, Phil Rizzuto, and Red Barber made up the broadcast team. NBC-TV broadcast the '62 World Series, with Mel Allen of the Yankees and Russ Hodges of the Giants handling the broadcasting duties. NBC also hosted the radio broadcast, with George Kell and Joe Garagiola. KRON Channel 4 carried the game in San Francisco, KTVU Channel 2 showed the game in Oakland, while KCRA Channel 3 beamed the game to the valley.

By then, most of the kids I knew had televisions. The neighborhood was a forest of metal antennas, except for those old-timers who still had rabbit ears sitting on top of their TV set. The games were broadcast in color, which was still pretty rare in those days. Not many people in Modesto had color sets, but a few kids I knew did. Now Gary did. It was another world. Valley Sporting Goods downtown had borrowed a color TV from Sanders Appliance Center and invited people to come down and watch the game. Asbill's did the same.

CHAPTER 55

Game Four – Monday, October 8 – 10:00 a.m. PST (1:00 p.m. EST) at Yankee Stadium

In Game Four, San Francisco unloaded behind starter Juan Marichal, who beat Whitey Ford 7-3. This would be the Dominican Dandy's only appearance in the Series and it came at the expense of lefty Ford, whose World Series magic seemed to be fading.

The game featured a rare break-out performance at the plate by the Giants' Chuck Hiller. An unlikely threat to the Yankees' power pitching, the second baseman had hit only twenty home runs in his eight-year Major League career. Those numbers didn't matter though, as he nailed a bases-loaded homer off Yankees reliever Marshall Bridges in the seventh, with the score tied 2-2. It was the first grand slam ever in a World Series by a National Leaguer and snapped a 2-2 tie.

In a strange twist, the winning Giants pitcher was none other than Don Larsen, who had pitched, exactly six years earlier to the day, his record-setting perfect game for the home team Yankees against the Brooklyn Dodgers. Billy O'Dell got the save. For the second time in as many games, a Giants catcher stroked a two-run homer, when Tom Haller hit one off Ford in the second inning.

Rumors travel fast, especially when they're fueled by jealousy. Only this was fact, not fiction. Susie, one of Kelly's friends, had told Barbara, who was going out with Todd, who told his friend, Dan, who had told Roy who told Gary who told me, while we were standing around in the activity court after lunch on Monday. We had just heard the final score of the game and things were looking good.

"Don't get mad at me," Gary said. "I'm just telling you what they told me."

I felt cold all over, like someone had kicked me in the stomach. It was the same way I felt that day in the park when Ernie kneed me. I didn't know you could feel this bad this fast. Everything sucked, especially stupid girls.

"Del Rio? She actually went to dinner with him at Del Rio?" I asked, my eyes narrowed.

"Yep, yesterday. A Sunday 'brunch.'"

"They weren't there with their parents? It was only them?"

"Only them. Two, alone."

"I just saw her Saturday."

"She moves fast."

"She told me she had to babysit."

"Well, she was, if Teddy was the baby."

"Butthole."

"Her or him?"

"Both."

"She told Joleen she kind of liked being treated like a princess. Guess he had someone chauffeur them around in some big, old antique car. He bought her a new dress and a corsage. All the trimmings."

"And she fell for it."

"Can't blame her."

"Sure I can."

"He lives in a different world."

"No lie. And it's not a world I've ever been to."

When I didn't call her that night like I usually did, she called me. That wasn't what a girl was supposed to do, but she didn't care what people thought. At least I knew that about her. My mom told her I was out. When I didn't return her call, she tried again. My mom covered for me again. She kept calling. She kept leaving messages. My mom kept fibbing. Finally, my mom refused to keep lying to "such a sweet girl who obviously likes you very much," as she said. When Kelly called again first thing Tuesday morning, Mom handed me the phone. "It's Kelly," was all she said.

I glared at her, but took it.

"Hey," I said into the phone and waited.

"I can explain," she said.

"Just leave me alone," I hissed. "You don't care anything about me. You'd rather hang out with the rich kids. Fine. Go ahead. I'll get along without you."

There was a long pause. She was patiently letting me blow off some steam before she spoke.

"My parents asked me to go with him. It was a favor. I wouldn't have done it if they hadn't asked."

"You said you had to babysit."

"I did, until this happened."

"You could've said no."

"You ever said no to your parents?"

"I don't know. Probably."

"Probably not. You're not that kind of person. Neither am I."

"I'm glad we're so much alike."

"It was lunch. That's all."

"Did you enjoy it?"

"It was very nice. Teddy treated me very well."

"Better than I did or could. Must be nice to be that rich."

"I don't know how rich he is, but I do know one thing. He's not a very nice boy."

"Did he try something?"

"He tried."

"Jerk!"

"He struck out," she said. "I told him I was going steady with you. He said that's why he asked me out."

"I knew it," I said. I stopped. "Wait, did you say 'going steady?'"

"I did."

"Are we?"

"If you're game."

The whole world suddenly got much brighter.

"I am."

Game Five – Tuesday, October 9 – Postponed

Game Five – Wednesday, October 10 – 10:00 a.m. PST (1:00 p.m. EST) at Yankee Stadium

Game Five was scheduled for Tuesday. It was postponed due to rain. Even the east coast was getting battered. It dried out enough for the game to be played the next day, Wednesday, October 10.

Hot-hitting José Pagán drove in two runs with a single in the third and a home run in the fifth. As with the previous games, both teams were locked in a tie late in the game. This time, it was Tom Tresh's turn to be the hero. With the score knotted 2-2 in the eighth, the New York rookie hammered a three-run shot off Jack Sanford, who lost the game despite putting up ten

K's in 7 1/3 innings. Ralph Terry, who had gone 0-4 in Series games before this one, finally managed to cross over in the fifth game, winning 5-3. With the Series returning to San Francisco, the Yankees had the edge, three games to two. The Giants were facing sudden death. "But we've been coming back all year after being counted out," Manager Dark told reporters. "We'll fool 'em again." The Giants would have to get up off the floor at least one more time to tie the Series and twice to win it.

Mother Nature was about to bat.

CHAPTER 56

Travel Day – Thursday, October 11

The Yankees and Giants were coming back to California. I had one more shot. I wasn't going to let anyone stop me this time. My dad was fading fast. I didn't know then how little time I really had.

Thursday was a travel day for the teams. Gary and I rode our bikes home after school. I stopped at his house, like I did every day. Gary was unlocking the front door when we heard the phone ringing inside the house. Gary got the door open, rushed in, and grabbed the phone.

"Hello," he said and listened. He turned to me and held out the phone. "It's your mom."

I went numb inside.

"Hi, Mom. What's up?"

"You need to come home. The ambulance just took your father to the hospital."

My dad was on the second floor of City Hospital downtown. It was the same hospital and same floor I had been on when I had ruptured my spleen last February. The smells and sounds brought back all kinds of unpleasant memories as we walked down the hall to my dad's room.

He smiled as all six of us trooped in. He looked pretty good, considering.

"Hey, here's my brood," he said to the nurse, who shook a thermometer and then slipped it into his mouth to take his temperature.

"Handsome family," she said.

"It is," he mumbled around the thermometer.

She checked her watch, removed the thermometer, and glanced at it.

"Now, promise me you won't get too excited, Mr. Wright," she said.

"I promise," my father said, as he crossed his heart.

She left and us kids flung ourselves at our father, smothering him in hugs and kisses. He returned the affection, like a puppy let out of its cage.

"That's enough," my mom said, gently. "Let him breathe."

We all backed away and moved to stand by the window.

I looked from my dad and mom to us kids, and realized we were standing in birth order. Oldest to youngest, left to right. The way we always did. *Funny*, I thought to myself. *We almost always stand in this order when we're together.*

I remembered a photograph of the family taken during some long-forgotten Valentine's Day. Mom and Dad stood in front of us. We stood in birth order, facing our parents, each holding a hand-made paper valentine. That photo made me think of one of our Disneyland trips. We were walking along the beach somewhere and my mom stooped to pick up an abandoned, rusted toy automobile. She started to cry. "What's wrong?" I asked her. "Nothing," she replied, then hugged me until I couldn't breathe.

"How you feeling, hon?" Mom asked my dad, as she gave him a big kiss.

"Ewww," we all said in unison.

"A little tired," he said, chuckling.

"I'm going to run them home and feed them dinner. Roy's mom is coming over to keep an eye on things and I'll be back."

"Can I stay?" I asked.

"Fine," my dad said.

"You sure?" my mom asked.

"Absolutely."

"I'll see if the Rawlings can come pick him up after I get back. I'm sure they'll be fine with him staying the night with Gary. I'll put some things together and drop them by later."

"Thanks, Mom."

"Okey-dokey, you two. Be good and I'll see you in a bit," my mom said, kissed us both, and herded my brothers and sisters from the room.

"That was a good game yesterday," he said.

"For your team. You guys can win it all tomorrow."

"Won't be easy now that the Giants have home-field advantage."

"Doesn't always work out for the home team."

"Usually does."

"You've got Ford going again."

"You've got Pierce."

"Should be a good match-up."

"If they play," my dad said. "That storm could really mess things up."

"I hope not. I think we're on a roll."

"How about letting a dying man's team win, son?"

I felt like someone had hit me with a baseball bat. That was the first time he'd said anything about dying.

"I didn't mean that, son. I meant to say I was tired."

"Dad, don't say that. You're going to get better. This is a great hospital with really good doctors. They can do anything."

"You are the ultimate optimist, Mikey. Always have been. No, you're right. Everything will be fine."

"'Sides, you need to get healthy enough to get out of bed and play catch with Mickey."

"I thought we were done with that?"

"Mom is. I'm not."

"Son, I've got a really big favor to ask. I want you to give it up. For me. Your mom's already stressed out and I don't want her worrying about you and me both. It's a wonderful thing you're trying to do and I would love to do it. But, it's never going to happen. Not now anyway."

He started to cough. Really cough. Worse than ever. He covered his mouth, then grabbed a bunch of Kleenex from a box on the portable table beside his bed. When he pulled the Kleenex away, I could see specks of blood. He quickly wadded them up and tucked them under his blankets. He pressed the call button and waited for the nurse.

"Mikey, can you go wait out in the waiting room? It's down the hall."

"I know where it is, Dad. Remember, I spent a few nights sitting down there watching the traffic lights change."

"That's right. I forgot. That seems so long ago."

"Not really. Just February of last year."

"We almost lost you."

"Thanks to baseball."

They had and it still hurt to remember it. The hospital was empty tonight. All the family and friends had left their loved ones to face the night alone. I recalled that February night, sitting in the second floor sun room, counting the seconds between the signal light changes at the corner of Seventeenth and H Streets. It was raining. The rain drizzles on the window pane gave the colored lights a surreal glow. Thirteen years old and alone in a hospital. Bleak, very bleak.

I recalled touching the bandage around my stomach as I sat there. It felt like it was holding in my guts. Maybe, because it was. Everything but the spleen the surgeons had removed. I thought about those long, sad nights as I stood there a moment, not wanting to leave my dad.

He closed his eyes. I adjusted the plastic ID band on his wrist, which looked exactly like the one I had worn several months ago. I placed my arm next to his. I compared our hands, palms, fingers, knuckles, fingernails, hair, and skin. Cut from the same cloth.

The nurse returned and I went down to the waiting room and settled into the same chair I had sat in the last time I was here. And began watching the signal light.

I often wondered, what if my dad and me were going somewhere together and we got in a bad wreck? We were both lying on the side of the road, fighting for our lives, which flashed before our eyes. Only I was seeing his and he was seeing mine. Would it be all that different? *Would it?* I wondered. I wanted to ask him if he thought about the same things I thought about when he was working in the yard, or fixing the car. Did he think about Mom, about what he hadn't done, about us kids, about growing up, about his friends, about how much he was drinking, about how much his back hurt, about how he'd rather be doing something else, about his favorite music, about life beyond this life, about watching the game with a beer, about how much work there was to do around the house, about how much money he owed, about his family? When he was feeling good and he was alone, did he dance around the room? Did he sing at the top of his lungs? Did he laugh because, at that moment, life was good? I wondered, *did he? Did he ever?* I remembered looking at all those old photos of him and Mom, smiling at the world that lay before them. All that hope and promise. I wanted to ask him about the FBI and why he wanted to be an architect. Before the story was lost with him. I wanted to ask him if he thought about those things. At that moment, I'm pretty sure he wasn't thinking about any of that. He just looked thin and very tired.

What had been idle speculation at the beginning of the school year now became a promise, as I waited to return to watch over my father. I would get a good education. I would go to college. I would get a good job, so I could take care of Dad, Mom, and my brothers and sisters. So I could do like he did. Maybe even more. Baseball was a game. This – life – wasn't. I would make him proud.

I mouthed the promise again as I sat beside my father's bed, once the nurse had asked me to come back in and had left us alone. He kept dozing off. He'd start himself awake, as if he were fighting falling asleep. I straightened the sheets. He woke up.

"How you doin', Daddy-O?"

"I'm a little scared," he said.

I didn't know what to say. I thought he'd say something like "Not bad" or "Okay." Something innocuous. Something to make me feel better. Something to hide the reality. I didn't want to know he was scared because there was nothing I could say, or do, to change that. I wanted to think otherwise, but I knew better. I just didn't have that kind of power. As much as I loved him, I couldn't save him.

"Of what?" I croaked.

"What's out there? What's next?"

"You'll take some time off, so you can get better. Then things will go back to the way they were."

"We'll never go back to the way we were, son."

"Just think positive, right? That's what you always told me."

"That's right. Think positive."

Then he was away, back deep inside himself. Alone.

CHAPTER 57

Dad woke up again when the nurse came in to check his temperature and empty his bed pan. He looked so weak. But, he wanted to talk. So we did. About school, about Kelly, about Mom, about the family, about him, about shoulda, coulda, and woulda.

"Do you regret not getting to go to college?" I asked.

"Yes and no," he replied. "I wouldn't have missed meeting your mom and having you kids for the world. You know that song we always used to sing?" He sat up a little and tried to get comfortable. He sang, breathless, a song that kind of summed up my parents' life. Every time I heard them sing "Let the Rest of the World Go By," which was usually in the car going somewhere, I realized that they really were pals "good and true." As he sang about wanting to "build a sweet little nest somewhere out in the west," I hoped he'd always be there in the front seat harmonizing with Mom and us kids about letting the rest of the world go by.

"I remember."

"That's all I ever wanted to do. College would have been great, but I would've been a different person and lived a different life."

"It's like that Robert Frost poem about the two roads, huh?"

"'The Road Not Taken.'"

"Yep, that's it."

"It's about choices. I chose you." He put his hand on my arm.

"What about the FBI? You could've carried a gun and chased the bad guys."

"After the war, I never wanted to see a gun again."

"You always talked about being an architect."

"I guess living in the valley as long as I did, there was something magical about all those tall buildings I saw in pictures. Just thought it'd be something I'd enjoy."

"Anything else you never did you wanted to do?"

"Play in the bigs."

"That would've been cool."

"But, no, nothing else. Well, except, I'm not done yet, right? Positive thoughts, right? I don't want to leave without finishing everything. I've still got a few songs to sing."

I thought about what the Wolfman had said.

Gary and his folks picked me up from the hospital about an hour later. Gary and I sat in his room listening to Russ and Lon and Don Sherwood on KSFO in San Francisco, which carried all the Giants games, talk about the Series, the upcoming games, and the weather.

"Man, we're so much alike," I said. "I knew exactly how he was feeling. It was almost as if I were looking out his eyes. He was scared. God, he looked so alone. I should've stayed."

"He was tired."

"This is my last chance," I said. "I need to get to San Francisco."

"Jeff's dad only had tickets to the one game."

"Too bad."

"Your mom will be bird-doggin' you. There's no way she'll let you out of her sight."

"I'm here, aren't I? Plus, she's got more important things to worry about."

"I'm really sorry he's not doing well."

"All the more reason."

"You still think playing catch with Mickey Mantle will make a difference?"

"All the difference in the world."

"So, what's the plan?"

"I need to get a car. Whatever it takes."

"You can't drive."

"Sure, I can. Dad's been letting me drive for years."

"Sitting in his lap and steering. That's not driving."

"Nah, he's let me drive with him sitting beside me. Out in the country. And I've driven around the block a few times and up at my Grampa Owl's ranch. And I've driven a truck at my dad's cousin's dairy. Aunt Cat let me drive a little on our way back from Chicago. Dad knows I'll be old enough to get my permit here pretty soon."

"In a year-and-a-half. You just turned fourteen, man. That's not just around the corner."

"I'll get Mr. Lowney to drive me."

"I doubt he's even got a license anymore. He looks too old to drive. Plus, he's half-blind. You ever look at his eyes? They're all glassy, like a blind dog's eyes."

"You're seein' things."

"He ain't."

"I'll figure it out."

"'Sides, where you gonna get a car?"

"I'll come up with something."

"Look, I'd rather not visit my best friend in Alcatraz."

"They put murderers and rapists there, not kids."

"Okay, I don't wanna visit you at Deuel or Juvie, either."

"You got a better plan?"

"How about I talk with Joey, my sister Lucy's boyfriend. This is right up his alley. He's a bit of a rebel."

"You really think he'd do it?"

"Sure, why not? He's not working. He's got time. And a car."

"A cool, cherry-red Corvair."

"Plus, he owes me. I haven't told my sister half the stuff he's done over the years."

"Good to be the little brother, sometimes."

"Amen to that, brother."

"Can you call him tonight? The game's tomorrow."

"Sure."

My best friend did what best friends do. He made the call and blackmailed his sister's boyfriend into helping out his buddy. It was all arranged. Joey would pick me up at eight o'clock Friday morning and we'd head for Candlestick. It meant I'd have to ditch school, but we'd already worked it out with Lucy to call the school and pretend to be my mom. My mom would forgive Lucy because they were good buddies and an awful lot alike. They had always gotten along. They were usually the ones yelling the loudest at our games and generally getting into trouble. They both got certificates from the coach at the end of each season for being our number one fans. They did all kinds of crazy things together, like chasing bullies with baseball bats.

The back-up plan was a go. Then the crap hit the fan. Or, should I say, Typhoon Freda hit California. It later became known as the Columbus Day Storm of 1962. It was one of the most intense cyclones to hit the Pacific Northwest since 1948. If it kept getting stronger, some forecasters predicted it could very well be the most powerful cyclone recorded in the U.S. in the twentieth century. Freda formed 500 miles off Wake Island in the central Pacific Ocean. It took nine days to cross the Pacific. Along the way, it became bigger when it merged with a cold front. By the time it hit California, it was only an "extra-tropical storm," but it was packing winds like a hurricane.

It exploded off Northern California, producing record rainfalls in and around San Francisco. The low moved northeastward, and then hooked straight north, as it neared southwest Oregon. The storm then raced almost directly northward at an average speed of forty miles per hour, with the center just fifty miles off the

Pacific Coast. It blew down trees up-and-down the coast. Flying debris killed several people caught outside, or in their cars. It passed through Oregon and into Canada, where it finally died.

Game Six – Friday, October 12 – Postponed

Freda didn't hit California head-on, so we didn't get the worst of it. In Central and Northern California, the record rains caused major flooding and mudslides, particularly in the Bay Area. Oakland set an all-time record with 4.52 inches of rain. Sacramento was hit with 3.77 inches. Over seven inches of rainfall were recorded in San Francisco. Enough to flood the outfield and parking lot at Candlestick.

The result? It was too wet to play Friday's Game Six at Candlestick, so it was postponed. In spite of the miserable conditions, all kinds of crazy fans camped out Friday night to get one of the 2,200 bleacher seats for Saturday's sold-out game.

Without a game to go to, I asked Joey to postpone our road trip. He was easy. Besides, he had nothing else to do. Now, we just had to keep it quiet.

Giants pitching coach Larry Jansen was happy with the delay. It meant giving Billy Pierce another day off before facing Whitey Ford. Billy was thirty-five, so he needed all the help he could get.

We all went to church that night. My mom, my brothers and sisters, and me. We were not big church-goers. When we did go, we went to the Congregational Church in the neighborhood. My mother even taught Sunday school there for a while. We were all baptized there. My dad had a disagreement with the Reverend Charlie Spencer about his politics and church contributions. My dad said he was squeezing the congregation to pay for a new Cadillac. We never went back. We occasionally did the usual holiday services, like Christmas and Easter. We became spiritual non-believers.

In 1962, Charlie Spencer ran for State Assembly as a Democrat. I guess he always had plans beyond church. Robert Bienvenu ran for State Senator. There were political ads in just about every newspaper and anything else with space and an audience, as well as candidate forums, lawn signs, TV commercials, mailers, and radio talk shows. It was overwhelming. I can't imagine how much money they had to spend to get elected.

I never really missed church. I guess I was a bit of a pagan. I'd rather be outside playing or watching baseball or football or doing chores instead of getting all dressed up and sitting on a hard seat for an hour-and-a-half listening to someone tell me how evil the world was and how I should repent for my sins. I didn't know I had any sins to repent for. Church and religion were just never a part of our lives. Plus, I never understood why it was that so many people were killed because of their religious beliefs. It just never made sense to me.

I was kind of interested in the Jewish religion because it seemed so practical. Some of my high school friends belonged to DeMolay, which was an organization of young men affiliated with the Masons. For the girls, there was Job's Daughters. It seemed like fun because they were always doing things and having dances. I guess my gauge of a good religion was how much joy they were spreading, not how much good they were doing.

Game Six – Saturday, October 13 – Postponed

Then the weather watch began. I was never much of a meteorologist, but I became one in those couple of days. We all watched and listened. Saturday was washed out also because the field was too wet to play on safely. Since Mr. Bellotti was a stockbroker, he had a teletype machine in his office at Fifteenth and Needham, so he could keep up with the news and the stock market. He could also track the storm, which he and the entire office were doing. Instead of posting stock prices, they were posting rainfall levels.

Not only could the games not be played, but it was too wet to practice, according to Candlestick's groundskeeper, Matty Schwab. Candlestick's adobe subsurface acted like a bathtub without a drain. Plus, the team owners didn't want their players getting hurt. Commissioner Frick quickly squashed any rumors that the Series might be shifted to another site. "Positively not," he said. "It will be played right here if we have to wait until Christmas." Of course, many people blamed Giants manager Dark for jinxing it. He had sat on a table at Yankee stadium after the fifth game and told reporters what everybody believed. "It never rains in California," he boasted.

The Yankees were getting punchy from too many hours spent playing poker in their hotel rooms at the TowneHouse Motor Hotel, which was owned by Del Webb and was located at Eighth and Market Streets, across from the Orpheum Theatre. Each day, each team would show up at the ballpark, hoping to get the game in. They'd get dressed out, but instead of playing baseball, they'd play cards. One columnist described the Yankees as caged animals. "We're all pokered out," grumbled Bill Skowron. "I like to poker once in a while, but I don't want to make a career out of it." Apparently, the Yankees were also complaining, and a little envious, that the Giants were at least at home with their families.

In interviews with radio, TV, and newspaper reporters, Yankees manager Houk was concerned that his team would lose their edge. He huddled with Dark, team owners Dan Topping and Del Webb of the Yankees and Horace Stoneham of the Giants, as well as General Manager Roy Hamey of the Yankees and Chub Feeney of the Giants. Both managers wanted their players practicing. Each club wanted to loosen up their pitchers, run all their players, take some batting practice, and just chase the fidgets that had developed during the delay. Dark said he was interested in working out mainly "for mental relaxation and to get the team back in the frame of mind for baseball." Plus, both managers had colds and they were ready for some sun.

Dark revealed that the Giants were working on a proposal to work out indoors at the Cow Palace. Hockey had been played there on Friday night, so it wouldn't be easy to get it set up for baseball. When asked if the Giants would have any problem with the Yankees using the same facility, Dark replied: "We'll certainly invite them to share any indoor quarters we may find."

Turned out, it wouldn't be necessary. Yankees owner Del Webb owned the AAA baseball team that played in my home town. The Modesto Colts played their home games at a field named after Mr. Webb. From 1954 to 1961, the team was known as the Modesto Reds and they were a farm club for the Yankees. In 1962, the Reds became the Colts, after becoming affiliated with the Houston Colt .45s, a new expansion team that started in 1962 and finished eighth in its first season in the National League. The Colts were part of the Class "C" California League. We fans weren't all that happy about the name change. We liked being called the Reds. Plus, we'd been the Reds for as long as I could remember.

CHAPTER 58

Modesto's first baseball team was organized in 1872. A March 22, 1872, article in the *Stanislaus County Weekly News* stated that, "although the players as yet had not evidenced much ability," they displayed "considerable muscle" and were "well backed with enthusiasm and vim." The following month, the *News* reported that the new team had chosen a uniform of red cap, red shirt, white pantaloons, white canvas shoes, and had selected the name of "Red Caps," in keeping with the uniform. The newspaper also suggested that the players should "perfect their skills and play according to the rules."

In the 1890s, the "Modesto Reds" played as a minor league team in a league that included Merced, Chowchilla, and Stockton. They travelled the circuit in a surrey pulled by four horses. In March 1904, a group of players and supporters gathered at Ramona's barbershop in Modesto to start a "base ball" club. Wade Howard was appointed manager. He had a budget of fifty dollars for uniforms and another twenty dollars to shape up the playing field.

Throughout the early 1900s, the Reds continued to compete as an independent, with hopes of joining a regional or statewide league, which would mean better competition and more money.

The Reds drew well and played pro-caliber baseball against amateur and semi-pro teams. Of one game against the visiting San Francisco Relays, the *News* wrote: "[The Reds] knocked the ball so far and so often that the boys from the fog belt tired themselves out chasing it."

The March 23, 1906, issue of the *News* announced that the "unbeaten and invincible Modesto Reds" were challenging any baseball team in the San Joaquin Valley, even the American Association – which later became the American League – and the National League. The boys felt that they were "equal to it" and were "chuck full of ginger," said the *News*, adding "bring on your champions from the tall grass of Merced and the mud flats of Stockton, anywhere in fact." The article also noted that people would be willing to pay "two-bits" all summer just to watch the Reds "eat 'em alive."

The Reds' challenge to other teams "anywhere" must have gone far and wide, because the Chicago White Sox made an eight-day train trip to Modesto to play the Reds on March 7, 1910, in a game that "was close from start to finish," according to the *Daily Evening News*. This event was extremely popular, as demonstrated by the 2,000 in attendance at Modesto's Baseball Park, and "every man, woman, and child who could get the price of admission, or who could find a hole in the fence, was on the grounds rooting for the Reds." The score was 1-0 at the beginning of the ninth inning when the White Sox blazed ahead and won 4-0 despite the cold, fog, wet grounds, and long train ride that "shook a lot of pepper" out of the Chicago boys.

Throughout the 1910s, the Reds were proving they were ready to play in the major leagues. In 1911, the Reds hosted two professional teams. They lost 5-0 to the Boston Red Sox and dropped two more to the Tacoma Tigers of the Pacific Coast League. The Reds finally got to be part of a semi-pro league in 1912 when they joined teams from Stockton, Oakland, San Francisco, Galt, and Sacramento to form the California State

League. The Modesto nine won the first half of the season and the team from Stockton won the second half. The Reds lost the best-of-three series. In 1914, the team became a farm club for the San Francisco Seals of the Pacific Coast League, while again playing in the resurrected California State League.

Over the years, Modesto was the site of spring training for a number of teams, including the Salt Lake City Bees in 1916. The Reds were also affiliated with various major league teams, including the St. Louis Browns (1948), Pittsburgh Pirates (1949-1952), Milwaukee Braves (1953), New York Yankees (1954-1961), and Houston Colt .45s (1962).

The Modesto team played in the California League from 1946 until 1962. The California League was founded in 1941 by a combination of Major League and Pacific Coast League clubs. The charter members were the Anaheim Aces, Bakersfield Badgers, Fresno Cardinals, Merced Bears, Riverside Reds, San Bernardino Stars, Santa Barbara Saints, and Stockton Fliers. Only six teams were able to complete the inaugural campaign, since Riverside and San Bernardino ceased operations midway through the season. The league dropped to four teams the following year, as the Bakersfield Badgers, Fresno Cardinals, and Santa Barbara Saints were joined by the San Jose Owls. In 1941, the California League was classified as a "C" League and would remain that way through 1962. League operations were suspended for the duration of World War II on June 29, 1942.

At the conclusion of World War II, the league resumed play with six teams. In 1946, the Bakersfield Indians, Fresno Cardinals, Modesto Reds, Santa Barbara Dodgers, Stockton Ports, and Visalia Cubs took the field. The San Jose Red Sox and Ventura Yankees joined the circuit in 1947. Bill Schroeder, who had organized the league, served as president through 1947. At that time, six franchises were owned by Major League teams and two, Modesto and Stockton, were independent.

Under the leadership of Jerry Donovan, California League president from 1949-1955, attendance skyrocketed after the war, reaching a peak of 789,940 in 1949. The Bakersfield Indians, Fresno Cardinals, Stockton Ports, and San Jose Red Sox all drew over 100,000 fans. In the mid-1950s, one of the league's most colorfully named teams, the Channel Cities Oilers, represented Santa Barbara and Ventura.

With the increased popularity and availability of television and home air-conditioning in the 1950s, attendance throughout Minor League Baseball began to dwindle. In the middle of the 1955 season, the Channel Cities Oilers franchise moved to Reno, Nevada, and would remain a league member for thirty-seven more years. Former Major League infielder Eddie Mulligan became league president in 1956. The California League retained its eight-team structure until 1959, when it dropped to six teams for three years.

One memorable exhibition game from the early years pitted the Modesto Reds against Casey Stengel's National League All-Stars, with the ceremonial first "pitch" dropped from an airplane. The Reds became one of the first baseball clubs to field an all-Japanese-American team in 1949. By that year, Modesto's active semi-professional baseball team was in need of better facilities. After years of playing league games using open fields and, later, an enclosed facility where admission was charged, the Reds finally got a new home. Owned by the city and located near the Municipal Golf Course, it was officially named Del Webb Field, after Webb, who had been a semi-pro baseball player himself and had played with the Modesto Reds in the 1920s.

Delbert Eugene Webb was born in Fresno, California, on May 17, 1899, the son of Ernest G. Webb, a fruit farmer, and

Henrietta S. Webb. Webb dropped out of high school to become a carpenter's apprentice. In 1919, Webb married Hazel Lenora Church, a graduate nurse. In 1920, Webb worked as a ship fitter, and the couple lived with his parents and two younger brothers in Placer County, California.

Webb's scholarly career was cut short in high school when, in 1915, financial setbacks afflicted his father, then the president of a California gravel company. After completing his freshman year, Webb fell back on two boyhood occupations: baseball, which he had been playing semi-professionally since age thirteen, and carpentry. For the next twelve years, he moved around California, working as a carpenter exclusively for companies with baseball teams, which allowed him to make some extra money. A bad bout with typhoid fever when he was twenty-eight and a sore arm ended his major league ambitions. As a result of the typhoid fever, he moved to Phoenix, Arizona, to recover.

Phoenix, in spite of its depressed economy, attracted Webb, like many others, in search of a healthy climate. Eager to return to the ball field, Webb violated a league residency requirement, which he had missed by one day. Unable to play and unwilling to do anything halfway, he ended his baseball career forever in 1928 and began concentrating on construction full-time. He was soon moonlighting as a contractor.

That same year, he was working as a small contractor building a grocery store. One day his paycheck bounced and his employer disappeared. The grocer asked young Webb to take over the job and Del E. Webb Construction Co. went into business. Its total assets: one cement mixer, ten wheelbarrows, twenty shovels, and ten picks. He landed many military contracts during World War II, including the construction of the Poston War Relocation Center near Parker, Arizona. Poston interned over 17,000 Japanese-Americans and, at the time, was the third largest "city" in Arizona.

Webb was associated with Howard Hughes and golfed with Hughes, Bing Crosby, Bob Hope, and Robert and Barry Goldwater. In 1945, Webb and partners Dan Topping and Larry MacPhail purchased the New York Yankees for $2.8 million. Webb and Topping bought out MacPhail in October 1947.

In 1948, in Tucson, Arizona, Webb was contracted to build 600 houses and a shopping center called Pueblo Gardens. This was a prelude to Sun City, which was launched on January 1, 1960, with five models, a shopping center, recreation center, and golf course. The opening weekend drew 100,000 people, ten times more than expected, and resulted in a *Time* magazine cover story. Sun City was the first major retirement community in the country – an idea that not only transformed the Phoenix area, but had a major effect on the sociology of the vast numbers of Americans who had, or would eventually approach, retirement age. Webb was always proud of the part he played in developing active retirement living. He said, "When I see what we've built, it's the most satisfying thing that's ever happened to me."

Webb also developed a chain of motor hotels under the "Hiway House" name and more "formal" hotels called "Del Webb's TowneHouse." He built the Las Vegas Flamingo hotel for Bugsy Siegel. He later owned his own casinos, the Sahara and the Mint in Las Vegas, and the Sahara Tahoe at Stateline, Nevada. By the 1960s, the Del E. Webb Construction Co. was one of the largest in the United States.

Although it was too wet to play ball in San Francisco, Modesto was dry as a bone. Del Webb consulted with Tom Mellis, a longtime friend of Yankees General Manager Roy Hamey, and Colts business manager, Jerry Pepelis. Mellis was a former president of the Modesto Reds, as well as one of the founders of the California Relays and the Sportsmen of Stanislaus men's club. The Colts agreed to invite the clubs to hold practice at Del Webb Field.

There was a bit of history of Modesto being used by major league clubs during rainouts. The field was used by the San

Francisco Seals in the early 1950s for their Pacific Coast League spring training when they were rained out of their Sonoma County camp.

CHAPTER 59

Commissioner Frick ordered Game Six postponed again after inspecting the field. Although it was sunny and clear, the field was still too wet. Standing in ankle-deep water, the Commissioner announced: "It's a cinch we'll get in the game tomorrow if there is no more rain."

Another decision was soon made. The public first heard about it on KSFO, as Russ and Lon broke the news, then on KFIV, KTRB, and in the Sunday *Modesto Bee*. The *Bee* was delivered in the afternoons during the week and in the morning on Sunday. There was no Saturday paper. As soon as the paper was delivered before dawn that Sunday, it was confirmed. The headline read: "Giant, Yankee Teams May Work Out Today in Modesto." Word spread like wildfire, especially in Modesto and the surrounding communities. The Yankees and Giants were coming to the Central Valley. My prayers had been answered. It was a glorious day.

As the Yankees boarded the bus for Modesto, Whitey Ford said it all: "I never thought I'd look forward to a two-hour bus ride." And that's exactly how long it took to cover the ninety-four miles to Modesto.

People started arriving at Del Webb Field around ten o'clock. By eleven, the crowd had grown to 3,000. By noon, when the

Yankees arrived, there were 5,000 on hand. Within hours, an estimated 16,000 fans would be waiting to get the 2,500 available seats to watch the two teams work out, including me and Gary. We got an early start, so I could do what I needed to do. Gary Sr. drove us down to the park in their '51 Chevy. On the way, we stopped at Bi-Rite Market to grab some doughnuts. Gary got a Nehi Orange, his usual. I got an RC Cola, my usual. Gary Sr. got a Burgie beer, his usual. Ah, the breakfast of champions.

It was a good thing we hit the road when we did because the traffic started backing up right away. The Modesto Police Department had to call up reserves to help out, including deputies from the Stanislaus County Sheriff's Department and officers from the California Highway Patrol.

The Yankees pulled into town first. They drove directly to the Sportsmen of Stanislaus Club, a men-only athletic facility located next to Dryden Municipal Golf Course, on the south edge of town and just south of Del Webb Field. The Tuolumne River meandered lazily to the east and south of the golf course and club. Owner Webb had made arrangements with the SOS to serve lunch and make the locker room available, so the players could change. The bus arrived around noon. The players had a nice steak lunch and changed into their road grey uniforms. They piled back onto the bus and drove the short distance to the field.

Gary, his dad, me, and most of the other fans were waiting by the main entrance to the park, thinking the teams would come in that way. I was straining to see over the crowd to catch a glimpse of the bus when a pair of hands covered my eyes. Surprised, and a little pissed, I ripped the hands away, spun around, and saw Kelly. She smiled, but stopped when she saw my face.

"Sorry, I thought you'd be happy to see me," she said.

"I am," I said, "but right now I've kinda got something I need to do."

"That thing for your dad?"

"Yes," I said, more than just a little distracted.

I abruptly turned away to see if the bus was coming. When I turned back, she was gone. I scanned the crowd for a moment, but couldn't see her.

"Girls," Gary said.

"Ain't it the truth," I replied.

"Wait until they become women," Gary Sr. added.

"It's always about making a choice. Why is that? I have to choose between her and baseball, her and my friends, her and my family, her and my father. It shouldn't be that way."

This was another character trait of mine that wasn't particularly attractive. I seemed to always blame others and never took personal responsibility for things I did, or things that happened to me; even though that was one of the most important lessons my father tried to teach all his children. Along with using our own good judgment, he expected us to take responsibility. He would patiently explain to me, if I had just done something I shouldn't have and had blamed someone else, that I was in control of my destiny. I hated it when he'd end our talk by saying, "It's all up to you." I couldn't admit it was my fault, or it was all up to me, because I never liked to be wrong. I always had to be right. It became almost a disease. I'd rather blame someone else than admit I'd done something, or said something, I shouldn't have. It was always someone else's fault. I could always find a reason to blame the teacher if I had to quit music, blame my coach if we lost a close game, blame the teacher if I didn't do well on a paper, or blame Kelly if we got in a fight, which is what I was doing at this moment. It wasn't a flattering feature of my personality, but it was all mine, like my chipped front tooth.

Just then, a bus horn sounded and the crowd roared.

The chartered bus carrying the Yankees pulled into the asphalt parking lot and, instead of navigating toward the front gate, it turned a hard left and headed toward the green wooden left field fence. There was a gate there that all the visiting teams used to enter the park. Panicked, everyone broke through the line of

Modesto Police Department officers and ran after the bus. I took off and sprinted around to the right of the crowd hoping to get to the gate first.

All of a sudden, I found myself sprawling face-first on the unforgiving asphalt. My hands and knees skidded along the tarmac. Stunned and skinned, I rolled over and gingerly got to my feet to see what I had tripped over.

"What the heck," I thought, as I looked at my hands.

Just then, a shadow blocked out the sun. I looked up to see the leering face of Teddy Jensen. He had tripped me. Now, he loomed over me, grinning.

"Just wanted to show you what I got," he gloated. He held out an autographed ball. "Got this at the SOS. My old man's a member. We had lunch with the Yankees. And guess what? I got to sit with Mickey. And he signed this." He tossed the ball lightly in the air. "I don't see what the big deal is. He's just this guy, you know."

"The greatest baseball player ever."

"Yeah, a baseball player. He didn't cure cancer, or the common cold. What makes him so special?"

"He's a good guy."

"Couldn't tell that by the stories he was telling. Made my ears red."

"Knock it off," I yelled, as I jumped to my feet to face him.

"All's I'm saying is you better be careful who you put up on a pedestal. It's a long fall."

"You don't know what you're talking about."

"Well, I have to admit he was nice to me and all the other kids in the room. When I told him my dad was sick, well it just broke his heart. Sound familiar? He felt bad for me. That's when he gave me the ball."

"I'm not sick, Teddy," a man's voice said. "Are you lying again?"

"No, dad," Teddy replied. "I was just showing my new ball off to my old friend, Mike, here."

Teddy's father looked down at me. "You okay, Mike? You look a little skinned up." My palms and knees were both bleeding. "What happened, son?"

"I tripped over something," I said, glaring at Teddy.

"Like what? This lot's pretty flat."

"Must have been my own feet. I do that a lot."

"Well, be careful." Just then, he snatched the ball Teddy was still tossing up and down. He looked it over and held it out to me. "Here, maybe this will make you feel better."

I looked longingly at the ball. "No, thank you, sir, it's not mine. I'm going to get my own."

Mr. Jensen pocketed the ball and looked past me at the crowd. "Well, you better hurry. They're getting off the bus."

I spun around, took a look, and took off. I yelled, "Thanks," over my shoulder as I dashed away.

As I ran, I thought, *Teddy's pops doesn't seem like a half-bad guy. Maybe all those stories I'd been hearing were wrong.*

Manager Ralph Houk led his coaching staff, trainers, and players off the bus and through the player entrance along the left field foul line. By the time I pushed my way through the crowd, the entire team was off the bus, through the gate, and onto the field. Except for one.

Tom Tresh stopped at the bottom step and looked out over the sea of faces and gazed upward at the beautiful, blue October sky.

"Now, this is baseball weather," he said to no one in particular. He stepped down onto the asphalt just as I elbowed my way through the crowd. "Well, it's that bad penny again," he said, gazing down at me. "What'd you do, sport? Looks like you slid head-first into home plate on a really bad Hoboken field. You okay?"

"I'm fine, Mr. Tresh. Just a few scrapes. Is Mickey still on the bus?"

"Nope, he was one of the first ones off. Probably in the cage by now. See you inside," and he headed through the gate. One of the police officers shut the gate behind him.

"You know Tom Tresh," a voice behind me said.

I turned to face a tall, sharp-angled, blonde kid that looked a couple years older than me.

"Sort of," I said. "He gave me an autograph once."

"Wow," the kid replied. "I wish I'd gotten here sooner so's I coulda gotten one, too. None of the other guys did."

"Guess they just want to play some ball."

"Me, too," the kid said. "I play varsity for Downey. I want to be just like them." He stuck out his hand. "Name's Joe. Joe Rudi."

"Mine's Mikey." I waited for it. And he delivered.

"Mouse or Mantle."

"Neither," I answered. He looked puzzled. "Never mind," I said. "I need to get inside."

"I'm staying out here. Get me some foul balls. And maybe get one of them to sign 'em."

"Good luck," I said.

"Same back at ya," Joe said.

I rushed back around to the front entrance, dashed through the gate, and tried to find a seat in the bleachers. Inside, there was a standing room crowd of about 6,000. I wormed my way into a spot behind the home team's left-field dugout, where the Yankees had collected. The old wooden stadium was packed to exploding. The next day, the *Modesto Bee* described it this way: "Men in pressed white shirts and ties lined the wood grandstands behind the batting cages and boys peeked through knotholes in the center field fence."

The Colts didn't charge admission, which was nice of the owners, and they didn't open the concession stands, which was a lot of lost money. One of their staff handled the public address system, announcing the names of each player who stepped into the cage to thunderous applause. On the steps of the dugout, Yankee second baseman, Bobby Richardson, was being interviewed by a reporter from the *Modesto Bee*, as a photographer took some photos.

"I'm impressed with these fans," Richardson said. "The people are the most orderly, most patient, and most pleasant I have seen in a long time. A lot different than our New York fans."

"What do you think of the facility?" the reporter asked.

"The dirt part of the infield is kept as well as that in Yankee Stadium," the Yankees' second sacker replied. Emilio "Butch" Pierini, the Del Webb groundskeeper, who was standing nearby, smiled when he heard that.

I saw a kid posing for photos with Roger Maris. I thought to myself, "What a lucky guy." Then, I wondered, "Who'd he know?" Just then, I heard a huge roar as Mickey stepped into the batting cage. He had been standing behind it talking with Yogi Berra and Whitey Ford. He took a few practice swings and stepped into the batter's box. The batting practice pitcher started firing away. Mickey rocketed shots all over the field, including a few monster blasts over the fence. In the parking lot, men raced boys to catch up with the bounding balls, as they ricocheted off the parked cars. Mickey then switched to take a few left-handed. And sent a couple more careening off the outfield fence. Mickey's hits sounded different than the other guys. It wasn't a thud, but more of a ring. There was no mistaking who was hitting when you heard that sound.

When Mickey was done, Yogi stepped up and the crowd applauded him even louder.

"Feels like déjà vu all over again," Yogi announced to the spectators. Everyone laughed, but me. I was watching Mickey and trying to figure out how I could get on the field and get to him. I was just about to jump up on the top of the dugout when I heard a scream. Some little kid, who had been sitting on the wooden outfield fence in left field, had fallen onto the field. Now he was darting around the dirt warning track trying to find a way back up on the wall. He was trying to avoid the police because the radio had said the police would arrest anyone who got onto the playing field. Finally, a policeman caught the boy and, instead of hauling him away, placed him back up on the fence. The crowd applauded.

I knew now that the police would be extra vigilant about keeping people off the field. I worked my way up the aisle from the dugout, turned left behind the backstop, and walked over to the visitor's dugout along first base. I was hoping to find an opening where I could yell and get Mickey's attention.

CHAPTER 60

I finally found a good vantage point and was inching my way closer to the dugout when another huge roar went up. I looked in the direction of the noise just in time to see the left field gate open and the Giants step onto the field and make their way down the left field line.

The Giants had changed out of their street clothes into their home uniforms and had a short team meeting in the dreary, dilapidated, and cramped home team clubhouse, which was located in a long metal hut behind the fence along the third base side of the field. It was pretty depressing. They probably all felt like they'd gone back in time to their own minor league days; the days of cold food, cheap hotels, bad facilities, and day-long bus rides. Everyone had ridden the team bus to town, except the "Say Hey Kid," who drove over in his Cadillac. When the Giants trooped onto the field, they were greeted by the thunderous applause saved for the hometown favorite.

After they dropped their bags, some jogged around, while others played catch or pepper until they could get loose. It didn't take long. You knew they'd finally relaxed when they started razzing each other and giving the bat boys a hard time. The Yankees and Giants players mingled on the field. Shaking hands, hugging, and poking one another in the ribs. You'd never know they were in the middle of a tense championship battle. They looked like players on competing company softball teams that hadn't seen each other in a while and always seemed to be facing one another each year in the championship game. Yankees manager Houk walked up to Giants manager Dark and said, "It's all yours, Alvin. We dug up a few holes to get you used to it."

"Thanks, Ralph," was all Dark could say in return. He then told his guys to "hit until you feel good."

Mays took a few warm-up swings in the cage. When he was done zinging line shots all over the field, the fans began to call for Willie McCovey to take some cuts. Big Mac stayed in the outfield, running wind sprints and shagging flies. A lot of the Yankees stuck around to watch the Giants work out. Some finally started drifting toward the left field gate and the parking lot. When I looked back to the field, Mickey was gone. I caught just a glimpse of his number seven as he jogged out along the left field line toward the Giants. The rest of the Yankees began collecting all their gear, to make way for their rivals. Mickey stopped to shake hands with Willie Mays. They chatted briefly, then Mickey headed out the left field gate. From '51 to '62, their paths always seemed to cross.

Suddenly, there was an empty spot behind the dugout where I'd been standing. I raced back along the concrete walkway running parallel to the backstop, down the ramp to the concession area behind the left-field stands, and toward the parking lot and the waiting bus. I was hoping I could catch the Mick before he could get on the bus.

I skidded to a halt at the door to the bus. Bruce Henry, the Yankees' traveling secretary, stood there holding a clipboard and a checklist of player names.

"Is Mr. Mantle on board?" I asked, almost too breathless to speak.

"Sorry, son, he decided to jog back over to the SOS Club to catch a steam before we head back. If you hurry, you might catch–"

I was gone before he could get the last words out.

I was fast, having won all kinds of blue ribbons in the fifty-yard dash and team relays, but not as fast as Mickey Mantle, even with his trick knee. Mickey, on two bum legs, was still a world-class sprinter. I hurtled south on Neece Drive. When I got to the National Guard armory, the road split. Right was Rouse Avenue and left was Neece. I had come to a fork in the road, as Yogi would say, and I took it. I sprinted down Neece, figuring that was the way Mickey would go since it was a direct shot to the club. I bolted past the Guard base and made a beeline for the front door.

When I reached the main entrance, I burst through the door. Panting, I said, "Has Mickey Mantle come through here?"

"He's in the locker room," the attendant said.

I spun and headed for the locker room door, which was just to the right of the reception desk. I didn't get far. The attendant jumped from his chair, stepped out from behind the desk, and blocked my way.

"I need to see your membership card."

"I don't have a card."

"Why not?"

"I'm not a member."

"Well, then, you can't go in."

"Mickey's not a member, either."

"He's a guest."

"Well, I'll be a guest."

"You have to know a member."

"I don't know any members," I blurted out. Then I stopped, thinking. "I know Teddy Jensen."

"Did he give you a guest pass?"

"No, I just thought I had to know a member."

"You do, but you need them to sign a guest pass, or have them let us know you're coming. Your name needs to be on the guest list."

"Was Mickey's name on the list?"

"It was."

"What member does he know?"

"Mr. Tom Mellis."

"Come on, I really need to see Mr. Mantle. It's a matter of life and death."

"I somehow doubt that," the attendant said, crossing his arms and blocking my way.

"Look, my father's dying. He loves Mickey Mantle. All I'm trying to do…" And the enormity and desperation and hopelessness of what I had been trying to do all this time, and was still trying to do, suddenly hit me. "…is ask Mickey Mantle to play catch with him before…" I sobbed. "Before he dies."

"Look, bud, I'd love to help you out, but I could lose my job. I don't know you from Adam's off ox and they've got very strict policies about guests here. You wouldn't want me to lose my job, now would you?"

"No, I suppose not."

"So, why don't you stick around and maybe your friend Mr. Jensen will show up and let you in."

"That's not going to happen," I replied, totally dejected.

"Well, then, I can't help you. Sorry."

"More sorry than you'll ever know," I said and, eyes downcast, I turned and headed for the door.

"Hey, man, really sorry about your dad," he said.

"Me, too," I answered, as I pushed open the front door and stepped out into the bright October sunlight.

I walked slowly back to Del Webb field. I trudged inside and finally found Gary and his dad standing at the very top of the grandstands behind home plate.

Then it was over.

The fans left the park around three o'clock when the last of the Giants trotted off the field.

While the Yankees steamed and showered at the SOS, the Giants had a late lunch on the bus, feasting on sandwiches made up by the company that sold concessions at Candlestick Park. Harry M. Stevens Inc. had been the concessionaire for the Giants for almost three-quarters of a century, having started with the club in 1894, when they were still in New York. Turns out, the original Harry M. Stevens was also the inventor of the hot dog. Apparently, he got the idea to serve warm food in 1901, when the frostbitten fans at New York's Polo Grounds got tired of ice cream and Cracker Jack and peanuts. He ordered up some long, skinny, German sausages and told his salesmen to sell them from portable Hot Water tanks. When Ted Dorgan, a sports cartoonist for the *New York Post*, asked him the name of the new concession item, Stevens said, "Red hot Dachshund sandwiches." The cartoonist couldn't spell "dachshund," so he called them "hot dogs." A great American fast food was born.

A few of the Giants, who had quit the workout early, had snuck over to the SOS for a steak lunch before manager Dark corralled them and got them back on the bus to head home to San Francisco. I would find out later that Mickey had held up the team's departure while he signed even more autographs. He never could say no. The Yankees and Giants headed back to San Francisco, prepared to resume the Series on Monday afternoon. I just wish I'd had the chance to ask him.

"I choked, Dad." The words gushed out of my mouth, like a torrent caused by Typhoon Freda, as I stood beside his hospital bed in the darkening room, staring down at my black Puma running shoes. "It was the bottom of the ninth, bases loaded, and

I couldn't deliver. I had my chances. A bunch. I just didn't get it done. He's a great guy and I'm sure he would've done it if I could've just asked him. Then stupid Teddy Jensen tripped me and then he took a steam and I'm not a member of the club and I got in a fight with Kelly…and…and I'm really sorry, Dad."

I looked up to see why my dad was so quiet.

"What's that?" I asked, staring at the hardball he held in his shaking right hand.

"You came through in the clutch, son. You did good," he said.

I took the ball and gently caressed the royal, ink-pen blue autograph of Mickey Mantle. When I looked up, my dad gingerly pulled on a sweat-stained Yankees hat. It fit like a glove.

"Look good?"

"Looks great." I instantly recognized it as the hat Mickey had just worn not two hours ago.

Dad took off the hat and showed me the underside of the bill. It, too, was signed by Mickey. He flipped the bed covers back to reveal a Yankee athletic bag. He unzipped it and withdrew its treasures. An autographed picture, travel jersey, bat, and glove. And a handwritten, signed note, which my father handed to me. I carefully and reverently took it, as if it were the Declaration of Independence, and read it:

> Podner, you can beat this. I've probably had more injuries this year than I've ever had in my career. I was down for a while, but never out. It's tough, but you can do it. Good luck. P.S. You've got one heck of a son there. He's a persistent little prairie dog. He wrote, he called, he chased me to Anaheim and Chicago. Even found my mom and gave her a note, which she sent on to me. I hope she didn't scare him too bad. She's got quite a bark. When I heard what he was trying to do, I made sure I tracked you down to meet the man who raised a boy like that. I wish I could have done the same for my father. He was the bravest man

> I ever knew. No boy ever loved his father more. I let him down. Mickey Mantle, #7.

"You met him?" I gushed.

"He stood right where you're standing."

"Did you get to play catch?"

"No," my dad answered.

I looked at him a moment and said, "Then I didn't do what I was supposed to do."

"But, you did."

"No, I was supposed to get him to play catch with you. He didn't."

My dad stared at me, looking so very sad, and replied, "He said he wanted you and me to do that."

I was speechless.

"What else did he say?"

"He apologized to you. He said, 'I'm only human. After all.'"

I helped my father out of bed, we grabbed Mickey's glove and my glove, which my mom had dropped by after my dad had called her to tell her what had happened, and a practice ball Mickey had left with my dad, then we walked out into the cold, harsh, sterile hospital hallway, and lit it up with the rhythmic sound of horsehide hitting leather. We played for what seemed like an eternity. We gathered a crowd. Of other patients, their families and friends, nurses, doctors, and hospital staffers. As my father and I finally played catch. With an assist from our new teammate and friend, Mickey Mantle.

My father and I didn't play catch in the sterile hospital hallways very long that day in October. When he finally got tired, which happened pretty quickly, I walked up to him and gave him the biggest bear hug I'd ever given anybody. I held on for dear life.

CHAPTER 61

Game Six – Monday, October 15 – 12:00 p.m. PST (3:00 p.m. EST) at Candlestick Park

On Monday morning, Gary, Roy, and I trudged through the activity court on our way to our first class. Kids were crisscrossing the open space trying to beat the bell. As a group of cheerleaders passed on the other side of the court, they revealed Teddy and the Eights. Teddy was looming over a kid. The little guy was handicapped and had to walk with braces and crutches. I stopped. Gary and Roy followed suit.

"Here we go again," I said.

Teddy kicked a crutch out from under the guy, who stumbled, but didn't fall. Teddy laughed, then looked at his posse. They didn't. Teddy frowned. He reached for the other crutch and Micah grabbed his arm. Another of the pack picked up the fallen crutch and gave it back to the kid. Each of the Eights stepped in front of Teddy and turned their backs on him, forming a wall between him and the kid, who leaned into his crutches and limped away. The Eights followed, each one pushing, or elbowing, Teddy as they passed. Teddy just stood there, shoulders slumped, arms slack at his side.

"Karma," I said. And the three of us headed to class.

Thanks to a couple days of sunshine and three helicopters hovering over the field, the sod at Candlestick was soon dry enough to play. The Giants were rested and ready to even the score.

For Game Six, Alvin Dark made one change, substituting Ed Bailey for Tom Haller at catcher. He said he decided to switch because "Pierce and Bailey work very well together." The game was a battle of left-handed starting pitchers. Billy Pierce outdueled Whitey Ford with a complete game three-hitter, as the Giants evened the Series at three wins apiece with a 5–2 victory. The Yankees' only runs came on a Maris solo home run in the fifth inning and an RBI single by Tony Kubek in the eighth. Orlando Cepeda had three hits and two RBIs. The Series was knotted.

Kelly and I stood in the middle of the sand box at Graceada Park. I had ridden my bike to meet her as soon as school let out. Her mother had driven her and now waited in the car at the curb.

"I'm really sorry," I said.

"You're not the one to apologize," Kelly replied. "It was me. I was being selfish. You were trying to help your dad. And it's baseball. I can't compete with that."

"If you only knew how wrong you are."

"I just wanted you to myself," she added.

"I get that. Believe me, I understand."

"I'm glad."

"But, you've got to share me."

"And you me."

"What do we do now?" I asked.

"Do you wanna dance?"

"Right here, right now?"

"You afraid?"

"Not anymore."

"Let's dance."

"Watch your feet," I warned her.

"I've got two."

And we did.

Game Seven – Tuesday, October 16 – 12:00 p.m. PST (3:00 p.m. EST) at Candlestick Park

Game Seven of the Series was a classic. I stayed home from school that day and watched it on Channel 3 with my dad in his hospital room.

"And now the title rides on the final game," announced Mel Allen. "It's D-Day at Candlestick. Six months of baseball now spirals to a climax in just one game."

The rain delay meant Ralph Terry would start Game Seven instead of Jim Bouton. Terry had been beaten badly in the '60 and '61 postseason, and he had given up Bill Mazeroski's Series-winning, walk-off home run in '60. But, this year, he had finally lived up to his potential, turning into the best in the league. He was especially tough against the Giants. Jack Sanford, the ace of the Giants' staff, started for the home team.

The two veteran pitchers battled to a scoreless tie through the first four innings. The Yankees finally got it started with a single run in the fifth, when Tony Kubek grounded into a double play with the bases loaded. It was the only run of the game going into the bottom of the ninth. Terry had retired the first seventeen Giants. As the goose eggs on the scoreboard stretched into the late innings, the Giants band behind the centerfield fence started playing "Bye Bye Baby" even louder, hoping to inspire the home team.

Matty Alou pinch-hit for pitcher Billy O'Dell, who had relieved Sanford in the top of the eighth, and drag-bunted for a single. Older brother Felipe tried to sacrifice Matty over to second, but fouled the ball off and finally struck out. Terry then struck out Chuck Hiller, who had also tried to bunt Alou over.

Willie Mays took two balls, as Terry tried to work around him, and then shot a double into the right field corner. The field was still pretty slick. If Roger Maris hadn't got there in time, Alou would have scored. But, Maris was able to race over, cut it off, and gun the ball back in quick enough to cut-off man Bobby Richardson, who relayed it home to keep Alou at third. When Terry raced to back up the play behind the plate, he slipped in the mud and fell.

The Giants now had runners on second and third with two out. Houk came out to check on Terry and ask him who he'd rather pitch to – Willie McCovey or Orlando Cepeda. "I wouldn't have wanted to pitch to either of them," Terry later said. "McCovey was about six foot four and could hit the ball 500 feet, and Cepeda wasn't called the Baby Bull for nothing. McCovey batted left-handed, Cepeda right. But, if we walked McCovey to load the bases, another walk would tie it. Either way, all of a sudden we went from having the Series sewn up to being one pitch away from losing it. One base hit, and we were done for."

Terry and Houk decided they didn't want to load the bases and risk walking in the tying run, like the Dodgers had during the tiebreaker game of the National League playoff series, or allowing the runner to score on a wild pitch, which would also tie it up. Houk believed Terry could handle the big lefty instead of Cepeda, who was swinging a hot bat. During the regular season, Mays had forty-nine homers and 141 RBIs, McCovey had twenty home runs and fifty-four RBIs, while Cepeda had thirty-four homers and 140 RBIs. It was a line-up that was almost as deadly to opposing teams as the Yankees' famed Murderer's Row of the 1920s.

Houk wasn't one to over-manage. He figured it was Terry's game to win or lose, since he'd gotten them this far. Terry figured he would work McCovey inside, so he couldn't extend his arms. If he walked him, it was no big deal since there was an open base. Terry's first pitch was a slow curve that McCovey smashed foul down the right-field line. Terry followed with an inside fastball that handcuffed Big Mac. McCovey adjusted mid-swing, extending his arms. He crushed a line drive toward right center. Mantle broke to his left, hoping he could get to it before it hit the gap. McCovey later said it was the hardest ball he had ever hit. The ball looked like it was going over Richardson's head. Instead, the topspin made the ball sink. Richardson moved to his left, shot his glove up in the air, and snagged the ball. Two feet either way and the Giants would have won. Terry had been given a second chance after being the goat the previous two years and had made the most of the opportunity.

Here's how George Kell called the last out on NBC Radio: "Ralph Terry gets set. Here's the pitch to Willie. There's a liner straight to Richardson! The ballgame is over and the World Series is over!" On the TV side, Mel Allen added, "The Yankees win 1-0 on a brilliant, clutch effort by Ralph Terry, the hero of the twentieth World Championship won by the New York Yankees." The Yankees had won their first Series in 1923. Of the forty Series played between 1923 and 1962, the Yankees had won half of them. They were a legitimate dynasty.

The Giants' dream of a World Series banner became just that. There would be no fireworks. No ticker tape parade. "Just a foot higher," Willie Mac murmured after the game.

Del Webb was one of the first to go into the Giants' clubhouse and congratulate them on a great Series. He also thanked Modesto for welcoming the two clubs. "Our teams really needed that exercise," he said.

The Yankees celebrated in the bar at the Del Webb TowneHouse. They caught a late flight, singing and talking most of the night, and arrived at New York's Idlewild Airport just before dawn the next morning. The terminal was almost deserted. When a reporter asked manager Houk if he expected a crowd to greet them, he replied, "A guy would have to be crazy to come out here at this hour." Ralph Terry said he was "really weary" and added, "All I want to do is get some sleep," which he did before playing a round of golf that afternoon.

Soon after the Series ended, *Peanuts* cartoonist and Giants fan Charles M. Schulz drew a comic strip with Charlie Brown sitting glumly with Linus, lamenting in the last panel, "Why couldn't McCovey have hit the ball just three feet higher?" Later, he drew an identical strip, except in the last panel Charlie moaned, "Or why couldn't McCovey have hit the ball just *two* feet higher?"

Once again, the mighty Bronx Bombers had been able to hold off a worthy opponent. It was the twentieth time they had won in twenty-seven appearances. It was the tenth time the Giants had lost in fifteen attempts. Every game was closely matched. They won in spite of having failed to win consecutive games at any point in the Series. Maris and Mantle hit a very weak .174 and .120 respectively. Mickey only got three hits in seven games, including a double off Jack Sanford. Their less-than-stellar stats were certainly a compliment to the Giants' pitching staff, especially considering that "The M&M Boys" had posted a combined 178 home runs in the previous two seasons.

This Series would be remembered for its record length of thirteen days and its dramatic conclusion. It was the second longest postponement of a World Series since 1911. The Giants were in that one, too. Pitcher Ralph Terry was named Series MVP. The Giants had a better batting average, earned run average, hit more home runs, triples, and doubles. And still lost. It was torture.

CHAPTER 62

The World Series wasn't the only exciting news happening in the world. The United States had been spying on Cuba with U-2 planes since discovering missile launchers on the island. President Kennedy went on television and told the American people that missile bases had been found that were capable of reaching the United States with nuclear warheads. He would be ordering an air and sea blockade to keep Russia from shipping military equipment to Cuba. The Cold War suddenly got very hot and we thought the world might actually come to an end. At school, people were listening to their transistors again, but not to baseball. Between classes, I'd be in the boy's bathroom and guys would be asking if there was any news. Anything about how close the ships were to Cuba. Our teachers talked about nuclear weapons, the Soviet Bloc, and Communism in class. We started doing drills again.

The Russians had agreed not to send any new offensive weapons to Cuba. Following Kennedy's announcement of the blockade, Soviet Premier Nikita Khrushchev refused to cooperate with the quarantine. After a tense several days, the U.S. and Soviet Union finally agreed on a formula to end the crisis and the

Cuban missile bases were dismantled. We had gotten really close to the nuclear war we had been worrying about for all these years.

The rest of the world was praying for peace, but I was praying my father would never go away.

Unfortunately, he did. My father passed away at 12:30 in the afternoon on Monday, November 12. We never made it back to Disneyland to be Mr. Disney's guest.

A few days later, I was sitting on the bench in Pike Park when Mr. Lowney sat down next to me.

"I'm really sorry, slugger," he said. "He was a good man. A real straight-shooter. You could always count on him."

"I don't know what I'm going to do."

"Go on. That's all you can do. Take care of your mom and your brothers and sisters. You're the man of the house now. Make him proud."

"I can't."

"When you lose someone close, you don't think you'll be able to handle it. But, you do, and life goes on. That's the way it's always been and always will be."

"It feels like it did that day I got kneed in the stomach."

"It will get better. Growing up means letting go. It's time to let him go, Michael."

Mr. Lowney stood. He unpinned the baseball bat pin from his jacket, closed the pin, and handed it to me. He put his hand on my shoulder before walking away toward the baseball diamond. As he stepped across the base path and onto the dirt infield, he disappeared. Like some kind of cheesy science fiction movie. I shook my head and looked again. He was gone. I rubbed my eyes and looked again. Still gone. I took off running for home.

We gathered at Dad's favorite restaurant downtown to say goodbye and remember his life. He used to go to Gervasoni's every day for lunch with the guys from his Pac Bell crew. The place was filled with our family, our friends, his co-workers, and people he grew up with. We had assembled a couple of easels holding posters covered with photos of him at different stages of his life. There was food, alcohol, music, and dancing. All the things he loved. We sang the old songs and did the jitterbug. Gary spun Mom around the floor and almost pulled her arm out of the socket. It was quite a night.

As the Wolfman had said, a hero is a man who does what he can and the best he can for others and the common good. My dad was my hero. He was kind-hearted, patient, dependable, honest, and constant. He loved his wife and us kids, and gave us a home to grow up in safely and as we chose. He trusted us, respected us, and encouraged us to do well. He taught us to sing, dance, work hard, play pinochle and baseball, finish the job, never give up on ourselves or others, be on time and fair, never lie or cheat, do the best we could, give people a second chance, and use our own good judgment. He truly illustrated how to live the right life by living that life. He never judged us, never abandoned us, and always defended us, even when we screwed up. He and Mom sacrificed their lives to assure the fulfillment of ours.

I missed him every day.

Mickey Mantle was my other hero. He won his third, and last, American League Most Valuable Player award that year. Tom Tresh was named AL Rookie of the Year, while Ken Hubbs of the Cubs won the NL award. Maury Wills just beat out Willie Mays for the MVP in the NL. Dodger Don Drysdale edged out Jack Sanford and Billy Pierce of the Giants for the Cy Young Award. Elroy Face of the Pirates and Dick Radatz of the Red Sox won *The Sporting News* Fireman's Trophies for the top relievers in each league. Mantle, Richardson, and Terry of the Yankees won Gold Gloves, as did Mays and Jimmie Davenport of the Giants.

In an interview with *The Sporting News* after the season, Ralph Houk was asked, if he had a choice of centerfielders, who would he pick, Mays or Mantle? "There is nobody alive better than Mantle," said Houk. "I've seen him do too many things. I'd just as soon have him run as Maury Wills. When you need a base stolen, Mantle will steal it. He doesn't steal as many but, when he goes, he makes it."

Mantle finished the year with eighty-nine RBIs and thirty home runs in 123 games. He led the American League in on-base percentage (.486) and slugging percentage (.605). He finished second in the league in batting with an average of .323. He turned thirty-two during the 1962 season. He had a good year and the fans loved him. It was that year that Mantle may have begun to realize that his best days might be behind him. Maybe that's why he was such a fan of the Willie Nelson country song that said, "Today's gonna make a wonderful yesterday."

Mantle would play his entire eighteen-year Major League Baseball career for the New York Yankees as an outfielder and first baseman. He won three American League MVP titles and played in twenty All-Star games. He won the Triple Crown in 1956. Mantle appeared in twelve World Series, winning seven of them. He still holds the records for most World Series home runs (18), RBIs (40), runs (42), walks (43), extra base hits (26), and total bases (123). He is also the career leader in game-ending home runs, with a combined thirteen: twelve in the regular season and one in the postseason. He is considered one of the greatest players in baseball history and perhaps the greatest switch-hitter of all time. Mantle was elected to the Baseball Hall of Fame in his first year of eligibility in 1974, along with teammate Whitey Ford. Mantle retired in the spring of 1969, following the 1968 season, at thirty-seven. He didn't die before he was forty, like the rest of his family and like he thought he was destined to. He died in 1995, after battling liver cancer. He admitted that his lifestyle had hurt his family and his game. "I'm not gonna be cheated," he would say. As the years passed and he put forty in his rear-view mirror, he would often repeat a phrase his friend and Dallas neighbor, football great Bobby Layne, used to use: "If I'd known I was gonna live this long, I'd have taken a lot better care of myself." Mantle asked his friend, country singer Roy Clarke, to sing "Yesterday When I Was Young" at his funeral because Mickey thought it summed up his life pretty well. Mantle's epitaph read simply, "A great teammate." In 2006, the U.S. Postal Service issued a Mickey Mantle stamp.

In 1962, I learned what it meant to be selfless, to think about others before myself, and to not be afraid of the unknown. I realized that I couldn't control everything in my life, that stuff happens and nothing ever goes as planned. Most importantly, I discovered that expectations weren't real, loneliness was absolute, change was inevitable, and laughter was essential. I became a believer in the power of positive thinking.

Mickey Mantle became, and remains, my favorite baseball player of all time.

Epilogue

"It's over." Those were the final words Kruk said. The Giants' 2011 season didn't end nearly as dramatically as Richardson stabbing McCovey's screamer, or Wilson striking out Cruz. It was less a bang and more a whimper. We were in the division race and the wild-card battle right up until the last week of the season. We lost the division race to the Arizona Diamondbacks, finishing eight games out. We lost the wild-card race to the St. Louis Cardinals, who went on to win it all.

The season had started with so much promise on April 8. The emotion of watching Brian Wilson run the championship pennant out to the flagpole in center field at AT&T Park, where it was hoisted into the blue San Francisco sky, plus the drama of the ring ceremony. All that hope. Dashed. "Let's do it again," was the chant of the day. But, we didn't. What if Buster and Freddy Sanchez hadn't gotten hurt? What if the Huff Daddy had hit like he did in 2010? What if Showtime hadn't done the documentary? What if the Beard had been healthy? We had a long list of those "what ifs" that allowed us to say, "Wait 'til next year," and kept us coming back each year. I guess the baseball Gods just turned their backs on us, laughing when we told them our dream of repeating.

If the Giants had won a mere handful of additional games, we would have been in the first round of the playoffs against the Philadelphia Phillies. Injuries and poor offense made it tough for our game-starting pitchers to win. The season-long joke in Philadelphia, who lost in five to St. Louis in the National League Championship Series, also rang true in San Francisco. It went something like this: "Manager Charlie Manuel tells the starting pitcher before every game, 'For us to win today, you gotta go out there, pitch a complete game shut-out, and hit a home run.'" It was sad, but true. Our starting rotation couldn't do it all, although they tried, so there would be no post-season torture and no defending our World Championship. The bid to repeat as World Series Champions was over for the Giants on September 24, 2011, a Saturday night in September, when Cy Young winner Ian Kennedy earned his National League-best twenty-first win and the Arizona Diamondbacks blasted us, 15-2. We remained World Series Champions until October 28, when Chris Carpenter, who started three of the Series games, and the Cardinals beat the Texas Rangers again in a nail-biting seventh game.

Then it was time for the long wait until the Giants returned to Spring Training.

A smile curled on my lips as that same old sun warmed my face on this November afternoon forty-eight years later. As I remembered that magical year, I wrapped my fingers tightly around the brand new Rawlings baseball, held it up to the sun, and dreamed of that day in February 2012, when pitchers and catchers would once again report to Scottsdale. And the cycle of the eternal game would begin again.

My son and I joined the rest of the crowd as we yelled, tooted horns, and waved goodbye to the back of the last of the floats. I recalled the words of Duane Kuiper, as he stood at the podium in front of City Hall with the smiling faces of the 2010 World Champion San Francisco Giants arrayed behind him. "Thanks to the gentlemen here, the torture is over." And it was.

We never stopped believing.

Mickey Mantle, Willie Mays – 1962 World Series

Reprinted Courtesy of National Baseball Hall of Fame Library, Cooperstown, New York.

CPSIA information can be obtained
at www.ICGtesting.com
Printed in the USA
FSOW04n1304151016
26120FS